BETRAYAL

Also by J. Robert Janes

The St-Cyr and Kohler Mysteries

Mayhem

Carousel

Kaleidoscope

Salamander

Mannequin

Dollmaker

Stonekiller

Sandman

Gypsy

Madrigal

Beekeeper

Flykiller

Bellringer

Tapestry

Carnival

Non-Fiction

The Great Canadian Outback

Geology and the New Global Tectonics

Earth Science

Rocks, Minerals and Fossils

Airphoto Interpretation and the Canadian Landscape
(with Dr. J.D. Mollard)

Thrillers

The Hunting Ground

The Alice Factor

The Hiding Place

The Third Story

The Watcher

The Toy Shop

And for Children

The Rolly Series

Danger on the River

Spies for Dinner

Murder in the Market

Also: *Theft of Gold*

The Odd-Lot Boys and the Tree-Fort War

BETRAYAL

J. ROBERT JANES

MYSTERIOUSPRESS.COM

OPEN ROAD
INTEGRATED MEDIA
NEW YORK

Cover design by Neil Alexander Heacox

978-1-4976-4159-4

Published in 2014 by MysteriousPress.com/Open Road Integrated Media, Inc.
345 Hudson Street
New York, NY 10014
www.mysteriouspress.com
www.openroadmedia.com

For Gracia who,
in her quiet but determined way,
made me go back at it again and again.

Author's Note

Betrayal is a work of fiction. Though I have used actual places and times, I have treated these as I have seen fit, changing some as appropriate. Occasionally the name of a real person is used for historical authenticity, but all are deceased and I have made of them what the story demands. There is, in so far as I know, neither a village of Ballylurgen nor a Castle Tralane, but Ireland being what it is, there could well be both, though surely not where I have put them.

BETRAYAL

There are lies, and then there are lies.

1

The raindrops were big and singular, and as they hit the steaming dark-blue bonnet of the car, each made a metallic thud that signalled it would burst to pieces. Hunched over the steering wheel, Mary Ellen Fraser tried not to concentrate on them. Their sound was one thing; the sight of them destroying themselves quite another.

Down from her, the gravelled, rut-gouged road narrowed to a single lane before the first of the frontier posts whose tin-roofed hut had the glaze of the forlorn, then it sprang across a small wooden bridge, low and hugging a narrow stream before climbing gently up the long slope to the second of the frontier posts and yet another tin-roofed hut. The North was in the distance: Ulster and a war on over there; the Free Zone here, the Republic, the South and no war here—no continental war, that is. Just neutrality.

Boulders, cleared and heaved from the pastures on either side, hemmed in the road so that no one, not herself or anyone else, could make a break for it. Not on 9 September 1941, not at any time, though the boulders looked as if they'd been here for centuries, and probably had.

The field of fire was therefore clear. The enclosing hills sloped up and away, and it would only take one bullet from a .303 Lee Enfield rifle to do the job. She'd slip, she'd fall, would get up and try to run, and it would happen just like that. Right in the centre or her back, right between the shoulder blades from which her nightdress had slipped, right where Erich Kramer had first put his hands but down a little further, yes down to where his fingers had traced out the soft contours of her seat before lifting her into his arms, she now to lie face down in the turf of an Irish frontier field out in no-man's-land.

The pungent smell of the turf came to her, the acidity of its tiresome smoke, the frugality of its burning, then of course, the dampness of the house—Georgian it was—and the smell of old books some of which would lie open here, there, everywhere on the arms of the chairs, the sofa or on the carpeted floor where the dog hairs were thickest. The cushions . . . Dear God in Heaven, why couldn't Hamish have set his bloody books aside for once and put a stop to what was happening to her?

'That isn't fair. No, it really isn't. It's myself who's to blame.'

The smell of hot engine oil came to her, then the mustiness of the fabric which covered the seat and the rancid dog smell of the throw rug in the back. The newspaper, which was still folded beside her, unread, gave off that inky smell which the dampness only reinforced. A copy of the *Irish Times*. Yesterday's. Bought in Dublin, of course. Dublin.

A straggle of cars and carts, two butcher's vans and the lorry of Michaelson's Fine Olde English Marmalade lay before her, just down the slope, still in the South and waiting in the rain. *Van* and *lorry* and things like *bonnet* she'd got used to very quickly. Oh yes she had.

On the other side, up the long slope from the stream, an almost equal lineup waited to get into the North. There wasn't a sight of anyone coming through to the South. Not a soul. It was like a migration of motorized cattle and horse-driven carts waiting silently in the rain at a ford, some getting across only to be held up by another barrier and a whole lot of silly damn questions. Always questions.

Why the delay? Why the bloody hell did this have to happen to her? Usually there were only one or two waiting, or none at all. It wasn't even the main road from Dublin which passed to the northeast of here through Newry.* It was just the one that headed north to the west of Slieve Gullion and made its way through the bogs and fields and the green-grass hills. Not a restricted road. Not one of those.

They'd have spotted the car of course. Even as they were thumbing through some poor sod's passport, or going through his motorcar with the look of Jesus about them, they'd have given a glance down the long dip in the road and up the far slope to her poised at the top of this little hill.

Yes, they'd have seen her all right. They'd have recognized the car.

'Been to Dublin again, have you, Mrs. Fraser?'—she could hear one of them saying. The Garda first, and then the others over there in the North. Which of the latter it would be she couldn't tell for they often took turns but always seemed to sound the same.

'Would you be good enough to get out of the car, m'am? Sergeant Dillaney will be wanting a word. We'll have the keys, please. Oh and sure there's nothing to worry about but two bottles in the boot for the doctor but no sign whatsoever, now was there, of the silk stockings for yourself?'

Unavailable those were, and not seen since before the war, but

*Southern Armagh being predominantly Catholic.

7

none of them would understand why she was here. Not the Garda nor the Royal Ulster Constabulary and the British Army. She wasn't from either the South or the North, wasn't of recent Irish descent, not for several generations back, wasn't even what you'd call British or Anglo-Irish, was simply from limbo. Yes, limbo.

Two tommies, their bayonets slicing the pregnant raindrops, stood to attention on either side of the road at that far post. A captain of the British Army did the checking; the Ulstermen, the Constabulary and the custom's guards being shunned today, though they'd have done the preliminaries, made one roll down the side windscreen, et cetera.

The captain was thorough. The Army wore slickers of oily brown and greenish brown camouflage to shield them from the rain, but his was thrown back over the shoulders as if he wanted everyone to see the medals. As if he *had* to have them seen.

A DSO with bar from France, from the defeat at Dunkirk, the others too. The battle ribbons.

Captain James Allanby—'Jimmy' for short. Wounded twice and then again. Washed up here so far from the fighting he wanted. A hard, bitter man. Not unhandsome but looks . . . why looks weren't everything and she hadn't been fooled by Jimmy. God no, but she *had* been deceived by Erich. Yes, she had.

'I've let him make a bloody great fool out of me and now I'm going to have to pay for it.'

Irritably running her gloved hands round the steering wheel, she shivered once and then clamped her knees together, said, 'Dear God, you stupid man, I have to pee!'

Jimmy Allanby would only have looked at her in the way drill sergeants do, and she'd have to wait, have to simply tough it out. An hour—would it take that long? Never mind trying to make a break for it, never mind getting herself shot out there. Never mind that it would only be recorded as a 'mistake.'

Jamming the gearshift into first, she released the handbrake and let the four-door Austin roll slowly downhill until, again, she was forced to stop. Now all she could see was the back of the marmalade van. Michaelson's of Armagh had been making the stuff since 1832. Wars hadn't stopped them. Through thick and thin, troubles and rebellion, and wasn't it typical they'd plastered on the logo—WORKING FOR THE BOYS UP FRONT*—and yet had had the gall to drive into the South so as to get unrationed sugar** and Sevilles when in season, all in the name of the precious *war effort* everyone talked so much about these days as if it was holy or something, as if they would just love to be up at that front too, giving old Hitler their best!

'I'm being unkind. I'm letting my troubles bring out the worst in me.'

The lorry lumbered ahead one space. The rain came down and the back of the lorry shut out everything else, made her world darker than she wanted, Hamish's voice coming to her, 'Mary, why must you go again? You were only there a fortnight ago.' The accent so of Edinburgh unless he deliberately used Glaswegian, he really wanting to say, 'My girl, I know damn well what you've been up to.'

'Would you rather I took the train this time?' she had asked.

He'd not turned from her. 'No . . . No, of course not. The

---

* Believing it too difficult and troublesome, the British government did not introduce conscription in Northern Ireland.
** Official rationing began in Britain in July 1940 but was never as strict in Northern Ireland. In southern Ireland, it began later, in May 1942, and again it was not as harsh. Although private motoring was banned in the South on 30 April 1942, it didn't completely cease until early in 1943. September 1941 thus gives a 'window of opportunity,' though this was fast closing. Early on in the war, tea—which had become scarce in southern Ireland and rationed in the North—led people to travel into the North to obtain it, while those there travelled south to buy sugar. There was also, of course, a vigourous, if clandestine, black market, the border being almost impossible to thoroughly police.

motor's far more comfortable and convenient. It's only that . . . well, you know how people are. There's bound to be talk.'

'I can't help the dentist wanting to do more work.' She'd been anxious—scared stiff he'd insist she take the train, but had it shown? Hamish could be so perceptive.

'But Dublin . . . Surely we could find someone suitable here? MacCool perhaps, in Armagh? They say he's very good,' the very pronounced as *vaery* or *vairie*, the good like *goude*, he stubbornly laying it on a little thicker.

'MacCool's not like Dr. Daly. He's not a dental surgeon, Hamish. It's a wisdom tooth—the upper left. Impacted. I've got to have it out.'

So much for lies and now what? No swollen jaw, no stitches. Not even a visit to Dr. Daly should Hamish think to have telephoned Dublin, just the rest of Saturday in that fair city and then . . . then on Sunday morning early, the long drive and finally out along the coast road to Kinsale and beyond. Erich had said, 'Make sure you take the car,' and she had wondered why but had had no chance to ask, had only found out later, yes, later.

It had been so necessary yet so noticeable. There'd been far too few other cars. And Hamish? she asked. Hamish would put his fingers against her cheek and say, 'It must hurt,' and she would have to pull away and shake her head, would have to duck her gaze to his tie and whisper shyly, 'I missed you, darling,' while she tightened it and leaned in to brush a cheek against his as she always did at such times.

Yes, she'd have to lie.

Awakened in the dead of night at Kernével, the requisitioned villa of a Breton sardine merchant near Lorient on the Atlantic coast of France, Admiral Karl Dönitz, Flag Officer U-boats, allowed a faint smile as he gathered his thoughts. Though the letter he had reached for had been dated last Thursday, it had not come by the usual Red Cross channels but by secret wireless transmission from Dublin early on Sunday morning to the Abwehr's listening post outside of Hamburg. They, in turn, had immediately sent it on to Berlin, a delay that could not have been avoided. XB Dienst's code breakers had since been given the code within its code, but neither the bearer of the letter nor the Dublin agent would have known of its contents, nor anyone else for that matter who might have intervened. Only Saucepan (*Tiegel*)—"Tieg"—the Vizeadmiral Huber, now a prisoner of war in Northern Ireland, and he had known of that inner code. Huber had also made certain that had the letter been intercepted, it would have initially been seen as totally fitting and innocuous.

4 September 1941

Dearest Heidi,

How kind of you to send us warm socks and shaving soap. We have little news but are fit and in good spirits. Table tennis, soccer, chess and our daily exercises—seven times around the compound, can you believe it?—these pass the time. But oh for the taste of schnapps and a cup of your coffee or stein of Berliner Kindl, and afterwards a dance, my cousin, with the most beautiful of girls.

Your affectionate Tieg, as always.

Just as when he had first decoded it early on Sunday morning, the message took Dönitz back to his days as a naval rating, to command of a submarine in the last stages of the Great War, to capture and the status of a prisoner of war himself, and now to Kernével.

He glanced up at his orderly. 'Ludi, give me a few moments

with this and that other business. Some coffee, yes, and a glass of schnapps.'

In May the *Bismark* had been sunk, and with it the Grossadmiral Raeder's hopes for a sea war on the surface. In June the Führer had launched Operation Barbarossa, the invasion of Russia, thus opening the war on two major fronts in spite of serious objections, and now there were the Murmansk convoys to contend with as well as those of the North Atlantic, both from Canada and sailing together. Too few boats to intercept them properly, too few experienced men, too little rest—they were dying like flies out there in spite of the successes: 325,000 tons of shipping sunk in May; 300,000 tons in June, but only 90,000 in July and even less in August.

Alarmingly increasing losses. Matz in U-70, Prien in U-47, Schepke in U-100, all lost; Kretschmer in U-99 taken prisoner. More deaths and more men as prisoners of war.

No matter how hard he had sought normal reasons—bad weather, the increased hours of daylight in summer, better protected and faster convoys, Dönitz knew it had to be something else. Spies among the French workers in the repair yards and submarine pens here at Lorient, at Brest, St-Nazaire, Bordeaux and La Pallice, a new or enhanced system of direction finding, a reason. It seemed as if the British knew of his every move, yet each time he had raised the wireless issue with Berlin, that same infuriatingly obstinate answer had come back.

'The matter is simply not possible. The integrity of our Hydra codes is being constantly monitored. *Nothing* has come up to suggest that there has been *any* breech of security.'

Nothing. From Kernével, so far removed from Berlin, and with but a slim staff of six experienced young officers, he directed the Battle of the Atlantic. Everything—the final bringing together of intelligence, its analysis and planning, the sending out of commands came from here, from two quite modest rooms, simply charts, charts and more of them, U-boat logbooks, messages, graphs of tonnages sunk, and graphs of U-boat losses.

Wireless security had been a problem he and Huber had discussed in Wilhelmshaven, and now here was this 'letter' from his old friend. Both of them had known absolutely that Berlin would listen hardest only to firsthand reports and that those who could bring a consensus of opinion were even better than those who could not.

Decoded, the message had read:

Most urgent put bearer of letter in contact with IRA. Imperative arrange escape Kapitänleutnant Erich Kramer Tralane Castle.

More had not been given, though much more had been implied, for Huber had included that one word which, if found in any such Red Cross letter home, would bring the news no commander would want. *Kindl*: codes may have been compromised.

It was now Tuesday, 9 September. By 0410 hours last Sunday Ast-X Bremen who ran the Dublin agent, had received confirmation from Berlin and had sent Dublin its signal to proceed. And now here was the message that had awakened him:

Contact made. Heidi in motion.

Dönitz knew he had another even more pressing matter to attend to and that he would have to use Hydra and could not concern himself with what Berlin would offer the IRA in exchange for Kramer's escape. U-85, lying in wait some 96.5 kilometres to the south of Greenland's bleak Cape Farewell, had sighted a large and heavily laden convoy steaming slowly eastward before turning south into what had become known to the enemy as Torpedo Junction. All the convoys now used the northwestern approach to the British Isles, with a final passage to safety through the North Channel between Fair Head in Northern Ireland and the Mull of Kintyre in Scotland.

He'd taken to using a new tactic, stringing his boats in wide arcs across the convoy routes, raking them like a giant comb. He knew the loneliness, the tension, that keyed-up feeling Gregor and all the men aboard U-85 would be experiencing because, unlike so many in Berlin these days, he had done it all himself. He could even put himself into the boots of the merchant seamen from Halifax and Sydney, Nova Scotia and could sense the fear they must feel.

'Signal the others of the Markgraf group to concentrate on U-85's convoy.'

There were seven boats in the group, U-85 being the most northerly. They'd begin the attack in the evening as darkness fell. In the interim, he'd see what the British did. If they directed the convoy northward towards the Greenland coast, the ships would have little room to manoeuvre and he'd know for certain that the enemy had decoded his wireless signal.

Or would he? Even with Huber's warning in hand, he still knew the British could well have some new means of detection. Perhaps Kramer would be able to shed some light on the matter, but what, really, would Berlin do about this Irish business? Would they offer the world so long as the IRA broke the Kapitänleutnant out of that castle?

Kramer . . . Begrudgingly Dönitz had to admit that Huber's choice had been wise. But the IRA? They were unreliable—governed by whim, totally involved with their own cause, and not to be trusted.

'Ludi, send our friends in Berlin something they will have to pay attention to: *Most urgent. Hydra believed compromised. Initiate Triton.*'*

Adding a fourth wheel to the Enigma encoding and decoding machine that every one of his boats carried, would give the British something to think about.

'And the IRA, Commander? Berlin will want an answer.'

'Yes, of course. *Imperative agree IRA demands secure release and safe return Kramer.*'

'Mrs. Mary Ellen Fraser?'

'Hello, Jimmy. What's on? Has someone escaped from the castle?'

'Not bloody likely. No . . . no, it's nothing so easy to take care of as that. Some IRA bastard set off a bomb in the tube station at Charing Cross and killed a little girl.'

'So all the borders in creation have to be closed while you . . .'

'A little girl, Mrs. Fraser. A child of seven. She was finally on her way out of the city to an aunt in Staffordshire, the mother having refused to include her among the evacuees at the outbreak of hostilities.' In September 1939, with the invasion of Poland, though London's evacuations hadn't really begun in earnest until a year later. 'Look, I didn't mean to suggest it wasn't important.'

'Of course you didn't.'

Water pouring from the peak of his cap, Allanby reached for

---

* This change from Hydra to Triton began in the late autumn of 1941 and was essentially complete by February 1942, but was only done with the Atlantic U-boats, though it resulted in huge increases in convoy losses there. Elsewhere, Hydra continued to be used by surface naval vessels and Arctic U-boats and was read by the British, who eventually mastered Triton.

her passport and held it just inside the window so as to shelter it from the rain, but as the backs of his fingers touched her, she stiffened in alarm and moved away a fraction.

'Sorry,' was all he'd say, she staring straight ahead now but catching sight of the corporals with their Lee Enfield rifles and their bayonets.

'Has something happened to your sergeant?' she asked tightly, not turning to look at him, for he'd lowered the passport.

'Sergeant Stuart's inside the hut. Would you care to see him?'

'Not really. Is it necessary? I've only been to . . .'

'To Dublin and back. Look, I don't make the custom's rules, do I, Mrs. Fraser?'

'And I'm not carrying contraband or IRA fugitives, am I?'

'No one said you were.'

'Stuart's not the one I should see then, is he?'

Jimmy opened the door for her and waited. The rain came down, the droplets breaking on the shiny black toes of his boots. Water ran from the creases in his khaki trousers. It clung to the Sam Brown belt, the pistol in its holster, the brass buttons of his tunic and the medals.

Allanby saw her defiantly swing one stockinged leg out of the car and then the other. Always neat as a pin, he'd be thinking. Good legs, nice ankles, that soft woollen frock coming well below her knees, he giving her a hand now, for one had to do that sort of thing, especially if one wanted to. . . .

She standing at last in the rain, no hat, just getting drenched because . . . why because it would be better that way.

A tall woman with dark reddish brown hair worn shoulder length, and greenish brown eyes, which were wide and searching, sad and distant but saw only the bayonets and the rain.

Jimmy let go of her and stooped to duck his head and shoulders inside the front seat of the car. Mary waited. She wouldn't run, wouldn't lower herself to that. Not yet. Not now.

He swept his hands and eyes over everything—looked under the seat, opened the glove compartment—rummaged about the side pockets, found nothing but the maps . . . Oh God, the maps.

Now it was the ashtray. 'I didn't know you'd taken to using tobacco,' he said, wondering why she was still hanging about.

'I don't,' she answered tensely.

'Then whose are these? That husband of yours swears by his pipe.'

He dumped the ashes into a palm and closed his fist about the three cigarette butts that had been forgotten, she remembering them too late, remembering a lonely road in the South with the sound of the sea not far, some ruins, an old abbey, the wreck of a castle . . .

'I . . . I don't know whose those are. You'll have to ask my husband.'

'Inside, I think,' he said, taking her by the elbow. 'Sergeant!'

'Sir?'

'See that Mrs. Fraser's bags are fetched and check the boot and spare tyre for contraband. Oh, and bring me those maps from the pocket of the right front door.'

Trapped, that's what she was. Trapped inside this bloody hut with the rain hammering on the tin roof and the water dripping off the hem and sleeves of her coat and from her nose and eyelashes. 'Look, I can explain. Jimmy, I wasn't doing anything I shouldn't have been.'

He unsnapped his rain cape and hung it up. Then he walked around behind the counter on which the sergeant would all too soon have one of the corporals place her bags. Jimmy was a strong man—fit in the body now that the wounds of the flesh had healed. Square-shouldered, the ramrod stance made him only a little taller than herself. He was clean-shaven, too, with dark brown eyes, a hard-cleaved nose, hard wide brow, bony cheeks and a belligerent chin. What more could one have expected, but the slicked down, dark brown hair that was parted on the left and cut too short?

'First these,' she heard him say, he tumbling the cigarette butts on to the counter while ignoring completely the constables and the custom's men who'd taken momentary shelter by the stove.

Mary looked at the cigarette butts that now lay on the polished brown linoleum of the counter, the scent of prewar lemon oil coming faintly to her on the stuffy, smoke-filled air. 'I . . . I gave someone a lift into Dublin. He . . . he was a farmer. He used the ashtray, I guess. I can't remember.'

'Going in to market, was he?'

'Jimmy, *please*! You know how it is. A bit of company. I . . .'

Allanby found a blank sheet of typing paper on the nearby desk. Still ignoring the Ulstermen, he rolled the cigarette butts into a tidy packet and put them away in the left breast pocket of his tunic.

One of the corporals brought her two suitcases and slung them on to the counter. The sergeant brought the maps, Jimmy nodding to one of the custom's men and curtly saying, 'You may do the necessary, Mr. O'Toole.'

That sandy-haired, portly individual flipped quickly through her things, ignoring the plain cotton step-ins as if they were poison but lingering lightly on a half-slip and the white flannel of her nightgown. She could almost hear him saying, 'Was it cold in them parts, m'am?' 'Them parts' being the South, along the coast road and not far from Kinsale late on Sunday before heading back to Dublin on Monday, but he wouldn't have known any of this.

The maps were being sorted. She signed the declaration papers—two bottles of Bushmills—it was so hard to get whiskey in the North even though the Bushmills distillery was there; and yes, silk stockings hadn't been seen in Dublin either since before the war.

Reluctantly Mary paid up the duty. 'There's nothing else but the motorcar to settle, Mr. O'Toole. My husband has posted the bond on a more-or-less permanent basis, as you know.'

One third the cost of the Austin. Each time a person entered the North behind the wheel of a car, the bond was handed over in trust; the same when entering the South. You'd think they might have at least got together on this. You'd think that every car owner who had passed through here had been in the used-car business. You'd think that by now they'd know her well enough, but oh no. Every time it was the same.

Every time but this.

Jimmy ran a smoothing hand over one of the county maps. 'Been down to Kinsale, have you, Mrs. Fraser?' he asked, suddenly looking up at her with nothing in those dark brown eyes of his but the emptiness of a military man in a time of war.

'Kinsale?' he asked, reminding her of it.

'Of course not,' she heard herself answering. 'Hamish and I did want to take a little holiday this past summer, but . . .'

Again her shoulders lifted in that shrug of hers. 'But what?' he asked.

He wasn't going to leave it. 'But work at the castle didn't allow for it. That map's from summer. That's why the Old Head of Kinsale and Roaring Water Bay have been circled in pencil.'

She'd remembered it from summer—perhaps. She'd forgotten about the cigarette butts. Allanby thought then that he'd best let her forget about them. Mrs. Mary Ellen Fraser was thirty-two. There were amber flecks in the large brown eyes with their touches of green—one noticed them when she was at one of the staff do's in the common room. One noticed her, one had to, but did lying make the amber come out? She had the blush of windburn about her, the cold of the rain against her cheeks, but was it also from the salt spray of some hidden little cove? She liked the sea, liked it a lot, liked being alone, too, the young wife of a Scottish country doctor—not a good one, not really. One who had messed up his life some place down the line and had been ditched by the first wife because of the drink only to find a niche in which to sit out the war. Bloody old Ireland and all that it entailed.

'Are you done with me?' she asked tightly.

'No, I'm not quite done with you.' She wasn't beautiful, but handsome. Yes, that's the word he wanted, but defiantly proud of what? Her body, her mind, her place in things, or what she'd been up to?

Something, by God. Something!

The rain had plastered the hair to her brow and made its thickness cling to the whiteness of a slender neck and the broad collar of her coat. Her chest rose and fell quite easily enough. Calm now, was it? he wondered, even with all the others stealing little glances at her. What the blazes had she been up to?

'This farmer you gave a lift to. Describe him for me.'

So he'd decided to press on with it regardless. Yet again then, she would shrug, thought Mary, but this time would pull off her gloves as if they were soiled. 'About seventy-five, I should think, and speaking Erse in spite of my telling him I couldn't understand a blessed word. Blue eyes—lots of the Irish have those, don't they, Jimmy? Wrinkles—he'd have had those too, wouldn't he, Captain? You see, I wouldn't really know, now would I, my eyes being on the road?'

Allanby waited. At some hidden thought her lips curved

gently upwards in a faint and hesitant smile, then she said, 'Sheep. He was into sheep and potatoes, this much I do know.'

'And he was over seventy,' he muttered, exhaling the words and wondering why she had bothered to taunt him.

'He also smoked cigarettes without a filter. Hand-rolled— I'm sure if you look, you'll find a few stray shreds of tobacco on the seat or the floor.'

'Sergeant, have a look, will you?'

'Sir.'

'Check the odometer, too.'

'Sir.'

'Jimmy, I haven't done anything wrong. I didn't go to Kinsale and I didn't pick up this . . . this IRA bomber. How could I have?'

'But you did do something, Mrs. Fraser.' He'd abruptly turn from her now. 'Mr. O'Toole, what was the odometer reading of the motorcar when it left here three days ago on Saturday early?'

O'Toole found the form, but played magistrate with his eyeglasses and tone of voice. 'The odometer read 7,263 miles, sir.'

He did lisp the *sir* but one had best ignore it for the moment, thought Allanby. It was near enough to twenty-one miles from the village and the castle to the border here. Another three and a half to Dundalk, then twenty-one to Drogheda and another twenty-five to Dublin. Close on seventy miles, then, and one hundred and forty on the round trip with another twenty thrown in to bugger about. That would make it one hundred and sixty, a goodly distance these days but petrol wasn't rationed in the South, not yet, just damned expensive.

The sergeant came back to give another salute and another crashing of his heels. Must he? cringed Mary.

'Tobacco flakes as the lady has said, Sir. Odometer reads 7,434 miles.'

Allanby watched as the softness of another smile grew to sharpen the windburn, and he realized then that it was at moments like this that the handsomeness passed into beauty.

'Are you satisfied?' asked Mary, seeing a hardness she didn't like enter his gaze. Was he still offended that she'd no time for him socially? Of course he was.

'Mr. O'Toole, have you any reason to detain Mrs. Fraser? If not, she's free to proceed.'

O'Toole closed and fastened the catches on her bags. As he handed them to her, his puffy eyelids lifted in feigned distress. 'We'll be seeing you again, Mrs. Fraser. Say hello to the doctor, will you? Tell him October's best in the second week, with a passable in the third. I'm away to fish the Blackwater then myself. Sure and it would be grand if the two of us could . . .'

He left it unsaid in shyness perhaps, or in feeling out of place, and suddenly she felt a rush of warmth and sympathy for him and answered, 'Thanks, I will. Everything all right about the motor?'

'As right as rain, m'am. Now be off with you while I hold the troops at bay.'

She chucked the cases into the backseat but paused before getting into the car. Allanby watched her through the window of the custom's shed. He noted straightness, the defiance, the determination and wondered why she'd taken it upon herself to let him see her this way.

The rain came down the glass, blurring his image of her. A fine young woman—heady, the Irish would have said, as of a filly that needed to be trained for the course.

Corporal Donaldson raised the barrier and she drove on through without a second look or wave, knowing she'd be followed by their eyes. Until the car was out of sight, Allanby watched it. She'd stop some place down the road to dry her hair a bit and shake the water from her coat, would try to calm herself.

Unknown to him, Mary nipped into the bracken round a bend and had a pee. Then she stood out in the rain, gazing steadily back towards the frontier which could no longer be seen.

London's underground station at Charing Cross was a shambles. Blood-spattered bits of charred clothing seemed everywhere. One of the child's shoes was broken at the heel, they no doubt second-hand and either purchased at a church jumble or picked up from one of the collections for those who'd lost their homes. A lisle stocking had caught on the shoe's buckle and had been dragged off—Churchill knew it had, the force of the explosion being such that the poor thing had been thrown some distance.

A button lay beneath the shoe—had it been from her overcoat? he wondered. She would only have had the one coat, such were the restrictions on what could and could not be taken by evacuees, so as to limit the amount of baggage to a single suitcase.

As he picked at the debris with the end of his walking stick, Winston Spencer Churchill let his moist blue eyes sift over the carnage. The fire had fortunately been quickly extinguished but even now pools of water still lay in the shallowest of hollows and the stench of wet, charred wood and wool and smouldering rubber stung the nostrils.

'Prime Minister . . .'

'Yes, yes, what is it?'

'MI5's Listeners have reported renewed clandestine wireless transmission from Dublin.'

Unfortunately only snatches of an earlier message, sent on Sunday, had been intercepted. 'Well, where is it?' he demanded.

Detective Inspector Franklin handed Mr. Churchill the thin brown envelope on which had been stamped, ULTRA, the Prime Minister ripping it open.

Silently those lips with their clenched cigar moved as the blessed thing was read:

0417 hours 9 September 1941 signal from VV-77 Dublin reads: Contact made. Heidi in motion.

Involuntarily Churchill closed a fist about the thing, crumpling it and the envelope before letting sentiment return. 'Ireland,' he said, though Franklin could not know precisely what he was on about. 'Dear old Ireland again. Find this IRA bomber for us, Inspector. Stop him before he gets across the Irish Sea, and if you cannot manage that, then get him afterwards.'

Again he returned to the damage, to a mass of splintered wood and the scattered possessions of a nation whose people had been forced to be constantly on the move.

Running from the Blitz was one thing; from the IRA another. Southern Ireland had steadfastly remained neutral. Britain had been denied naval and air bases it desperately needed, especially in the battle for the Atlantic. Always there had been talk of the Nazis opening a second front in the Republic; always he had tried to preach caution lest too swift and injudicious an intervention set the Irish aflame.

They'd never succeed in taming them, of course, but there were those in Whitehall and the War Office who would be only too willing to bomb the daylights out of Dublin.

Contact made. Heidi in motion—what were they up to now? 'Confound it, Inspector, must we stand like ruminants before the ashes of our haystack while they play elsewhere at fire? See to this, and see that the child's mother—I gather the father is abroad with our forces so she must bear the pain alone—see that she has both the best of comfort and support in her hour of need.'

With the recovery, on 7 May 1941, of codebooks from the trawler *München* and then on the ninth of that same month, the capture of U-110's Enigma machine and its codebooks, the decoders at Bletchley Park had been hard at work deciphering the wireless traffic of the German Navy. Not every attempt was successful. There were delays—changes in the Enigma settings. None of it was easy.

The codes of the Abwehr, the counterintelligence service of the German military, had also been broken, and sometimes Abwehr Hamburg's listening post would re-encode a message using an Enigma cipher machine before transmitting it to Berlin.

Perhaps a double dose of salts in this case. In any event, a tiny break that could well mean much. From an IRA bomb attack in Charing Cross Station to a second front in Southern Ireland was not impossible, given the nature of some of the Irish, but since the darkest days of 1940, de Valera, their prime minister, had taken the hint, never officially stated, and had all but wiped out the IRA in the South. It could be that the rebels wished a last-ditch attempt or that the Nazis wished to embarrass the British government and force the Americans into a firmer neutrality should dear old Ireland fall under the bombs of the RAF.

It could be the Nazis and the IRA had something planned for Northern Ireland whose air and naval bases in Londonderry and Belfast were crucial to the U-boat war.

It could be anything.

Striking a match, feeling security paramount and things

hastily tucked into a pocket subject to loss, he held it to the Ultra signal and waited as it burned until thumb and forefinger could wait no longer. 'They are insidious, Inspector. Insidious! Get them before it's too late!'

Get this Heidi for us.

It was on the 6.00 p.m. news. Mary heard it clearly from the foyer, a repeat notice. The bomb had gone off at 11.00 a.m. killing Nora Fergus and maiming thirteen others. Scotland Yard were asking members of the public to come forward of their own volition if they had any knowledge of this tragic event.

To attack the tube stations was horrid—the Blitz was still on; well, the bombing anyway. It had been terrible in May of this year, five hundred bombers in one night alone, waves of them. People used those stations during the raids. They slept in them, made tea, had singsongs to cheer themselves on.

'Sure and it's a terrible thing, Mrs. Fraser. Now you mark my words, m'am, there'll be no good come of it. None at all.'

'Now, Mrs. Haney, please don't get yourself upset.'

'Upset is it, and me wrung dry already? I had to send Bridget home again today, I did. But you'll be taking some tea. Dublin to your satisfaction, was it?'

'Yes. Yes, Dublin was fine.'

'But there was a delay at the frontier?'

'Yes. Yes, there was. This . . .'

'This anarchist! Sadist! Hitler himself could be no worse.'

'Mrs. Haney . . .'

'I'll bring it, m'am. A good cup of tea will set you to rights, that and a change of clothing, I'm thinking. There was no news of this terrible trouble in Dublin, was there then?'

'I . . . I didn't see the papers. I . . .'

Ria O'Shane O'Hoolihan Haney gave her the look she reserved for wanton harlots who sold their bodies in the streets of that fair city. She tossed her head knowingly and clucked, 'Dentist, was it?' beneath her breath before departing to her kitchen.

By himself, Dr. Fraser was a saint, a prince of a man. With that young wife of his, the poor soul didn't know what to do, and that was the God's truth, it was.

Leaving her suitcases in the foyer, Mary found the will to climb the stairs. Exhausted by the border crossing, she dragged herself up to her room knowing Mrs. Haney would be listening for her, knowing too, that in all this Georgian loveliness—and it was lovely—the echoes sounded and the sounds of them ran straight to the kitchen.

'How could I have forgotten those cigarette butts and the maps?' she asked herself. Had there been anything else? Dear God, she hoped there hadn't. Jimmy . . . Jimmy was on to her.

Dressed in a robe, she hurried along the corridor to the bathroom but in passing the head of the stairs, thought to call down to say she'd be taking a bath, but then thought better of it. For one thing, there was the boiler and its firing up—an hour at least—for another, there was Mrs. Haney.

Instead, she found a towel and went back along the corridor drying her hair and wishing the house was warm, not damp and cold. It wasn't that she didn't like Mrs. Haney or want at least to tolerate the woman, it was simply that given a measure of fairness and tact, they might well have got on, but that could never be. Not now.

Mrs. Haney didn't knock. The woman had the tray with the silver service and all, and very nearly dropped it.

'Mrs. Fraser . . . Well, I never! I . . .'

No chance to cross herself, and speechless for once, but

Mary could hear her saying to all and sundry, 'As naked as a jackdaw plucked of its feathers, she was, and that's the God's truth, the brazen hussy!'

'You can put it on the table over there by the window, Mrs. Haney. I was just trying to dry my hair at the electric fire.'

'And the rest of you,' muttered the woman, clucking her tongue loudly enough for the sound to be heard in the kitchen.

'Perhaps, then, the next time you'll knock?'

And her not covering herself at all, at all, swore Ria silently. Just standing there with the towel in hand, her backside to the electricity and that zebra-striped robe of hers down around her ankles, everything she owned just hanging out for all the world to see. Like fruit they was. Like young melons or over-ripe Bartlett pears! 'I'll let the doctor know you're home when he comes in.'

'You do that, and the next time I'm away and coming home, you make sure Bridget or yourself builds a fire in my room.'

'Had you but telephoned, m'am, it would have been exactly as you wished.'

Lord save us but Mrs. Haney certainly knew how to put a person in her place! It was all about to start again. The house and Hamish, the lies, the village, its telephone line and electrical wires crisscrossing above a rain-swept single street, a track, a lane that ran between a straggle of tiny houses, too few of them Protestant so as to equal things out for all, the poverty of the place, the ignorance, the ingrown insularity, the castle and its prisoners of war.

The castle . . .

Erich Kramer . . . Erich who had been the captain of a German U-boat. Erich who had asked her to take a letter to his 'cousin' in Dublin. Some cousin! She'd been tricked into helping him. Deceived!

For love? she asked and said, her back still to the electric fire, 'You silly fool. Hamish is the one who loves you. Hamish would rather die than see you come to harm.'

Hamish didn't come home for supper nor did he ring to say what was keeping him. She ate alone in the smaller of the two dining rooms, the echo of lonely Crown Derby, Waterford crystal, and Georgian silver being all around her, as was the flickering of a solitary candle.

At 9.00 p.m. he still hadn't returned or rung, nor at 10.00. At 11.00 she heard the pony trap, heard him softly chastising William, the stableboy, for having not gone home. At 11.45 she found him in the library but did not tell him she had come downstairs. Instead, Mary stood out in the corridor, the sight of him framed by the white trim of the doorway.

He was sitting by the fire, on the couch at the far end of the room, it being one of those sloppy, comfortable things with large, cushioned arms, a faded olive-green to beige cover and slips that hung loosely and were nearly always rumpled. Having been quickly gone through, a newspaper was strewn about as if impatiently thrown away, some of it on the floor, some on the inlaid fruitwood of the coffee table, the rest on the cushions.

The dog was asleep at his feet, and the white marble of the chimneypiece with its neoclassical columns and its crown of laurel leaves was beyond him. Was it Burke's *Landed Gentry* that he was now reading yet again, or the *Farmer's Almanac of 1937*, or *Chum*, one of his boyhood books? Hamish read widely and with such vigour and absorption, not even a vengeful, parsimonious librarian could stir him from it, and yes, he read voraciously when angry and upset.

The salmon and the trout rods, the basket creels and long-handled landing nets, boots, hats and tackle boxes were in there, too, in their usual jumble, along with the pith helmet from India and the spiked iron one of the German soldier he had had to shoot and kill in France, in that other war.

As always, too, he wore the same grey-flecked Harris tweed suit and waistcoat his rounds demanded, the same trousers with their stovepipe legs, the same blue tie with its multitude of tiny fleurs-de-lis in gold.

The necktie was a thing a French girl had given him years ago and Mary knew she must remind him of that girl and that this had probably been one of the reasons they had married.

The drapes were drawn, the blackout being observed in this place but not in the South, never in the South.* Belfast had been bombed in April and again in May. Terrible damage and loss of life,** but since then the Luftwaffe had left Northern Ireland alone and the country had gone back to being just what it was, the centuries of silence and the fight, of course, their precious 'Rebellion.'

The gold-rimmed eyeglasses were perched well down on the bridge of his nose. A hank of thinning hair, once reddish blond, now of sand and getting grey, hung over the right side of his brow. He seldom gave a care for such things. Perhaps he once had, but in all honesty she felt Hamish was trapped by time, circumstance and profession, he wanting only to revert to his essential self.

Just what that was she hadn't quite decided.

---

* Southern Ireland never had a blackout, but rather a dim-out later on in the war.
** Pilot-navigator error during this raid saw two bombs fall on Dublin, they thinking they were over Belfast where, in addition to the 700 in April, another 150 were killed.

'Mary, I've awakened you.'

He started to get up—uncrossed his legs and closed the book, threw off the dust of his subconscious as she brushed a cheek against his own and momentarily hugged him.

'I couldn't sleep,' she said.

'Dublin go all right?' he asked as she turned to sit in the armchair by the fire. Her chair, his sofa, and the dog not even stirring or taking any notice of her.

'Yes, fine. Easier than I'd thought. And you? You're late.'

'Another incident at the castle. A second lieutenant this time. The Leutnant zur See Bachmann, a nice boy, Mary. Only twenty-four and a great pity it had to happen.' More he wouldn't say but they both knew the truth would soon be out. Nothing stayed buried for long in these parts. Not unless the Irish wanted it that way.

'Please don't distress yourself, Mary. War makes prisoners of us all. It makes men do things they oughtn't.'

And here she'd thought he would be upset with her. 'Would you like a nightcap?'

'Bushmills?'

'In the cabinet. I could only get two, though.'

The newspaper was the copy of the *Irish Times* she'd bought yesterday, and she knew then, as he went to get the whiskey, that Hamish had taken a look in the car himself and had retrieved it. He'd been talking to Jimmy. He would know all about what had happened at the border.

'A little water?' he asked, not turning to look at her.

'Yes. Yes, I'd like that.'

Hamish was almost old enough to have been her father. Fifty-four and not worrying about it, though. Not looking it either. Not really. A grand, tall, humble man with loose arms and a jacket that hung on him giving lots of room because he liked it that way and often had to pull the sleeves up or take the blessed thing off.

There were wrinkles, especially at the far corners of his eyes. The complexion was ruddy, the face broad and very Scottish with a full, if sometimes frightening nose and a chin that jutted out to accept both wind and rain with equal disregard.

There were bags under his eyes, a sag to the cheeks—he'd been biting himself with his back molars and had said over breakfast once, 'I'm beginning to fold in on myself.'

As he handed her the cut-glass tumbler, their fingers touched and he stood before her, stood there looking down at her wondering, was he? Wondering what he was going to do about her? He had that look about him, had it in the smoky warmth of greeny-brown eyes that searched for answers now and could not be defied for long.

But then, on some sudden thought, or perhaps because of something he'd been reading, he smiled, and at once this was reflected in his eyes and she felt herself slipping back to him and wanted to say, to shout, 'Don't make it any harder!' but could only smile wanly up at him, knowing that she would remind him of the girl he'd found in France and the one he'd rescued from the shores of Loch Lomond in the spring of 1939.

She took a sip. Fraser sat down opposite her on the sofa, wouldn't touch his whiskey yet, he thought, would just stare at it and wish away the gulf between them, though Mary couldn't really know this nor how much he wanted simply to forgive and forget. 'The IRA are trouble, lass. A great deal of it. Captain Allanby had his reasons for being insufferable—orders from the top, no doubt, and word that someone close to this bomber, if not the man himself, would try to slip back into the North at that crossing, though why any of that lot would bother is beyond me. A border crossing when they've the whole of the border to slip through? It defies reason, but an order is an order, the High Command omnipotent, and no matter the consequences.'

Still untouched, he set his whiskey aside to take out his pipe and tobacco pouch.

'The Belfast organization is by far the strongest at the moment,' he went on, choosing not to look at her but to busy himself. 'They've the whole of the nine northern counties to slip into and away, not just the six of Ulster, and as anyone knows, they're not to be tampered with.'

'Jimmy was just being insufferable, Hamish. He knows I can't stand him—I wish I could, a little, that is, but I can't. I've had nothing to do with those people—how could I have?'

Still he would not look at her. 'My thoughts exactly,' was all he said and, striking the match, brought it to the bowl of that pipe of his to look down its length at her.

'Scotland Yard are certain Liam Nolan was the man who set off that bomb and took the life of that little girl, Mary, the poor wee thing worried only about having to leave her mother. Nolan's been keeping himself out of sight since those Belfast bank jobs they pulled off last spring. Gone to ground, as they say, but . . .' He waved the match out and flicked it into the grate. 'But perhaps the Yard have got it all wrong.'

Mary knew she would have to say something, but that she'd have to still the panic in her. She didn't know of this Nolan; Brenda Darcy had said nothing of him. Nothing! 'Wouldn't it make more sense to think the Irish Sea would stop him in wartime?'

'There are fishing boats. They still do get across—the IRA, that is, and others.'

It was her turn to stare emptily at her whiskey. Her voice lost, she sadly whispered, 'It seems such a horrid thing to have done. Utterly senseless.'

To let his gaze settle on her would take some doing when her eyes were downcast like this, Fraser warned himself, but he'd have to look for signs and not give in. He knew she was an enigma to him, that beneath the lie of innocence a herculean struggle was going on, that she had a conscience, a strength and depth of character he'd yet to fathom.

The slender hands that had been folded in front of her flattened themselves against her thighs. 'I didn't go to the dentist, Hamish. I . . . I just had to get away again. This place . . . You know how it is. I know you do. I stayed at the White Horse Inn on Wilton Terrace, overlooking the Grand Canal. I went for walks. I . . .'

Those lovely eyes of hers lifted to meet his gaze, she giving him that shrug he knew so well. 'Mary . . . Lass, there's no harm in that. Did you enjoy yourself?'

Must they play this game? 'Not really. I missed you. I . . . I felt awful.'

Fraser told himself to say nothing of the cigarette butts they'd found in the motorcar—Jimmy Allanby was just being himself, a bitter, lonely, overly suspicious man with a chip on his shoulder and one she knew well enough. *Och*, he would reach for his glass—aye, that's what he'd do.

But he didn't. Mary heard him get up. He set his pipe aside and stepped around the coffee table. 'You must be tired,' he said, and she felt him take her by the hand, wished he'd say something sharp—anything!—before it was too late.

In the morning, the rain had gone. A grey mist hung over the fields and woods, and in the gardens behind the house droplets of water lay on every petal and on all the blades of grass.

Each day had its hushes. The most intense was, of course, not just before dawn but as now when the light of a struggling sun tried to break through the tops of the most distant beeches which stood dark in clusters on the endlessly rolling crowns of the drumlins, and the land, with its meadows, fields, hills and hedgerows of mossy stone and bushes or bracken gave to the world but a whisper and the brown-eyed cattle returned from their milking.

Mary stopped by the bridge where the Loughie ran dark amber with its taste of peat and the reeds were turning brown. Breathing in deeply, she listened to the hush, picking out the faint sound of Parker O'Shane's lead cow and best milker, named Mary just like herself. Though she wouldn't go there today, the sly laughter and swift asides of each exchange came readily enough, Parker with his gumboots mired in cowpats and sucking on that fire of his just as Hamish sucked on his. These visits, she knew, were bright spots in this life of hers, but was it a day for confessions?

Getting on the forest-green Raleigh with its wicker carrier basket up front, she started out again, a lone woman on her bicycle amid the green, grass-green of a landscape that had gone to grey with a mist whose trailing tendrils felt their way into every hollow.

The house, situated a good three miles from the village of Ballylurgen, was some twelve miles as the raven flew to Armagh in the County Armagh. She'd had such an idea of the place, such a picture of it when Hamish had first told her about it. Romance and him wanting to get away from the war, wanting to keep her safe from it. Escape.

There were a good four acres of gardens to look after or let go—mainly the latter—a stable of sorts and a stableboy because Hamish preferred to use the pony trap, what with the petrol rationing and all, and the wagging tongues of the critical.

Besides the gardener and William, there were Mrs. Haney

and Bridget, so a staff of four she'd just as soon have liked to dismiss long ago for various reasons. Love at first, and privacy, but then . . . why then, the slow and patient withdrawal. Whose fault had it been? Her own? Hamish's? Had they both expected too much of the other? Had this place simply got to them, made her vulnerable but not let her realize how it must have shown?

In any case that was all over and done with, but at the crest of Caitlyn Murphy's Hill, the girl who had died up here during the Troubles just like Nora Fergus, Mary stopped to look back and away to the north, to the house and beyond.

It *was* lovely. Georgian as she'd said so many times. Not the usual Georgian of Northern Ireland. Solid—still exuding wealth, position, power and paternalism. Well-built by one Royal George Morton in 1770 and not all of that pale grey Armagh granite, but mainly of English brick from Kent, and with only the granite at its corners, sills and lintels or above the front door and in its three low steps.

The trim had been painted white but was green in and under the eaves and over the shutters which were never closed, not since her arrival anyway.

The drive was circular, the broad oval of the fishpond being enclosed by gravel. The fountains were of beautifully sculpted, bronze-green naked boys riding dolphins and misbehaving. There were three of them, the water pissing outwards in long streams so that against all other sounds at night, one had a constant urge to urinate.

'I'm being wicked,' she said. 'The water has now been turned off and the pond drained. The pipes were corroded.'

The house had eighteen rooms plus kitchen, pantry, mudroom and laundry, not to count the attic. It had its wings of equal size and of two storeys, dormers on the fourth floor of the main and a grey slate roof with six good, sturdy chimneys and fireplaces in all the important rooms.

Bay windows, too, and a solarium full of hothouse plants— a jungle—on the ground floor at the back, overlooking the gardens.

Yes, it was lovely, and yes, Hamish had bought it especially for her, but was it not also, like the land, inherently sad?

Royal George Morton had been well settled by his family, with land holdings in excess of some 582 acres most of which he'd all too soon gambled or drunk away. In the end, he had died of a bullet to the brain from a horse pistol. Not suicide, nothing so grand as that. Murder, foul murder but 'justified, the Lord God willing, for debts unpaid,' Mrs. Haney had said often enough, 'and the dishonouring of a young girl.'

The next owner and the next had apparently fared no better—did Ireland do that to its immigrants or was it simply the flowering of Mrs. Haney's velum-bound Celtic mind?

It had to be true. And now? she asked but refused to speculate. She knew that Erich Kramer wanted desperately to escape, but that there must also be some very important reason for him doing so and that every day, every week now only made it worse not just for him but for the Reich. It had been Mrs. Tulford at the White Horse who had arranged everything, the disconnecting of the odometer and its reconnecting later, a goodly supply of petrol too, and the meeting with Brenda Darcy late on Sunday out along the coast road to the west of Kinsale. Three cigarette butts in the ashtray and grim last words, cold, so coldly given. 'You're in it now, Mrs. Fraser. Don't ever think you can get out.'

Hamish had introduced her to Erich some seven, or was it eight—could it really be eight months ago? Hamish loved to play chess. As the castle's doctor he'd taken to spending an hour or so in the prisoners' common room, formerly the great hall, or in the library, polishing up on his German and filling himself in on the other side of the war: what was past and what they thought might happen, especially now with the Russian campaign going so well for them. Like herself, he was starved for intellectual companionship which the German officers could supply. A dangerous thing perhaps, but tolerated by Major Trant and encouraged by Colonel Bannerman.

'Anything to keep them peacefully occupied,' the colonel had said once and it had stuck with her.

Because she had a smattering of *Deutsch* from college—long forgotten, most of it—Hamish had encouraged her to help out with the library. She had borrowed books from his own and had been buying them in the flea markets of Armagh and Newry when occasion allowed, but it *had* been Hamish who had started it all by introducing them. 'Erich, this is Mary, the light of my life.'

All castles have names and histories but the truth was, there was little to this one. It was situated in a parklike setting of large trees surrounded by lawns and formal gardens overlooking a small, man-made lake, a damming of the Loughie, hence the name *Lough Loughie*.

Tralane Castle wasn't really a proper castle—not in the ancient ruins sort of way. It was, however, one of the largest castle-country houses in Ireland and had been built between 1798 and 1812 or thereabouts, so well after the house.

It had its crenellated battlements, its round towers of pale grey granite, a square Keep some eighty feet high, the Union Jack flying proudly above both it and the towers. There were the chimneys, a ground floor and three storeys with tall, windowed rooms—caverns some of them. Its rambling corridors and narrow passageways sometimes led to equally narrow, hidden staircases. There were dungeons, too, and cellars like she'd never seen before.

Milk rooms and tack rooms and stables and lots of places where there could be pallets of straw and the quick rush of forbidden things done in secret while a comrade or comrades kept a lookout and you knew this and yet you did it anyway, lying half-naked on that pallet while betraying both husband and country. A half-hour, forty minutes once and the sheer terror of being discovered, but of course it hadn't begun in the castle at all, but in that beautiful Georgian house.

And only then, later, in the castle's infirmary once, and later still, why Erich worked things out and they had used other places in there. Clever . . . he was always so clever with these. Erich had his people, his men, and they did exactly as he said. Orders always, though she'd not thought of them as that at first, but of course he'd been their captain and still was.

There were barbed-wire enclosures—two rings of these, with guard dogs and torch beams in the night, and searchlights too, if necessary, and a single pass gate with barrier bar and armed sentries.

Hesitating now, Mary approached the opposite shore of the lake. There was a small clearing here, the tall trees of a woods on the other side and a view of the castle across the water. Standing alone as nearly always these days, she got a grip on herself. Three swans, ever white and majestic, yet serene, cruised gracefully by.

One hundred and eighty-two German officers were prisoners of war in that castle. Some, like Erich, had come from U-boats, others from downed aircraft, ships at sea or armies on land. Mostly they were guarded by men of the last war, by

Anglo-Irish of Scottish descent, Protestants too, and therefore reliable, or so it must be thought.

And of course there were the regulars from the British Army. Guards with more than one purpose: Captain James Allanby and his commanding officers, Major Trant and Colonel Bannerman. They had the garrison at the castle and did other things like watching border crossings when needed or searching out fugitives in the hills and houses.

There were four British divisions stationed in the North because it was still felt necessary. Jimmy had been right, though. 'Not bloody likely,' he'd said. To escape from Tralane Castle wouldn't be easy. One had, however, the whole of Ireland in which to hide, the temptation of it and the IRA who might, given the right incentives, be willing to help.

Hamish had been right, too. In the North, the IRA were still quite strong and well disciplined. In the South, a series of reversals had left most of their leadership in prison and the rest in a shambles. Brenda Darcy hadn't said this. One picked that sort of thing up as it seeped out of the ground at your feet or dripped from the skies above.

When 10.00 a.m. came, Mary started out again. There were 915 acres of grounds attached to the castle, all of it in the hands of the British Army on a lend-lease basis, hence a lonelier than usual road whose verges had been mown by work gangs of German officers.

Under guard, of course, with Thompson submachine guns, Lee Enfield rifles and sometimes Webley service revolvers.

All the furnishings had been sold at auction in 1922 to pay the taxes so the castle wasn't that pleasant a place, if one was looking for that sort of thing.

At the entrance she was told plainly enough, 'You can't go in, Miss. Tralane is out of bounds to all civilians.'

The warning signs had said as much. 'But . . . but I'm looking after the library? I've brought some more books. Look, I know you're new here, Sergeant, but I'm Mary Fraser, the doctor's wife.'

She might just as well have been Saint Jude or Joan of Arc for all he cared.

'I'm sorry, madam, but we have our orders.'

'Is it because of what happened last night?' She'd forgotten about the Second Lieutenant Bachmann and should have remembered. Had Hamish tried to warn her?

The sergeant, tough, hard and in his late forties, gave her the once over and, unsmiling, un-anything, simply said, 'I wouldn't know about that, Mrs. Fraser. My orders are to turn away all civilians until further notice.'

'Even the greengrocer's van and the butcher's?'

He waited, saying nothing further. She was up against the British Army again, and hadn't it taken special permission to get her in here in the first place? Hadn't it only been because this *was* Ireland and the prisoners *were* officers and gentlemen to whom honour was their bond, or should have been, Colonel Bannerman wanting to keep them content, or had he? Hadn't he and Major Trant seen in her presence a means of finding things out, she naively repeating what she'd overheard at times even to Jimmy?

They'd given no hint. None whatsoever. Sickened by the thought, Mary tried to calm her voice. 'Sergeant, please ask Captain Allanby to let me know when things are back to normal.'

Turning at his nod, she began to walk the bike away, only to remember the books, but she couldn't tuck a note into any of them, couldn't chance asking that they be given to Erich or one of the others, since she'd mentioned Jimmy's name.

'Sergeant?'

'Yes, miss?'

'Mrs. Could I ask that you see that these books are delivered to the library?'

'Library's off limits until further notice.'

All recreation, such as it was, must have been cancelled, but had it all been for nothing, the trip South, the meeting with Brenda Darcy, the crossing of the border?

Back at the house, Mrs. Haney didn't wait. 'A hanging, m'am. A hanging!'

Bridget Leahy, all of seventeen, was jumping. 'By the *neck* it was, m'am, and he one of their own!'

'But not one enough, I'm thinking,' said Mrs. Haney with a grim, sharp nod, she waiting for some response while Bridget remained wild-eyed and all over the place, but Mrs. Haney chose not to discipline the girl in front of others.

'Sure and didn't I tell you they'd be up to no good in that place and you being turned away like that,' the woman said, fiercely clucking her tongue. 'You was turned away, Missus Fraser? Am I right now, m'am? Sure it is that I am.'

'Mrs. Haney . . .'

'M'am?' and she looking pale and bleached about the gills and coming into the kitchen like that for answers now. Answers!

Wanting to shout at her, 'Don't you dare insinuate such things!' Wanting to wipe that brooding Celtic look from that thick, brown-brow of a face with its swift brown eyes that saw everything, Mary said, 'Nothing . . . It's nothing. Bridget, would you do a bit of tidying up in the doctor's library for me, please?'

Ria reached for the long-handled iron spoon that hung above the cast-iron range but paused. 'Bridget! You bring me them taters from the garden like I asked you.'

'Mrs. Haney . . .'

'M'am?'

42

'Oh never mind! Just never mind!' Retreating quickly, visions of the woman followed of their own accord. The front, the back, the side—all were nearly of the same dimension—a tower of strength, a pillar of it, the woman standing firmly in her kitchen, her territory where others, the owner's wife and mistress of the house, her employer, for God's sake, were persona non grata, the jade-green skirt being hitched up, the off-white blouse with its bits of lace her mother's likely, *and* two bulky knitted cardigans, the outer being unbuttoned always, the inner, the newer, being buttoned and of a deeper green!

The carpet slippers were for around the house because they 'eased,' spelled *aized* her feet, her bunions, spelled *boonians* and the sagging woollen socks were 'of the army,' and, 'for the warmth of a morn.'

'Oh damn that woman, damn her anyway!' swore Mary under her breath as she stopped in the foyer to check the morning's mail.

There was nothing from Dublin, thank fortune, but there was a letter from Canada, from home. Opened by the censors and then resealed. Posted a good four months ago and come all the way across the Atlantic by convoy to England under threat of German U-boats and then by packet across the Irish Sea.

Nothing stopped the Royal Mail, not even a war.

It was a letter from Frank Thomas's mother, but she'd leave it for a moment, and climbing the stairs, went along to the bedroom Erich had used, to stand in its doorway feeling lost and alone.

Erich had needed to have his appendix out early in March. Things had gone well but he'd been run-down and after some weeks in the castle's infirmary, still hadn't been right: a fever that doggedly came and went. A low-grade thing that would suddenly flare up for no apparent reason.

Puzzled by it, Hamish had gone to the colonel, and Erich had been brought to the house. He'd spent a fortnight here—over a week in bed and then a few days around the place, but had Hamish seen it coming? He had had to go out on a call. She'd gone downstairs with him, hadn't been sleeping well and had heard him get up. It had been late—nearly 2.00 a.m. She'd asked if he'd like her to come with him but he had only shaken his head in that way he always did, and had told her to go back to bed, Mrs. Haney and the others never sleeping in the house. Erich . . . Erich had caught her all but in darkness on the up-stairs landing. Her back had hit the wall as he'd kissed her and she'd tried to pull away.

'Don't lie about it. You wanted him,' she said. Even now she could still feel how her nightgown had slipped from her shoulders as it had fallen to the floor.

But to understand how it could happen in the castle—in a prisoner of war camp—one had to understand the workings of the place. The British and the Anglo-Irish of the British Army were always about, but there were no armed guards within those parts of the castle that had been assigned to the prisoners—just guards without their guns. At any moment one or more of them could come into the library and often did—everything was always more or less in a state of flux and she was always accompanied in any case, and always there would be at least one of them standing at the door.

Being officers, the prisoners weren't locked into rooms or anything like that. They were fully responsible for their own well-being and had duty rosters organized, even their own cooks. They organized their own recreation and had the run of the central courtyard—acres for soccer, which they played nearly every day after their calisthenics.

There were lectures, too, on history, on bridge building or

making wine, even on things like fishing and tying flies for salmon or trout—oh, they had them on any number of subjects and were a very diverse group. They built beautiful model ships, played cards, wrote letters home, received Red Cross parcels and had somehow managed to acquire two Ping-Pong tables.

Music was a favourite, of course, but mostly a choral group for which she was always trying to find new scores. They had a piano the Catholics in Armagh had sent along with two accordions, a gramophone and stacks of records. Hence the 'parties' now and then when things were going well and they were especially behaving themselves, which was exactly what Colonel Bannerman wanted most, of course. Even a bit of beer and once . . . why once, a drop of whiskey—she'd mentioned the absence of a bottle to Hamish and he'd only touched his lips and said, 'Sh!'

Many of the men simply walked and talked among themselves or to her if they could, using up their precious tobacco rations and trying to follow the war without news beyond what they were allowed to be given or learned from the clandestine radio they'd built—they must have. But the guards could not be everywhere at all times, and they could be distracted, singled out, cut off, isolated. One of Erich's men would keep a watch. Another would act as a discreet relay, a third watching yet another approach, their exit if needed.

Together, she going first or following at a distance, they would manage to slip away. It hadn't happened that much—five times, that's all. Just five since here, since when it had first happened. Well, since Erich had left the house. Each time there had been the apprehension, the terror of discovery, the shame of such a thing, but the incredible sexual tension that fear and darkened corridors and empty rooms could bring, the presence of others close by. Had they listened? They must have.

She'd been a fool, a terrible fool.

When Fraser found her, Mary was sitting on the edge of the bed. The last of the sunlight caught her and he wondered why she'd come in here to read a letter from home, and he thought he knew the reason.

'Lass, what is it? What's happened?'

Awakening to his presence, she didn't want him to see that there were no tears. 'Frank's been killed. Four months ago. April twenty-fifth, in Egypt, at a place called the Halfaya Pass.'

Hamish had been told that she'd been engaged to Frank Thomas, an up-and-coming lawyer from Orillia, in Ontario, Canada, and that they'd broken it off for some reason, but he had never once asked that of her.

He took the letter from her; Mary let him read what there was of it.

If only you and Frank had married. If only you hadn't thrown him over like that and run away.

It had taken her more than three-and-a-half years to make that crossing to England, an interlude she'd have on her conscience for the rest of her life, but he'd say nothing of it now, though he'd waited long enough.

2

Ballylurgen held its market day three times a week, 'for want of something better to do,' Mrs. Haney would always say, though the thought didn't bring a smile to Mary. Halfway between the house and the village, an old road took off into the woods and hills to Newtonhamilton some ten or twelve miles to the southwest, if one was foolish enough to attempt such a thing. Once over the first of the hills, this road began to peter out among the whin before passing through crowding blackberry canes, elderberry, stunted hawthorn and apple trees that had gone to ruin. At the Loughie there was a small wooden bridge now half rotted through and so overgrown one couldn't see the rot at first.

Stopping on this bridge, she got off her bike. Instinct warned that she wasn't alone—instinct and that emptiness the land could bring, the silence through which the trickle of the Loughie came as it made its way between the green grass of the banks.

Yes, she wasn't alone. Her heart began to race, she to regret ever having suggested that if it were best, she might be contacted here on the first of the week's market days, held each Tuesday. Another lie to everyone else—Hamish included but Mrs. Haney in particular. She would have to say she'd had a puncture—an excuse for not having gone into the village.

The rotten, sometimes fallen-in timbers at her feet came into view, she not budging. Around a half-sunken log, the water, always dark, gurgled, the smell of peat and rotting vegetation joining that of forgotten apples, but then there was the warm scent of blackberry leaves.

Nearly two weeks had passed since she'd come back from the South. There had been no chance whatsoever of getting into the castle. Determined to find the man or men responsible for the hanging of the Leutnant zur See Bachmann, Jimmy Allanby, Major Trant and Colonel Bannerman, were equally determined, as were the High Command in Belfast and Derry, to find and kill or bring to justice one Liam Nolan, now dubbed by the press as 'The Mad Bomber of London.'

The British Army would turn the whole of Northern Ireland upside down if necessary. Nolan's photographs hadn't been complimentary. Jimmy had thrown them down on the coffee table in the main living room at the house and had demanded, 'Well?'

'Well, *what?*' she had asked, sitting on one of the sofas with her knees clasped.

'Is that the man you gave a lift to?'

'Certainly not. I've never seen him before.' But why had he suspected her? Why?

As if in answer, Nolan stepped on to the road at the other end of the bridge. The grey tweed cap, open-collared blue work shirt and blue-black jacket of heavy serge, the boldness of stovepipe trousers and black boots were like those of a dockworker. The arms hung loosely at his sides, the hands thin and long-fingered, the wildness of a grin lighting up swift blue eyes that taunted, took her in, stripped her naked, no doubt, and laughed at her predicament while coldly assessing her.

The face was narrow and thin, the features sharp, the hair that washed-out shade flax has after it's been beaten and the sun has yet to come out.

'Mrs. Fraser, it is. Mary, I believe.'

The shock was not that the photographs had told her so little, but that the voice hadn't been what one would have expected. The accent was soft and that of a man with an education and a very good one. But a man of what? she wondered, not moving a muscle.

Thirty-two—was he that old? Six feet, two inches or so in height and weighing perhaps 160 pounds, but all arms and legs, he not moving a muscle either, the cheeks pinched, the nose thin and long, the end of it tilted up and to his left, the imp, the eyes beneath and well back of the brows as if looking out from a cave.

One would never know what to expect from him, and at once this was the thought that frightened most and would, she knew, linger with her. Nolan . . . Liam Nolan.

Unseen, except out of the corners of her eyes, two others stepped on to the road, one on either side of her, another man and a woman. 'What is it you want with me?' she asked, her voice leaping as she tried to be calm and not betray herself.

Nolan touched the peak of his cap in deference. 'A word, that's all, m'am,' the *all* so soft and melodious it went with the *A* of his *m'am* and was like the spilling of flour on a pastry cutting table.

'But not here,' said the woman sharply. Grinning swiftly, darkly, this one clamped a cold, moist, pudgy hand firmly over her own right which held the bike pulled in tightly against a hip.

It wasn't Brenda Darcy but a suggestion of her, both in the coarseness of the face and lankness of the reddish brown hair. Sisters, then?

The woman was probably four years younger than Nolan and there was a hardness to her sea-green eyes that could not be avoided. A chipped, upper left front tooth automatically drew a second glance for the whole half-corner had been knocked away at an angle of forty-five degrees and it lay next to a gap no woman would have wanted.

'Enough of this hanging about,' said the other one who was at Mary's left, he crowding her so closely she could smell the stale tobacco smoke on him.

They rushed her into the woods—there was no time to object, only for Brenda Darcy's words to come back. 'You're in it now, Mrs. Fraser. Don't ever think you can get out!'

Nolan, having leapt nimbly from the end of the bridge, was in the lead, then came the woman and lastly the other one who had a revolver jammed into the waistband of his trousers and had his hand on the seat of the bike, he pushing her and it along so that she was forced to run.

The path only appeared at the crest of the first hill, she out of breath and feeling the ache in her chest, her heart hammering. They went down across a valley where the bracken and the gorse gave evidence of a former pasture. All too soon, though, they were climbing again, each of them looking back to make sure they'd not been followed; Mary looking back, too, to catch in the eyes of the man behind her the thought: You're dead if you've betrayed us.

Numbed by this thought, and still rushing along with the bike, they drove her up a steep rise and into another bit of woods only to take off suddenly at an angle to the left, Nolan turning aside so quickly the woman stepped on his heels and stumbled in her haste to follow. Again and again it was woods and hollows, dips and hills—once, though, a clear stretch of fields that were dotted with sheep, the perspiration streaming from her until at last, at another change of direction, they came to the edge of a clearing and the track of an even older road.

'You're to go ahead now, Mrs. Fraser,' said Nolan, turning at last to step back the few paces that had separated them.

What was there in that look of his? An emptiness . . .

'You'll find Padrick Darcy's smithy but don't be afraid. Just go inside with the bicycle and close the door. We'll be along soon enough.'

'Don't try anything funny,' said the woman.

'How could I? I *don't* even *know* where I *am!*'

Nolan flashed her the grin of a towheaded urchin who had just got away with something, then nodded to the others and they were gone.

Gone, leaving her here all alone in the middle of nowhere.

A red squirrel scolded fiercely from among the limbs of a nearby oak, driving her away from the hill and down to the road. Water mint, bog cotton, and lady's tresses, now gone to seed, grew in the ditches among the holy grass. A jackdaw didn't like the intrusion. A wren flitted nervously away, flying straight into the sweeping grey beard of an ancient hawthorn.

Padrick Darcy's cottage and shop had lain empty and abandoned for at least two decades. Both buildings were of that rough, flagged stone typical of the Irish countryside but had, however, been roofed with slate and had withstood the weather and the wasting better than most.

The door to the cottage, seen some distance from the smithy and uphill from it, was of coral pink but faded and with that horizontal cut across the middle that broke it into halves but could only have let in the wind.

A horseshoe, rusty and nailed upside down to the flaking whitewash of the smithy door, met her gaze. The smell of autumn was strongly in the air but never like that of Canada, never the scent of the maples. Masses of tiny white daisies were everywhere and of waist height so, too, the bees.

The black iron latch, high on the door, came open easily enough. With a nudge from the front wheel of the bike, and a last hesitant look thrown anxiously over her left shoulder, Mary pushed on into the place. At once the stench of old horse piss rushed at her, and then more gradually, the smells of charcoal and the sulphur of cherry-red or white-hot iron whose sparks would have flown about as the iron was beaten flat or hammered into shape.

Among the clutter there was space enough to lean the bike out of the way and light enough coming in through the windows and through gaps in the roof above for her to see quite well enough.

A litter of discarded horseshoes lay strewn about the massive anvil. A forgotten wagon wheel, its rim newly fitted back then, leaned against a heap of bolt boxes, lengths of iron strapping and bars of the same as if, in waiting so long, the owner of the wheel had simply departed and the blacksmith had been taken away to be hanged.

All of it should have gone for scrap metal, of course. All of it, but no one would dare to touch it.

The brick hearth of the forge held only soot and cold ashes, and the nubby droplets of once-molten iron and slag.

Mary stood in the silence fighting off childhood memories of Orillia, of Alliston and points thereabouts, of a river Boyne that was not in Ireland at all, but had once been a very fine trout stream, lying as it did under the high, bleak crown of Sharp's Hill in Ontario, Canada.

She touched the sooty brick and saw, chalked on the bricks of the chimney, the dates and accounts of bills owing, Padrick Darcy having kept things straight that way. His leather apron and heavy leather gauntlets were mouldy and next to the filthy dark remains of a woollen, cable-stitched pullover whose left sleeve, having often been yanked at, was the longer, for the blacksmith would have gathered it into his fist to keep the heat of the tongs from his hand.

So much for gauntlets. Big and cumbersome they were, and had been, she remembering a moment, a flash in time when the blacksmith at home had flung his off in disgust.

'You've been in such a place before.'

Startled, for she hadn't heard anyone come in, Mary turned to search the door, finding nothing. Anxiously she ran her eyes over the clutter, saw the dust, the cobwebs, the ruins of a lifetime of labour and poverty, but saw no one at first.

Then only the one called Liam Nolan.

Like a scarecrow cut out of blue-black serge, he was standing in the shadows of a far corner, framed by the upright shafts of a pony trap and backed by a clutter of harness. 'How did you . . .' she began, breaking off the question to ask, 'Where are the others?'

'Keeping a watch, so it's only myself you have to contend with.'

He hadn't moved an inch. 'Did you really do it?' she asked.

'Is it so important to you?'

A shaft of light from the roof had fallen on her. 'Yes . . . Yes, I think it does matter. You see, I once had a little girl of my own but had to give her up before I came to England.'

Nolan drew in a breath and held it before saying, 'Then it's sorry I am to have troubled you. Tell your friend it's off.'

'She's seen too much of us, Liam.'

'Fay, I told you to keep a watch.'

'Kevin's looking after things. His cousin's come to join us.'

Nolan swore softly under his breath, his voice rising to, 'That's all we need.'

'Oh, and is it now? And who was it that saw you into Eire? Who was it, I'm asking?'

Fay Darcy had spoken through the gap that had been left by a missing pane of glass in one of the windows. The round, chubby cheeks and chin appeared jaundiced in the half-light.

The woman turned away suddenly and gave a low whistle. In no time the one called Kevin had joined her and they crowded inside.

'The coast is clear enough, Liam,' he said. 'Let's settle this and be away.'

'I wasn't followed to that bridge where you met me. No one has any reason to do that.'

'Oh?' It was the woman who had asked this. 'A "You"-boat captain is it, Mrs. Fraser? Handsome, I take it?'

'Fay . . .'

'Liam, you shut yours. Why're you doin' this, Mrs. Fraser? For love, is it? It *can't* be for patriotism, now can it?'

'It's all a mistake. Look, I didn't know anyone would be involved other than Erich's cousin. I simply delivered a letter for him in an envelope to which I had attached a postage stamp. I was to mail it to a German address if she wasn't at the White Horse Inn.'

'Taken past the sentries at the castle, was it? That's treason, I should . . .'

'Fay . . .'

'Kevin, be quiet. She's got jam on her fingers.'

Fay plucked at a sleeve of Mary Fraser's brown velvet jacket. She took in the soft yellow mohair pullover and the plain white cotton blouse with its tidy little Peter Pan collar that was buttoned up close and tight around that milk-white slender throat. Everything she saw spelled 'kept woman,' including the green tartan skirt which was not of the Fraser Clan at all and therefore must spell ignorance of such things.

'D' you know what an Orangeman is, Mrs. Fraser?' she asked, forcing her way round the one called Kevin to stand behind her now.

Again Mary found herself looking at Nolan whose eyes flashed mischief as they flicked back and forth between her and the Darcy woman.

'An Orangeman's a Protestant,' she said at last, swallowing tightly at the intended humiliation.

'A Prod she says, boys. A blackhearted booger with murder in his heart, Mrs. Fraser, and the blood of his manliness in his hands. And me with his knackers to show for it!'

'Fay, cut it out!' swore Nolan angrily.

'Why should I?' she shot back, baiting him.

'Because this is getting us nowhere.'

'Then she's all yours, Your Eminence, and only the more so if you were to bed her.'

'Liam, pay her no mind.' The one called Kevin stepped closer to Nolan. Offering a cigarette, he held the match for him, then lit his own.

Kevin had the wiry, short, curly jet black hair of some of the Irish, but his dark grey eyes squinted out from under dark, thick brows that slanted away and down. A man of forty or so. A man who kept himself back a bit. Stocky and of shoulder height to Nolan, the expression one of, Well, what are we to do with you now?

The hairline was receding at the sides. The mouth was wide, the lips slightly parted. Sharp cleavages cut across the corners of the lips, slanting in towards the nose while two strong troughs shot up the middle of the weather-beaten cheeks to meet the crow's-feet at the corners of his eyes.

Did he have to wear glasses, and by not doing so, was he trying to hide this from her? she wondered.

Kevin . . . Kevin who?

The ears stuck out a little more than they should have, and the chin was cleanly shaven and round.

'Give us an answer then, Mrs. Fraser,' he said at last, knowing that she had memorized the look of him. 'Tell us why you're willing to help a German U-boat captain.'

Was he the leader after all?

Nolan frugally pinched his cigarette between thumb and forefinger as he drew on it, cupping the hand over the glowing end to protect it from rain and wind out of habit perhaps or from the darkness here out of common sense but was it not also a sign of someone who had spent time in prison? she wondered, glancing quickly from one to the other of them.

The Darcy woman still hadn't moved from behind her.

'We're waiting,' said Nolan softly. 'We can't wait much longer.'

'I . . . I think I'm pregnant—carrying his child.' It was to Nolan that she'd chosen to say this.

'Another mistake?' asked the Darcy woman with a sharp snicker.

Mary refused to answer.

Kevin O'Bannion noted the pride. She was like a queen of old at the end of a battle that had been lost. 'Will you betray us?' he asked suddenly, and she found then that he, too, had a look that could not be avoided.

'I don't want to hurt my husband. He doesn't know about the . . .'

'The baby,' breathed Fay with just the right amount of excitement and wickedness.

'The baby, yes. I . . .'

'You've been cheating on your husband, have you?' taunted the woman. 'Answer me!' she shouted.

'Yes. Yes, I've been . . . been cheating on him.'

'Then she'll do as we ask,' sighed Nolan, 'or the husband will be told of it and there'll be more than one body to bury.'

They'd kill Hamish, not just herself and the child.

O'Bannion took her by the hand and, wrenching the palm upwards, pressed the cold, gun metal of his revolver into it. 'You'll carry this into Tralane, Mrs. Fraser, and you'll pass it on to your friend as a token of our interest. You can tell him he'll get cartridges enough when we're satisfied.'

'The castle's closed and off limits,' she blurted, tearing her gaze from that thing only to see him squinting at her all the more.

Then he said, 'That business will soon pass, though we can't wait long. Liam, here, must get away. Germany would suit him fine. Tell your friend we'll pry him loose of Tralane and get him out of Eire for a price. Tell him, too, that we've been in wireless contact with his people and that they've asked us to give him this.'

'The gun?' she blurted. Wireless contact . . . Was Mrs. Tulford of the White Horse Inn a German spy?

'No, this,' said O'Bannion, handing her a small, torn slip of paper. 'Latitude north, sixty-five degrees, thirty-two minutes, eighteen seconds; west longitude, seventeen degrees, twenty-four minutes, nine seconds. That's where they've said his U-boat is supposed to have gone down. U-121,* Mrs. Fraser. You can tell him that, too. No doubt your friend has something he desperately has to tell his people in Berlin. No doubt he hasn't

---

* Scuttled with many others in May 1945.

let you in on the fact that he's the one who's been chosen to escape. He's used you, and I'm wondering if that submarine of his really did go down or if the British didn't capture it and his codes and encoding-and-decoding machine?'

O'Bannion saw the sickness come into her eyes, but the moment soon passed. Not only could she get a grip on herself if needed but she'd figured things out for herself and had seen glimpses of truth in what he'd just said.

The Germans would have to know if U-121 had been taken and not scuttled off the Orkneys as had been reported in the press of last January. They'd have to know if the British were not now reading the German navy's coded transmissions.

'He wants to escape. I know he does,' she said emptily, 'but he hasn't said this to me.'

Her eyes were downcast, she trying to fight back the tears. 'You'll do as we tell you,' said Nolan—Mary knew it was him, and that he wasn't the leader after all. Grimly she nodded and tried to face them, begged herself to do so.

Fay touched the woman's lovely soft hair, making her jump and look up.

Kevin was the one to say, 'We've a meeting place, Mrs. Fraser. When the right time comes, we'll tell you of it.'

'You'll be blindfolded,' said Fay. 'I'll be the one what comes to take you there.'

They left her then—left her in the middle of nowhere again but with a British Army service revolver, she standing alone amid the clutter, weeping buckets and not knowing what to do.

'Bastards!' she softly blurted. 'You're all bastards, Erich especially!'

Kevin O'Bannion watched her from the seclusion of the woods. Mrs. Mary Ellen Fraser pushed the bicycle out into the fleeting sunlight to stand there a moment. Then she did a curious thing for a woman who must surely wonder what must happen to her in the end. She lowered the bicycle to the ground and ran trailing fingers through the thickness of the waist-high Michaelmas daisies that crowded about her. Slowly, as if coming out of a dream and not a nightmare, she began to gather a bouquet and to smell them frequently, as though to banish the stench of what she'd just been through.

When enough of them had been gathered, she found a wisp of straw and wrapped it tightly around the stems several times before tying it. First the gun went into the carrier basket, then the folded jacket and lastly the bouquet. He was impressed, for she would use the bouquet as a talking point if stopped on the road and questioned.

Leaning the bicycle against the wall of the smithy, she picked her way through to the house. Hesitantly she nudged the door open a crack to peer in and then, finally, to step inside, causing him to be dumbfounded at such a summoning of courage and resilience. He knew she'd find among the refuse on the window sill, the cast-off boots whose laces were gone, knew she'd find the faded amber of forgotten photographs, the dark brown empties of Guinness, the broken teacups, littered straw and cobwebbed gas mask Padrick Darcy had once used in the trenches of France. The enamelled plaque of the Christ, too, with the words, *Wherever I am hung, I am present.*

Mary knew she was being watched even as she looked out through the window and tried to appear preoccupied, and when, having set down a still half-filled, stoppered bottle of tincture of iodine, she brushed the dust from her fingers and decided that it was time to leave, she came outside.

Kevin—she still did not know his last name—met up with her on the path, she saying only, 'It was cruel of you people to have left me like that, but I got over it soon enough.'

'Are you really carrying his child?'

'You'll have to wonder about that just as I'm wondering myself.'

The water was hot and when she had lowered herself into the tub, her skin grew pink. Steam floated about the place. Stretching out, Mary tilted back her head and shut her eyes, let herself go limp, went right under. She had to unwind, was still far too tense. It had taken guts to have ridden into Ballylurgen with that revolver in the carrier basket but she'd forced herself to do it, hadn't wanted them to think her weak, had known they'd somehow still be watching. The Irish made good sausages and even though rationed, she had managed a pound and some kippers. One couldn't trample kitchen toes at home, though, so she hadn't bought someone else's soda bread and barmbrach that was light with beaten eggs* and yeast yet so well speckled with dried fruit she had momentarily forgotten the war. Both Catholic shops of course, both Republicans, it being that sort of day.

A fruit tart and then a custard one had been for herself, secretly and hastily eaten on the road home but enjoyed . . . yes, enjoyed, crumbs and things dribbling down her chin in spite of feelings of guilt, of starving, war-torn children, and then a few shortbreads—had she been eating for two, or simply because she'd been so darned scared?

In a rush, she surfaced, gasping for air as the water coursed off her. She had wanted to see Parker O'Shane at his farm. Wizened, bent, thin and with a sharply pinched face, Parker's skin

---

* Eggs were extremely scarce in England but plentiful in the North and the South of Ireland, as were butter, milk, and other farm produce, both regions being predominantly agricultural at the time.

had the look of oak tannin. Bound leather was always at the knees of his trousers and down over the laces of his boots, not canvas there for him, the pipe clenched and the scythe going with the rhythm of the centuries. 'A cutting of the hay it is, missus,' he'd always say. 'And you like the blush of an April morn. Them cows of mine be powerful eaters.'

Parker was Mrs. Haney's half-brother, so he had the inside track on herself both ways and yet they had a common bond they could explore and enjoy. A trade-off she had welcomed, thereby having gained his respect, a rare thing for an Irishman and not given lightly to an outsider, especially not in these troubled times.

But she couldn't have gone to see him today. Parker would have noticed the burs and weed seeds that still clung to her clothes, the mud on her shoes. He would have known she hadn't just been 'out and about' but precisely where she'd been, and if not by those, then by the look in her eyes.

Again she tried to let the warmth sooth her, but Mrs. Haney would hear the silence, for the bath was directly above the kitchen range, the woman wondering at it, for a body ought to be scrubbing a body's skin to 'murder and Creation' with the bristles of a murderous brush.

Carefully budgeting the prewar glycerine soap, she did a thorough job of it, and always there was the blessed relief of gurgling water as it ran away and took its time, giving some few moments of privacy.

They had her right where they wanted. She couldn't go to the police or to Jimmy Allanby—Hamish's life had not only been threatened, he'd be ruined, devastated.

Everything came back in a rush, the Darcy woman, Liam Nolan and Kevin . . . Would Parker let slip that one's last name if she was careful—had she stooped so low as to use the only friend she had apart from Hamish? Was Hamish really what she should call a friend? It had been ages since they'd been away together. They'd once been very much in love. It had been good, hadn't it?

But then Erich had come between them and the war, the castle and Hamish never refusing to help others when needed.

There were stacks and stacks of books in with all the rest of his things. Dickens, Dumas and Kant—she had to find something big enough. Balzac . . . Mark Twain . . . Moliere, Tolstoy, Burns, Darwin, Kant again and such a jumble. It couldn't be a favourite. He had such a mind for his books, such a memory . . .

The Thackeray, then. *The Virginians*, an illustrated copy.

Even as she touched its red leather binding, intuition told her to leave it, but having come this far and needing it, there was no turning back.

Upstairs, in her room, she cut out almost the whole of the inside of the book before jamming the revolver into the gap. The gun just fit, even its cylinder, but the muzzle did cause a slight bulge in the top of the pages when the book was closed.

Burning the scraps in the grate, she took some string and bound four others with it: a Dumas, *The Man in the Iron Mask*; Mark Twain's *Tom Sawyer*; Kant's *Critique of Pure Reason*, in the original German; then the Thackeray; and lastly the Dickens, *A Tale of Two Cities*.

She would leave the bundle on the floor beside her desk with all the others she had prepared. Each was of five, six or seven books, so as to always have something.

They let her into the castle on Friday at just after 2.00 p.m. From the gatehouse and the barbican with its armoury, offices and living quarters for the guards, it was a walk of several hundred yards across the bailey, the huge courtyard that was enclosed by the walls, the house and the towers.

Clutching her bundle of books by its string, Mary started out alone, for the corporal who had accompanied her had been told to go no farther. That, in itself, was unsettling—always someone would escort her right to the library and *not* up to the top of the keep. But what made her even more uneasy was the sheer and utter absence of another living soul.

Only the flapping of the flags came to her, and the solitary sound of her own steps on the metalled surface of the road. One hundred and eighty-two prisoners of war, their guards and guard dogs were here someplace, yet there wasn't a sign of any of them.

It made her think that the truth was out and that they were all watching her—Hamish especially, because he would have been let in early this morning. Colonel Bannerman and Major Trant would both be with him, spiffy in their uniforms but of so vastly different characters and abilities: Trant harshly military and always thinking the worst; Bannermann, the good fellow who was prepared to sit out the war here because the British High Command knew he was of no other use.

Then, too, there was Jimmy—Captain James Allanby. Mary knew he had ordered this, that he must be watching her from the top of that bloody keep. He'd see the books and wonder about them, would hate her for having never paid the slightest attention to him at any of the staff do's. Arrogant—did he think that of her? Did he not sense that she had instantly come to feel there wasn't something quite right about him?

A lone woman, dressed almost as she'd been the other day. The brown velvet jacket was a favourite. It went with so many things and it had lots of useful pockets, had been brushed thoroughly, brushed of its seeds and burs, brushed to that sheen only a good quality of velvet can possess. Didn't it compliment the beige skirt and sand-coloured knee socks, her brown Oxfords, her eyes most of all?

Still there wasn't a sign of anyone—not up on the battlements of the enclosing walls, not anywhere within the bailey below them. Nothing, either, from the many tall windows of the castle house proper, but would the sun and the drifting clouds not block those out with glare or reflections?

Access to the keep was either from within the castle via the second storey, or by the stone staircase to a forebuilding that went up to that same floor. Mary took the latter because she'd been told to, but paused only once to look back across that wasteland.

Cannon were positioned at the four corners of the parade square. A flagpole stood in its centre. Five flags then—at least five. She picked out three of them. The wind . . . the wind atop the keep must be gusting hard.

Reaching the iron-studded, oaken door at last, knowing how heavy it would be, she set the books down to use both hands and brace a foot against the sill. A rush of cold air hit her, she being momentarily blinded by flying dust. Straining now, she pulled the thing open and struggled to retrieve the books, finding this all but impossible unless she threw a shoulder against the door.

It slammed so hard behind her, the sound of it reverberated in the emptiness, making her cringe and hurry on beneath a high stone arch whose portcullis hung above her like a grill of iron teeth set to come crashing down, a lesson in castles for which she might once have been grateful. Boiling oil and hot boulders or iron-tipped arrows would have rained through the murder holes, though this was only a pseudo-Norman castle, not a real one, but was Jimmy watching her through one of them? Would he cut the string and search through the books, he and Major Trant and Colonel Bannerman, the three of them in front of Hamish?

The corridor was nearly seventy-five feet in length, and at the end of it, more stairs began again and it was still so very silent, it made her shudder.

Jimmy was waiting on the battlements some eighty feet above. The wind was freezing. It drove the flag above him to desperation, and at first he didn't say a thing, and she thought then that it really was all up for her, but she wouldn't beg, not even for Hamish's sake.

A Vickers machine gun covered the bailey. One of the merlons had been taken down so as to widen the embrassure and give the thing a greater field of fire. Sandbags helped to buttress the gun and its crew of three.

Two sentries, armed with Lee Enfields, stood to attention in the wings. Was she to be arrested?

'Well, Mrs. Fraser, good of you to have come. Major Trant thought you might like the view. I hope you're not dizzy.'

'Jimmy, why this? Why up here? What's happened?'

She was looking positively ill. Allanby hesitated, asked harshly of himself as he had many times before, Why the bloody hell did Hamish Fraser have to have a wife like this?

Her eyes were moistening rapidly—was it simply because of the wind, he wondered, or because she was afraid of what she'd been up to? 'The prisoners are confined to their barrack rooms until further notice.'

'Then why the machine gun?' demanded Mary, seeing nothing in his gaze but the brutal emptiness of an accuser.

'They're allowed an hour of exercise under Sergeant Stuart's command—push-ups, calisthenics, a forced run of three miles around the compound.'

The bailey and its ring road. 'I see,' she said, turning away to look out over the place and catch glimpses of other machine guns and other sentries on the high points, on subordinate towers and along the battlements of the intervening walls. Had they always been up here? Had there always been so many, and why would Jimmy let her see them if he knew she was meeting Erich Kramer in secret and would be bound to tell him?

'They've threatened to break out, have they?' she asked, unable to keep the sarcasm from her. Like Fay Darcy, Jimmy had chosen to stand directly behind her, the gun crew and sentries hearing everything, of course, because normal conversation was impossible and one had to all but yell.

'They've hanged an innocent man, Mrs. Fraser. A man who had no use for their Nazi doctrines and was strong enough to have said so.'

'An informer?' she asked too swiftly, biting back the tears, knowing that it really was all up for her.

She was still clutching her latest bundle of books by its string. A gust of wind flung her hair about, she still not turning to face him. Crying now, was she? he wondered. Allanby knew he wanted to break her, wanted to smash that infernal pride. 'That husband of yours has threatened to take his bitching to London, to a higher authority than the British High Command in Belfast. To put it bluntly, he wants to mollycoddle murderers—Nazi swine, Mrs. Fraser. There's a war on.'

'And some of them have been pretty badly wounded.'

Must she always rankle him? 'Our authority can't be challenged. There is the law of the land to be obeyed. British law.'

'Then why let me in?'

Allanby wanted to shriek, 'Look at me, damn you!' but would hold himself in check and every bit as erect. 'Because, as a measure of our good faith, and in hopes one of them will come forward, the colonel's decided to allow the library to be reopened three afternoons a week.'

'From two until four?' she asked, knowing Hamish must have raised hell.

'On market days.'

Stung by this, Mary turned to angrily face him. He *couldn't* have known she had agreed to meet Nolan and the others on those days. He couldn't! Yet still there was that emptiness. Jimmy was watching her far too closely. A raw, tough, and unfeeling man when it came to war, and this *was* war, but had they been using her all along to find things out? Had they? 'The conditions, Captain? What is it you people want of me?'

Allanby noted the distress and the bitterness—she had realized well enough that she'd naively repeated things overheard, but he'd not smile in triumph, not yet. He'd take her by an elbow and guide her over to one of the merlons, would force her to look straight down. 'That you say nothing of this meeting either to those bastards in here or to that husband of yours, and that you will report everything to me that you see and overhear.'

'My German's useless.'

'You studied it at college. I've seen you suddenly turn when things were said by them.'

'My first in third-year university classics and modern languages is far too rusty. Besides, I simply won't do it.'

'I didn't think you would.'

'What's that supposed to mean? A deal . . . some sort of deal?'

'Make of it what you will.'

'Wait and see what happens—is that it, Jimmy?'

Her lower lip was quivering; her cheeks were tightening. By God it was good to have her like this. He'd break her, he really would but would only say, 'Yes, wait and see.'

Mary went first, she hurrying to keep ahead of him, the two of them pitching down the stairs and along each length of corridor, faster now, their steps resounding until she was practically running. At any moment she knew she'd burst into tears, would throw the books down and . . .

Allanby snatched at an arm. Missing it, he tried again and managed to yank her to a stop, her chest rising and falling in panic, she struggling to find the will to face him.

Only as her chest eased, the tears plain enough, did he let her have it. 'Colonel wants to see you in the staff common, madam. You're to come along now.'

Bachmann . . . The Leutnant zur See must have told them everything.

Tea—the real stuff—had a seductive quality about it. When taken clear the way she sometimes did, it looked like bog water but was warm and that was supposed to reassure a person who was in trouble with the law, was supposed to make her feel that things might not be so bad if only she would loosen her tongue, and yes, the colonel really did have his supplies of tea.

All the prelims were over, the intros so to speak, the false bantering, the too many hellos and mock surprise at her entry. Colonel Bannerman was sitting in one of the heavy leather armchairs the British Army had found for his use, Major Trant in another, and Hamish . . . Had it been Hamish who had put the cup and saucer into her hands?

It had been the orderly. A plate of sugared biscuits—ginger perhaps—was passed, she shaking her head, Hamish saying, 'Now, Mary, at least try one. Mrs. Bannerman made them especially.'

For what? For this inquisition? Hard as bullets they were

and therefore to be dunked, she letting him and the others return to their talk, they all stalling—holding back the worst until the last and keeping it in so as to make her suffer all the more.

The bundle of books was now on a side table nearest Major Trant who liked to use a short, ivory cigarette holder and to cross his knees when observing trapped women.

Trant was in his early fifties—fit like all the rest of them except for the colonel. He had very dark brown eyes and no sense of humour that she could ever discern. None of that searching emptiness. No, Trant always knew beforehand exactly which direction to take and what the subject was thinking.

He was an expert in interrogating prisoners of war. It was his specialty. Inadvertently she must have given him lots she'd overheard, fool that she'd been.

The chin was narrow, the jaw and cheeks cleaved upwards in a V to the small, but still cauliflower ears he'd belligerently earned in the ring at Sandhurst. The brow was narrow, the dark black hair short and crinkly, the nose aquiline, one might have said had it not been broken, the eyes of medium spacing but small and darting under jet black brows that were thin.

There were sun blotches—he'd spent time in the Far East, had been a liaison officer attached to the Hong Kong police force, it was said. A man of medium height but one who always seemed to be at eye level with whomever he was addressing. Trant didn't 'talk' in the normal sense of people who are at ease with themselves and with one another, at least not that she had ever witnessed. He 'addressed,' his colonel in particular.

In another life and at another time, Colonel Dulsin Bannerman, 'Dulsey' for short, would have been the epitome of a country squire. Something out of Fielding perhaps.

Robust and short, the uniform stretched at the buttons,

he was bound in by the Sam Brown belt. Bannerman tried to please everyone. He liked an 'easy ship,' liked his accounts to be 'square.' He had the bluest eyes of any man she had ever encountered—far bluer than Erich's or even those of Liam Nolan, of that unnatural blue that signals something wrong in the character, something hidden.

The short blond, carefully trimmed hair was now faded, washed-out and turning to the very pale grey he had accepted long ago. A man of some sixty-seven years and past 'retirement.'

Snatches of their conversation came to her. The British had airfields and army and naval bases in Northern Ireland. There was a training camp for 'special forces.' The factories and shipyards in Belfast were back to normal, or nearly so. Nothing worth listening to. Just dross to lull her for the big event, but then, suddenly out of the blue as it were, and from the colonel, he having poured himself another cup of tea and reaching for another biscuit, 'Are we agreeable, Dr. Fraser?'

The doctor set his cup and saucer aside, *and* his pipe, Mary realizing that for the first time ever in her thoughts, she had referred to Hamish as 'the doctor.'

'Colonel, I want two periods of exercise for them each day and a return to their games of soccer. *Och*, it takes the steam out of them, man. You know it yourself. Am I no' right, Major?'

'Dr. Fraser, we've got to find the killer, or killers, of that man. London won't have it otherwise. Orders are orders,' said Trant.

'But surely locking them up won't work? Put them off their guard. Loosen up.'

'Admit that Second Lieutenant Bachmann was an informer, that it?' went on Trant.

'Yes. He was one of theirs. They . . .'

'Had a right to exercise their own brand of justice?' demanded Trant, uncrossing his knees and getting up to slosh tea, bloody tea, all over the carpet.

But not on his precious uniform, thank God.

Hamish wasn't going to back off. Mary could see this at a glance. 'These men are prisoners of war,' he said. 'Under the articles of the Geneva Convention, I ask again that you allow them sufficient exercise *and* food, *and* recreation to maintain normal health. I also want my patients transferred to civilian hospitals where they can get the proper prostheses and physiotherapy. You can't keep those poor men waiting forever!'

'Damn it, man, there's a war on,' shouted Trant.

Had he met his match? wondered Mary. Hamish drew himself up—the colonel knew what he was about to say but did Hamish deliberately let him intercede?

'Now, now, gentlemen. A compromise, isn't that right, Mrs. Fraser? A happy medium, with some privileges being withheld until such time as . . .'

'As hell freezes over?' demanded Hamish. 'I meant what I said, Colonel. I'll go to London if necessary. I'll see the prime minister himself.'

'A fat lot of good that'll do,' snorted Trant.

'Aye, but not if I were to talk t' th' press first, Major. The American press.'

He'd done it now. He'd said the stupidest of things. 'Why not let me help?' she heard herself saying. 'I could . . .' She shrugged. 'Listen more carefully, I suppose. The men do say things to each other that they might not say when near anyone else. I've known it for some time and . . . and have always wondered if I oughtn't to speak to you about it.'

Silently Allanby cursed her for not having earlier agreed to do as he'd asked, but was she now trying to bargain with them? She hadn't even glanced at him once since coming into the room.

Trant knew he'd best give Jimmy a nod, for she'd just agreed to do what Bannerman and himself had had in mind for her all along, but had it been clever of her, a last desperate gamble to stay the arm of the law, or was she simply getting back at the captain? Interrogating a woman like Mrs. Mary Ellen Fraser would be like having a damned fine meal in a damned fine restaurant, especially when picking the flesh out of the snail.

It was Dulsey Bannerman who said, with tongue in cheek, 'We wouldn't want you to spy on anyone, Mrs. Fraser. They're being sent to camps in Canada as soon as a ship becomes available. It's only that we'd like to clear the matter up before they leave us.'

Canada. Dulsey had done it perfectly, thought Trant. She had been struck by the news, and struck hard.

All of them were watching her now, Mary knew. Hamish in particular. 'More tea, madam?' asked the orderly, she feeling herself give a nod as Jimmy went over to the books to cut the string.

'A Dickens,' he said, flipping through the pages before passing it to Trant who then handed the book to the colonel, who said with boyhood appreciation, *David Copperfield*, oh my. Do they really want to read this?'

'Some of them are learning English, Colonel. I thought reading Dickens might help.'

'You do get on with them, don't you,' said the major, but it wasn't given as a question, more as a statement of fact. Trant could easily have gone through the books himself and yet had let Jimmy do the job so that he could watch her, she being momentarily distracted.

It was coming now—Mary knew it and, setting her cup and saucer down, forced herself to look at Hamish, to plead with her eyes for understanding, to beg it of him.

He wasn't 'old.' He was looking lost, though, and was worrying about her.

'A Mark Twain,' said Jimmy as if it were trash and *Huckleberry Finn* not one of the finest novels ever.

That, too, was flipped through and then the others, he passing each of them to Trant who deliberately took his time before handing each of them to the colonel.

'Nothing,' he said.

'Perhaps you've been wrong then, Captain,' she heard the colonel say.

'Perhaps.'

That had been Trant, of course, but thank heavens she had left the gun at home this time, wanting to find out how things were.

They talked about the IRA, about the Garda's secret list and of how, under de Valera's government, they had very nearly been cleaned out of Eire and destroyed forever.

They talked about how the Dublin Armoury had been robbed of more than one million rounds of .455 calibre ammunition—enough to fill five or six large lorries, but that the silly buggers had then had no place to hide the stuff and the Garda had made a clean sweep and got back far more.

Yes, they talked and said more quietly and firmly that de Valera's government had been and still were scared stiff the IRA would try to link up with the Nazis and that Britain, being Britain, would rush in to occupy the South if there was so much as a hint of its ever happening.

'Hence, Nolan had to come up here,' said someone, the colonel she thought.

'Has there been anything new on him?' That had been Hamish.

It was Trant who said, 'Only that one of the Darcy sisters was recently seen in the vicinity.'

'As was Kevin O'Bannion,' said Jimmy, watching her closely, too closely, but failing entirely to realize that he had just given her Kevin's last name.

'He's the second-in-command of the Northern Ireland group,' said Trant. 'A cold-blooded killer, Mrs. Fraser. A terrorist who'll let nothing, not even his own people, stand in the way.'

'A rebel,' bristled the colonel, reaching for a slice of his wife's pound cake.

'Rumour has it that O'Bannion and the Darcy woman have met up with Liam Nolan and are hoping to get him out of Ireland.'

Trant had said that, his knees again crossed.

'What we would really like to know, Mrs. Fraser, is if you've overheard anything useful in this regard—the other's a foregone conclusion, I take it.'

Again it wasn't a question but she answered in the affirmative, knowing Hamish would only say, 'Mary, how could you?'

'The Darcy woman, Mrs. Faser?' reminded Trant. 'You were recently in the South. Captain Allanby . . .'

'Yes . . . Yes, I was there. I gave a lift to a farmer, that's all. I heard nothing useful—how could I have? I didn't even know of the bombing until . . .'

'The bloody news was splashed all over that newspaper you had on the front seat of the car. The whole of Dublin must have been abuzz!' said Allanby.

Mary leapt to her feet, waiting for the accusations. She would face each of them in turn, would try not to disgrace herself. 'I bought that for my husband. I was in a hurry and . . . and didn't even look at it.'

'Or hear what the vendor must have been shouting?' asked Trant.

'That is correct, Major.' It was all she could think to say, but Jimmy had clenched and unclenched his fists and was still doing this.

'Perhaps you've been wrong then, Captain,' said Bannerman before repeating his earlier comment about Nolan having come north, but adding, 'and that's an end to it for now. An end.'

'You lied to me, Erich. Lied!'

'Mary, I couldn't help it. I had to.'

'Did you? What about the man who was hanged?'

'That business has nothing to do with us. Nothing!'

'They think it has! They know all about us. I'm certain they do. Certain, do you hear? He must have told them!'

'*Ach*, Bachmann knew nothing. The British are lying.'

'You're to be moved to Canada.'

'When?'

'I . . . I don't know. As . . . as soon as a ship becomes available. Perhaps you'd best tell Berlin that, hadn't you? Otherwise one of your own might just torpedo you.'

Canada! Everything counted on time. Everything! Mary could see him thinking this as he glanced both ways along the darkened corridor towards the light at each end. Franz Bauer and Hans Schleiger were watching out. Bauer, she had never liked. Bauer.

'Which of them said we were to be moved?'

He still didn't have a care for what she'd just been through.

'Well?' he demanded.

'Colonel Bannerman.'

'Not Trant? Not Allanby?'

'Bannerman. I've only just come from having tea with them. Tea, Erich!'

He couldn't know that right up until the last she had thought herself done for. Again he glanced towards each end of the corridor, still kept his hands planted firmly pressed flat against the wall on either side of her, still kept a little distance but now something suddenly went out of him and he gave that fleeting smile she'd come to know.

'I've brought you trouble,' he whispered. Nearly all of their words had had to be given in whispers, some urgent, some not. That warmth he had for her came into his eyes, that momentary rush of a faraway look.

'I ought to hate you,' she said. 'This thing between us can't go on and had best stop.'

Kramer laid the backs of three fingers against the smooth softness of her right cheek and immediately felt the flush of heat in her. Furious with him, she was rightly feeling betrayed. Something very frightening must have happened. Trant or Allanby, or even Bannerman must suspect her. As always though, the nearness of him triggered signals in her, but had she realized she was fighting a battle she could never be allowed to win?

He'd touch her lips and let his fingers linger there, had best look steadily into her eyes and say it with meaning. 'I love you, Mary. That still hasn't changed.'

'You don't!' she said, jerking that head of hers away as far as possible to glare accusingly at him through the semi-darkness. 'It's crazy of us to meet so soon. Jimmy Allanby is on to something. What I don't know, but . . . but something.'

The corridor was off the library. Usually blocked by locked doors at either end, it had, for some reason, been left open, forgotten in the rush of things perhaps, the British having carted everything back—Kramer could see her thinking this and worrying about it. Always she was the worrier, a useful plus for them.

The library had been in a shambles—still was, for that matter. Stacks of books had lain everywhere, they having all been confiscated and returned by the guards. Several of the men were busy sorting through and putting them on the shelves. She'd be missed—he could see her thinking this, too, she always noting the bits and pieces of uniform that had been saved as their ships or boats or aircraft had gone down. A blue tunic on one, a pair of grey-green trousers on another, felt-lined flying boots on yet another.

'Erich, *please*. I must go. The corporal who came with me is new. He'll be watching for just such a thing. Trant will have told him to. Trant, Erich.'

'Will I see you again?'

Vehemently Mary shook her head. 'We mustn't. It's far too dangerous. There are things that have happened since I last saw you, things I have to . . . to think about.'

Erich didn't ask if there had been trouble with Hamish, or anything like that. Indeed, even though he must need to know what had happened with his 'cousin' in Dublin, he didn't ask about it. He *knew* she needed time and he *was* willing to give her that, even with Canada on the horizon.

Tapping her lightly under the chin, he gave a gentle chuckle. It was not that of a man who would have had a tanker within the cross-haired glass of his periscope, not that of a man who must have shouted time and again, 'Fire numbers one and two!'

Kramer took her hands in his and held them against his lips, felt the trembling in her, the uncertainty, knew there were things he had to ask but that they'd have to wait. She'd be worrying about his wanting to kiss her now, would be wondering if she would still be able to resist. Was she wet? he wondered and thought it likely. Lies . . . he had told her lies—she'd be telling herself this, would be shouting it at herself.

As his lips found hers, she tried to draw away but then . . . then threw her arms about his neck as he pressed her against the wall, her skirt rucking up until suddenly he let go of it to slide his hands under pullover, blouse and brassiere to take each nipple firmly between a thumb and forefinger.

'I can't, Erich. I mustn't. Hamish . . .'

A button must have popped off her blouse. A button! Mary knew she couldn't have heard it hit the floor at their feet, he not leaving her yet, she now pressing her forehead against his chest.

More couldn't be said, for one of the lookouts—Bauer, she thought—hissed 'Vanish!' in *Deutsch*, and they parted, she going one way, Erich the other.

The sheets were cool and crisp and smelling sweetly of hay and roses and autumn. Deeply troubled by the day, Mary slid further down and pulled the covers up about herself. Mrs. Haney and Bridget did such a good job of things. No spite, no venom. Just clean sheets, ironed to beat the blazes beside the kitchen fire.

I hate myself, she silently said. No matter how hard she tried, the image of an Allied freighter going down at night in mid-Atlantic wouldn't leave her. Another seven thousand tons of shipping, that one. Hamish and she had listened to the news on the wireless, and then she had gone up to bed, to huge blessings that were so often taken for granted, to shelter and clean sheets now warming with her body's heat.

'You wanted him,' she said softly to herself. 'Admit it, damn you. You secretly hoped he'd take you right then and there. . . . I needed reassurance, that's all.'

From him? she silently asked and answered, Erich doesn't love you. He can't! That freighter would have lain like a thin, mast-bristling silhouette on the ocean's dark horizon. He would have watched as they'd got closer and closer to it and then, as the torpedoes had struck it, he'd have seen the explosions flash brightly through the pitch darkness of the night as they ripped the hull right out of it.

Bathed in that terrible light, men would have run this way and that in their confusion and panic, trying to cut the lifeboats free, the boats then dangling over the side as the ship listed suddenly, so suddenly, it would have upended in a ball of fire and hiss of steam before slipping below the waves to give the death rattle of bursting bulkheads and boiler plate.

Not speaking, Hamish had looked at her, she not saying anything, either, each of them wondering how many survivors there could possibly be from that one ship alone? The men on watch perhaps, but definitely not those who had been below decks in their bunks or the engine room—how many tons of shipping had Erich's U-boat sunk, how many lives had been lost to the cold, cold waters of the North Atlantic because of him?

The news had gone on to other things, she knowing Hamish had still been watching her. Leningrad was under siege, Moscow threatened. Near Kiev, in the Ukraine, more than seven hundred thousand Russian soldiers had surrendered to the enemy.

London had been bombed again.

And in the North Atlantic, a convoy out of Halifax, in Canada, had been savagely mauled by a wolf pack of German submarines. Seven ships had been lost—not just that one freighter. Two hundred and eighty-four men were known to have died or gone missing and yet here she was, clean, not covered with Bunker C and freezing, lying only in fear of losing everything, of disgracing herself and those who counted most, of dyingtoo.

'Mary, what is it?'

When she didn't answer, he said, 'Is it the loss of those men? There is no feeling in war. Men have to kill without feeling. It's the only way. We have our own U-boats. Had the shoe been on the other foot, it would have been the same.'

Mary knew he was thinking of Erich and herself, of the man he'd befriended, the patient he had cared for and trusted, the wife as well.

Fraser sat down on the edge of her bed. He thought to tell her that on the late bulletin they'd announced that one of the U-boats had been sent to the bottom, and that this must mean the Royal Navy had some new means of detection.

He thought to tell her that he understood. He tried to reach out to her, only to pull back at the last and then to reach out again.

As his hand came to rest on the back of her head, she heard him gently saying, 'What is it, lass?' and when she didn't answer, felt his hand slide down under her hair to the nape of her neck. Even as she went on and on and couldn't seem to stop herself or say a thing, he worked at relieving the tension in her. The feel of his hands was like some magical balm. He knew she was desperately in love with Erich Kramer and that it couldn't have been easy for her at the castle today, and when she had finally settled down a little, he said, 'Our Ria says you're all a-rattle these days. Like a chicken she once knew as a girl. "The poor creature had its head off, it surely had, Doctor, and ran about the yard trying to peck up its dinner before climbing into the nest to lay four brown eggs and die. *Four*, it was, I'm telling you, Doctor. Ah and sure it was a tough *ould* bird it was. Stewed to string and still like binder twine!"'

Grimacing, clamping her eyes shut, Mary tried to stop herself. Hamish *loved* these people, was in sympathy with them, with the very heart and soul of them.

A meeting place, Kevin O'Bannion had said. Some place along the coast—in Donegal perhaps? Somewhere hidden so well, the Germans could bring in a U-boat to take Erich Kramer and Liam Nolan off and how, please, had Erich known of the White Horse Inn and Mrs. Tulford, how?

Pushing herself up on one arm, she turned to look at him. 'Hamish, make love to me,' she said—nothing else. She had to have him in her, had to feel the warmth of his ejaculation, had to have a reason for what had happened to her body, had to lie.

At midnight she awoke to the sound of a single aircraft. The pillowcases were damp. Hamish hadn't come to bed with her.

On Thursday she wasn't feeling well and didn't go to the castle in the afternoon. On Saturday it was the same.

No breakfast for fear she'd throw up and let the news out. Weak tea and a biscuit at dinner. Something solid for supper, and then, after Mrs. Haney and Bridget had left for the day, two ham sandwiches with mustard and a glass of porter.

---

* While there were rationing restrictions and periodic checks, farmers and other rural people, as here, tended to fare much better than those in the urban centres.

3

Fay met her in the orchard at the far corner of the garden. The Fraser woman had been gathering windfalls, it being Sunday and the one day the woman had the kitchen to herself. The rotten, sour-sweet cider smell of the apples was all around the twat, as were the yellow jackets. 'You're a fancy woman, Mrs. Fraser.'

'Don't you *care* if someone sees you from the house?'

The voice was shrill; Fay shook her head. 'It's the rebel's curse and cause t' be a rebel. The more we stand out, the more we succeed.'

Hamish was in the house. Hamish . . . Mary set the basket down. 'I can't go through with it. I can't betray my country and my husband.'

Brave words now were they? 'We'll see about that then.'

'What's that supposed to mean?'

She was agitation itself. 'That you're to make of it what you will. Slut, I'm thinking. See what happens to sluts who bed those they're not supposed to and then refuse to do as they're told.'

'Wait . . . Please wait. Don't you see it's not easy for me to take things into Tralane? The guards always check.'

Fay turned to swiftly close the distance between them. The woman's cardigan had come undone, a button had been lost from her blouse. 'By guards, you mean Captain Allanby.'

'Yes . . . Yes, him.'

'What's he to you then?'

With a toss, the Darcy woman threw back the hank of reddish brown hair that had fallen forward over her brow and let an insane look come into her sea-green eyes.

'Nothing. I *don't* exactly like him.'

'But he fancies you, does he? You're quite the looker. Always in heat, is it? And there's Jimmy Allanby himself panting at your heels and wanting to lick the arse off you. Am I not right?'

Mary waited for her to shriek, 'Answer me!' but it never came.

Fay touched the place where the button had gone missing. 'You've lost something, deary. You want to mend a thing like that, you do, what with all them men lusting after that body of yours.'

Involuntarily Mary felt the gap. She'd forgotten all about the button. She should have gone back into that corridor to look for it, knew she'd been far too upset. 'Wait . . . Please wait,' she called.

Fay turned to look at her from under the last of the trees. 'Objecting is it? Not obeying orders? Well, you watch and you wait, and you'll learn soon enough.'

The Fraser woman crouched to grab and throw apples at her—any of the damned things. Stung repeatedly by the yellow jackets, the woman never once took her eyes from her, the juice and the pulp of those now clenched running like blood through her fingers, but she'd not cry out, not this one, though the pain must be hurting her something terrible.

Fay was impressed but didn't care to let on and walked away without another word.

It was Hamish who pried Mary's hands apart in the kitchen and said, 'What have you done?'

'Stung myself rather badly, I'm afraid.' Had he seen them talking? Did he now know what she was up against? If he did, Hamish didn't let on. He washed the pulp and juice from her hands, then found his tweezers and removed the stingers, after which he bathed the stings with methylated spirit and swabbed them with cotton wool that had been dipped in vinegar.

'Now go and lie down for a bit. We've apples enough.'

'I didn't want to waste them. I really was trying to help out. Mrs. Haney . . .'

'*Och*, I know you were and that Ria's been on another of her rationing crusades. A cup of that blackberry tea perhaps, and then a walk? Would that suit?'

'Yes . . . Yes, of course. You know I always enjoy our walks, but let's have the rosehip with a touch of her honey. It will please her if we do, and at least then I can then tell her that we did.'

And not lie. Mary's hands could only be throbbing like blazes, yet she acted as though immune to it.

They'd had their 'tea' and then their walk. They'd had their supper in by the fire and had gone to bed after the news. Hamish never closed his bedroom door. Doctors who are always on call can never do a thing like that, for the telephone might ring at any time.

His light had still been on at 11.00 p.m. and then at midnight. He was reading again. Robbie was lying on the bed beside him. The two of them were snuggled up, the dog as asleep as dogs ever get, which simply meant that Robbie would be certain to have heard her, she standing out in the corridor.

Robbie went everywhere with Hamish. A Sheltie with an absolutely gorgeous coat and a clear, crisp mind, he embarrassed her with his loyalty. It was as if the dog knew she wasn't behaving properly and had therefore shunned her. Oh, he'd shake a paw and come if called but one could tell his heart wasn't in it.

Mary hesitated. There were so many feelings crowding her— guilt, loss, fear; a cold, sheeting fear that terrified, for Fay Darcy had meant what she'd said, but a need also to tell Hamish everything, to talk it out and see what was best. To confess, to say, I've been cheating on you.

Another page was turned—had he seen the Darcy woman and herself and thought to say nothing of it? *Nothing*—Hamish who knew a lot more about the IRA and the local people than he ever let on? He would know what she'd been going through, would try to understand. That was his very nature.

She would have to do something. There couldn't be any questions as to who the father was, not for her sake and not for his. She would have to face up to the rest of it, too, ought, really, to confide in him since only he could help her.

He nudged the reading glasses further up on the bridge of his nose. The pale light from the lamp brought out the softness of the reddish tints in his sandy hair, making him look gentler, kinder, calmer than she'd ever seen before.

Though it hurt her knuckles, she knocked and said, 'Hamish, I have to talk to you. Can I come in?'

The dog looked up, saw whom he had already known was there and, saddened by the thought, laid his muzzle down again. There was such a look of dismay in Robbie's eyes, it was as if she had not just disturbed their peace but would come between them.

'Robbie, go and lie on the carpet, there's my wee lad. Mary, is it your hands? Do you want a sleeping tablet?'

She shook her head and managed a smile. 'No, they're fine. Lots better. The swelling seems to have reached its peak. I only wish they hadn't stung me between the fingers.'

Robbie slunk off the bed and went to curl up on the carpet. As Fraser watched, Mary came to stand where the dog's paws had first touched the floor. She was wearing the dark blue velvet dressing gown he'd bought her a year ago this coming Christmas, when such things could still be found, but what was there in the look she gave? A plea for understanding? A 'Hamish, I don't just need to talk?'

'What is it?' he asked, but she didn't answer. Instead, she let the robe fall about her ankles, himself pulling back the covers.

With a brief, self-conscious smile, she slid in beside him and snuggled down. 'You smell nice,' she said, giving him a contented sigh and meaning it too, no doubt. 'Did you know that?' she asked suddenly, twisting to look at him before settling back. 'Hamish . . . Darling, why can't things be like they used to be? I need to be with you some of the time, even if you're out on a call. I need to have someone I can talk to, like we used to. Something's come up and . . . Well, it's more than I can handle on my own.'

Dear God, she'd come to him at last. 'Light on, or light off?' he asked.

She had shut her eyes anyway, must be wondering how best to begin.

'The news was terrible, wasn't it?' she said. 'Everything indicates the Germans are going to win.'

Fraser felt how hot her hand was, she taking his own to tuck it under an arm. 'Does Erich believe this?' he asked, letting her sense the tightness in his voice.

Mary gave a shrug. 'I haven't seen him yet, but the others all believe it. A few months, a year at most and then they'll be free again.'

Almost to a man, Fraser knew they could be arrogant when they wanted, too young most of them to know what war was really like, too fit, taken too early perhaps. Officers, of course. The pick of the crop, the ones who had joined up first, Nazis some of them, not all, but those who had hanged one of their own certainly must have been, though he'd not say any of this to her. He'd wait.

'I've become a symbol to them, Hamish. A "good" person among the enemy. Someone they feel they can trust. Someone they can joke with and talk to, and be themselves.'

'It was wrong of the colonel and the others to have asked you to spy for them. You mustn't do it, lass. It's far too dangerous. They won't find the men who hanged the Leutnant zur See Bachmann, not even if you were to listen and repeat every word you had heard.'

'Who did it? You must have some idea.'

'Is that what you wanted to discuss?'

'Not exactly but . . . but it's a part of it. It must be.'

Fraser reached out to switch off the light. Sliding down under the covers, he turned on to his side and laid a hand fondly against her cheek. '*Och*, with you I'm at a loss; with Robbie I know exactly what to do.'

'I'm not a dog,' she said, feeling the nearness of him now, the warmth.

'Of course you're not, nor would I have it.'

'I'm not the girl you lost in France, nor the wife you used to have. I wish I was that girl, Hamish. Sometimes I really do, but I'm not.'

It's Erich, isn't it? he wanted to say but couldn't bring himself to do so. Again she snuggled down against him, this time with her head in the crook of his arm.

'You're such a good man, Hamish. I don't want to see you hurt. There are things I have to tell you and I want so much to say them.'

It began to rain, and they listened to it gusting against the windows, Mary plucking at his pajama top until finally managing to slide a hand in under. 'I like the feel of the hairs on your chest,' she said.

'I *am* partial to having you feel them.'

'Are you really?' she asked, pushing herself away to sit up and look down at him through the darkness.

'*Och*, you must know that. What is it? What's been troubling you?'

'So many things I don't know where or how to begin.'

Mary pulled off her nightgown. Shutting her eyes, she kissed him on the chin and snuggled up again, wanted so much to say, 'Make love to me, my darling,' but felt it wouldn't be right of her. Guilt and Erich lay between them, the child as well. 'Come in me, Hamish. I have to have you in me.'

Fraser kissed her then and slid her arms about his neck but suddenly she began to cry, couldn't seem to stop herself.

'Mary, please tell me what it is before it's too late.'

Her knees came up on either side of him, he wanting her no matter what and tearing at his pajama bottoms, trying to get free of them.

It had to happen. Hamish needed the offer doubt would hold; she needed it too. 'In, my darling. In,' she begged.

A rain of gravel hit the window. Another burst followed, he penetrating her deeply only to curse and withdraw. 'Oh damn and blast it! What the blessed hell's the matter now? I'm not a bloody vet!'

Robbie was barking like crazy and leaping about in the darkness, the two of them having forgotten all about him.

Another blast of gravel hit the window, giving the telltale tinkle of broken glass as Hamish fumbled blindly for something to wear, she scrambling out of bed to thrust his pajamas at him.

A woman was standing in the darkness and the rain, clutching a shawl about herself and keening up at them. 'Doctor . . . Doctor, come quickly. Oh, please, Doctor. Something terrible's happened.'

'Mrs. Haney, what is it?' he yelled, leaning well out of the window.

'Doctor, it's Caithleen O'Neill. She's in the field back of Ned Cassidy's cowshed.'

Hamish let a roar out of him, a cry of despair at the insanity of things. Turning swiftly from the window, not bothering even to close it, he shouted, 'Put the light on, Mary. For God's sake get dressed and don't hang about. I'm going to need you. Don't just stand there gaping at me. Get some blankets!' as if she were to blame for what had happened, as if he knew all about things and the worst had happened to someone else.

Hamish had never spoken to her like this before. Never!

Knowing Mrs. Haney would see her nakedness against the light and that it would have to be enough for gossip's whispers, Mary ran to the window to look down. The child would die within her as she died herself. It would never be born, not properly. There would be no time for that but she might lose it as she died and that would start them talking.

The rain came down in buckets but she heard it as at the frontier, the headlamps shining out into the night. They were on a lane that ran beneath overhanging branches and between low and tumbled walls of stone. Ned Cassidy must have taken his milk cart along it thousands of times but had never once lifted a finger to maintain the blessed thing. The lane wasn't just a typical Irish boreen but a prideful example of it, the ruts being overly deep, the boulders huge. At every turning there was either the empty blackness of a field or a wall of brush and trees that threatened to dent the top of the car.

Hamish drove with grim determination, and for the first time ever, she realized exactly how well he knew his way about the countryside. They hadn't needed directions from Mrs. Haney in the backseat who had offered them in any case *and* a litany that had stretched back to the Troubles and beyond, the woman having never once touched on exactly what had happened to Caithleen O'Neill, though Hamish knew—Mary was certain of this.

In low gear, they reached the top of a hill and started down but when they came to the bridge, it looked so like the one Liam Nolan had been on that day she'd met him. There were bushes on either side, a timber lay half out of the water . . .

Panicking, she heard herself shouting, 'Stop! It's broken, Hamish. I've been here before.'

"Tis no more broken than I am, Doctor,' said Mrs. Haney. 'More likely awash, I'm thinking.'

'Wait here, then, the two of you, while I have a look.'

'No, I will!'

Mary scrambled out and ran into the light, and they watched as she bent to the sheeting rain, clutching her coat collar close, her boots now ankle deep, the Loughie rising by the moment as the torch was shone around.

Fraser saw her step gingerly on to the bridge, she turning now in uncertainty to look with disbelief at the soundness of it.

'It's as I've said, Doctor. No more broke than I am. Your missus must have been thinking of another.'

Yet still she didn't want to believe it. Finally Fraser saw her look up and heard her shout something. Rolling down the side windscreen, he stuck his head out and yelled, 'Is it clear?'

Mary fought her way back to tell him there must be a steep hill on the other side, a thing he'd have known in any case.

'And the bridge?' he asked, wondering which one she'd thought it must have been.

'Solid,' she said, no longer paying the rain any mind.

'Hop in, then, and we'll give it a go. Hang on, Mrs. Haney, and say a prayer for us.'

The lane ended in a cattle gate on the steep side of yet another hill. From there they made their way uphill to the cattle shed which was in the ruins of an old abbey. There was a lantern on and at first they thought the girl must have been brought in out of the rain, but this wasn't so. Bits of her clothing law strewn about in the straw and the dung. The cattle mooed or stared or bawled. A pitchfork leaned against the wall, the sound of the rain being everywhere.

Mary stooped to pick up a blouse, Hamish angrily saying, 'Leave that, for God's sake!' and they went back out into the rain, he grim and determined, so much so that he was soon well ahead of them.

Caithleen O'Neill was down in a hollow on the other side of the hill. A scattering of men stood around her, three of them holding lanterns, Hamish pushing on through. . . .

Mary flung up a hand to stop herself from crying out at the sight of the girl. Mrs. Haney said, 'Dear God forgive them, the poor wee thing.'

The girl, a direct descendant of one of the High Kings of Eire, or so it was claimed, lay on her side, stripped of her clothes, shorn of her lovely hair and covered in tar and feathers from head to foot.

She was shivering, was whimpering and trying to say the rosary as the rain beat down on her. A girl of seventeen. Mary had seen her out walking with one of the men from the castle, a boy of nineteen, a British tommy.

Hamish hesitated and she knew then that he was afraid but not for himself—never that. 'Caithleen . . . Caithleen, it's me, Dr. Fraser. Now you're not to worry a moment more. You're going to be all right because I'm going to see to it.

'Mary, pass me my bag. Someone shelter us with one of those blankets. A lantern, one of you—dear God, don't you dare defy me. A lantern now, I say!'

It was the closest he'd come to cursing them, though the tarring wasn't of their doing and the girl but a leper now.

When Mary held the bag open for him, she saw the tears and understood that they weren't just for Caithleen but for herself.

The kitchen was warm, the mug of real tea as strong as the Irish could make it but good to hold. As Mary sat alone on a bench, Mrs. Haney muscled another soup kettle of water on to the stove.

Warm water, rationed soap and rationed butter would be used, but lastly. Already wads and wads of used cotton wool and gauze lay about the floor. All the bottles of surgical benzene had long since been drained. Poor Hamish was now using those of methylated spirit, eight brown bottles of which had come from the pharmacy in Armagh, he having asked her to ring Trant first to request all that he'd had in the castle's infirmary before then asking her to beg them to send someone to Armagh for extra lanolin as well.

It would take him the rest of the night. She knew he wouldn't stop until he had the girl tucked in upstairs. He was washing her off in the mudroom. Both its window and door were wide open to air the place, yet the fumes were everywhere and he was worried about them, kept glancing at the door whenever he could, kept muttering to himself.

Her head bowed in shame, Caithleen stood with fists clenched at her sides and eyes clamped shut. The tar was now in streaks and brownish-black smears through which the whiteness of her skin showed. When the worst of it was removed, they quickly used the warm water, soap, baking soda and lanolin, the butter too. Mary knew he'd never seen anything like it before, that it couldn't have been worse.

'Darling, let me take over. You need to rest.'

'Would you get Caithleen another cup of that tea, Mary? With lots of sugar and none of that damned saccharin. Add a dram or two. It won't hurt, will it, Caithleen? Now surely it won't.'

Mary held the cup to the girl's lips, Caithleen letting the tea trickle down her throat and never once opening her eyes, but each time the lips were touched, the girl stiffened in alarm. 'Don't cry anymore, Caithleen. Please don't. Hamish is taking good care of you. Mrs. Haney's still here, in the kitchen. We're all going to look after you.'

They came to the house then. They'd been out hunting rebels half the night, were drenched to the skin, but hadn't found a thing: Jimmy Allanby, Sergeant Stuart, and six of the men. All were armed—Lee Enfield rifles, Thompson guns, and a Webley service revolver for Jimmy just like the one she still had upstairs in her room.

Hamish didn't look up. He kept right on gently bathing a spot before scraping at it with the dinner knife. 'What's the meaning of this, Captain?' he asked—none of them would have noticed the flicker of anger, none of them would have realized that he must have been worrying about them all along.

'A word, that's all,' said Jimmy, taking things in quickly. 'That girl has to tell us who did this, Dr. Fraser. My orders are to . . .'

His shirt sleeves rolled well above the elbows, Hamish straightened to face him. The broad suspender straps swelled outwards as he drew in a breath. He was the taller by a good half-head. 'Since when do orders supersede medical necessity?'

Jimmy had taken off the grey woollen gloves the Army used when in battle in the rain and cold, but hadn't pulled off the black beret with its regimental badge.

'Look, I don't want trouble, do I?' he said.

'Nor I,' said Hamish softly. 'Kindly ask your men to step outside. There's to be no smoking in here and that *is* an order, Captain. It really is.'

Jimmy searched Hamish's expression for signs of weakness. Mary knew he was thinking him a failure, that he'd had to leave Edinburgh in disgrace and that he'd taken to the bottle, but what Jimmy didn't know, what none of them had realized, herself most especially until now, was that Hamish had come by choice.

'I'll ask it of you again, Captain. Kindly remove your men from my mudroom.'

'Sergeant.'

'Sir?'

'Place Dr. Fraser under arrest.'

Hamish must have known what Jimmy would do, for when seized by the arms, he didn't resist. 'Caithleen,' he said, tossing the words to her, 'this animal is going to ask you some questions. It's your right to say nothing. *Nothing*, Caithleen. Do you hear me, lass? Mrs. Fraser and I will back you to the hilt.'

For this he was shoved from behind and pinned to the wall with one of the rifles and three of the men holding him there. Mary used her fists and voice, kicking savagely at Jimmy and shrieking that he was cruel and a bastard. 'You're only doing this because the sight of you sickens me,' she cried, Hamish shouting, 'Mary, for God's sake, a spark!'

Caithleen broke into sobs. Mrs. Haney came roaring through from the kitchen, her rolling pin upraised, only to be shoved aside, it clattering to the floor as coats, hats and scarves showered down around her from their hangers. Pushed up against the wall beside Hamish, forced to watch in silence, they waited as Jimmy walked around the girl. He'd say it only once—he had that look about him: cold, brutal, fed up with the Irish and with the way the war had been going for him.

'The names, Caithleen O'Neill. Fay Darcy, am I right? Was it Fay who tore the clothes from you as you shrieked at her?'

There was no other sound, the girl steadfastly gazing at the wall beyond him.

'Liam Nolan was with the Darcy woman, wasn't he?' said Jimmy. 'So why you, Caithleen? Why the example?'

Allanby let his eyes travel down her naked back until they came to rest on her rump. She'd a good figure—far better than most of them. A real 'slip of a thing,' the Irish would have said.

He wouldn't touch her yet, wouldn't make her jump and flinch by doing that. He'd simply say it suddenly from behind her left ear. 'Listen to me, girl. Kevin O'Bannion didn't order this. Kevin's far too smart, so he's split from Fay and Nolan, am I right?'

How could she possibly have known, she screaming her heart out as they'd grappled her to the ground? wondered Mary, sucking in a breath as Jimmy came to face the girl again, even to letting his eyes run swiftly over her.

Hamish had had to cut the hair closer. One breast was free of tar, the other still had a few feathers clinging to it.

Again Jimmy said, 'Listen to me, girl,' this time grabbing her by the chin to press his face close to hers. 'I want the names of those who did this to you and I want to know why. So what if you've been making eyes at one of my men and walking out with him of a Sunday? That's been going on for months and we know he hasn't been poling you because he's told us you're a good girl, so why this, Caithleen? Why all of a sudden?'

'She can't answer,' said Hamish. 'Her voice is gone.'

'SERGEANT.'

'SIR?'

'Silence that man if he opens his mouth again. Well?' he asked. 'They cut off your hair, girl, as though you'd been letting that boy pole the daylights out of you. They sheared you like a sheep, bent you over and shoved that brush . . .'

'JIMMY, STOP IT! Please stop it. You'll get nothing from her that way.'

Allanby didn't turn to look at her. He simply said, 'Corporal Hamilton, take Mrs. Fraser into the other room.'

'No, damn you. I'll stay. I'll . . . I'll be quiet.'

'The alcohol . . .' said Hamish, only to have a hand clamped over his mouth and his head banged back against the wall.

'The methylated spirits,' said Jimmy softly. 'Caithleen, I know you can hear me. I'm going to take out a cigarette and light it but first I'm going to gather these swabs about your feet.'

Caithleen clamped her eyes shut. Clasping her hands in front of her in prayer, she shrieked, 'I don't know who did it! I don't!'

Jimmy took the cigarette out and tapped one end of it against the case to let her know he wasn't kidding, then opened the packet of matches.

'Jimmy, don't. Please don't.'

Allanby hid the elation he felt. Turning swiftly from the girl, he took two strides and demanded, 'Well, what the hell have you to say about it then? You've been hiding something. I know damned well you have.'

'She'll go up like a torch. You know she will. You can't threaten her like that.'

'And not carry through—that it?'

Did he hate her so much? wondered Mary. He struck the wooden end of the match against the sandpaper of the box, dragged it along next to the girl's ear, letting all of them hear it plainly enough.

'Fay Darcy,' blurted Caithleen.

'Lass, you mustn't,' breathed Hamish.

Her head was bowed. Caithleen knew they'd all be looking at her, she naked and covered with tar and feathers, her lovely hair gone, her hair . . . Her *da* would want her to keep shut— everyone would no matter what happened to her.

A match. A cigarette. The flames and her screams as she threw herself about on the floor and died.

'Fay Darcy, my cousin Sean, and . . . and my uncle Jack.'

'Are they hiding Fay?'

The girl nodded. Mary watched in dismay as the life seemed to drain from Hamish, all the years of trying to help others, all the wars, the insanities of men against men, women and children. 'You've as much as killed that girl,' he said on being released. 'I shall try not to despise you for it, Captain, but don't ever cross me again.'

Jimmy simply ordered the men out into what was left of the night and departed from them without another word or gesture. Given the mood of the times, Mary knew they'd hang Jack O'Neill and the cousin, but first they'd make them talk.

'Mary . . . Mary, I spoke harshly to you. Earlier it was. Can you ever forgive me?'

'Hamish, it doesn't matter.'

'But it does, lass. It wasn't right of me.'

'Mrs. Fraser, how good of you to call in like this.'

'Colonel, with all due respect, my appearance here was ordered by yourself.'

And my, but wasn't she looking upset about it? 'Now, now, my dear. *Tut, tut.* That more books for the men?'

'Of course it is.'

'Tea?' he asked, coming round the desk to take her coat himself, to let his hands momentarily rest on her shoulders and smell the clean, bath-soapy smell of her.

'Just a cup, then,' Mary heard herself answer, he still standing behind her. 'I haven't much time and must get back to the house.'

He'd clear his throat now, thought Bannerman, would lift her coat away and say, 'Um, er . . . How is the . . .'

'Victim, Colonel?'

Oh my, oh my, and touchy too. 'The girl, Caithleen O'Neill.'

Mary knew she would have to put him on the defensive. She couldn't have him flipping through the books. 'A little better, if one can ever recover from such a thing. Colonel . . .'

'My dear?' he asked, indicating the couch. He would set her hat, coat and scarf nearby, so as to have them in sight. 'You were saying, Mary?'

Always he had addressed her as Mrs. Fraser. 'It wasn't right of Captain Allanby to have done what he did, Colonel. Hamish and I are very upset. My husband . . .' The blue eyes widened in mock anticipation. 'Colonel, my husband has gone to Belfast to lodge a formal complaint. He'll cross over to England if he has to. Hamish *will* see the prime minister. He won't stop until things are set right and that girl looked after.'

Travel was far from that easy, and she knew it, but even so one should affect the grimacing, fatuitous smile of a squire who had just lost out on the purchase of a beagle bitch. One should offer her a cigarette, knowing she didn't use them and that this would unsettle her further, then put the carved sandalwood box back on the coffee table so that she could see the camels on its lid, the one mounting the other.

Her knees were primly together, giving no sight of leg beyond that which hands and tartan skirt couldn't hide. She was wearing the velvet jacket again, had a rather splendid cairngorm pin in silver at the throat. Fraser? he wondered. Older men so often made fools of themselves with younger women, and she half the doctor's age. 'You mustn't take what happened too seriously, Mary. Captain Allanby was just doing his duty. This Nolan must be apprehended. The Darcy woman is a part of it, and they did terrify that girl of yours. We mustn't forget that, must we?'

'And Caithleen's uncle and cousin, Colonel? Did they have to beat the Jesus out of them? The Jesus. That's what people are saying.'

He'd best shrug, then, and gush a little, best get her even more agitated. 'These times are difficult. War is war, and never easy.'

He'd a hand on her knee, and damn him for looking at her the way he was! 'Colonel . . .'

'Tea, I think,' was all he said. The adjutant brought it, the colonel indicating that she was to pour when steeped. Facing each other, they waited.

He'd give her time, thought Bannerman. He would show

her that she was like warm putty in his hands. 'Now, Mary, what's all this you've been hiding from us? Captain Allanby is certain you . . .'

'Jimmy's got it all wrong, Colonel. I've nothing to hide. How could I possibly have?'

Bannerman let his gaze move appreciatively over her. He would make her think that given the right incentive there might be merit in a little extramarital dalliance. Yes . . . yes, that's what he'd do, knowing it would unsettle her all the more. 'I must say you look particularly fetching. The rough weather suits. You've a divine blush.'

'Colonel, what is it you want with me?'

He would choose not to answer, would take a sip of the tea she'd just poured and ask for the sugar she'd forgotten to offer. Real sugar, no less.

It only flustered her all the more. 'You're upset with us, Mary, and needn't be. Friends, that's what we are. Friends in house. Hamish will be turned back. You know it as well as I do, so let's get that out of the way.'

'And Caithleen?' she asked, looking up from her cup to see him staring at her as a man does a woman he's about to seduce. 'Colonel, that girl will be killed if she stays in Ireland.'

'An O'Neill,' he said, as if savouring the last name and not the tea. 'The girl could be got out, I suppose. Of course, if you . . .'

Sex—was this what he wanted of herself? It was, thought Mary. Flustered, she said silently, Oh damn, what the hell am I to do?

'A job in a munitions factory,' he said, drifting off into thought himself. 'Manchester, I should think, or Sheffield. After the hair grows in—couldn't have it otherwise, now could we? She could work as a domestic, though, for a few months. Now there's a thought. Yes, by heavens she could. I've a sister in Nottingham. Gwen would be glad to have this girl of yours. She'd be just the thing.'

'Colonel, exactly what are you asking of me?'

'In return?'

No smiles now, no phony airs or pompous colonel stuff, just the business of a squire who knew what he wanted. 'In return, yes,' she said, setting her cup and saucer aside and waiting for it now.

Bannerman knew he was surprised that she had even condescended to listen and not bolt from the bloody office. He hadn't lost the touch then, had played her right into the trap he'd set for her, she now so unsettled, those lovely eyes of hers found it hard to even face him. 'That's a nice pin you're wearing. A cairngorm, is it?'

'Yes. Hamish bought it for me before . . . before we were married.'

'Getting on well, are the two of you?' he asked. He'd now play the father confessor.

'Hamish and I have always got on, Colonel. We're two of a kind.'

That so? he'd ask with lifted eyebrows, but the look she gave in return was steady and only then did she say, 'Of course.'

'Of course *what*, my dear?' he blandly asked.

Mary reached for her cup and saucer, had to have something to hang on to. 'Only that we do get on, Colonel. I love my husband very much and wouldn't want to hurt him in any way.'

Oh my, oh my, she'd given him her answer after all. 'Then you'll tell me everything, won't you?'

Flustered—angry with herself for having let him lead her on and showing it, Mary heard herself saying sharply, 'There's nothing to tell. How could there be?'

Captain Allanby had been so certain the woman was up to something behind their backs. Everything that had happened to the O'Neill girl pointed that way, but then Jimmy had it in for Mrs. Mary Ellen Fraser. Burned before the bed, as they say. Love was such a damned silly thing. Sex . . . now sex was something quite different. Over in an instant after a good ramming.

'What books did you bring this time?' he asked, catching her unawares and causing her to momentarily glance at them, revealing an anxiety one could only find troubling.

Again those puffy eyelids with their faded brows were lifted in question. Mary knew she was trapped. 'A Dumas,' she said emptily. '*The Man in the Iron Mask. Tom Sawyer*,' she went on for there could be no stopping now. 'Kant's *Critique of Pure Reason*; Thackeray's *The Virginians*, and . . . and a Dickens. *A Tale of Two Cities*.'

'You'll not mind if I take a quick look through them, will you? It's just a formality. You do understand?'

She mustn't hesitate. 'Please do. You can borrow any of them if you wish. Perhaps Mrs. Bannerman might like one.'

She wasn't going to let him reach those books alone, though, had quickly set her cup and saucer down and had got up. 'I'll just get the scissors, then, shall I?'

Mary knew he had caught her out, that he'd planned it all along. In a way she was glad it was over. The strain of the last few days had been almost more than she could bear. By the time Hamish got back from Belfast, she'd be in prison—safe perhaps from Fay Darcy and the others.

Bannerman had handed the scissors to her and she'd not even realized it.

'Now, now, my dear, you mustn't think we're so bad. Captain Allanby means well, but he has his orders just as I have mine.'

Then cut the bloody string for me! she wanted to scream,

but all he said, she turning from him now to hide her tears, was, 'We need to know everything you can tell us about Erich Kramer and what he's been up to. That suit?'

One had best take her by the shoulders and play the father figure, felt Bannerman. 'This chappie, the Second Lieutenant Bachmann, Mary. He was so useful to us. It's a pity they had to hang him, a great pity. Now run along, there's a good girl, and do your stuff.'

Their steps rang hollowly in the empty corridors. Again not another soul was about. Where once she and the guard might have passed groups of men smoking and chatting, or simply hanging about, there was only the emptiness of a castle vacated by its baron and cleaned out by the auctioneers.

The library was in an anteroom off the far corner of the great hall, in what might, in Norman days, have been called a bedchamber. The passageway Erich and she had last used ran from this chamber to another and smaller one. From there, another corridor led to a spiral staircase that gave access to both the floors above and those below, but—and this was important—that staircase wasn't the main one.

Try as she did not to dwell on it, Mary knew that Jimmy Allanby must have deliberately left those corridor doors open.

She and the guard came to the foot of the spiral staircase but went straight on past it. She'd lost the button up there and Jimmy had somehow found it. They had put two and two together and had agreed to turn a blind eye for a while and use her even more than they'd already been doing.

There was nothing else she could conclude. Jimmy would keep that button until needed.

Button, button . . . As she and the guard hurried away to

the main staircase, each step echoed up the word and Mary saw herself in that corridor, saw Erich yanking at her blouse and felt the button pop off and roll away.

It was such a simple thing. Dear God, what was she to do? She was caught between the British Army and the IRA. If she refused the latter, they'd strip her naked and cut off her hair before tarring her and showering on the feathers; if the former, they'd see her arrested for treason.

And Erich? she asked. Erich *couldn't* be in love with her. How could she go through with the things they all wanted of her—Fay Darcy and Kevin O'Bannion; the colonel and Major Trant and Jimmy Allanby; and Erich . . . yes, Erich most of all?

Must she betray her country?

'Mrs. Fraser, m'am. We're here.'

'Wha . . .? Oh. Oh, thank you, Corporal. About an hour suit?'

She was as white as a sheet. 'An hour it is then, m'am.' He touched his cap and left her, didn't hang around as they usually did.

The great hall was huge—some sixty feet in length, by forty-five in width. Erich and his group had measured it as they'd measured everything else. They'd drawn up plans of the castle, knew things she suspected the British didn't even know.

Secret plans that were kept hidden in the metal tubes of their bunks—this much she did know, for she'd overheard it once. And yes, those locations had probably been changed again and again.

Galleries at the ends of the upstairs corridors gave out on to the great hall. The hearth was massive and smoke-blackened but its chimney was hidden and didn't run all the way up to the vaulted ceiling some forty feet or so above because it was, after all, not a Norman castle but something far, far newer than that.

The hall was empty of furnishings, empty too, of the men, each of whom would wear those rescued bits and pieces of their uniforms as badges of their heroism and measures of their rank.

Mary knew she would have had to smile at them had they been here talking, giving her smiles of their own and the appreciative looks of young men who'd been without a woman for some time.

Men who knew—some of them in any case—that she and Erich Kramer had been lovers. Had been—yes, that was the way it would have to be.

As she started out to cross the hall, her steps echoed up from the squared parquet of white-and-red Venetian marble, and when she came to its centre, she was forced to stop.

'Where are the men?' she asked.

Trant heard her voice as if from the hollowness of a cannon barrel. He had come to stand in the farthest gallery from her. But was he gazing down upon her like the lord of the manor? he wondered. It felt like that, up here in the gods as it were, she looking alone and lost with that bundle of books clutched to her as if about to drown.

Allowing a trace of jocularity, he said, 'The men will be along in a moment. It's good of you to have come so promptly.'

'Why promptly?' she wanted to shout up at him. 'Are they still under house arrest?'

'Still being stubborn, I'm afraid,' he said, not leaning on the balustrade but placing his hands lightly there as one of the Norman kings might have done, she the Irish serving wench he would use.

Trant wasn't after her body, though, only her mind and what she could divulge. Did castles always breed suspicion, intrigue and contempt? she wondered.

As he continued to look at her, Mary passed beneath, knowing now that they *had* agreed among themselves: Trant, the colonel, and Jimmy Allanby. Jimmy.

Setting the bundle of books on the library's table, she hurried to the corridor to yank on the door's handle, realizing that Trant had made damned sure it would be locked and off limits.

Had he the button?

They were all around her now, she existing on two levels, the one so friendly and outgoing—she had to keep up the mask of that—the other bleak.

The line-up was long and stretched well out into the great hall. Everyone, it seemed, wanted to take out books. Usually Oberleutant Werner, a first lieutenant, helped at the desk. A pilot in the Luftwaffe, Philip had been shot down over the Channel and had been fished out of the water. One of the lucky ones, he'd always say, but today he wasn't here, and she kept wondering why.

There'd still been no sign of Erich. The Thackeray still sat on her left, her hand always straying nervously to it. More than once, far more, someone had tried to pick it up. The Dickens was gone, the Mark Twain—all the rest of what she'd brought in.

Franz Bauer stood waiting. A Leutnant zur See just like Second Lieutenant Bachmann had been, Bauer had been one of U-121's officers, still was for that matter.

'Captain wants to speak to you,' he said in his broken English while handing her a book to be stamped out, any book. Mary had never liked him, had always thought him a bit uncouth and not to be trusted.

'I can't come. Not today. Tell Erich he must come here and

that's all there is to it. I've got something for him. Next? Oh, hello, Helmut. How's the arm coming along?'

Helmut Wolfganger gave her a grin. An Oberleutnant zur See from Idar-Oberstein, he had the look of a farm boy, though thirty-five, was blond and blue-eyed, but painfully thin.

'You're all alone,' he said. 'The arm's fine.'

Mary saw that he was taking out one of the other Thackerays. She hesitated, looked up at him even as he noticed the book on her left and reached for it. 'Don't, please. Just leave it. That's for Erich.'

Wolfganger gave her another of those grins of his before taking his book back and saying, 'He's a lucky man, Mrs. Fraser. I hope the doctor doesn't mind.'

When Erich finally did come into the library, the level of conversation fell to a hush and she knew then that something really was going on among the prisoners and that more than a few of them were now aware that she was a part of it.

'Mary, what do you want? I was in a meeting. Policies . . . the way we do things here. It . . . it couldn't be helped.'

Policies? Escape perhaps? Erich was wearing his peaked white cap, his *Schirmmutze*, the dark grey woollen turtleneck pullover too.

'*Liebling*, what's the matter?' he asked, concern in his deep blue eyes.

'Nothing. I've found a copy of that Thackeray you wanted. Don't . . . Please don't open it here. Just take some others with you.'

Kramer felt the weight of the book and the bulge. 'I didn't ask for any Thackeray.'

'Erich, please just do as I've asked. It's . . . it's already been stamped.' He wouldn't go over to the shelves to get some others. He just stood there looking down at her.

Kramer slid a forefinger into the book and felt the gun but knew there was more to this, much more. 'They've contacted you,' he said. He'd let his face break out into a generous grin but would that ease her mind?

'Yes, they've contacted me. I've done what I had to.'

There was no smile from her, no sign of the relief there ought to have been, she turning from him now and still all wound up about it, but what else? he wondered. Did the British suspect her of aiding the enemy?

'We have to talk,' he said, turning away to say, 'Franz, the lady needs to visit the toilet. Oblige us.'

'No! Erich, listen to me. I can't. Major Trant will only be watching for something like that.'

So it had been Trant after all and now she was noticing that the room had fallen to absolute silence as it should have.

Erich motioned for the men to leave, and they did in trickles so as not to make their leaving too obvious. Even though some were of higher rank, they obeyed as if he was in command of them, but he wasn't in command of herself, was he? she had to silently ask.

Kramer reached across the table that separated them, she ignoring the outstretched hand, he beckoning with it now.

'It's finished between us, Erich. It has to be.'

Grabbing her by the wrist, he pulled her after him, took her in between the rows of shelves and forced her to face him. 'Who gave you this?' he demanded.

'The IRA. Who the hell did you think that "cousin" of yours would contact other than Berlin?'

'Then you *have* made contact and Dublin has been in touch with C-and-C U-boats.'

He was relieved—she could see this at a glance but . . . 'You don't love me. You never did.'

Some women were easy, some more difficult, but all needed that little something. He'd close the book, he decided. He'd take two others from the shelf she'd her back to, would sandwich the Thackeray between them. 'I do but I know you must be finding it hard to believe. I have to get away.'

'Why?'

She was watching him too closely—was angry and afraid, and struggling with her conscience, even feeling a fool.

When he didn't answer, she turned to leave, only to feel the touch of him on her hand and ask, 'Were you responsible for the hanging of that man? Is that why you have to get away?'

'I had no part in that.'

'Then who did?'

'You know I can't tell you. How could I?'

Had he been one of them? Had he given the command? 'It's what they want me to find out. The names of all who were responsible.'

'It's impossible.'

'Is it? If I don't get the answer, Bannerman and Trant will accuse me of helping you and of betraying my husband and my country, and if they don't, Jimmy Allanby will.'

They had put it to her then, or at least had got her to believe they had.

Something went out of him then and an apologetic tone crept into his voice.

'You're caught between us, aren't you, *mein Schatz*? The British, the Reich and the IRA. Can you ever forgive me?'

Mein Schatz . . . my treasure. He was so close to her now. The cap was set at a rakish angle, and she realized then that he'd have worn it that way at sea. 'I must go. Look, as far as you and I are concerned, it is finished. It has to be.'

Then why tremble at the nearness of him, why search for

signs that it wasn't? Kramer set the books aside. He'd have to let her see how it really was for a man like himself. Giving her an understanding nod, he said, 'It's not right of us to leave things this way. Take the gun back and tell them it's all off no matter what C-and-C U-boats and Berlin have sent over the wireless to Dublin. I'm staying here until the British ship me off to Canada. It'll be easier then. A few months, nothing more.'

Apart from their having won the war, he couldn't mean it. He really couldn't.

Kramer turned his back on her. He would leave the books on the shelf she faced, would leave the gun, would let her make a grab for them and say:

'Erich, wait! Darling, I . . . I had to know.'

Franz was signalling that they'd best hurry it up, so *gut, ja, gut*, but had she really fallen for it?

He waited, his back still to her, and when she handed the books to him, he heard her saying, 'They've a meeting place they'll use. I don't know where it is, but will try to find out. Somewhere on the north coast, I think. In Donegal, most likely. Somewhere your people can bring a submarine in close enough to take you off.'

'And you, Mary. You. I'm not leaving you behind. I couldn't.'

Was he lying or simply trying to make things easier for her? she wondered. He hadn't asked what the IRA would demand in exchange, would have to leave all that up to others, to C-and-C U-boats and Berlin, and to wireless contact with Dublin, but she would have to let him kiss her. She mustn't pull away, mustn't let her doubts show, must give herself to him and give herself time.

Trant was waiting for her in the corridor when she had closed up the library and crossed the great hall. Falling in beside her, they continued on towards the main staircase.

'You never wear lipstick when you come to see us. I find that curious.'

'You can find it any way you wish, Major. I simply choose not to during the day. There's a war on and good lipstick is rather hard to come by. The kind that is available bothers my lips.'

Long after he had left her near the foot of the stairs, Trant continued to watch her, then went back to open the doors to that other corridor and find his way from there through to the library.

Thackeray, he mused. *The Virginians.* Dulsey had memorized the titles of the lot she'd brought in today. It had been sharp of the colonel to have done that, but then Bannerman was an old hand at such things.

Kramer . . . had she given him the book? All the others had been accounted for, so that must have been it.

A note . . . had she passed him a note?

'Now, Doctor, you're not to worry yourself. Sure and that wee slip of a girl is feeling terribly out of sorts and hiding herself away upstairs, but Bridget and I will keep a close eye on her.'

Hamish was sitting in the kitchen at the big deal table Mrs. Haney used to roll out her pastry and do everything else. One of those huge cups the Irish sometimes use was in front of him, but was it carrot, rose hip, dandelion or blackberry tea? Hamish always went along with the 'expeerimints,' even though slices of ham, freshly baked brown bread, butter—not margarine yet—and a plate of scones were there too.

'You're a wonderful woman, Mrs. Haney. As God is my witness, I don't know what I'd do without you. Mary still not back?'

'Likely walking in the fields and woods, and it's yourself be worryin' about her too. She be doin' a powerful lot of walking about these days, she does, Doctor. Now she does.'

Oh how they avoided things, the two of them, sparring with each other like that. Wisely, though, Hamish never questioned the alchemy of the kitchen. He laid a slice of ham on one of liberally buttered bread, could just as well have been out fishing were it not for the stoop to his shoulders.

Mary waited out in the corridor, seeing the two of them through a gap in the door. It was well after dark and yet he hadn't questioned this nor had Mrs. Haney thought to raise the issue of her not having even come in for supper.

'Is she meeting someone?' asked Hamish at last, not wanting to let things show. 'A bunch of tinkers perhaps? Mary's always been fascinated by them.'

'Tinkers is it?' snorted the woman. 'God would wish it so, Doctor. Indeed He would.'

Fastidiously he took time with the open-faced sandwich he'd made and carefully cut it into quarters. 'Then you've heard something?' he hazarded.

Mrs. Haney sprinkled on a last dusting of flour before muscling the rolling pin over the pastry dough so quickly and robustly, Mary found jealousy intruding her thoughts. The woman was so capable, so solid. Like one of those round tower houses that had been built a thousand years ago and stood out all over the landscape, some having been more lately refurbished in payment of a ten-pound note to London.

'I have, Doctor. That I have. Parker O'Shane, that disreputable half-brother of mine, God save him, saw her on the old tote road to Newtonhamilton the day we had them sausages from Mr. Brian Kelly's butcher shop. She'd been picking the Michaelmas daisies.'

'There's nothing wrong in that, is there?'

'Not with bunches of them growing along every roadside from here to Killarney and Ballyshannon. It's the broken bridge on that old bit of road what worries me, Doctor. You'll be recalling the one we had to cross the other night.'

'How could I ever forget it,' said Hamish sadly, but remembering, too, to take a generous bite and reach for his tea.

Mrs. Haney set the rolling pin down, after first having given it the wringing scrape of an encircling thumb and forefinger. She went over to the stove to get the big teapot she'd brought from her own hearth, the doctor's not being good enough. Refilling his cup with its ink, she slung one over for herself, took but a grain of the sugar, and sat down across the table from him. Rationing or no rationing, the Lord always helped those who helped themselves, and of course there was the black market too, and connections, always those, but worry had entered the woman's gaze, fear and an honest concern that puzzled, Mrs. Haney not liking her.

'Doctor, did she meet someone at that broken-down *ould* bridge, I'm asking? Parker, he said she had burs and weed seeds all over her like enough to fit an English setter with fleas.'

'Liam Nolan?' asked Hamish, the name barely whispered.

'The same, Doctor. Is it not what you yourself have been thinking?'

'Mary would have told me. She'd not have kept a thing like that from . . .'

'Doctor, what is it?'

'Caithleen . . . I was thinking of Caithleen.'

'I've sent Bridget up to keep her company. Now you're not to worry yourself. Caithleen?' asked the woman, she prodding, probing, wanting answers herself.

Hamish stared at the bread and ham on the plate before

him, then glanced at the wall clock beneath which Mrs. Haney had hung one of those hideous aquatints of the Christ in hand-painted luminescent tones.

Mary started into the room. 'I've been out walking and thinking, Hamish. I'm sorry if I worried you, darling. I know it's well after dark. Belfast bad? They turned you back, didn't they? The colonel said that they would.'

'Lass, where have you really been?'

'Out walking. If Mrs. Haney had thought to ask William, she'd have been told my bicycle was in the shed, so I couldn't have been far, could I?'

'But it's not safe for a woman to walk about at night alone. Not after what's happened. Not with . . .'

'With the hills being combed by British tommies? No, I guess it isn't. Mrs. Haney, I'd like a cup of that tea, please. It's freezing out there. Shouldn't you be home yourself by now?'

Ria gave her a look that would have whipped a dead donkey to life. Bolting up from the table, she stormed over to the door to yell at the top of her lungs, 'Bridget! Bridget Leahy, girl, her ladyship is home and we can be away now. Away it is, and me with a husband who's not yet had his supper these past three hours. Three it is, Mrs. Fraser. Three!'

'Mary . . . Mary, what's wrong?'

'Nothing. I just had to have a think. I wasn't far, Hamish. I was in the garden.'

Waiting for Bridget and Mrs. Haney to leave the house, she poured herself a cup of tea—dandelion it was and horrible. Roasted to death and pulverized. Grimacing, she said, 'The colonel will arrange for Caithleen to be taken to his sister's in the Midlands.'

'In return for what?'

Did Hamish now know everything? 'For my cooperation.'

BETRAYAL

*   *   *

On Thursday morning she was at the bridge again but they didn't come. Perhaps they were hiding out in the hills and too afraid, perhaps they were back in the South and hadn't been able to get a message to her.

Dismayed at not finding them, for they had to meet—there'd been no word from Mrs. Tulford in Dublin either—she rode into Ballylurgen. Irish villages weren't like those in England. They were more like some she'd seen from the train west on the prairies of Canada, if one took away the grain elevators and the endless horizons. A straggle, then, of houses along an empty road with gaps between and the damned loneliness of it all stretching away for miles around.

She knew she was being unkind, that it was just because things had been going badly for her. Ballylurgen was no better, no worse than any other village of two hundred souls. It had a Catholic day school, the boys out playing hurley in the yard and Father O'Donnell in his cassock with the wind flapping at it to make him look like a tall, gaunt old rook in a sea of shouting to which the shrill blasts of his whistle did not the slightest bit of good.

She stopped on the road, for the school and the adjacent church were not the usual, but a little ways from what might be termed the heart of the village. One of the boys was particularly good. Very fast with the stick and the eye. Goal after goal to the dismay of the opposing team and the cheers of his mates.

They'd choose up sides again tomorrow and Father O'Donnell would see that the boy was on the other team.

The wind blew at her skirt. Mary grabbed a fistful to bind it to her legs. After a rain, the light over the fields and hills with their hedgerows seemed always greener, sharper, clearer as if washed.

Another gust came, a stronger one. She grabbed her tam, letting go of the skirt which billowed well up above her knees before she could beat it down.

Seen from the bell tower of the church, the Fraser woman was wearing knee socks today but not the Stewart Hunting of a green tartan skirt. Instead, it was the soft, greyish white of the Stewart Dress with its lines of red, green, yellow and that lovely shade of blue.

O'Bannion kept the field glasses trained on her, now that he'd seen the coast was clear. As so many times since they'd first met, he thought her not just proud and pretty, but beneath it all, tough and determined, and he wondered then, as he stood out of sight and the shouts of the boys came up to him, what she'd do.

That business of the O'Neill girl couldn't have gone down well with Mrs. Mary Ellen Fraser. 'Necessary,' Fay had said and he'd known enough not to have challenged her, the larger issue being far more important, but would the threat of a tarring be enough? Would that woman out there not find herself forced into such a situation, she'd throw herself away and betray them all in one last proud act of defiance?

The wind tugged at her hair. She continued to watch the boys, and the shrill blasts of the whistle seemed only to make her forget her cares. He knew it was but a moment for her, a brief escape. He found a gladness in himself and wondered at it harshly before setting it coldly from him.

Dublin had got through to Berlin again. They'd had the rendezvous already chosen for the Nazis, a place right under the noses of the British, right where they'd suspect it least, but the Fraser woman mustn't get wind of the location until the end.

There must be no chance of her giving that away. Everything had to go like clockwork. The exchange had to be made. The Kapitänleutnant Erich Kramer and the information he would be carrying in return for much, much more. For everything.

He would have to watch what Fay and Liam said to the woman. He had the thought that she would try her damnedest to find out the location of the rendezvous. She would want to know that desperately because by now she must have had inklings that for her, life would take her no farther. They'd have to kill her.

O'Bannion let the glasses settle on her one last time. She was laughing. Not knowing that she was being watched, she was taking delight in the play of small boys and the antics of an old priest.

When the ball came out on to the road, as it often did, she madly set the bicycle down and ran like the blazes after it, wound up and pitched it back. 'Haroo!' he heard her yell, and he wondered then again if he hadn't softened towards her, and he knew that this would only get in the way and that she'd use it if she could, that she'd use every little thing she could to betray them all.

4

Kevin O'Bannion was watching her from beneath a hawthorn whose berries were scarlet, the thorns some three inches long and of a deep purplish brown. The leaves, having turned to russet, were falling about the ruins over which the ancient branches had spread, Mary hearing them and nothing else.

He'd been leaning against the inner part of one of the stone walls, smoking a cigarette and waiting. 'So you've come at last,' he said, as if there could have been any doubt in the matter, as if the note someone had left in her carrier basket in Ballylurgen—she in one of the shops—hadn't been found by her and read.

'Yes, of course I've come,' she answered tightly, not stepping closer but having tucked the bike out of sight.

No danger then of them being seen from the road. 'Did you take him the gun?' he asked. She was even prettier now that he had a chance to see her up close without Fay and Liam around.

Mary found suddenly that, unlike the walk out from Padrick Darcy's smithy, the nearness and aloneness of herself and O'Bannion unsettled her in more ways than one. Perhaps it was that closed-in feeling the walls exuded, perhaps the absence of the others. In any case, she didn't like the feeling and found she couldn't understand it in herself.

He was no longer squinting at her and when he asked about the gun again, she said, 'Yes, I took it to him. It . . . it wasn't easy, though. Major Trant and Colonel Bannerman suspect I'm up to something, as does Jimmy Allanby.'

'I thought they might. Did you tell Kramer he'll get the cartridges when we're satisfied with the negotiations?'

'No . . . No, I didn't.' What was there in that look of his?

'Was he glad to get the gun?' he asked, smiling knowingly.

Mary tensed. 'Yes, he . . . he was glad to get it.'

Then she'd been upset by Kramer's elation and had been worrying ever since. 'Why didn't you tell him the gun was empty?'

His sudden harshness was frightening; the dark grey eyes held nothing now, no sympathy, no attempt to understand how difficult it had been and still was.

Well? his look demanded. 'I didn't, that's all.'

'Is it that you're continually needing lessons?'

'It was despicable what you people did to Caithleen. An act of cowards not rebels.'

'Cowards, was it? From what I hear, your Captain Allanby was no better.'

'He's not my "captain." I despise him as much as I . . . Look, I didn't mean that. I . . .' They were all alone. The road wasn't far but she'd never make it and he knew it too, had seen her thinking this.

'Oh but you did mean it, Mrs. Fraser. You despise us more than you do Jimmy Allanby, but he would have torched that girl and then what would you have believed?'

Mary glanced away. Suddenly she had to avoid his scrutiny,

couldn't seem to bring herself to face him. 'It's not important what I think. What is important is that I'm to take the girl to Dublin this weekend. I'm to put her into the hands of the authorities there who'll see she gets safely over to England.'

'Good.' O'Bannion gave her a moment to consider the terseness of his response, knew then that she'd have to be broken gently, knew, too, that she hadn't even wondered why the Brits had chosen Dublin instead of Belfast which was one hell of a lot closer and far more logical. 'You've made a deal with the colonel?'

She would have to face him. 'Yes, but it has nothing to do with you and the others.'

'You're full of surprises. Enlighten me.'

She mustn't tell him everything. 'They want me to spy on the prisoners for them.'

He'd let it come as a sigh. 'Correction. They want you to tell them who hanged that man in there.'

'Yes.' The wind, gusting in the enclosure, tugged at the wiry black hair that was receding from his forehead but was still thick and crinkly. 'Am I to stay at the White Horse Inn again, or is it now too dangerous?'

'Is it that they suspect you're up to something else?'

'I wouldn't know. How could I? Trant and the colonel are together in this, as is Allanby. I may never know how much they're aware of until it's too late. In the past they must have heard me repeating things the prisoners had said, but . . . but stupidly I hadn't been aware of their having used me like that. It's probably why Trant and the colonel agreed to let me into Tralane in the first place. They knew I'd be bound to pick things up and pass them on.'

She'd been thinking things over, all right. Muscling that pretty little head of hers around it all. 'There's a slab of stone next to that wall. Let's sit out of the wind. We'll be safe enough for a while.'

Mary knew she'd no longer have to face him when they leaned back against that wall, but why had he suggested it? To put her off her guard, to pry everything out of her while there was still time, or simply to be alone with her so as to get to know her better? With Fay Darcy and Liam Nolan she could almost gauge the trend of their thoughts; with him it was more difficult. He still hadn't told her if she was to stay at the White Horse again, still hadn't told her anything much.

'Why are you doing this?' she asked.

She had smoothed that tartan skirt of hers over those shapely thighs, had leaned back and was feeling grateful for the chance not to have to face him. Best then to let it come easy, best not to rattle her too much. 'Because we have to. There's no other way of looking at it for us. Too much has happened in the past.'

As if to emphasize this, he took out his revolver but said suddenly, 'Don't be frightened,' and breaking the cylinder open, let one of the cartridges fall into his hand, knew absolutely that she must be bone-terrified.

The slug was fat and ugly and she'd know it soon enough, but had he been too conscious of her feelings? wondered O'Bannion. Was the woman getting to him with those downcast eyes of hers? 'You're to take this to Kramer, Mrs. Fraser. Tell him we've been in contact with C-and-C U-boats via Berlin. They want him badly, and we'll know soon enough if they'll pay the price.'

'Which is?' she heard herself asking, but he wouldn't tell her, of course, for he'd gone from trying to be considerate, to being brutal and that could only mean he had been angry with himself for letting his thoughts show.

O'Bannion pressed the bullet into that palm of hers and closed the fingers over it, just as he'd done with the revolver at the Darcy place. He took out another cigarette and, lighting it, sat back with the gun still in his lap.

Inhaling deeply, giving her a moment, and why not? he said, 'You'll be told when it's all arranged and not before then. Your German must know something vital, Mrs. Fraser. Have you any idea what it is?'

She'd have to give him something. 'Only what you said before, that the British may have captured Erich's boat with all its codes and things.'

'He could send that over on Mrs. Tulford's wireless and probably already has in that first message you took to her.'

'Not if he was afraid of jeopardizing the escape and Mrs. Tulford herself. But . . . but it might be more than that—some new device we have for detecting enemy submarines. That would be vital information Erich wouldn't want to trust to just anyone, wouldn't it?'

She had used *we* and *enemy* without having realized it, had been searching for reasons herself. He'd not say anything then. He'd see if she ran on with it like a fellow conspirator.

'Perhaps they've all come to a consensus of what's been happening to their U-boats,' said Mary. 'Erich's U-121 was supposedly sunk in January but there have been others since—at least three that I know of have officers in Tralane.'

O'Bannion knew that he was impressed but that her figuring things out for herself could be both a good and a bad thing. Berlin wanted Kramer—that was clear enough. They might well pay the price they'd been asked, and then again, they might not. The Germans were far from easy. They didn't trust the Irish any more than he and the others trusted them, and she'd have reasoned this out too. No doubt Kramer's superior officers had agreed to let him be the front man because he'd succeeded in being intimate with her but Kramer would not have been given the Tulford woman's address. He'd have had to get that from someone higher up and that could only mean they must be wanting to break someone else out with him. She would not have been told this, but had she thought of it? If so, she was definitely not saying. A woman then who could go on giving her thoughts aloud and yet still hold something back even when afraid the next bullet could well be for herself. And if not that, then the hangman's noose.

The wind teased the cigarette smoke from him, she catching whiffs of it now and then, she exuding a sensuality he found troubling, for she wasn't really aware of it, but was it fear that made her like this, he wondered, or simply the nearness of him?

'Mrs. Fraser . . .?'

'Yes?' she asked, stiffening in alarm at the sound of his voice.

'Has Kramer said he'd take you with him?'

The nod she gave was that of a realist. Still staring at the bullet, she felt the metal of its brass casing, then that of the lead slug.

As she put it away, he heard her saying, 'I don't want any killing. One won't be of much use, will it?'

As if that, in itself, made it easier for her conscience.

Exhaling the last of the smoke, he quickly stubbed the cigarette out and brushed away the soot mark, saw her notice this, a woman then who, even though afraid, could find the will to search for every little detail in the hope it might be useful.

He'd give her a grin and let her in on it. 'You never can tell who'll come by to have a look.'

'Isn't one of the others watching out?'

She had pinned her hair back at the sides and had tied it behind with a bit of brown velvet to match, but several strands had come loose down there on the road by the school and the sunlight had found these, bringing out the coppery tints, the cloud shadows only darkened.

When her throat tightened under such a scrutiny, he said almost brutally, 'For now that's all. Tell Kramer you'll be in touch with Mrs. Tulford. You're to stay at the White Horse right enough. See if he gives you anything for her to send over. It's my bet that he won't, but ask it of him anyways. Tell him you have no other choice but to find out which of them were responsible for the hanging of that man. If he wants out badly enough, then he has to cooperate.'

'But . . . but why? What's it to you people whether Trant and the colonel find out who hanged that man?'

He'd let her see him drop his eyes down over her. Involuntarily she pressed her hands against those thighs, failing entirely to realize how provocative the gesture was. 'Why the interest in a hanging that wasn't one of ours? Is it not obvious?'

When she shrugged, he let her have it, 'Because you're going to have to lead the British into thinking you'll cooperate. They won't have it any other way, and you know that as well as I, but you must always keep them waiting for a little more even if you do chance to find out who was responsible.'

Long after he had left her, Mary remained sitting with her back to the wall, exhausted by the encounter. Shutting her eyes, she let her hands move firmly down over her thighs right to the knees then slowly back up and down again, trying to ease the tension only to realize that she'd been doing this as he'd looked at her. Had he thought to get her to believe she could seduce him into being careless?

He would know she wasn't fool enough to think such a

thing. Then why had her hands been on her thighs like that when she'd known he was looking at her in such a way? Had she secretly wanted to feel the touch of him?

'I hate myself,' she said, and getting up, went over to her bicycle to leave the ruins to the softly falling leaves.

The shed was behind the house and well off to its left. As Mary turned in at the drive, the last of the light streaked the sky, etching the plum-coloured clouds that lay like flat, elongated strings of mountains in the west.

Riding under the copper beeches—immense things, they were—she went into the deeper darkness of the wisteria whose long arbour stretched almost to the stable. Hopping off the bike, she walked it along the path that turned off here to the shed, she cursing the sound of the sprocket, for she didn't want to have to talk to William just now, didn't want to have to talk to anyone.

The shed gave out on to the gardens and was used for all sorts of things. Tools, firewood, peat and vegetables, apples, paints and turpentine, the smells of these being everywhere. A kind of sanctuary.

Leaning the bike against a pillar post, she picked her way through to the workbench. The house was in total darkness, the blackout curtains all thoroughly drawn. Mrs. Haney never let a chink of light escape. Every evening now Bridget would be sent out to check, then the two of them and William would be off home. They didn't live far—about a mile back of the garden along a path across the fields.

Mary knew that it couldn't be easy for them to make that walk, that each evening now, it would be getting harder and harder. Caithleen would have to be taken to Dublin, and the sooner the better.

There were baskets and pots of bulbs on the bench—tulips, daffodils, hyacinths and crocuses—things they'd forced and had had around the house last winter. Hamish loved gardening, loved so many things . . .

What light there was gave a rippled mirror-sheen of darkness to the windowpanes as she listened to the wind, to the sound of the crickets and then to that of William's quiet and deferential knock at the mudroom door.

He'd be told to see if her bike was back. She had about two minutes and in that time so many things to think about.

A thin film of grease still clung to the bullet. Reaching out, she picked up one of the daffodil bulbs, pressed her middle against the edge of the workbench, was momentarily lost to the bullet and the paper dryness of the bulb, she seeing Hamish in the garden in his old clothes, for he loved nothing better unless it was his fishing. She knew she would never be able to face him with the truth of what she'd done, that she mustn't ask for his help—they'd kill him if she did, but softly said, 'Darling, please help me before it's too late.'

'M'am, is that you?'

Had William overheard her? He was standing in the doorway, his silhouette all too clear. 'Yes. I . . . I was just putting my bike away. You can tell Mrs. Haney I'll be there in a minute. She can leave now, if she wants.'

'M'am, it's Caithleen. She be in a terrible state. Mrs. Haney is beside herself with the worries and fearful the girl will come to harm.'

'All right. I'll come with you.'

Blinking at the unaccustomed light, she saw at a glance that Bridget was the one in trouble and that Mrs. Haney was indeed beside herself with worry. The woman didn't wait.

'M'am, would you please be going up them stairs to that

poor wee girl? Bridget and I have tried everything. 'Tis the flood itself, and she wrung dry yet producing the waters of Babylon.'

Could nothing go right? 'Isn't Dr. Fraser home?'

'He is not, m'am. He's been away to Tralane this whole time, he has. Arguing his case, pleading with them to listen to God's good sense. But was you not with him? The doctor did say he'd be picking you up in Ballylurgen or along the road. It is a Thursday, is it not? Market days be library days at the castle. We all thought . . .'

Had Hamish seen her walking the bike across those fields to the ruins? Had he *stopped* the car and not honked its horn, but stood at the side of the road watching her? Did he *know* with whom she'd met?

'M'am, was you not with him, then?' asked the woman.

'No, I wasn't. I was out.'

Out was it? Mary could see the question rise in Mrs. Haney's gullet but would have to ignore it. 'Bridget didn't tell Caithleen I was to take her to Dublin, did she?'

Ria wrung her hands. 'She did, m'am, and that's the way of it.'

'But Dr. Fraser warned you all to say nothing of it.'

'He did not, m'am. 'Twas yourself what did.'

'And is *that* why you let Bridget tell her? Mrs. Haney, I really wish you'd . . .'

'M'am, let us make a bit of peace between us. The girl was trying to kill herself. Bridget found her in the bathroom with the doctor's razor.'

'She didn't! That's simply not true!'

The deal table separated them, Bridget looking up from it now to be silenced with a glance.

'The Lord knows I would wish it wasn't so, m'am, but 'tis. Caithleen being such a good Catholic knows only too well what awaits her if she should ever do such a terrible thing, and she with ground Sheffield ready enough to slash her fair wrists!'

'But why, Mrs. Haney? Why?'

'Why indeed, m'am? Because that girl has lost her love, her home, her friends and family—everything that counts for a girl of seventeen. She knows her uncle and her cousin are in prison for what she said, and no amount of caring seems enough. Bridget thought that by telling her she was being sent to England, Caithleen would stop, but 't has only made her worse. Now the girl wants to go home, Mrs. Fraser. She knows she's going to die no matter what.'

'They'll kill her.'

'Then go you up and try to talk her out of it before she runs off on us and we find her in Lough Loughie or hanging from a tree.'

The bedroom was in darkness, the girl lying on her side facing the wall. Mary knew she had been secretly avoiding her, that the sight of her brought only panic and remorse. 'Caithleen, it's me. I'm so sorry this had to happen to you. It wasn't supposed to. Things . . . things just got out of hand, I think. The colonel's sister will look after you. Hamish . . . Hamish will see that there's enough money set aside for your clothes and such, and that you'll not want for anything.'

It sounded so damned paternalistic of her, so bloody British, thought Mary.

'"Not supposed to," and not meant for me, Mrs. Fraser?'

Hamish came into the room with Robbie and told him to put his muzzle on the edge of the bed. 'Caithleen, this won't hurt a bit, not if you hang on to my wee dog. You need to sleep, then we'll sort all this out, no fear, you understand?'

Hiking the girl's nightgown, Fraser rubbed a spot on her

seat with an alcohol swab, then found his hypodermic syringe and, glancing up at Mary, spread thumb and forefinger over the smooth, soft contours before jabbing the needle in and rubbing the spot again. 'There, it's done, Caithleen. There'll be no more talk of your killing yourself, do you hear me, lass? As God is your witness, swear you will put the thought right from you.'

He pulled the nightgown down, began then to gently rub the back of Caithleen's neck and shoulders. Perhaps five minutes passed, perhaps a little more.

'She's asleep. She's gone off, Hamish.'

'*Och*, I know she has. You look as though you could do with some yourself.'

'Will the colonel really let me take her to Dublin on Sunday?'

And why Dublin? Why not Belfast or even Derry? 'He wants another week.'

He's holding out on you—Mary could see it in the look he gave. 'And when that week's done?'

The truth at last, was it? 'It could well be another and another. I tried to reason with them, but they wouldn't listen.' Gently he brushed a hand over Caithleen's head. 'Robbie, stay.'

'Let me, Hamish, just for a bit.'

'And when she awakens?'

'I . . . I'll try to make her understand.'

'To salve your conscience?'

'Yes. Yes, that's it exactly.'

'Ah sure, and isn't death an Irish pastime, missus? Come like the skirts of mist at morn to sweep in over them lovely hills and stretch out Her fingers to touch and take at will.'

They'd been talking about Caithleen. 'Parker, you can't mean that.'

'And why not? Isn't it a self-evident fact that the Irish do be killing each other since long before the time of Christ Himself, not to mention St. Patrick? I do believe 'tis written in them blessed stars above, missus, and in the potatoes and all below. There be no end to it.'

His gumboots were mired in cowpats, the herd was bawling from the pasture, the pipe smoke particularly fragrant—had Hamish been talking to this stooped little man whose eyes were like lumps of anthracite and whose skin really was the colour of oak tannin and like something that had been left in a bog? 'You saw me on the old tote road to Newton-hamilton.'

And she accusative of it. 'That I did, missus, and you the picture of heaven itself with your jacket off and folded up and that bunch of Michaelmas daisies in your carrier basket. You was wearin' a smile so lovely it touched me heart, it did.'

'It didn't, Parker, because I wasn't smiling.'

'No, missus, you wasn't.'

'Did you see anyone with me?'

O'Shane drew on his pipe. The two of them, each now with a foot up on the lowest rail, were resting their arms on the gate to the highest of his fields. From where they were standing, the land fell away to the banks of the Loughie in the valley below.

He'd have to tell her something. 'Well now I did and I didn't, missus, and that's the truth of it.'

'You told Mrs. Haney you'd seen me—she's the source of that pipe tobacco you're smoking.'

One could seldom get away with a thing. 'I did, that I did. She asked it of me, missus. That woman has a nose for trouble like a sow after rats.'

'You hinted at it first, Parker. Ria then pried it out of you. She bribed you. Bribed you with my husband's tobacco—stolen tobacco.'

Mrs. Mary Fraser was so dismayed, O'Shane was afraid he'd lost a friend. 'It's what I didn't tell her that counts.'

'Then you *did* see someone with me.'

She had come all the way up here just to ask it of him, she had, was that afraid Ria had not only found out she had met someone at that old bridge but had gone to have a look at it herself.

'I did, missus, and I didn't. Them bushes was in the way and you the clearer of the two, him keeping to the cover like. But I've kept it to myself, I has. I was hoping you'd tell me yourself, you see. There could be any number of explanations—the world's full of them and me with ears big enough to take in the lot.'

Mary wished she hadn't come. She'd been hoping that what he'd have to say would have cheered her up. 'Can I ask that you not tell anyone, not for a while? Not even Hamish, Parker. Not until it's . . . it's over.'

Had it come to that? he wondered, fearing for her. 'Of course, missus. I be the very soul of discretion. You have my word on it, if I'm to keep you as a friend.'

O'Shane gripped the hand she had thrust out. He wanted to say the O'Bannions were always a bad lot, the Darcys far worse. He wanted to tell her that Liam Nolan was excitable and inclined to do the very thing she'd least expect, but he would have to hold his tongue and merely nod because that was how one kept death from the door.

There were thousands of buttons in the box but none to match the one she'd lost. Alone in her room after lunch, Mary dumped the box on the carpet and began to spread the things.

There were buttons and buttons. They went back through the years from Mrs. Haney's own scavenging to that of her mother and grandmother. All had been avid collectors, the things picked up in streets, shops, churches, shrines and on pilgrimages, at county fairs, too, and cattle auctions, in theatres as well and on trains, even out in the countryside on picnics and no doubt in the most unlikely of places.

Pins had also been a priority—straight ones, bent ones, safety and dress. Needles, too, and bits of thread and gold and silver brocade. She *had* to find a match or replace them all. Jimmy Allanby would have found and kept that button to confront her with it no matter. The more she searched, the more anxious she became. It had been horrid of Parker to have said that of death with such cheerful acceptance, as if there really could be no stop to the killing, as if it had been preordained.

The blouse had cost Hamish a fortune in Edinburgh. He'd remember the day he'd bought it for her, would remember how pleased she'd been. It wasn't often, was it, that a husband intuitively knew not only quality but what suited best? An impromptu gift, an impulse—hadn't *that* been what had pleased her most?

Of course it had, but Jimmy would show the button to him.

Mary lost herself to the hunt. Things were strewn all over the carpet now. Among the pins there were the flags of an independent Ireland, those of the Ulster Orange and King Billy, as if the keeping of the one negated the throwing away of the other. When a pair of bare feet appeared out of the corner of her eye, she looked up to see the ankles and then the hem of the flannel nightgown. The girl had the loveliest sea-green eyes, dark at some hidden thought, light with intent, but widely set under the fine brush of brows that were just a touch darker than the chopped-off hair.

'Caithleen, it's good to see you up. I've lost a button. Come and help me find a replacement.'

The blouse was spread over a nearby chair and was ever so grand. Caithleen tried several mismatches just to see what would happen, and when she found a perfect one, hid this. Mrs. Fraser was worried, she was, and not inclined to let up, so the blouse was something special and the losing of its button rather important. 'Did you look where you thought you might have lost it?' she asked.

The girl's accent was soft and melodious. 'Under the bureau and bed, behind the sofa downstairs in Hamish's study. Just about everywhere, I'm afraid.'

And her not wanting to look up but hiding her eyes away. 'Buttons are always going missing. Me mam . . .' Caithleen bit off the sentence. 'I'm always losing them in the worst of places. Albert, he . . .' She bit that off too, let Mrs. Fraser hunt some more, noticed the quickness of her fingers, the agitation and felt the fear.

'Did you mean what you said last night?'

Mary wanted so much to tell her, to say again that it oughtn't to have happened to her at all, but of course she couldn't say that. Not yet, maybe never.

'I was mistaken, then, was I, Mrs. Fraser? I guess I was just so upset, my mind said crazy things to me.'

The lake was a mirror of darkness over which the first droplets of the coming rain sent their rings of ripples. Mary stood with her bike in the clearing, looking up from the water to the castle beyond the other shore. She had brought two bundles of books this time but didn't think she could go through with it. Hamish had come in late last night, had hardly made a sound, but she'd seen him standing in the doorway to her room, had hoped he'd come in, had waited, knowing that he was struggling with himself and that, at the last, he had turned away.

Caithleen had been awake and he'd gone in there for a moment, the girl whispering, 'Dr. Fraser, why is this happening to me?'

In the morning, he'd been up and out of the house well before Mrs. Haney and the others had arrived, had hitched the pony to the trap—was good at things like that. Like his gardening or his fishing and the tying of trout and salmon flies, there was much she didn't know about him. No criminal charges had been laid over the abortion. Hamish had done it for humanitarian reasons—she had always felt this even though he had never said and she'd had to find out by going to the hospital in Edinburgh and demanding an answer from one of his former colleagues. The girl had been thirteen years old, the father the girl's own, but the man had drunkenly raised a terrible row that too many others had heard. And then? she asked. Hamish had saved herself and she had saved him, and for a while it had been good.

Above the castle, the Union Jacks hung limply in the rain. Some were folded in on themselves, others wrapped about their flagpoles and not a sign of anyone up on the battlements or in any of the towers. Perhaps the distance was too great. She'd best be going, had best get it over with. 'Be brave,' she said. 'Do it because you have to.'

Whether in rain or sunshine, the first sight one had of the entrance to the prison was of barbed wire in accordion coils strung between and over log Xs. There was a barrier bar that could be raised or lowered just like the ones at border crossings, the guardhouse being somewhat more substantial yet even more bleak and with printed instructions that were tacked to one of the walls, the warning signs, the sentries with their rifles and, sometimes as today, one or two of the dogs.

Mary rode towards that thing she'd come to dread because, once in, there was no turning back. She handed over her pass, said, 'I want to see the colonel, please.'

'Colonel's away, miss.'

'Then Major Trant.'

All the ringing up on the field telephone, the request, the orders and the answers she heard and yet didn't hear, was conscious only of the rain, the wire and the castle whose gatehouse and barbican were at the end of the road.

'Miss?' She must have said yes, because he went on. 'Major Trant will see you in staff common, miss. If you wait at the main door, Private Summers will show you up.'

Miss . . . why had he called her that when her pass clearly gave her married name?

Her ring . . . Mary glanced down at her hand and realized that she must have taken it off and left it beside the bathroom sink. There was nothing for it but to continue—she couldn't turn back, not now.

The gatehouse at Tralane had two octagonal towers set astride the central passageway, each of some three storeys. Access was by a stone bridge instead of a drawbridge, but there was a portcullis of spiked iron bars hanging up there, with murder holes for quicklime, arrows, hot stones and boiling oil just as before.

The archway went clear through to another bridge and portcullis, so one had another dose of it, the gatehouse being backed by what was called the barbican—two round towers with square, interconnecting floors—six of these, so that the battlements rose up ahead of her, unseen now, but as a rampart.

Trant had his offices on the third floor of the barbican. That was where they had the interrogation rooms and where the careful sifting of intelligence was done, the gleaning of carelessly given words about submarines, aircraft, cruisers, tanks or heavy guns. Bombs too—anything that might be useful, including especially that which was repeated by unsuspecting female volunteer librarians.

The lounge was on the fourth floor—bedrooms and living quarters on the two other floors she supposed, though the colonel and his wife didn't live in the castle, just Jimmy and the major and the men.

Mary was shown into the lounge and told to wait. The chairs and sofas were all of that much worn morocco that had been fashionable twenty and thirty years ago, the room looking like that of a dingy, down-at-the-heels men's club. Ashtrays on stands, the rudiments of a bar—locked up, of course. A few newspapers, a couple of magazines, centuries old, dim lights, not on, the windows serving that purpose. A photograph of His Majesty, King George the Sixth.

The prisoners were standing in the rain. They were formed up across the Bailey in long lines that ran away from her, the men rigidly at attention, all 182 of them—no, 181, wasn't it? The Second Lieutenant Bachmann and . . . and then those, too, who were in the infirmary . . .

Mary began to count them, only to discover that at least some forty or so new arrivals had been received. She tried to find Erich—could spot the *Schirmmützen* of the U-boat captains—there were now five of these, but she couldn't see him and wondered if he wasn't in one of the interrogation rooms below her—Trant would have done that sort of thing. He'd have known she would go over to the windows and would see them all standing out there, so cold and wet Hamish would hear of it.

Pulling off her gloves and coat, she removed her beret and paced about, returning frequently to the windows, only to see the men still standing at attention. They'd all get pneumonia. It was just damned stupid. Why were they doing it to them, why were the men taking it so stubbornly? It was as if there'd been a funeral or something and they were all on parade to honour their dead.

'Mrs. Fraser, sorry to have kept you waiting, but it couldn't be helped. What can I do for you?'

'Are they still under house arrest?'

Her voice had leapt; he'd give her the offering of a brief smile. 'If you mean, are they still being recalcitrant, then yes.'

'But surely they'll become ill?'

'That? Oh that . . .' He'd go over to the windows now to stand beside her. 'That's of their own choosing. Marvellous discipline. Saw them like that in the stadium at Nurnberg in '36. The Nazis have no equal for it. Beautifully trained robots.'

'How long have they been like that?'

'Two hours. Since the dinner they refused to eat. A minor complaint about something Quartermaster Deeks had supplied their cooks. Now what can we do for you?'

Even as she turned from the window, Mary knew the men were breaking rank to go indoors, yet their being out there couldn't have been solely for her benefit, could it? Trant *was* an expert in the psychologies of interrogation.

'I have to take Caithleen to Dublin this Sunday, Major. The girl's suicidal. There is also, as you well know, the danger that those who were responsible will come back to finish the job.'

There were more, then, than the girl's uncle and cousin, were there, to say nothing of Fay Darcy? 'If they had wanted to kill her, they'd have done so.'

'She tried to . . .'

'We know all about that. Your husband has already told us.'

'Then why won't you let me take her to Dublin on Sunday?'

'Because it can't be arranged. Transport is at a premium these days, Mrs. Fraser. Space has been requested. When it becomes available, we'll let you know.'

'You just want to see if I keep my side of the bargain.'

'I'm sure the colonel would find that most unkind. More books?' he asked.

He had changed topics so suddenly, he could only be trying to catch her out. 'Yes,' she hazarded. 'You can look through them if you wish.'

A tough nut, was she? 'The Thackeray you brought the last time. Any idea who borrowed it? The colonel's wife has expressed an interest.'

She shook that head of hers, but he'd take his time with her. 'We can't seem to find the blessed thing. No one seems to have heard of it.'

'But it must be somewhere?'

She had been genuinely unsettled but had managed to keep control quite nicely. '*The Virginians*, was it?'

To turn away from him would only make things worse. 'There were some lovely illustrations—lithographs, not woodcuts. Hamish . . . Hamish is very fond of them. I do hope nothing has . . .'

'You don't like me very much, do you, Mrs. Fraser?'

'Should I?'

She'd been caught by that little confrontation and had weathered it well, but was now suitably flustered. 'No, of course not.'

He would take out his pocketknife and cut the strings, felt Mary, would notice that she was heading back to the windows rather than watch as he flipped through the books. Why *couldn't* he just condemn her and get it over with?

Trant saw that she had her back to him. She had worn a beige suit today, with sand-coloured knee socks and those brogues of hers. The regular little Scottish mistress, made over from Canada, he snorted silently. Tall but not too tall. A good figure, if one was interested in such things, good posture, good shoulders and afraid, so damned afraid he could smell the fear on her.

There'd be nothing in the books this time, so she either had it on her person or hadn't brought a thing and was simply worried about the Thackeray.

Then what the devil had she brought in that one? 'You weren't here on Thursday.'

There was no one out in the bailey now, not a soul. 'I was busy elsewhere. Didn't Hamish tell you?'

Best not to answer that, best to leave her worrying. 'The Thackeray, Mrs. Fraser. The men have refused to give it up, now why do you suppose that is?'

But he had *said* no one had heard of it! The urge to say, *A love of literature,* was almost more than she could bear but she would have to hold her tongue. Things must be all over for her, he having simply played her along, she having let him.

'That book,' he said.

'I . . . I haven't the slightest idea, Major. I'm not very fond of Thackeray—haven't read him in years. Not since I was at Trinity College—the one in Toronto, Canada, not Dublin.'

'Who borrowed the book?'

'Kramer, I think. Yes, it was Erich Kramer.'

'And yet he denies this?'

'Is that why they were all standing out there in the rain?'

Trant set the last of the books down on the couch where she had left them. He would let her do the tying up, would leave her just as she was with her back still to him.

Mary heard him leave the room.

The men began to gather in the great hall and come into the library. Philip Werner was back, and Mary was glad to see him. A bad cold, he said, grinning at her in that way small boys do who have successfully skipped lining up at school and want to tell their friends about it. Since a lot of them knew little if any English, books in German were at a premium. Philip chatted away their disappointment but knew she was doing the best she could with promises or editions, if not in *Deutsch*, then in French, Italian or Spanish—things once left by sailors in Newry and picked up for a song in the fleas. Blood and gore, most of them, or hot romances. Repeated requests to lending libraries and to private citizens were constantly being made. Anywhere she could get them, she did, but it was never easy. Far too often she was asked why she was doing 'anything for the enemy.'

Everything went as usual and this, too, wasn't easy. Philip *was* so darned nice and such a good friend, Helmut Wolfganger, too. Those who could speak English all tried to chat her up. As usual they wanted news of the war and she was forced to tell them yet again that she had been specifically forbidden to discuss it.

Orel had fallen—it had been on the news last night. Bryansk and Vyazma were caught in pincers. Thousands and thousands of Russian soldiers had either been killed or taken prisoner. It would have made Erich and the others happy, would have made their standing in the rain less an act of punishment and more one of heroism, but she couldn't tell them, and the news really was terrible. The Germans seemed to be winning on every front.

They had all had to change out of their bits and pieces of uniform, though. Rank had vanished, as had regimental unit and service. All had been levelled in this way, and she wondered if Trant hadn't done it deliberately so that she could see them for what they were: German and Nazi, even though many of them were so nice and not Nazis at all? Time and again, to reassure her, they had said their quarrel wasn't with Britain, many that once the Communists had been crushed in the East, peace would be made in the West, an honourable peace; some that it was the Soviets, the Bolsheviks and the Jews who were responsible.

Seeing her lost in thought, Werner gave her a questioning look to which she returned an uncertain smile. 'Another hour, Mrs. Fraser. It's good of you to do this for us.'

How many times had she heard that also? 'Two hours, Philip. Because of the delay, I've told Private Summers I won't be leaving until six, if that's all right.'

Werner grinned sheepishly and scratched his head in doubt. 'Has the private asked the major if this is possible?'

'Could you go and see, please?' It was all so coy—Philip knew something of what had been going on between Erich and herself—all of them must.

He grinned again and, pushing himself away from the table, reached for his crutches and said, 'For me, it will be a pleasure.'

Mary picked up the latest pile of returns. Several of the men came in and she knew Philip had stopped to talk to one of them, to Helmut Wolfganger. There were whispers, for Helmut was looking gravely at him, and then at herself, she starting in among the shelves to hear only snatches of what was being said in *Deutsch*. 'It's a good thing . . . Bachmann when . . . did . . .'

Angrily shoving the books into any place she could, she called out, 'Helmut, wait, please. I . . .'

With a warning, he shook his head but she asked it of him anyway. Had they been talking about the second lieutenant?

'You are mistaken, Mrs. Fraser. We were discussing the weather.'

There was no humour now in either of them, no kindness, only a warning that was all too clear. She couldn't have been wrong about them. She couldn't!

The bullet hadn't been in any of the books she'd brought in today. It was resting against her left instep. Only once in a while had it bothered her and each time someone had asked—Private Summers most of all—she had said a nail must have come through from her heel, or there was a stone, that she would check when she got the chance.

Philip came back to report that 6.00 p.m. would be fine with Major Trant. They worked, she filled in time and when Franz Bauer came for her, she knew Erich would be waiting.

Just next to the washroom there was a narrow set of stairs that spiralled up to a series of corridors and rooms, some with doors, others without. At a landing, she turned quickly off to her right and ran along the corridor until she came to another set of stairs.

Running up these, Mary flung open the door at the top, then closed it behind herself and leaned back against it, her heart hammering. Always it was like this. The fear of knowing Trant and Jimmy Allanby and the guards would be watching for just such a thing. The fear of what she was doing, of betraying Hamish and her country, herself as well and all for what? For loving one of the enemy? Did she really still love Erich? How could she?

'*Liebling*, it's good to see you.'

He had come in through the other door, was suddenly here and grinning at her. 'But . . . but what is this?' she heard him saying. 'You're out of breath.'

Kramer put his arms about her, the woman hesitating, knowing she mustn't, that everything in her was telling her she was a silly damned fool, that the IRA would kill her if she didn't go through with it; that the British would if she did. *Ach*, he had his work cut out for him, would kiss the tip of her nose now—*ja*, that would be best. Even though she pulled away, he'd not let her get off so easily, would give that gentle laugh she liked so much, would brush a hand fondly across that brow of hers, tracing out the lines of worry, kissing it now, murmuring, 'Worries, such worries I've brought you. Can you ever forgive me?'

Gently, hesitantly, he found her lips, but she tried to break away, he laughing now as he lifted her up and swung her around before hugging her as if dearest to him, he burying his face in her hair, her lovely hair. 'You smell wonderful,' he said. '*Ach*, it's safe for a while. Private Summers will be diverted by a display of naked young ladies such as he's never seen before.'

'Photographs, I hope,' was all she said, she growing serious again and asking, 'Were you cold out there?'

He grinned and shook his head. 'Martin Hauser filled in for me. He was in the infirmary. Such a soaking they got, Mary, and all because of a missing book!'

Erich had lent his cap to someone else. 'Trant knows I gave that book to you.'

And still worried. 'So? What if he does?'

'Why weren't you out with the others?'

Was it to be that way with them? 'Me? I had some things to do.'

Things he couldn't tell her. Things like places he could not have measured or explored without some sort of a diversion to occupy the guards.

Mein Gott, but she was needing reassurance. He would run his hands up and down her arms, would say, 'Please don't worry so much. I burned the book in our stove. Your Major Trant suspects this but what he doesn't yet know is that you're missing seventeen others. When he realizes what must have happened, he will be told in no uncertain terms that we need more and better fuel for our stoves. Coal instead of peat, I think.'

If she thought to say they were like a bunch of schoolboys, she didn't. He would touch her hair, then, would lay a hand against her left cheek, would feel how nervous she was, how uncertain still and quivering.

Leaning close, he whispered, '*Liebling*, may I?'

Mary knew that if she didn't let him kiss her, things might only go from bad to worse and she might have to take the bullet home, yet if she did let him . . .

He wrapped his arms about her and lifted her up, she pressing herself against him. 'Erich . . .' she managed, turning quickly aside only to find his lips again and again until, finally, she had broken away.

Was demanding of herself why she would do such a thing— Kramer could see this in her. 'Was Thursday a bad day for you?' he asked, resting his forehead against her own.

Erich would take her if he could, and she knew this now. He would try to get her down on her back or on her hands and knees, but would she let him? 'I had to meet with Kevin O'Bannion. He . . . he gave me something for you.'

She looked for signs, for reassurance perhaps. As she pried off her shoe, he got down on his knees, would let her feel his every touch. It was always best with women like this, the constant teasing now light, now firm, the coolness of the room rushing in on her as the stocking was removed. She'd be worrying about being away too long, that she would be missed and had best get back. She'd be thinking of Trant or Allanby and the guards rushing in on them. 'I've missed you, Mary. I wish . . .' He would kiss her bare foot now, would run his hands up her leg. 'A bullet? Only one?'

'O'Bannion said there'd be others later,' she heard herself saying, but had Erich noticed how desperately afraid she was not just of everything else but of herself?

He looked up at her with that thing in his fingers. 'So they are playing games with us, are they? One at a time only makes it all the harder for you.'

'Erich, I overheard Helmut and Philip in the library. Were they involved in the hanging of that man?'

Kramer swore under his breath. 'Trant has no business asking you to spy on us.'

'But were they? He'll only ask if I've heard anything, and Kevin . . . The IRA are demanding that you tell me something so that I can put Trant off and let him think I'm cooperating. It's . . . it's one of their conditions. They need time to . . . to work things out.'

'So, it has to be business for us after all, has it?'

She mustn't weaken, must just get back to the library. 'Were they involved?' she asked, reaching out to lay a hand on his head, he still on his knees.

'Tell Trant what you overheard. I can't stop you, but neither can I betray them.'

Then they *had* been involved. 'I wish you'd just say it, Erich. It would make things so much easier for me.'

'And I wish they would just ship us off to Canada. I'd miss

you, but can wait. It wouldn't be for long in any case. Has there been anything further on that?'

She shook her head, still hadn't removed her hand. 'When are you going to Dublin next?' he asked.

He still hadn't got to his feet; she was still leaning against the wall. 'It's being deliberately put off—I have to have something for them in return. That's . . . that's how it is.'

'Were the people who would help us responsible for what happened to that girl?'

'They . . . they also want to know if there's anything you would like to send over by wireless.'

The tarring had been done as a warning to her, then, and they had chosen to make a regular little courier out of her, so must have been satisfied. 'No, there's nothing to send over. Berlin must want them to get me out, otherwise they would have severed all contact right away.'

He was lost to it now, was thinking it all through as he must, but would he also wonder where things might lead for her? 'Have you any idea of what the IRA will want in return?'

It was not the time to smile, even if softly. 'You're worried about their taking innocent lives. Of course you are and so am I. This war, this whole business . . . So few of us have any say in things, it's just not fair, is it?'

'Guns and ammunition? Explosives?'

She had asked it as if knowing it must be true and hating herself, but had she not been a little grateful for what he'd just said? 'Or money, *Liebling*. Lots of money in small bills probably. In British one- and five-pound notes.'

'Do we have to go through with this? Couldn't we simply stop right now?' Mary told him what had happened to Caithleen. 'She . . . she wanted to kill herself.'

He'd not let on that they'd already known, would simply

say, 'It's been terrible for you, hasn't it?' and let her feel his hands on her legs.

'I mustn't,' she said.

His hands moved up to her thighs.

'Erich, *please!*'

'Hush, *mein Schatz*. Hush. Let's steal the moment while we can.'

'No! It . . . it has to stop!'

She'd be glancing at each of the doors now, would be worrying about their being found out. When her underwear reached her knees, she tried to pull it up, but one must be ready for just such a thing and tighten it about her ankles. '*Please!*' she said, those eyes of hers clamped lest the sight of him make her want it all the more, her fists clenched at her sides, his hands on her bare ass now, she trying to turn away from his kisses only to find out that she couldn't.

When he stood to push his trousers down, she took his *Schwanz* in her hands when given it, was used to this, but he'd trace a finger down her chin and open her blouse, would have to fondle her, have to make her believe that it was love.

She was wet, all right, had been wanting it in spite all the objections, the clitoris stiff and rising to his touch, she gripping his cock harder and harder. He'd let her see the mist in his eyes as he came—yes, yes, that would be best, but first herself. He had to get the bitch to cry out for it so loudly she'd have to smother herself with a hand and let him have her any time he wanted.

Mary felt the release. She shook, she tried not to cry out, tried to stop herself, but came and came, saw that look come into his eyes as he ejaculated until limp.

Turning aside, hating herself, she wept, and he left her just like that.

*   *   *

'Wolfganger?'

'I didn't hear all of what they said, Major. My German's simply not that good.'

'But it sounded like, It's a good thing we hanged Bachmann when we did?'

She was standing before his desk like an errant schoolgirl, couldn't seem to bring herself to face him directly. 'Well?' he demanded.

'Yes, then. I . . . I suppose so, but . . . but it could just as easily have been, It's a good thing *they* hanged Bachmann when they did.'

'Meaning Wolfganger and Werner knew all about it but weren't directly involved, that it?'

Must he snap at her?

When she didn't answer, Trant offered a cigarette but didn't ask her to sit down. 'Library go all right?' he asked.

He knew damned well he hadn't turned on any lights, was deliberately letting darkness overtake the office. 'I can't find the Thackeray,' Mary heard herself saying stiffly. 'I'm sorry. We did look. We asked every . . .'

'You and Werner?'

Must he startle her? 'Yes. Apparently it's not the only book that's missing. Eighteen of them can't be accounted for.'

He raised his dark eyebrows as he lit a cigarette. 'I see,' was all he said.

'May I go now? It's . . . it's getting rather late. Hamish . . . My husband doesn't like me to be out after dark.'

'Mrs. Fraser, why do you suppose Wolfganger would have said, "It's a good thing they hanged Bachmann when they did?"'

'I've no idea.'

'But surely something must have happened to make him say that? Did Werner pass some information on to Helmut who in turn said, "It's a good thing they . . ."'

'Major, *please*! I really must go. I've no idea what was said beyond what I've already told you, and no idea whatsoever as to why it should have been said at that particular moment.'

'The two of them in the doorway, that right? Was it crowded? Who else was with them—come, come, Mrs. Fraser, surely you can remember that much?'

'I can't, and you've no reason to subject me to this . . . this sort of thing.'

'An interrogation, is that what you're thinking? My dear woman, this is far from that sort of thing. I am merely trying to determine why Wolfganger should have said . . .'

'Stop it! Just stop it! I *don't* know.'

It would be so easy to break her now. She'd been unsettled and preoccupied when she'd come into the office. Dust must have been caught in her eyes. The bloody stuff was always blowing about. Could have picked it up anywhere, could have been crying, too.

'I'm sorry if I've upset you, Mrs. Fraser.'

It wasn't fair of him to have kept her standing in front of his desk like some sort of criminal. She would have to force herself to look up, to look steadily at him and not feel as though he knew what she'd just let Erich do to her. To her!

He'd let her wait, thought Trant. He'd have her in each day for a session if he could, and he'd save one of the interrogation rooms just to let her experience what it was really like.

When she turned away to leave, he said, 'I'm not finished with you yet.'

It was all but dark in the room.

'Mrs. Fraser, have you heard anything about a plan to escape?'

Even before she could answer, he had switched on the desk lamp, had caught her in its glare and made her shield her eyes. 'Of course I haven't. Had I, I would immediately have told you.'

'Or the colonel,' he said softly, she still wincing at the light.

'Yes, or Captain Allanby.'

He'd adopt the air of the good host now and startle the living daylights out of her. 'Captain,' he called out. 'Good of you to have joined us. Mrs. Fraser was just telling me Kramer and the others burned a bunch of her books in their stoves. Now what do you make of that?'

To give credit where credit was due, thought Trant, Allanby stayed over by the door, letting her wonder not only where he was but how long he'd been there, but a conciliatory tone would be best. 'Mrs. Fraser, the prisoners may seem a nice group of men to you and your husband. Oh I know they're far from home and feeling lonely, many of them. It's not a normal life any more than it is for our chaps over there. Like monks, I should think. But they are German officers, Mrs. Fraser, and up to mischief all the time.'

'Then perhaps you should have them stand out in the rain more often.'

Oh my, oh my, a spark of fight, was it? Well, good—yes, that was all to the good. She'd not been here on Thursday but he'd leave that, would let her continue to puzzle over why he hadn't pressed the issue.

Motioning her to come closer, he took out a folder and laid some drawings on the desk—floor plans of the castle done precisely in pencil with measurements clearly indicated in metres and notations written in *Deutsch*. She would have to lean well over the desk to see them.

'They've been digging a tunnel, Mrs. Fraser. From what used to be the brewhouse here in the cellars, out to a copse of oaks not far from the perimeter, so you see,' he said, looking up at her, his face close to hers, 'they do intend to escape. They think about it constantly, and we must continually be on the alert for such things.'

Was that the fear of discovery he saw in those bedroom eyes of hers, he wondered, or simply the fear of knowing she was way in over her head?

He'd lower his voice to barely a whisper. 'They are desperate men, Mrs. Fraser. Please make no mistake about it.'

She really did have such lovely eyes—large and of a deep chestnut shade but with those tints of green and flecks of amber Jimmy must always think of. Poor Jimmy. Love was such a stupid thing and Allanby such a lonely man. They really must do something to stem that. The colonel had been absolutely right.

'Captain Allanby, would you show Mrs. Fraser to the perimeter?'

Trant had noticed that she wasn't wearing her wedding ring. He must have seen this earlier but hadn't said a thing then of it either.

'That's all for now, Mrs. Fraser. We'll see you on Tuesday, I take it?'

She was still bent over the damned desk, was still giving Jimmy a full view of that backside of hers, yet hadn't been able to make herself move.

'Well?' he asked.

'Yes. Yes, of course I'll come.'

As they walked along the road towards the barbed wire of the perimeter, Allanby broke the silence that she had always put between them. 'I met your husband on the old tote road to Newtonhamilton. He was having a look at the bridge.'

'Oh?'

She had definitely panicked at the thought. 'Then I met him at the Darcy place. Why do you suppose he was poking around there? He's a very busy man.'

Mary was glad that it was dark and he couldn't see her clearly, but she'd have to say something, couldn't just leave it, had best be calm. 'I've no idea, Captain. Hamish does love the countryside and he might have had a few moments to himself, though he gets few enough of them. Perhaps he was looking for another place to fish—he loves his fishing, but again he can't seem to find the time.'

'And the Darcy place?' he asked.

She mustn't hesitate. 'He's always had an interest in saving things from the past. It's in far better shape than most.'

Was it? But he'd not ask how the bloody hell she'd even known! He'd leave that for a while, would chalk it up on the bricks as Fay Darcy's father had his frigging accounts. 'Money would be needed. Lots of it,' he snorted. 'It's a good job that family you married into sold out when they did, though, in '28 and just before the crash. The old man made quite a bundle, or so I gather.'

'Hamish has three brothers and two sisters, Captain. That "bundle" as you call it, was shared equally after taxes.'

'And he's prepared to sink some into Irish history? Come on, Mary, that husband of yours is no fool. The Darcy place?'

'Captain, I'm very tired and must get home.'

'We'll put the bike in the boot and I'll drive you over.'

He would, too. 'That's very kind, but I'd rather be by myself. The air will do me good.'

God damn her anyway! He'd grab her by the arm and force her to face him. 'Mary, listen to me. I had to do what I did to that girl.'

'And Hamish and I have to suffer the consequences, as does Caithleen. Now *let* go of me, Captain. I'll walk the rest of the way by myself.'

Long after she had left him, Allanby continued to stare after her. She was like a moth trapped in a smoke-filled glass that had been turned upside down on a beer-sloshed table, the men all around and betting on how long she'd last.

'Mrs. Haney, I'm awfully sorry to be a bother when you're just about to go home. Caithleen and I did look through your button box but we weren't able to come up with anything. Would you have a button to match these?'

A button, was it? thought Ria, but the tone of voice and the look were those of apology, and she had no heart to let her tongue run over the hills with the doctor looking like a dog that had lost its bone and master.

Taking the blouse from her, she examined the gap. Given the right chance, Mrs. Fraser would come round, but would she be given that chance? 'A bit of material's been torn, m'am. I'll be wanting fine thread and a fine needle for that. And was there anything else?'

To say, I wish we wouldn't fight, I need you on my side, would do no good. 'Why, yes, there is. Have either yourself or Bridget seen my wedding ring? I thought I must have left it beside the sink upstairs, but it seems to have vanished.'

'Vanished, has it? Vanished my foot! Stolen most likely. Bridget . . . Bridget Leahy, you come here now, my girl. I want a word with you I do, and when I'm finished your ears will be ringing so hard you'll never again hear that Bing Crosby you like so much singin' "I Surrender, Dear"!'

'Mrs. Haney, *please*! I need a button, not a police inquiry. Bridget wouldn't have stolen my ring.'

'You leave this t' me, m'am. Leave it, I say! Bridget? Bridget, girl, you fetch that button box of my mother's and a sheet from the closet upstairs. Fetch Caithleen as well. Three pairs of eyes it will be, Mrs. Fraser. Three I'm telling you.'

Good God Almighty, why did the woman have to go on like this? 'Please don't flood the place with tears. We've had far too many of them of late.'

Tears was it? and look who had opened the floodgates! 'Just you leave it to me, m'am. Stand aside while I cuts to the quick of it!'

Lost buttons and lost wedding rings, was it now? And there was that half-brother of hers rolling his eyes to the heavens above while denying the two of them had talked at all, at all about the O'Bannions and the Darcys, to say not a blessed thing about Liam Nolan.

'There's something going on around this house, Mrs. Fraser, and I aims to get to the bottom of it, I does.'

She had left the kitchen, had vanished just like her ring. Caithleen came running only to have the sheet torn from her hands and flung over the kitchen table, snapped to make it fly and settle without a hand needing to smooth it.

'Now you put that box down and stand there before it, the two of you. Bridget! close the lid. That was my mother's, and before ever we searched, we said us a prayer, we did. So bow your heads now, I say, and draw your hands together in penitence.'

The two of them were a pair, Caithleen the taller, Bridget the plumper. Ria drew in a breath. Girls had to be dealt with firmly where stealing was involved. 'Now say after me, Dear God—repeat it now, the two of you.'

They did, and their voices were most humble and that was as it should be. 'Dear God, Who is the One and Only God, Father of the Son and Blessed Father to us all, I do swear on my grave to come and that of my ancestors back unto the tenth generation that I have stolen nothing from this house. Bridget, you being employed and all by that kindest of men, we'll overlook them Christmas raisins and currants I be saving and we'll settle on Mrs. Fraser's ring. Did you steal it?' she hissed, making the girl fling back her head as if struck.

Bridget burst into tears. 'No, m'am. No! I wouldn't do such a terrible thing. You know I wouldn't. I'm a good girl. I goes to Mass. I says my prayers. I . . .'

'That'll be enough, girl. Now look at that box of my mother's. See the inlay of it, do you? 'Tis the Star of David himself, it is, given in the circle of the world and come by ship from the very Plains of Abraham on the death to the third or fourth generation or more of a dearly departed relative. Now answer me again, girl. Did you take that ring because if you did, your heart is smaller than the smallest button in that box unless you repent and give it up this instant!'

The girl would have troubled Noah on the fortieth day, and him with the last of the doves in his hand. 'Fair enough, Bridget. Now don't carry on. I has to know, girl.

'Caithleen, you being a guest in this house and dear to us, I'll ask it of you too. If you did take Mrs. Fraser's wedding ring, it'll be a secret known only to the three of us.'

The girl didn't cry. Where there should have been tears there was only anger.

'I did not, Mrs. Haney. I wouldn't do a thing like that. The doctor's my friend.'

'Then let us find a button for that blouse.'

Caithleen wanted to say, There's no need. I have one, but

she held her tongue. Dr. Fraser had the wedding ring. She had seen him looking sadly at it, but when she'd come along the corridor towards him, he had simply tucked it away in his waistcoat pocket and had said nothing. Not a blessed thing, though he'd seen her looking at it.

5

The sound of the car was all that passed between them, the lights on the dash glowing dimly, the road ahead being dark, Hamish late as usual. Even on a Sunday he would be called away.

'Darling, I wish you'd say something. My ring will turn up. I didn't lose it on purpose.'

'And I didn't say you had.'

'Then what's bothering you? You know I can't stand your being upset with me any more than I can our having to go to another of these wretched do's of the colonel's.'

Deliberately he left his foot off the brake as they rounded a hairpin bend. Her stomach lifted. Bends and ups and downs had always been a problem, only the more so now. Her stomach felt so queasy. Every morning it was as if she couldn't keep a thing down. 'I wish you'd let me drive.'

'We'd never get there. Blame Mrs. O'Brian, if you like, for letting her son play Tarzan with his cousins on my day of rest. Blame the fathers, too, for giving the boys the ropes and iron hoops they thought the little nippers would need.'

'You're enjoying this.'

'I am not. You know I can never forgive Trant and the colonel for the way Jimmy threatened Caithleen and had us shoved about, but I have to keep up a pretense of sociability!'

'How much have you had to drink? Look, I know the Bushmills is gone. There was a half left last night when I went to bed.'

'You sound like a fishwife.'

'I'm only telling you the truth.'

He gripped the wheel with one hand and, digging into his jacket pocket, thrust the flask at her. Mary knew then that he really was upset with her but that he'd say nothing of it. 'I wish I hadn't lost my ring, Hamish. I really do.'

'Mrs. Haney questioned the girls. If I've understood it correctly from Caithleen, the Spanish Inquisition couldn't have been worse.'

'Please don't make fun of it. That girl has to go. She's upsetting Bridget and Mrs. Haney.'

'Mary, how can you say a thing like that when you know it is yourself she's upset?'

Hamish had always been one for the truth. Abruptly she turned from him to stare emptily out the side windscreen. After the 'Inquisition' she had searched the house, had even gone into his study, though it couldn't have been left in there.

'I didn't drink the Bushmills, lass. I took it up to Clarence Malloy so as to give the old man a bit of comfort. That flask of mine is empty.'

Instinctively she flung herself from the windscreen to hug his arm and lean against him, then to snuggle down with her feet curled up on the seat and her head in his lap. 'Don't hate me,' she said.

Fraser eased off on the accelerator. He couldn't let her go

into the colonel's without her ring—it wasn't right of him. They'd all notice. Dorothy Bannerman was a royal pain in the ass, and God knows, he hated these things as much as Mary, but had she taken the ring off on purpose or instinctively and not even realized it? She'd been at the castle yesterday. At breakfast this morning she'd been quiet, hadn't looked well and had got up suddenly to leave the room, he having only just broken the yolks of two poached eggs on toast. He'd found her in the conservatory watering the plants and looking pale.

Erich Kramer was far more her age, sensitive too, when he'd a mind, and intelligent—the two of them had several interests in common. They'd got on well—hadn't he seen it coming, fool that he'd been? Hadn't he encouraged it, if not for both their sakes then simply because Mary had been lonely and feeling so out of place, but now? he had to ask. What now? He had thought that once Erich had gone back to Tralane it would have been the end of the matter, but then had come the offer of books from the lending library in Newry and his own suggestion that she help out, since the librarian there had insisted on someone responsible being left in charge. Trant and Bannerman had talked it over at length, and had finally agreed.

Again he had only himself to blame but what the hell was he to do? Pull over to the side and switch off the motor?

She was asleep. Fraser knew this, felt it, had to ask, Exhaustion? and answer, Oh dear, oh dear.

'Mary . . . Mary, we're almost there. Do you want to straighten your hair?'

She stirred, got more comfortable and murmured, 'Darling, take me away from Ireland. Take me some place where I don't know anyone but you.'

'Is it Erich, lass? You can tell me if it is.'

'Erich? It's . . . It's just this place. It's got to me. I can't stand it anymore and yet I know I'm going to have to.'

Fraser felt an utter fool—angry with her for not being honest, angry with himself for wanting to pitch the ring out on to the road! Slamming the car into first, he started off again. Doctors had the right not to tape their headlamps to blackout pinpoints. He had compromised by going the half and leaving the centre swath free but felt like getting out and tearing the things off.

They got to the lane soon enough, the colonel and his wife living in a Tudor 'cottage' that was set in five acres of well-treed grounds near Armagh and solid comfort but Bannerman must have always looked out for himself, and Dotty, with her face powder, blush and creams, had simply tagged along. They had a poodle named Schnapps, a cat named Robustus, and two sons in the war, and they had a sign on a ramrod staff that had been cast out of Sudanese musket balls and was stabbed into the lawn to simply read: DULSE AND DOTTY AT HOME. *Och*, how many times had he vowed to steal the bloody thing and never had the courage?

Mary heard him fling it into the boot and knew then that he might well go on a bender that could last for days, that he was not only furious with her but with himself. Whiskey did things to him. First the talk, then the fun, and then the pain. He hadn't done that in a long, long time, not since she'd first known him and he'd come to love her.

The cocktails were over and they were just going in to dinner when Hamish rang the bell. They said their hellos and gave their apologies, his voice loud and boisterous. 'A fractured right humerus and the left femur, Colonel. Assorted bruises, abrasions and cuts, and a gash like the leavings of a hurley stick. I packed the lad off to Newry in his father's donkey cart with enough morphine to turn him into a dope addict.'

'All the Irish are the same. They breed them that way,' roared the colonel, in good form.

'Don't they,' shouted Hamish. 'Mary . . . Mary, lass, let me *tak* your *coot.*'

'Coats upstairs for the ladies, Mrs. Fraser. Third on the right. Can't miss it. Powder on the left. Hamish, glad you could make it. Been wanting to have a chat. Informally, if you get the gist.'

'Oh I do, Colonel. I do. Captain Allanby, nice to see they've given you a night off. Major, have the gates been left wide open?'

Mary could hear them from the top of the stairs and then from the bedroom whose bed was heaped with coats. So Jimmy was here and the major, and damn it, what was she to do? *Sit* with them at dinner? She'd throw up all over the place.

Somehow she got herself together and went down but didn't have to sit with either. Dotty Bannerman had given her Father Eugene O'Donnell on her right and the Reverend Frederick Mountjoy, pastor of All Saints in Belfast, on her left. Perhaps the woman had thought she'd be the cushion between them, perhaps the cement that bound these two old chunks of granite into some sort of conversational bridge.

There were, however, three RAF—smashing types, as the Brits were fond of saying—all in their uniforms with wings, five officers from the Royal Navy and a good sprinkling from the army, several WRNS (aka Wrens) and FANYs,* even two unattached but soon-to-be-attached Anglo-Irish girls by the looks they gave the boys, and assorted others both male and female.

It wasn't the usual, not quite. In fact, it was a darned sight different, and she wondered then as Father O'Donnell waited patiently for his turn to say the blessing, if the colonel and

---

* Women's Royal Naval Service, and First Aid Nursing Yeomanry.

the major hadn't done it all on purpose. To cut her off from Hamish and single her out in the company of younger people like herself. Younger people who were at war and on leave, something she'd know little of.

'Antisubmarine patrols out of Derry. It's jolly fast and furious when we see them and have a chance to run in, but terribly boring most of the time.'

'And cold. Bloody awful, I should say.'

'My da's a farmer. Sheep and cattle mostly, and the pigs. Me mam's a hairdresser and I'm a secretary.'

'My father's a lawyer and doing very nicely, I'll thank you kindly.'

'You lot should try the North Atlantic in gale force ten. Whips the tops right off the waves. Makes Jerry want to submerge just to steady the crockery.'

Destroyers, that one, felt Mary, but wasn't gale force ten the maximum, or was that twelve? They had had the soup and the poached salmon and were now on the main course. The chandeliers gave their light among the assorted crystal, the laughter and the conversation. Wineglasses were refilled constantly, no shortages here, not even a hint of them. The waiters had all been recruited from the hotels in Armagh and were very attentive in black bow ties and dinner jackets.

Snatches of conversation kept coming at her, glimpses of flashing blue and brown eyes, of white, white teeth, for the Anglo-Irish girls had cozied up to the two RAF across the table. The girls were plump-breasted things with necklines that plunged dangerously every time they leaned over, having deliberately dropped a fork or spoon. The one would toss her long raven-hair back; the other would bat her big brown eyes and smile.

'King Billy was the curse of all Ireland,' said Father O'Donnell briskly, the two clergymen talking across her as if she didn't exist.

'And Patrick, I be thinking, though there are those of us who would claim him as our own,' said Mountjoy with spittle.

'Father, would you pass me the cranberry sauce, please?'

'That I will, miss. As I was saying, Father Mountjoy . . .'

'Pastor . . . It's pastor.'

'That it is, if you're claiming it.'

'I saw you refereeing the boys at hurley the other day, Father.'

'That you did, miss. Now please don't interrupt me.'

Trying to tuck in a bite, she saw the two flying officers across the table laughing at her predicament. Flashing them a smile and shrugging with her eyebrows only made the Irish girls furious, but what could one do? 'Are you really on antisubmarine patrols out of Derry?' she asked. It was all but a shout.

The one nodded, the other grinned and said, 'Would we lie to you about a thing like that?' to which the Irish girls got huffy and the Royal Navy second lieutenant added, 'They haven't hit a thing yet, Mrs. Fraser,' and the Catholic priest pricked up his ancient ears.

'Mrs. Fraser, ah now I have your name and take cognizance of it.' Without her wedding ring, she was, and with an eye for the lads and the husband down at the far end making mischief with the wine.

'Aren't they very hard to detect?' she asked, hiding her left hand in her lap and leaning over the table so as to be heard.

'Very,' said the Royal Navy officer. 'Like the proverbial needle in the haystack.'

'I've seen lots of them,' said one of the pilots. 'From the air we can spot them better. Besides, we've got . . .'

'Jack, steady on. Ears, eh what?'

'Oh, sorry, Chris. Sorry. Need to keep my mouth zipped, Mrs. Fraser.'

'But are you detecting them better than before?'

He gave her a nod. The raven-haired girl tossed back her hair. 'My dad says there are lots of U-boats in the South, off Cork and other places.'

'In the West,' said the brown-eyed one. 'There are hundreds of places for them to hide. Dingle Bay, for sure. Thousands of little coves and no one in sight for miles around.'

Someone asked her jokingly how she could be so certain and she answered swiftly, 'My da knows more than pigs, he does.'

The Royal Navy officer suggested she should offer her services to the War Office to which the poor girl blushed crimson and said, 'Me mam's from Glenbeigh, so there, Your Highness, and my grandda's seen three of them German U-boats which is more than th' whole lot of ye have seen, I suppose.'

A girl of spirit. 'Good for you, Maevis. That's telling them,' said the raven-haired one looking darkly across the table as if this Mrs. Fraser was to blame for it all.

'Three?' asked the pilot named Jack. He wasn't going to leave it. 'Up Derry way we're seeing three a week sometimes. They come to raid the convoys.'

'Oh, and do they? Convoys is it? Ships from America, Erin. In the films, I'd be for sure and you, too, what with them eyes of yours that are such a lovely shade of violet and that ebony hair.'

They talked about America. One had best pick at the roast chicken and try a bit of the beef but definitely not ask Pastor Mountjoy to pass the forgotten horseradish.

Hamish was on his feet. Someone was dinging a glass, and soon everyone was following suit. 'Ladies and gentlemen, I give you His Majesty, the King,' he said, raising his glass. He had such a strong voice and good bearing when he wanted.

'The King . . . The King,' they all chimed in.

'And the war,' he said, looking down the length of the table towards her.

'Here, here,' shouted someone. 'The war.'

'Please let's not have any talk of that beastly business, not tonight,' said their hostess from the other end of the table. 'Dulsey, you know we agreed.'

She was really looking most dismayed and likely to blubber at any moment.

'Boys in a bit of a dust-up with Rommel's chaps,' apologized the colonel gruffly. 'Gone missing in action. We've been waiting for weeks for news. Sorry, luv. Dr. Fraser meant well.'

'Oh I did indeed,' said Hamish clearly, 'but what I meant was the U-boat war in the North Atlantic. May it go so well every one of the damned things is sunk!'

With the loss of all hands. She *must* look at him; mustn't concentrate on the mashed potatoes picked at in their gravy before her with bits of dressing—did they call it stuffing in England and Ireland? The cranberry sauce she had fought so hard to get had been left untouched.

'Are you finished, madam?'

'Yes. Yes, thanks.' Hamish had sat down at last, and the talk had gone back to other things, to films, to fishing, to books read and not yet read, to dancing and thoughts of Christmas leave to come. At least the talk here had. *And* religion. *And* the war between the North and the South. Would that blasted business ever end?

Hamish was looking rather pleased with himself. Though

she couldn't see them, she thought then that Major Trant and Captain Allanby must be sitting across the table from him and that he had said it as much for their benefit as her own.

'What is it you do in the war?'

'Nothing. I'm not in it.'

'But you want to be?'

'Not really. Look, I know that sounds as if I don't care about what's been happening but I do. I care passionately but . . . but it just isn't my war. I'm a Canadian.'

'But Canada's been in it right from the start. Half my old squadron were Canadians. Bomber Command is loaded with them, as are the Royal Navy and Army. Jack's navigator's from Winnipeg.'

He'd found her alone in the colonel's gun room. Flying Officer Christopher Blakely was about four years younger than herself, of the same height and with dark, wavy hair, a narrow, somewhat hawkish face, and deep grey eyes that seemed to say he really did want to know something about her.

She wondered where the Irish girls had got to, but then the sound of a record player started up—they'd rolled the carpets back.

'Most of the merchant ships that come over here have Canadian crews, Mrs. Fraser, out of Halifax, Nova Scotia and St. John's, Newfoundland. They're a damn fine lot of men.'

'Yes, I know, but you see, I came to Britain in the autumn of 1938 to get away from something, so I've cut myself off and now feel I'm neither Canadian nor British, or Irish for that matter, just someone without a country.'

Had she been trying to justify things to herself? wondered Blakey. That business about getting away from something couldn't have been easy, but best not to pry, best to simply say, 'Someone with all sorts of feelings then?'

She wished he wouldn't persist. 'Yes, that's just the trouble. They're all mixed up at the moment. Now if you'll excuse me, Flying Officer, I'd best rejoin my husband.'

'Hey, hang on a minute. Let's talk. It can't hurt. I'm . . . Look, you'd jolly well be doing me a favour, Mrs. Fraser. You see . . .' He glanced towards the door and the sounds of Glen Miller's band. 'I'm rather fixed at the moment—engaged, if you get my meaning.'

And very much in love? 'Tell me something then about the North Channel—anything, that is, that's not classified.'

'Why the interest—if you don't mind my asking?'

Had Bannerman or Trant sent him to her after all? 'I work with the prisoners at Tralane Castle. Some of them were on U-boats.'

Blakely gave her a sheepish grin and scratched the back of his head. 'Well, I'll be damned. You're a lot closer to them than we are. Who would have guessed?'

Again she wondered if he'd been sent to ask her things but that couldn't be. He was far too nice. And she thought then, as she sat down in one of the easy chairs, that his girl was pretty lucky, and she hoped he'd make it through.

'What are they really like?' he asked, genuinely wanting to know.

'A lot like yourselves. Young and very fit and eager to fight, but wanting lives of their own as well.'

'But incredibly tough and brave, I should think.'

He sat forward on the couch, resting his arms on his knees, wanting a cigarette perhaps, but not having one because he must have known by then that she didn't smoke.

'Jackie did shoot up a sub pretty badly and came back with the holes from their deck guns to prove it.'

'And yourself?' The image of Erich in his conning tower facing the strafing of enemy aircraft was all too clear.

Blakely lost himself in thought. It wouldn't be fair of him to tell her he'd seen men trying to swim in the sea with their clothing on fire and that there'd been nothing he could have done for them. 'London diverts the convoys up our way. It's supposed to avoid the massive concentrations of air and sea power Jerry has along the French coast, but it doesn't always work.'

When she didn't say anything, he carried on. 'The North Channel's heavily mined, Mrs. Fraser, so there's only a narrow passage, and the Channel itself isn't any more than ten miles across between Torr Head and the Mull of Kintyre. Mostly they hit the convoys well before then, but it's uncanny how some of them get past us.'

Again she didn't say anything, but was she forcing him to continue? 'The U-boats slip under the mines and through the nets to come up at night and wait. They can't remain submerged for all that long. Usually a few hours at most—that's how we get them sometimes. They're starved for oxygen by then, so they have to surface for air and to recharge their batteries. They cruise on their diesels, on the surface. Although they can receive wireless signals underwater, they can't send them and have to surface for that, but I expect you know all this.'

Had he and his crew sunk one, had that been it? Things had really got to him, and he had wanted to talk about it to someone. 'How many ships have you seen go down?' she asked.

He seemed startled by the question. 'So close to home? Seven. Jerry has the whole area divided into grid squares. Sectors fifty-four and fifty-five hug the north coast of Ireland. Fifty-seven is the worst because it's right in the narrowest part of the

Channel. Sectors fifty-one and fifty-four are just to the north. They call it the AM Block. I don't think what I'm telling you is classified, but just to be on the safe side . . .'

She'd give him a nod. 'Do they come in packs?'

'Wolf packs? Don't believe all the press tells us, Mrs. Fraser. Two or three U-boats are a lot to see in an area at any one time but the bottom's not too deep in the North Channel—about six hundred feet and just at the limit of safe depth for them, so they can and do lie on it.'

'Having picked up the sound of the propellers with their hydrophones, the asdic first, if there's a destroyer?'

Had the prisoners told her such, or had she overheard them, and in either case, what else? 'Then they wait for the depth charges, but they can tell one kind of propeller from another—they're very good at this, and I've known them to stay down until you'd think they must surely have all died from suffocation. Thirty-six hours once, with everything shut down, of course.'

Sweating in the heat and the closeness, the men remaining still and silent lest they give themselves away. 'They'd all be looking up every time a destroyer's propeller noise increased until passing over top of them.'

'And the depth charges begin to sink, but those have to hit the pressurized hull or explode very close to it, otherwise it's far too strong. But, yes, it can't be any more pleasant for them at times than it is for our own people.' She was really feeling it, was still lost to it.

'Did Trant and the colonel send you to me?'

She had such smashing eyes. 'Why should they have?'

A shrug would be best. 'It doesn't matter. You wouldn't understand and it would take me too long to explain. Now I really must get back to my husband.'

Blakely got to his feet to stretch out a helping hand. 'Will he mind if we have one dance?'

What was it in the look he gave her now? A need for understanding? It wasn't his fault he'd been ordered to talk to her.

'That dark-haired girl. Mrs. Fraser. She's got it into her head that she fancies me, but I'm off home soon to get married. Flying patrols is not like it was during the Battle of Britain. I've got a bit of time coming and really ought to make use of it. Besides, my girl would kill me if she knew I was out with someone else.'

That was fair enough and she'd let him lead her back. All the younger set were dancing. Having shoved the furniture aside, the floor was crowded. She and Blakely would have to slip quickly in between other couples and dance cheek to cheek, he with an arm about her waist, she with hers about his shoulders.

Hamish caught sight of them, and she smiled his way and raised a hand to indicate she'd forgive him if he behaved. Chris Blakely was a good dancer. Erin Ross had changed boyfriends . . .

'You enjoy dancing,' he said appreciatively.

Though she smiled at the compliment, he couldn't have seen this. 'Dancing . . . Yes, I do, but it's been ages since I've been out. Hamish . . . My husband's a doctor.'

'Was he the one who gave the toast to the King?'

A nod would suffice, though she wanted to say, He's really not that much older than myself. He does like dancing and he's not bad at it, only . . .

They came to the end of the piece and Blakely asked for another. Jimmy Allanby was looking at them and she didn't want a scene, not if it could be avoided. Besides, with Blakely she was safe, and for a while she needed that, needed the reassurance of someone who was completely neutral and unthreatening. And it felt good, so good, just to dance.

Eventually they broke for drinks and he found her a gin and tonic, but then Tommy Dorsey's *Moonlight Serenade* came on and it was such a good piece they went at it again.

'Someone's stealing my drink,' she said, catching sight of Maevis.

Blakely swung them around and chuckled. 'My gosh, I hope she doesn't get sloshed. Jack and I borrowed the squadron leader's MG. If we're not back with it in tiptop shape, we're for it.'

'How did you meet the girls?' she asked, leaning away from him a little. 'They're from Armagh, aren't they?'

'The colonel's wife fixed us up. I really didn't want to come.'

'You're missing your fiancée, aren't you?' He had a nice warm smile, and she felt he'd be honest with her.

'You bet I am, Mrs. Fraser. We've got to take the girls home, so I only hope there aren't any hitches.'

Like someone throwing up all over the seat or wanting something else. 'Then you're heading back to base tonight, to Derry?' He smoothly pivoted them around.

'Unless the colonel wants us here for breakfast.'

So that was it. Breakfast! Pump Mrs. Fraser and find out what you can. Tell her how bad things really are and kick a bit of gumption into her!

'Thanks. I must go.'

Leaving him standing in the middle of the floor watching, Mary barged through the others, made it right to the drawing room, then the conservatory.

'Look, what's the matter, Mrs. Fraser? Did I say something I shouldn't have?'

'No. No, it wasn't anything like that.'

He handed her a fresh drink and she took a nervous sip,

knew he'd see that she was still shaking, but she mustn't be angry with him over something he could not have known a thing about. 'I do want to join up. I think I need that, but can't. Not for a bit.'

'Then why not come back and dance? No strings attached, just friends.'

Everyone would begin to wonder about she and Hamish who had left her on her own, hadn't even bothered to come over. Not once! Oh damn. He was being stubborn.

Perhaps Erin Ross would cut in on them, and if not that one, then her friend. After all, the boys did have a motor car and these days . . . 'How did you and Jack get asked to the party?'

Blakely knew he was for it, but he'd be straight with her. 'The C.O. gave us our marching orders. Said the colonel wanted some RAF types who'd seen a bit of U-boat action.'

And could tell her about it if the seating arrangements were such that Mrs. Mary Ellen Fraser was stuck between two dry old sticks of religion. 'Did he ask you to tell me something of what you've been through?'

'Do you mind?'

'Not really. I know most of it anyway, but . . . but from the other side, of course.'

When they reached the dancing, Mary set her glass down on the table behind her. They tried to make idle conversation but it was no use. They watched the couples. Someone called out to Blakely. Suddenly everything was loud—the talk, the music, the laughter, even the sounds of the glasses. Colonel Bannerman was climbing on to a chair to give some sort of an announcement. He was waving a telegram. His wife was with him, so it was good news about their sons. 'The boys are safe, ladies and gentlemen. Safe! Found walking in the desert!'

Trant was nowhere to be seen and neither was Jimmy.

'Your drink, Mrs. Fraser.'

Distracted, she accepted the glass from the waiter without looking at him. The colonel's face was flushed. He was still waving the telegram, still couldn't believe the miracle that had happened. Tears of gratitude were running down Dotty Bannerman's plump cheeks, ruining her makeup.

Mary took a sip only to find the glass empty, wondered what on earth had happened to her drink, and turned quickly towards the waiter only to see that he had left.

Her drink was still on the table where she'd set it. Bubbles were rising in it, but lying against the base of the glass was a .455 calibre cartridge. She could see the number quite clearly, and damn, oh damn, what was she to do? That voice . . . The way he'd said her name.

Even as her fingers closed about the cartridge, she knew he was watching her, that somehow Liam Nolan had got into the house dressed as one of the waiters.

He would have been here all along. The colonel and the others—Major Trant and Jimmy—wouldn't even have thought it possible.

'Is there a problem?' asked Blakely as the clapping and the cheering died away and the colonel finally got down off his perch.

Shaking her head, she heard herself saying, 'It's nothing. I'd best go upstairs for a minute, though. I think one of my garters has come undone.'

'Wish I could help,' he said and grinned, 'but I'm spoken for, aren't I? Oh well, Erin of the Raven Hair will just have to be fended off. See you soon?'

'Yes, of course. I'd like that very much.' How had she kept her voice so calm? wondered Mary. They'd dance again. She'd have to now, she pregnant by a German officer and with an IRA bullet hidden in one of the cups of her bra.

She was tucking the bullet away, had her back to the door, when Nolan stepped quickly into the bedroom. A corner of his reflection was caught in the bureau mirror and long before his face was seen, she knew it was him, felt weak, sick, terrified—so many things all at once and couldn't seem to move. In a black dinner jacket, bow tie, white dress shirt and black trousers, he looked the rake, the cavalier, the debonair man-about-town, not the mad bomber of a London tube station.

'Mrs. Fraser, it is,' he said. She was still holding herself by the right breast, but had gripped it more tightly. 'Looking lovely in a dark brown velvet dress. A velvet woman is it?'

Very slowly the hand was withdrawn, but she'd not turn to face him yet, was terrified someone else would come and catch her at it.

Nolan gave her the brief smile of a small boy up to mischief, causing her to ask what it was he wanted. 'Don't you care that they might recognize you?'

He'd scare the living daylights out of her now, would play it hard. 'You didn't go to Dublin like you said you would. We were waiting for you and you didn't care to show up.'

'I couldn't! The colonel . . . He's put it off for a while.' It all sounded so weak of her.

'How's Caithleen?' he asked, startling her for he'd moved away from the open door and she'd thought someone must be coming.

'Fine. She's fine.' He'd not come any closer yet.

'You're not getting cold feet, are you?' he asked.

Nolan had a way of switching in an instant from the small

boy's delight with laughter in the eyes to an emptiness that frightened.

'I could scream for help,' she said warily, now watching him more closely in that mirror of hers.

'Try it and see what happens.'

'What is it you want? Please just ask it and go. I . . . I *can't* have anyone finding us together. Not here, not anywhere.'

'Ashamed of me, are you? And there was me serving up the beef to the major and the colonel and asking if they'd each like two slices. Rare was the colonel's, with the blood dripping from the knife and them china-blue eyes of his dancing with greed, to say nothing of the fact that all that grub was supposed to have been rationed.'

Someone must have started up the stairs, for he ducked his head out, only to pull back in. 'False alarm,' he said, enjoying her predicament. 'Are you cooperating with the major?'

The flaxen hair had been cut quite short and slicked down hard so as to be like that of the other waiters and all of the male guests. It was parted in the middle. 'I . . . I've given him two names.'

'But it wasn't enough, was it?'

He was smiling at her again. He had such a soft accent, she had to wonder where he'd gone to school and why he could be so refined at times and yet . . . 'No, it wasn't enough.'

'Did Kramer give you anything for us to send over on that wireless of the Germans?'

'Kevin said Erich wouldn't, and he didn't.'

She was like a wary little velvet mouse. The dress suited. She'd be as warm as toast in it and as fresh as a Michaelmas daisy, even to wearing a touch of scent behind those ears of hers. 'So it's Kevin, is it now?'

'O'Bannion then.'

'Do you fancy him, Mrs. Fraser?'

'Look, please just tell me what you want and go. It's crazy of you to have come here.'

Crazy was it?

He had moved away and at first she couldn't find him in the mirror, but then there he was standing by the bed.

'British Army mack's. FANYs, too, eh? Dark blue ones for the Wrens. Just what the devil's been going on down there, Mrs. Fraser? You spending all that time with a RAF flying officer and that husband of yours not having a care?'

'Bannerman thought it would soften me up if I talked to someone who'd been chasing U-boats.'

'And did it?' he asked, tossing a coat aside and then another and another—was he planning to take her somewhere? Was Fay Darcy waiting outside for them?

'Well?' he demanded.

'No, of course it didn't.'

'Berlin have been asking questions, Mrs. Fraser. If you'd thought to go to Dublin like you said you would, you'd have found that out.'

'I've already told you . . .'

Nolan pulled out her coat. 'Berlin are being difficult. They want the names of all of Kramer's superior officers—the German High Command in Tralane. They want proof that you've met with them. Get it!'

He tossed her coat on top of the others, looked as if he'd like to kill her and leave her body lying there.

'You and that husband of yours be out of here no later than one fifteen.'

Dear God, a bomb? Nolan could see the thought racing through that velvet mind like lightning.

'You wouldn't,' he heard her say, she trying hard not to cry. 'You couldn't.'

BETRAYAL

Had her voice betrayed her feelings far more than the moisture that had collected in those lovely bedroom eyes of hers?

When he stood behind her, his breath was warm and as he touched her dress, she couldn't help but flinch.

She did smell nice, thought Nolan, her hair like silk. He'd brush a hand down her arm, would let her think he'd mess with her. 'You want to watch out for Kevin, Mrs. Fraser.'

A bomb . . . Nolan had planted one in the house. It was in the smile he gave, in the way he was watching to see what she'd do. Turning quickly, she faced him, he stepping back a pace and instantly losing the smile. 'If you set off a bomb in here, everything at Tralane changes. They won't let me in because they won't be around to do so.'

'Or there'll be such a state of emergency they'll have turned the whole of Ulster inside out—is that it, Mrs. Fraser?'

'You know it is. Look, *please*! For the love of God . . .'

'Whose god? Why should I listen to any talk of God from the likes of you?'

Mary ducked but he didn't hit her.

'Maybe the Germans want us to blow this place to smithereens, Mrs. Fraser, maybe they think that copping this lot is a far better job than bagging that lover of yours, but it's leaving you with the thought, I am. Good hunting.'

'Nolan, please don't do this to me. My husband . . . the others . . .'

Right enough she could see the shambles the bomb would leave and hear the cries for help.

'Just tell me what you want of me.'

She had said it like a woman down on her hands and knees. 'Everything, Mrs. Fraser. Every little thing we ask.' He'd let her feel his lips brush over hers, would put a hand at the base of her throat, then both of them on those breasts of hers while feeling for the bullet.

'Don't, please don't.'

'Just remember what I said.'

The room was in darkness. Every second of every minute ticked away. Mary wished she'd not hear them, wished she didn't have the image of what must happen. All the upstairs rooms but one had been gone through and done as best she could, the bedroom with the coats first, she thinking that he could well have left it there in a box or hamper under the bed or tucked into one of the closets, but the trouble was, of course, that Dotty Bannerman and the colonel had umpteen boxes and suitcases and she couldn't possibly look in all of them, had been so afraid, too, that someone would find her at it and demand to know the truth.

Feeling for the light switch, murmuring came to her, sweet nothings, hot kisses and then, 'Oh that's lovely, Jack. You've such a grand one.'

They were going at it on one of the twin beds in Colonel and Mrs. Bannerman's room. Maevis had her knickers looped around an ankle. Her stockinged knees were up and Jack, with his trousers down, was lying between them, his face buried in the girl's breasts, she clutching him by the seat.

Blinding them momentarily with the light, Mary stammered, 'Oh, sorry.' Blushing crimson and feeling utterly stupid, she backed out but forgot about the light, Maevis saying, 'Shit! It's that doctor's wife,' but going right back to it.

Pressing her forehead against the door, her hand still on the knob, Mary heard herself whisper, 'Please help me find it.' She couldn't tell the colonel and the major that there was a bomb in the house. They'd ask her how she knew of it, and she'd have to tell them everything as everyone else ran outside.

It was 12.37 a.m. Straightening, she dried her eyes. If all else failed, she would tell them to clear the house with ten minutes to spare.

Then she would stay inside all by herself and that would be the end of it.

There were two telephones in the house. One at the foot of the stairs, she coming down them now, the other in the study. She could say she'd been passing by and had heard the thing ring. An anonymous caller, a tip-off. Didn't the IRA sometimes do that, especially if they knew the bomb could not possibly be found in time?

'Phone's out of order, Miss. Captain Allanby's attending to it. Wind must have blown a line down.'

A line . . . She'd forgotten all about Jimmy's being at the party.

Mary set the phone down. 'Thanks. It doesn't matter. I was just going to check with Mrs. Haney, our cook-housekeeper. She and her husband are staying with Caithleen.'

'It's grand news about the colonel's sons, miss. The party will be certain to go till dawn.'

'Yes. Yes, I suppose it will.'

If she told them about the bomb, she'd betray the IRA and Fay Darcy would make sure they got their hands on her. If she didn't tell them, there'd be chaos at precisely 1.16 a.m.

'You're enjoying yourself, Mary?'

'Hamish, shouldn't we be going?'

'*Och* no, lass. The night has only begun.'

Somehow she had found her way into the breakfast nook. Hamish was courting a bottle of single malt he'd pinched from the colonel's private store, was mellow by the look, not four sheets to the wind yet, but no doubt very near to it.

'You look particularly beautiful,' he said. 'The major, here, was only just saying it.'

Trant lifted his glass in a silent salute as sober as a judge and damn Hamish for getting himself pissed at a time like this! 'I think you've had enough,' she said, the fishwife again and knowing only that he'd rebel.

'Come and join us, lass. The major was saying you were being most helpful.'

Trant took in the stark beauty of despair, the haunted look of a woman on the run. 'Yes, please do.'

'I can't. If you'll excuse me, Major, I'll go back to the dancing.'

He pointed the way and when she went into the kitchen, patted the husband's arm in farewell and got up to follow her. She was looking at the kitchen waste, then in under the sinks, then up in the cupboards, first one and then another and with no time to lose, the staff being nudged out of the way if necessary and no explanations given.

She settled on two cardboard boxes that had been left beside the outer door, hardly had time to ask what they contained and when she heard, 'Favours for the ladies and gents, miss,' snatched up a knife and cut the strings.

Then her fingers went to a nervous stillness Trant found curious, for they had paused over the first of the boxes.

She teased the lid open—didn't have a care about getting that frock of hers dirty. Just knelt on the floor and began gingerly to take up each of the brightly wrapped packages. Some were smaller than others—cufflinks, no doubt. Others were lipstick size or longer and wider—pen-and-pencil sets perhaps. There were name cards and she glanced at one of these before leaving the first box to open the second.

'Looking for something, are we?' he asked, startling her.

'My gift,' she said, having turned back to the box. '*And* Hamish's, Major. He has to be at the hospital in Newry first thing tomorrow. If I don't get him home . . .'

It was no use, and Trant had seen this clearly enough. Hamish didn't ever *need* to be at that hospital or any other than Tralane's. Even here in Northern Ireland, the Royal Society of Medicine had taken that privilege away. Besides, he'd be drunk in any case.

'I just want to go home, Major. If you must know, I'm worried about Caithleen.'

'Then let me help you. One mustn't leave without one's favour.' What the devil was the matter with her?

They found Fraser's cufflinks and she set that one aside on the floor. 'And this is yours, I believe,' he said, handing the thing to her, she awkwardly taking it from him.

'Major . . .'

'Yes?'

She winced. 'Would you have the time, please?'

The time. She'd a watch on her wrist and the clock up there on the wall. 'Zero one hundred hours, near enough.'

'Thanks. Now if you'll excuse me, I . . . I have something to do.'

She ran from him, completely forgetting the much sought after favours. She was in the men's coatroom when he found her madly going through the pockets, she saying overly loudly that she simply had to find Fraser's car keys.

There were boots and shoes and walking sticks and mack's, caps and guns, Bannerman's Webley service revolver, his own as well. 'Mrs. Fraser, why not tell me what you're really looking for?'

Mary glanced at her watch and pushed past him, heading

for the living room, the sound of music and laughter growing, Maevis and Jack coming down the stairs but still looking
flushed and turning quickly away so as to avoid her, Erin Ross
and Christopher Blakely being nowhere in sight.

'Mrs. Fraser? Mrs. Mary Ellen Fraser?'

'She's over here,' shouted someone.

Blakely gave her a generous smile, so kind and understanding she wanted to scream at him to get out of the house.

'Mrs. Fraser?'

It was one of the waiters. 'M'am, you're wanted on the telephone.'

'But . . . but the line's been disconnected?'

'Line's been reconnected, m'am. You can take the call in the
colonel's study if you wish. I'll show you the way.'

It was 1.13 a.m. Mary hesitated. She wanted to shout,
'There's a bomb in the house!'

The telephone was warm but the line was dead. Thoughts
of Hamish came to her, she wishing he was holding her, but of
course he wasn't anywhere near, and when she went into the
breakfast nook, he was no longer there, nor in the conservatory.

There was now less than half a minute left. As she ran towards the music to warn everyone, she banged into one of the
waiters, heard the telephone ringing again even as it was answered and her name being called out again.

There was a cardboard box tucked against the bottom of a
radiator and under a chair in the foyer. Had she not come this
way, she would never have seen it.

'The telephone, Mrs. Fraser.'

The box was heavy. 'It's all right,' she heard herself saying.
'Just tell whomever it is that I've left for home.'

Seeing her letting herself out of the house, he called after her, 'Mrs. Fraser, m'am, he says you're to put the cake in the boot of your motorcar, that it's a present for Caithleen O'Neill.'

The rain beat against the car, the sound of it hammering in her head. Nothing had happened. Somehow she had made it to the car and had driven some distance from the house, only to stop at the side of the road and wait, herself saying, 'Hamish, forgive me. I did love you, my darling. You've been so good to me and I've been such a fool.'

The road ahead was lit up slightly by the headlamps. The wiper blades made their passes over the windscreen. Looking like the spun grey-blonde of an old woman's hair, the tall grasses along the verge had been beaten down.

Glancing at her watch, Mary leaned forward so that the faint glow from the dash would help, then switched on the overhead Hamish had yet to disconnect.

It was 1.57 a.m. and nothing had happened. Slowly, as in some horrible dream, she opened the box and took out the bundles, each of six sticks but there were no wires, no clock timer, no fuse, just the gelignite that was wrapped in stiffened, waxed brown paper, the bundles bound by electrician's black tape.

Nolan could so easily have blown them all to pieces. It was just a 'present' for Caithleen and yet another lesson for herself.

When her head began to fiercely ache, she rolled down the side windscreen, drank in the fresh air, but still sat with the bundles on the seat beside her not knowing what she was going to do.

How had the second caller known she'd found the box? The man who had answered the telephone must have told him.

In spite of the smell, which was like no other, she tucked one of the bundles under the front seat, pushing it well back of the wiper rags and tools Hamish had there. Then she closed the lid of the box and, turning the car around, drove slowly back to the house, trying desperately to clear her head of the fumes and to think, not panic.

Jimmy was standing in the rain with a torch and for a moment she didn't know what to say to him, just wanted to run and wait for the bullet to hit her between the shoulders. He had that look about him.

'Jimmy, I've found a bomb. I'm sorry I couldn't tell anyone about it, but the caller didn't give me much time. The only thing is, it didn't go off when it should have. There are no fuses, no wires, no timer. Just some sticks of explosive.'

'Why you?'

'Caithleen, I suppose. He did say it was a present for her.'

'And you took it where?'

'Down the road a piece.'

'You stupid, stupid woman. You could have been blown to bits!'

That instant told her much. Jimmy wasn't just interested in her but desperately in love. She saw it in the anger not just at her but at himself, in the way he yanked the box from her, in the defeat as he held it, the hope she'd understand how he felt and why it was hurting him.

'Say nothing of this,' he all but shouted, angered by her lack of response. 'Let the colonel and his wife enjoy themselves. He'll know soon enough.'

'Will you help me to get Hamish home when the time comes?'

Had it been a particle of yielding on her part? 'Yes. Yes, of course, I'd be glad to.'

Had she crossed a watershed? wondered Mary, struck by the thought, for now she couldn't tell him of the sticks she'd hidden, could tell no one of them, certainly not Nolan. But . . . but Jimmy wouldn't want to make too much of the incident, not when he'd been in charge of security, so at least that was something. She'd best leave the side windscreen rolled down the half, though, as if she'd forgotten all about it.

The tea was hot and sweet, and she took it in the Bannermans' kitchen not knowing really how long she had been sitting here. The cooks had left plates of sandwiches. The major had set an egg salad in front of her. There were two oatmeal biscuits as well but she knew she mustn't eat a thing.

She was very frightened and vulnerable, thought Trant. Jimmy had been slack—damned bad form for a man as good as he was. She had had two telephone calls, she'd said, but neither of them had been before she'd begun to hunt for that bomb, and why in God's name had the IRA not chosen to set the bloody thing off? To simply place a dozen sticks of gelignite in a cardboard box and throw the fear of the Lord into them didn't really make much sense, but he would have to leave all that for now. She had clearly been through enough. 'You ought, really, to get a medal for what you did. There are just a few questions I'd like to ask, but we can go over them another time.'

He set the favours on the table beside her sandwich, two brightly wrapped packages she couldn't have cared less about. Silly things, pathetic things, by the look she gave. 'Haven't they found Hamish yet?' she asked.

'Now just rest easy. The doctor will be found.'

Dead? she seemed to silently ask, but then she ducked away to the cup and saucer in her lap. Wishing he could pursue things, Trant knew it wouldn't be right of him and that he would just have to wait.

Somehow Mary finished the tea. The two Wrens came in to put the kettles on, so the party must be winding down. 'Major, what time is it?' she asked, knowing her voice must sound empty.

'Just after zero three hundred hours. Why not let me have one of the men drive you home? The doctor can then pick up the car when he's feeling better.'

And not drunk, was that it? 'I'm really all right, thanks. If I could just sit here quietly, I'd appreciate it.'

Jimmy and the major had kept the bomb to themselves. The Wrens looked as if they had had a smashing time. Both were bright-eyed, tussle-haired girls in their early twenties. After all, it was a young person's war and one had to take one's fun whenever the opportunity arose.

Trant went off to see about something and when one of the corporals who had been on sentry duty came to fetch her, she got up without a murmur. Jimmy would want her to see the condition he'd found Hamish in, but had Fay Darcy and the others hurt him or had he simply clutched that bottle by the neck as he'd stumbled blindly away to fall flat on his face among the cowpats?

Behind the topiary and the fishponds there were more of the rose arbours, and beyond them some walls, the kitchen gardens, the orchard and Mrs. Bannerman's potting shed.

Jimmy was waiting for them. There was another man with him, the two standing in the darkness beneath one of the trees. *Trant?* she wondered, the strong cider smell of the apples reminding her of their own orchard.

BETRAYAL

The corporal switched off his torch, Jimmy wanting it this way.

'Mary, it's not what you think.'

Mary! as if that sort of familiarity could ever have existed. 'Captain, I don't understand? Look, I've had enough for one night. What the hell do you mean: It's not what I think?'

Someone swung the beam of a torch over the potting shed. The door had been broken open, the panes of glass in its top half having shattered. Splintered wood lay about the lock but nobody in creation ever bothered to lock up a potting shed. The door had been kicked in by the flat of someone's shoe.

'He's dead,' said Allanby. 'Mary, I'm so . . .'

'Corporal Monaghan, see to Mrs. Fraser,' snapped Trant.

It *was* him. She felt the corporal grip her by an arm, threw him off and pushed past Jimmy, hitting the door with a shoulder as she stumbled inside, her voice rising . . . 'Hamish? Darling, it's me. I . . . Oh God, no, Hamish! No!'

He was lying face down on the pebbly floor among the shattered remains of several flowerpots. A litter of earth, bulbs and baskets lay about him. His shoes were caked with mud and one of them had come off and was next to his head. The tweed trousers were wet through and yes, he still clutched a bottle by the neck. Gin on top of Scotch and wine. Gin!

Everything inside of her collapsed. There was blood on the back of Hamish's head and when she touched it, her fingers were not warmed but left cold and sticky. 'Hamish . . . Hamish, what happened?' She had never seen him like this. Never!

Allanby took her by the shoulders to lift her away from the corpse but she threw him off and shrieked, 'Leave me alone!'

Trant crouched to lay three fingers against the doctor's neck. They all could hear the snores as he looked up, first to herself and then to Jimmy.

'I . . . Damn it, Major, I thought he was dead.'

He had hoped it true. Trant must have left them with a snort of disgust, for all Jimmy said was, 'Come on, then. Let's take him home. Corporal Monaghan . . .'

'SOR?'

Jimmy leapt. 'God damn you, Corporal! Don't you dare SOR me again or I'll have you up on a charge. Now get this man into the backseat of his car and be quick about it! I'll take Mrs. Fraser in mine and follow you.'

There was no thought of bathing Hamish's head or of making him comfortable, just that of disgusting old drunk who, by the stench, had urinated in his trousers.

In the late afternoon of the following day pools of water gave mirror images to the branches and the tall grasses that had, last night along the road, looked so like an old woman's hair.

Mary hadn't slept. Hamish had a concussion—Dr. Connor had come out from Armagh; a few days in bed had been insisted on. Caithleen was looking after the patient, and if not the girl, then Mrs. Haney and Bridget, the house having gone to the medicinal quietude of a mortuary, the rain coming down so much, standing at the windows of her own bedroom or in any of the others—Hamish's most particularly—had done no good.

'One of us has to apologize,' she had said after Dr. Connor had gone. 'It might just as well be me.'

Hamish had shown no signs of wanting drink and that, too, hadn't been right, for an alcoholic is driven to swill it for days on end. 'Och, lass,' he had said, 'I feel so ashamed of m'self, I could gladly fit the noose and pull the drop lever.'

He'd been watching her for signs of sympathy; she'd answered tartly, 'You behaved abominably. I ought to hate you for it.'

'Take th' colonel's signpost back. I canna rest knowing I've stolen it.'

'And six silver teaspoons. Would you have pawned them in Armagh on your next visit?' she had asked.

'There's th' half-pound of pipe tobacco, too, and six Havanas, no matter th' shortages, lass,' he'd said, implying the colonel had a black-market source for both items. 'Did you enjoy yourself?'

'Some,' she had answered gruffly.

'Lass, I've heard whispers of a bomb. Say it was na true.'

She had wished he'd not used that brogue. His head had been bandaged—he'd no memory of what had happened. A complete blank, he'd said. He had been sitting up in that acorn bed of his, two books open in his lap, several others lying about and the newspapers scattered. There'd been a well-fed fire in the grate, and Robbie looking sorrowfully up at her from under his hand.

'There was a bomb. I gave it to Jimmy.'

'Did you? That was good of you. I'm grateful. I dare say we all are.'

Mrs. Haney would have told him what had happened, and if not her, then Bridget. News travelled so fast. One couldn't keep a thing secret from the Irish. Not a thing. Not for long.

Suddenly she realized that she was sitting in the car at the side of the road opposite to where she had sat last night with that bomb, her mind going over everything. Trant would be bound to ask questions she'd have to answer. He'd be worried about the two telephone calls, would know that the lines had been down earlier and that she must have had a prior warning.

Try as she did, no answers would come and she started off

again to turn in at the colonel's and face the music for Hamish. Just how she would unload everything she didn't know. The truth perhaps, but would Dotty Bannerman understand?

Of course not, though the colonel would have been told of the bomb and the woman ought rightly to be grateful.

The colonel's adjutant met her at the door, one look being enough. 'What's happened?' she asked, handing him the lead sign on its ramrod post.

'Colonel and Mrs. Bannerman's sons were both killed in action, Mrs. Fraser. Was there something . . .'

'Killed? But I thought . . .'

'A bloody awful mix-up, I'm afraid. Colonel tried to send off a cable of congratulations and got back the truth.'

The rain came down, she awakening to it. 'I'm so sorry. Please tell them both how sorry Hamish and I am.'

'Was there anything else?'

'Only that the door to their potting shed was damaged and that my husband and I will pay for it.'

'I'll give Colonel and Mrs. Bannerman your condolences, Mrs. Fraser. I think this . . .' He hefted the sign. 'Had best go back in the lawn where it came from.'

She took the sign. He closed the door, shutting herself off from the house and from what she had really wanted to tell them, for the mix-up in telegrams could only have been Liam Nolan's way of saying he hadn't wanted the news to spoil the party.

The ramrod staff went in easily enough for the ground was spongy. Leaving the car, she walked round the house and through to the shed. The door would have to be replaced. As she stood looking at it, the sound of the rain on the white-washed glass came to her, and she smelled the apples, recalled each detail of what had happened.

Hamish could just as easily have been trying to hit someone with that gin bottle. There were grooves in the earth to the left of the path which showed clearly that he'd been dragged to the shed.

That right shoe of his had then been tossed in after him.

6

At dusk and then at dawn it was the same. The gossamer of a mist would wrap the hills, hugging the valley to lie like grey cotton wool atop the black, still waters of Lough Loughie. Across from her, Tralane Castle appeared as if from a distant land, a medieval stronghold whose flags, wrapped in the drifting mist, hung at half-mast.

Mary knew she couldn't help but feel terrible. She wasn't clever, was in fact a very ordinary person. At 2.00 p.m. today she'd present herself at the barrier bar and ask to be let in. There'd be one bundle of books. Short of a strip search, the bullet would be safe. No hobbling about this time. Why she hadn't thought of hiding it in her brassiere before, she'd no idea. False modesty perhaps.

Trant would want to question her, though, and not just about the bomb. He'd want answers she had as yet no idea how to give, would want more information about the hanging—would persist in that even though things had moved by leaps and bounds on to a new and far more dangerous plateau where something was bound to break.

Nolan had forced the issue—she knew that now. He and the others wanted her to meet with the German High Command. Erich was no longer enough. They wanted the names of the officers as proof she'd met them. The negotiations with Berlin weren't going well. Berlin was being difficult.

If she didn't meet with them and get that proof, Fay Darcy would see to it that her hair was hacked off, her clothes torn from her and her body tarred and feathered. They'd tie her to a post in some farmer's field or in the village, and Fay would kill her because Fay would do that sort of thing, and Nolan would watch as she did it.

A Webley service revolver had only chambers for six cartridges, but—and this was crucial—was Kevin O'Bannion using the deliveries as a means of setting the time of events to come? She must never forget that he was their leader and that what had happened at the colonel's house could not have been done by Nolan alone.

The swans came back and she watched them and the mist. The deaths of the colonel's two sons could only cast a pall on things, making security within the castle far tighter. There might, however, be a brief period in which grief overshadowed the anger and hatred such a loss would bring. Not that the colonel was a cruel and vindictive man. She didn't think that, not really. Only, that if she had lost two sons herself, it would be hard not to want to take it out on the enemy.

And Trant? she asked. Trant would realize this long before it happened, so he'd be planning to use it as best he could.

And Jimmy? Jimmy might want her love and friendship no matter the lie of it, but when the chips were down, he'd put duty to his country above all else and would be the harshest of them all.

Dew had condensed on the handlebars of her bike, and

on its bell and lamp. Hamish wasn't one for bicycles, not any more at least, but he had gone to great lengths to get her exactly what would suit best. At times he seemed to know intuitively what she needed, but he'd offered no answers, no explanations as to what had actually happened to him. Not that she had asked him outright. They'd played cat and mouse.

Pulling off her gloves, Mary rubbed warmth into her fingers only to again feel the absence of her ring. Did Hamish have it? she wondered. Caithleen had been giving her funny looks; Bridget had been in on it, Mrs. Haney shut right out but for how long?

Were there four bullets to go and then the prison break—was that how it was to be? A meeting place somewhere on the north coast most likely, and a rendezvous with a German submarine.

She'd lose the child. They'd be bound to find it aborted at her death and Hamish . . . Hamish would forgive her because . . . why because he was like that, like one of the swans gliding eerily through an Irish mist so that she could only catch glimpses now and then of what he was up to or thinking. Grand and dignified, wise and serene, but always holding himself back—was he giving her a chance to prove herself? Was this what he was really on about?

He hadn't been drunk and she knew this now though he'd used the threat of it to make her stay away from him at the party. That he suspected she was up to mischief was one thing, that he might well know far more than he was letting on, quite another. 'Darling, please be careful. Don't do anything stupid. Not with these people, not even if you think you know them through and through and better than they do themselves.'

Silently the swans departed, she wishing they wouldn't. Whatever had come between Hamish and herself ought not to have, but had he found out about Louise, about the little girl she had had to leave behind in Canada? Had that made him think her callous? He'd never said, but it could well have been that. If so, it was long past the time she should have talked to him about Louise, of how it had hurt so much to have to leave her, of how it still did.

'I was destitute,' she said, as if to that castle over there. 'Flat broke and without a hope or penny.

'Admit it, you just wanted to get away.

'I had to. No one was going to forgive me.'

She had worked her passage as cook's helper on an Italian freighter out of Montreal, and if one thought that had been easy, one had best think again, but the deal she'd made had meant that she could never write to Louise, never see her again.

Hamish did love children—there had been none from his first marriage. He wanted them and she had always known this. He'd view the giving up of a child as the ultimate act of betrayal. In that, he was only being the good, solid Presbyterian he'd once been, though he hadn't darkened the door of a church in years, not since the Great War. But he would think less of her, and yes, she had sensed this and hadn't had the courage to tell him, though as a doctor you'd think he'd have known she'd had a child. Weren't doctors usually the dumbest of people when it came to themselves and their wives?

He hadn't been what one would have called a good lover. His intuitiveness hadn't extended to the bedroom—perhaps that was why he read Freud? He'd been far too shy with her, far too passive, as if still in love with the wife who'd left him, as if he was bound to break things he had no desire to break.

Not cold. Not untouching, either. Just not touching enough. Not like Erich.

The shed, though unheated, was warmer than outside. Again she pulled off her gloves. Trant, like Nolan, had done the unexpected and come to her with his questions. His car was out front. She had, at best, perhaps three, maybe four minutes to collect her thoughts. The dynamite, wrapped in old burlap sacking, was hidden under the rafters above and behind stacks of old boards and windows, no problem with its smell, not here, for she'd splashed turpentine about.

The bullet was snug in preparation for this afternoon.

'I have no other choice but to face him,' she murmured to herself. She'd been doing a lot of this lately, she had to admit. 'He's chosen his moment wisely, when I'm least able to lie. He'll talk to me in front of Hamish.'

The two of them were in the study by the fire. She'd best extend the hand of friendship, best sound happy to see him. 'Major, you're early. It's good of you to pop in to see how Hamish is getting on. How are the colonel and his wife bearing up?'

Trant took her in swiftly but he would say nothing of the rosy cheeks, the coldness of her hand or the fact that for a woman who ought really to be exhausted and in bed, she'd been out and about so early herself. 'As well as can be expected. It's a dastardly thing to have happened but war is war, and the colonel certainly aware of this. Please.' He indicated she should join them. 'Hamish and I were just discussing it.'

'Mary, it seems that the real telegram did get through but was stopped at GHQ Belfast and a false one sent on.'

'How awful. How could anyone have done such a thing?'

'Our thoughts entirely, Mrs. Fraser. The IRA had a man inside, a Protestant no less. Needless to say, that man has been identified.'

'And caught, I hope.' Dear God, it was coming now—she could see it in his watchfulness.

He'd nod grimly, thought Trant. He'd give her a little as an opener, would let the husband flesh things out and get the two of them going. 'Apprehended as of two thirty this morning. One Tim Pat Sheehy, fifty-two years of age and twice decorated for service beyond the call of duty on the Somme.'

'The IRA are insidious,' said Hamish. 'Mary, the major says they've just suffered their final reversal in the South, that the organization has been smashed to pieces in the Republic, but that up here in the North we have the last stronghold.'

And now for a little more, thought Trant. 'Our informants tell us Liam Nolan and the Darcy woman are living in the rough, flitting back and forth across the border into the counties Monaghan and Cavan, as is Kevin O'Bannion.'

Their informants . . . Could she possibly keep the emptiness from her voice? 'County Armagh's home to all of them.'

Quite possibly she could have asked that of someone after the O'Neill girl's tarring. 'They know the countryside far better than we do, Mrs. Fraser. Captain Allanby's being given the runaround. If we use horses, they have a van or a lorry or motorcar and plenty of petrol. If we have those, they've got the horses or are on foot and so well tipped off they're miles from where they should have been by the time we get there.'

'The Darcy woman was seen in Kinsale with her sister, Mary. The Garda caught up with them but Fay escaped in a hail of bullets. The sister's been badly wounded and is not expected to survive.'

Trant had let Hamish tell her, but why? Was he now about to accuse her of having met with that very sister?

Fortunately Mrs. Haney chose to bring their breakfast. Coffee, jam, and toasted muffins. Three fried eggs each with rashers of bacon for the major and two kippers on the side for Hamish. A bowl of sliced apples and pears as well.

'M'am, will you be eating th' morn?'

Mary felt her stomach involuntarily tighten at the sight of

the food. 'Later, thanks, Mrs. Haney. A cup of that coffee perhaps, if it's not too much trouble.'

Trouble was it? and the missus about to show the world the bottom of her stomach but so china sweet it would make rock* run in the mouth! 'It's no trouble at all, m'am. I'll be sending Bridget in directly with another cup and saucer. M'am, a button cannot be found for that lovely blouse the doctor gave you in Edinburgh. Begging your permission, I'll be sending that wretched girl along to Ballylurgan the day t' see if Mr. Brian Kelly's wife can help.'

The butcher's wife. 'That's very kind of you, Mrs. Haney. Be sure to tell Bridget to thank Mrs. Kelly for her trouble.'

'She's a button box bigger than the Tower of London and a tongue to go with it, she has.'

The major had taken it all in, as had the doctor, thought Ria, but had she said something she shouldn't have? The missus was looking like she'd just had th' skean** run right through her! 'I will tell the girl not to waggle her tongue, I will, m'am. You need have no fears on that score, not from His Honour the doctor's house.'

'By jove, a superb breakfast, Mrs. Haney,' said Trant, clearing away Hamish's books and things. 'You've done us proud in these days of shortages. The army could use a woman like yourself.'

But which army—was that it? wondered Mary. Trant was deliberately hinting at things far back in the O'Shane, the O'Hoolighan, or the Haney past, but Mrs. Haney, by the look, was having no part of it.

'Them hens was my own, Major, as was the porker from which the doctor's share of that bacon did come.'

---

* Rock candy.
** The short sword.

Don't choke on it, Mary could hear Ria saying to herself and warmed to the woman in spite of what had been said about the blouse. 'It's all right, Mrs. Haney. I'm sure the major didn't mean it.'

Oh but he did, m'am, he did, Ria wanted so much to say but would rather slice off her tongue!

The door was closed but not softly, though one didn't jump at the sound of it, not when knowing beforehand of what must surely come. 'You shouldn't have done that, Major. Mrs. Haney is a very generous, kindhearted woman who has no patience whatsoever with the IRA, both past and present.'

'To which I would add, Major, that our Ria has seen too much of what they can and have done to want to see any more of it.'

Which was exactly what he'd wanted to impress on the two of them, thought Trant. He'd make no apologies, would rest content.

They began to eat, Mary to watch them as best she could. Trant, of course, suspected that things weren't right between Hamish and herself, and had obviously wanted to confront them together. Hamish, though, made no pretense of loss of appetite or ability to play the host. Between mouthfuls, the two of them chatted about the war, the country, the Irish—the whole sweep of things including the castle, he deliberately forgetting that he'd been brutally mishandled as had Caithleen, and had also been at loggerheads with them over the treatment of the prisoners.

Great lashings of black currant jam* disappeared, black strings among the runny yolks and the sop of bacon grease.

---

* Extra rations of sugar were made available at preserving time, though Mrs. Haney could have used honey from her own hives.

'That bomb you found,' said Trant, wolfing a mouthful of egg.

Nausea had to be fought down while waiting for him to get on with it.

'Judging by the size, Mrs. Fraser, I'd have said Liam Nolan was involved but he couldn't have been, or we'd not be here discussing it unless . . .'

He briskly cut off a piece of bacon. The 'coffee' was full of chicory but must be good—not tea, as usual—for he took another pull at it before shovelling the bacon in.

Droplets of yolk ran down his fork.

'Unless, what, Major?' she asked, glancing apprehensively at Hamish who was working on the kippers and looked as if he couldn't have cared less what happened to her.

Robbie got a small portion, just a taste.

'Unless Nolan had wanted to impress someone with the fact that he and his friends had easy access to us at any time.'

Trant waved his knife and fork to emphasize the point or perhaps to merely indicate it was only a suggestion.

'In short, Mary, was this Nolan not within the house itself during the party, did he not place that cardboard box under that chair, and if so, who was he trying to impress?'

'Won't this . . . this Sheehy tell you anything?' she heard herself ask, the sight of the kippers and oil and melted margarine making her want to throw up.

Hamish fastidiously picked a bone from pursed lips. 'Major,' she heard him saying, 'I have no doubt the man's as stubborn as the rest of them. Am I right now?'

Trant added a dash of milk to his freshened coffee. 'Time will tell, Doctor. Sheehy had obviously been coerced into helping them.'

'His wife and family held to hostage, then,' sighed Hamish, reaching for another muffin, the margarine and the milk laid on because of the major, not butter and cream, not the usual for Mrs. Haney.

'These people are all the same,' said Trant.

'Mary, the major would like you to go over things for him. As well as you can recall them, lass.'

His use of 'lass' was overbearing but she mustn't get angry, for that would only get in the way, and thank heavens the two of them weren't smoking. 'There were three telephone calls.'

'Three?' exclaimed Trant, caught by surprise.

'Yes. One very early on in the evening before the phone lines had been cut. The caller simply said that if I did exactly as I was told no harm would come to anyone.'

The morsel of dripping egg on his fork was momentarily forgotten.

'When would this have been?' he hazarded.

There was a slim chance they wouldn't know exactly when the lines had been cut and she'd have to take it. 'About nine thirty or ten—just after we'd got up from dinner.'

'A man or a woman?' asked Trant, having set down his knife and fork.

'The former, Major. All three calls were from the same person.'

Was she playing with him? wondered Trant. She'd not taken that third call. No, by God, she hadn't! 'Would you recognize the voice if you heard it again?'

'How could I ever forget? The accent was very soft and melodious, not harsh or broken or what one would expect.'

'Of an IRA bomber.'

'Yes, of course that's what I meant.'

'Who answered that first call, Mrs. Fraser? We know the name of the waiter who took the other two calls, and have questioned him, of course.'

Egg was now again dripping from his fork. 'I did. I had just come down the stairs and was right next to it.'

And bold as brass, but if she was lying, that husband of hers gave no indication of it beyond the slightest hesitation with the last of his kippers. 'And what did the caller tell you would happen?'

'Nothing more than I've already said. I presumed I'd be told in due course but when I went to use the telephone later to call home, I found it out of order. I was told the lines were down and that Captain Allanby had gone to see to them. The wind . . .'

'Yet you distinctly said but a moment ago that they'd been cut?'

'Of course. I assumed this, knowing as we all do now of the bomb threat.'

And as bold as brass again! 'And the second call?'

Slowly, deliberately Mary reached for a muffin. She would borrow Hamish's knife and spread black currant jam over the thing, Bridget now bringing her cup and saucer.

'By then I was very worried, Major. You see, I'd been trapped into talking to Flying Officer Blakely. Well, not trapped as such, but you know what I mean.'

Bridget filled her cup and poured the milk but gave her such a knowing look, Mary heard herself stammer, 'Thanks. You can go now. We'd been dancing, Major. Blakely had insisted on pursuing things. I . . . Well, if you must know, I also felt the caller must have forgotten me.'

'With the lines down?'

'Yes. Yes, of course.'

'Mary, lass, what made you think there was a bomb? The major saw you searching for it long before that second call came in?

'More correctly, Mrs. Fraser, suspecting that there might be one, why in God's name didn't you warn us?'

'I . . . I didn't know for sure, did I? Remember, please, that I'd not been told this by the first caller. I could just as easily have been wrong. Caithleen was home here with Mrs. Haney and her husband, but none of them would have been able to stop this . . . this Nolan if he'd wanted to kill Caithleen. I . . . I had to do as the caller had said.'

'Then it was Nolan?' asked Trant, his teaspoon poised over the saccharin Mrs. Haney had laid on especially for his benefit.

'Major, I didn't say he was the caller, only that Nolan might have been one of those responsible for what happened to her.'

'You've questioned the girl's uncle and cousin, no doubt?' asked Hamish, letting Robbie lick his plate.

'They'll both go to prison in silence,' Trant said with a touch of exasperation. 'Mrs. Fraser, what was the gist of that second call?'

'Nothing. The line simply went dead. He hung up.'

'Without a word? I find that curious. The lines have only just been repaired and all you receive is a caller who says nothing? Come, come now, Mrs. Fraser, you'd been hunting for a bomb.'

'They rang through right afterwards, but by then I'd found it, so didn't answer.'

'You simply said, "It's all right. Just tell whomever it is that I've left for home." That's calm fodder for a woman who was holding a dozen sticks of gelignite and her instant death!'

'I can't explain it any more than you can the act of a man who throws himself on a live grenade to save his comrades in battle.'

Hamish was impressed with her response, but Trant was only too quick to cut him down.

'Doctor, there were splinters in that cut you received.'

'As I fell, I hit the edge of a trestle table.'

'Did you have to kick in the door of that potting shed?'

He shrugged and managed to look sheepish. '*Och*, I was in a rage wi' m'self for being so tight.'

She had best say something. Trant suspected Hamish of lying, but more than this, he had wanted her to know it. 'Hamish and I've not been getting on, Major. It's my fault. I . . . I just feel so very out of sorts here.'

The truth when needed, was that it, well some of it, and given with downcast eyes? 'Mrs. Fraser, why do you suppose the caller told you to put the cake in the boot of your motorcar, that it was a present for the O'Neill girl?'

'Because he knew by then I'd found the bomb.'

'But you *hadn't* told him this?'

'Of course not. The waiter who answered the telephone must have. Didn't he?'

Trant set his knife and fork down on his plate at precisely the 6.30 a.m. or p.m. position. 'You've not touched your coffee.'

Or the muffin she'd spread with jam. He glanced at his wristwatch, got up without another word, and left the room before she could even see him to the front door, left her standing here waiting for him to accuse her, waiting until they heard his car start up and leave in haste, Hamish having let the silence grow between them.

'Darling, what did he mean by saying there were splinters in that cut on your head?'

'Only that he had talked to Dr. Connor in Armagh.'

A nod was all she could give. Like Caithleen, he had been left as a warning. Fay Darcy and the others could so easily have killed him and Trant hadn't been the only one to have realized this but Hamish was waiting for her to admit it.

'Will you be off to Tralane this afternoon?' she heard him ask.

'Yes, I suppose so. I guess I must.'

'You're not feeling ill, are you?'

'No, of course not. Just tired.'

Two minutes later Fraser heard her on the stairs; three and she was throwing up into the toilet. The whole house would have heard it.

Trant stood at the windows in his office with his back to her. He'd given no greeting, hadn't even had the courtesy to turn. As the door closed behind her, Mary came to stand before his desk. He was over on her right. There were three tall, leaded windows in the bay and he was facing the middle of them. The lights had been deliberately switched off prior to her entry. Though it was just a little after 2.00 p.m., the room appeared as if at dusk.

Still he would not turn. 'Liam Nolan, Mrs. Fraser. Educated at St. Patrick's School for Boys in Armagh. Taken at the age of seven by one of the priests and thrashed until the blood ran for being unruly and deceitful. He was sent home to Morlan Park, the estate of Lord Gilmore where his father was head gamekeeper. There the boy was stripped naked, tied by the wrists to the pump standard in the yard near the stables, and thrashed again and then again.'

'But he was only seven?'

'A fact that seems to have been ignored. Oh, his father wasn't an unkindly man, but the boy's keep at the school was being paid by Lord Gilmore. Nolan had, apparently, brought disgrace not only down upon himself but on the estate of his lordship. He held out for three days in the rain and the freezing wind, then his lordship gave in and the boy was put to bed.'

Trant was affecting a dryness he knew she'd find disconcerting.

'Needless to say, Nolan was no problem after that. Oh I

have no doubt he was every bit as unruly and deceitful—more so perhaps—but other boys got the blame and took the rap. Excelled at his schoolwork, was head altar boy and lead soloist until his voice broke, but not much at sports. Perhaps he saved all that up for his holidays home. Went to Trinity College, Dublin, on a scholarship. Ancient and medieval history with, of course, the usual Irish readings, the Book of Kells, that sort of thing. Just where and how he learned to make bombs, I wish I knew, but the problem is, Mrs. Fraser, Liam Nolan most certainly does know how to make them.'

Still she stood waiting for him to turn from the windows. He'd let her wait. 'Nolan was at Oxford, did you know that?'

'No, I didn't. Major, I've never met this Nolan. How could I possibly know anything about him?'

'My thoughts precisely. The point is, Mrs. Fraser, he seems to know of you—enough, at least, to have realized you wouldn't just hang around for another of those telephone calls of yours but would start hunting for that so-called bomb.'

When she didn't respond, the major rubbed the windowpane in front of himself to clear it of the fog his breath had caused.

'Just who were they trying to impress, Mrs. Fraser? Yourself, or someone else?'

Trant would know she would want him to face her and that she would be wondering what on earth was happening out in the Bailey.

'Well?' he asked, startling her.

'I . . . I've no idea.'

Yet she had described Nolan's voice over the telephone to a tee. 'He wouldn't have wasted twelve sticks of gelignite on trying to impress that girl, Mrs. Fraser. Not Liam Nolan.'

Were the accusations coming now? 'I've told you all I know.'

'What's he got in mind?'

'Major, I've absolutely no idea. How could I have?'

Surprisingly her voice hadn't risen, but they'd got nicely over the business of whether it had been Nolan or not. She'd not even realized that by speaking as if it had, she'd given away the fact.

He'd rub the window again. The Bailey was deserted, of course, but she'd not see this yet, the grass rather green for this time of year, but then, it was nearly always green.

The flagpole stood in the centre of the parade square, with four of Napoleon's cannon at the corners. Private Summers would escort her along a route she'd wonder at, taking her to the cannon only to leave her on the pretext of having forgotten something, and she'd be forced to wait out there all alone. Yes, that would be best.

But what must her thoughts be at such a time? he wondered. Guilt over the ugliness of a sordid little affair with Erich Kramer? Fear for her life, if Nolan and the Darcy woman were twisting her arm and that's what Kevin O'Bannion wanted?

Fear of betrayal then, and of being caught at it. Something . . . by God, something! That damned book she'd given Kramer. Thackeray, *The Virginians*.

'You can go now, Mrs. Fraser. Get me all you can on the Bachmann thing. Wolfganger and Werner have denied any involvement, but of course, they would.'

He had still not turned to look at her. 'You didn't tell them I'd overheard things, did you?'

'Don't be silly. They'll have figured that out all by themselves.'

The walk along the ramparts had been cruel—she not knowing why they were taking that route. They never had before. Private Summers had worn a black armband and had carried a

Lee Enfield rifle as if she was a prisoner and he the jailer who had despised her, which was so unlike him it hadn't made any sense either unless he'd been ordered to behave like that.

The rampart walk had run eastwards from above Trant's office to the Gosling Tower. From there it had taken them to Sir Guy's Spy, a cubicle sentry box with embrasures, then down a long slope of wall to the first of the east gate towers.

They had then walked out across the bailey and Summers had left her here at the flagstaff on the flimsy excuse of having forgotten something. The main part of the castle—its living quarters with all its many rooms and tall windows, was now off to her right, to the west.

As she stood looking southwards towards the barbican and Trant's office, Mary picked out the bay with its three windows and knew he'd still be standing there as she was here, each staring at the other across the football field of a no-man's-land of grass and empty space.

Would he be using field glasses? she wondered, hating the thought of it, the deliberateness.

Setting the bundle of books down, she slid her hands into the pockets of her overcoat. Trant would be asking himself questions about her, and she would have to remain like this, facing him for as long as it took to bring Summers back.

But it was lonely, was hard to bear, and the wind seemed only to echo from the surrounding walls and towers, there being no other sound. Two men with a Vickers machine gun had manned each section of rampart up there when she'd gone to meet Jimmy that time atop the keep and been able to see them from there. At the first of the east gate towers there had been a Lewis light machine gun. All had been waiting, all watching the bailey and the prisoners but now were they at the ready to fire on this one woman—was that what Trant had wanted her to feel by leaving her out here like this? That they would shoot traitors in times of war, even women? Or had he merely *wanted* her to remember what was up there, he thinking that she could well pass the information along, as she'd felt when with Jimmy? If so, why that opened a whole Pandora's box because it really did mean that they were using her to feed false information to the prisoners—that business of their being sent to Canada; this one of the defences when everyone knew men and guns were at a premium and the castle could not, out of necessity, be as secure as they'd have liked.

Did Trant suspect Nolan and the others had made contact with her for purposes of breaking the prisoners out? If so, he would have thought they'd ask her about such things. They'd want plans of the place, drawings, sketches, hence his showing her that sketch of the cellars and the escape tunnel they'd supposedly found.

Mary felt the wind as it teased the strands of hair that protruded from beneath her beret. It irritated the fine threads of the soft yellow scarf she wore. Though she had hardly taken her eyes from Trant's office, she sensed that the private hadn't yet been told to return.

Trant was making her feel as though Fay Darcy and Liam Nolan would tie her to the flagstaff if they could. He was making her hate herself all the more—Jimmy must have shown him that button he'd found. Did they now know beyond a shadow of doubt that she had been having an affair with Erich Kramer right within the walls of their castle?

Erich would be waiting for her. He'd be anxious—was that not a part of it too, this psychological warfare of Trant's, she still with a bullet for them, and why that bit about Nolan's past? Trant and Jimmy and the colonel must know where Nolan and the others had got that dynamite, yet he'd said nothing of this.

Scotland Yard would have followed up Nolan's trail in England both before and after the bomb incident at Charing Cross, yet that hadn't been mentioned either. And if the IRA were on the run in the South and smashed, did this not put Mrs. Tulford of the White Horse in jeopardy? And why that bit about Fay Darcy and her sister? Did they know she had met with Brenda? Had they been watching the sister's house in Kinsale for just that reason?

If Brenda Darcy should die of her wounds, that would only make Fay more violent, but had Trant wanted her to see this too?

'I hate you, Major,' she said. 'I absolutely loathe what you and Jimmy and the colonel stand for because you're using me just as is everyone else.'

Trant gave her another fifteen minutes. There would have been no thought of his undressing her with those field glasses of his, no danger of his finding the bullet. Trant wasn't like that, not while on duty, and he was always on duty, yet she knew then that he had wanted not only to provoke her into thinking things over but into doing something rash so as to betray herself.

Would he leave her out here all night if he had to, leave her to the prisoners, to men like Bauer just to see what would happen? Would he not care tuppence about her so long as he got what he wanted?

Philip Werner was sitting at the desk in the library when she came in. His crutches leaned against the wall behind him. The hello he gave was subdued but she wouldn't pursue things because there was no sense in that. Philip knew only too well she had ratted on them.

It was Helmut Wolfganger, though, who trapped her between the rows of shelves to whisper, 'You should look a little closer, Mrs. Fraser,' he nodding towards the desk where Franz Bauer awaited her return.

Mary touched his hand. 'Helmut, I'm sorry. I . . . I had no other choice.'

Wolfganger grinned. 'So now you give them the truth, or do you hold it back until you need it?'

He couldn't have been ordered to tell her this—he couldn't! 'I hold it back.'

Wolfganger nodded in that curt way Germans do. 'But you watch yourself very carefully. Don't let our Franz get too close when others are not around.'

Bauer saw the light of fear enter the bitch's eyes and understood he'd been fingered. *Ach*, when you've hanged a man, the rule of law prevails. Murder was murder and the Kapitänleutnant's *Hure* knew it too.

'The Oberst Karl-Ernst Tatlinger of the Luftwaffe, the Generalmajor Walter Storch of the Army, and Vizeadmiral Dietrich Huber. Those are the High Command at Tralane. Berlin will already know of this, through the International Red Cross.'

Tatlinger, Storch and Huber . . . 'Erich, you must tell them that I have to meet with all of them in person.'

'That's impossible.'

She had run all the way up the stairs, had bolted along the corridor and up yet another flight, could hardly catch her breath. 'It's no more risky than what I've been doing, is it?' she managed. 'The IRA are insisting and want proof I've done this.'

'Why aren't the negotiations proceeding swiftly?' he demanded, his tone of voice something she had never heard before.

When she didn't answer, but only looked questioningly at him, he asked for the ammunition and had she brought any this time. 'One? Why only one?' she heard him say.

Had she been such a fool as to believe he was in love with her? 'Because they are in control and what they say and do goes. It's something we have to discuss. A lot has happened since I last saw you.'

'Then tell me!'

'I can't. There isn't time and even if there was, the IRA would want me to tell it to you in the presence of your commanding officers since they are the ones who ultimately must make the decisions.'

Her chest was still rising and falling. There was none of that uncertainty he had come to expect, none of her needing reassurance.

She would have to tell him, thought Mary, since he was looking at her as if he doubted her loyalty. 'Berlin are refusing to go through with things unless there is further proof. You have to understand that the IRA not only mean business but that they will set the terms and the time and place. No one else.'

Irritably he ran a hand through his hair. 'Berlin will never agree to that and neither will Tatlinger and the others. It's finished.'

'They having come this far?'

'These IRA people of yours must want a great deal.'

They weren't her 'people' but she wished he'd not said it. 'I don't really know what they want. I'm only doing what I've been told to because I have no other choice.'

If he didn't soften, they'd lose her, thought Kramer. '*Li-

ebling, of course you're doing all you can. It's stupid of me to be angry but I have to get out of this place and the sooner the better.'

But with no thoughts of escape when in Canada, then? 'Look, I must get back. Trant hasn't given me much time today.'

'Then go. I'll speak to the others. You'll hear from me on Thursday.'

'Come yourself. Don't send Bauer.'

He would give her the boyish grin that had never failed to warm that heart of hers, would take her by the hand and kiss her fingers. 'Trant has forbidden me to visit the library. If I burn books, I'm not fit to borrow them. It's really very stupid of them but we go along with such things because they are so stupid and we can use them.'

'And Bauer?' she asked, betraying a nervousness he found curious and . . . and funny—did he find it amusing?

His look grew serious. 'Franz knows what to do. He's a good man in a pinch, Mary. The very best.'

The clearing in the woods on the opposite shore of Lough Loughie offered a haven and a chance to think on the way home. The swans cruised by in the gathering dusk while the castle seemed to welcome its shroud and the mist began to rise off the water.

Trant hadn't wanted to speak to her on the way out and that, in itself, was disconcerting enough, but Erich had said, 'Franz,' in that way a man does when he's lived in close company with other men and has come to know their every strength and weakness and to either respect or reject them.

Bauer wasn't Erich's Number One. He was somewhere further down the chain of command. Perhaps he'd been in charge of the engine room—he had that way about him. Out of necessity, U-boats had short chains of command—five officers and a crew of fifty or so, all cooped up for weeks on end, months too, sometimes. The pale blue eyes that were always without a hint of feeling had never failed but to make her uneasy. The faded, washed-out blond hair and pale, thick brows, bony, pasty face with its freckles and the squat solid build all spoke of the engine room. Bauer's hands were those of a pipe fitter—big, strong, thick fingered and fleshy, the nails clipped short but with dirt and grease under them always. A man who knew her body was being used by his captain and who laughed at her predicament but gave no outward sign of this beyond his not trusting her for a moment.

Try as she did, Mary couldn't avoid the thought of he and Erich living together for months on end. They'd have gone on leave in Normandy, in Brest perhaps. Had their good times, their laughs—returned to base from a successful tour of duty to wreaths and bunches of flowers, a brass band and medals. To pretty French girls who would want to party. To whores who'd be willing to do something else—Bauer would be like that. No time for the girls who wanted a drink or a dance at least. Simply first in line, he slinging his duffel bag over a shoulder and heading off alone to the nearest *maison de tolérance* for a clean-out just like his diesel engines. No feeling for the woman he was having sex with, no compassion, just the rut so as to get it all out of his system.

Then back again to the North Atlantic.

Erich had said so little about his men. Hans Schleiger, who had often kept watch for them too, was a bit older than Bauer—perhaps thirty and vastly different. Tall, thin, well educated, well mannered, good-looking—lots and lots of attributes and yet, a good man in a pinch. He'd have had to have been because Erich would not have tolerated sluggards. Not Erich.

Schleiger had managed to save his heavy grey turtleneck pullover, the leather trousers and the towel he had wrapped about his neck just before going up into the conning tower that last time. He had even kept the red glasses they put on belowdecks to accustom their eyes to the darkness outside, so he'd been up there when it had happened and they'd lost their boat.

A man who could still laugh at himself and the world, though. One of the elite.

Yes, they were a close group of men. They did as they were told and withdrew into themselves to form a fighting unit, even at Tralane.

Erich had two other officers with him who could have been on watch at times—those pictures of naked girls Private Summers had been shown? Had one of them, or both, singled Summers out while she and Erich had made love in that tiny room—love? Hadn't it simply been sex for him and she nothing but a fool as she'd felt earlier today? She still hadn't been able to learn the names of these two officers but had those been deliberately kept from her?

Unsettled by the thought, she switched on the headlamp of her bike, but remembered the blackout regulations and quickly turned it off, the road becoming dark and unfriendly.

Private Summers hadn't been his usual self—no jokes, no comments about the war, the world, the weather and the wife. Had he been hauled on the carpet and forced to tell Trant about those pictures? Had that been it?

If so, then Trant would know Summers had been purposely distracted, yet he hadn't said a thing about this and she'd managed again to meet with Erich. Same place, same time, well almost, but had Trant allowed that meeting to take place and had one of his men watching for it to happen?

The thought was more than she could bear.

Hamish was reading aloud, in by the fire in the study. Caithleen was wearing the white flannel nightgown she'd been loaned, and was curled up on the hearthrug at his slippered feet, with Robbie resting his muzzle in her lap. There was some question of refreshment, then the reading got on to horses and Robbie stirred at the mention of them. Someone had been asked to stay to dinner but had declined as a brave general should, asking only for time to feed his horse and have a glass of water for himself.

George Washington?

Mary started into the room. Robbie looked up, torn between objecting at the intrusion and ignoring it. Caithleen sat up. Hamish closed the book, but kept a finger in place. 'Lass, you're late. Mrs. Haney and Bridget and William went home a wee bit early. Your supper's in the warming oven.'

'What were you reading?'

As if she hadn't known. '*Och*, Caithleen and I were discussing the prospects of America. It's *The Virginians*. I could na find that copy I had wi' those lovely lithographs but we settled on another.'

'*The Virginians.*'

'Aye. 'Tis a story of much interest. Robbie was quite taken wi' it.'

He would use that brogue, knowing it would upset her! 'That copy was destroyed in one of the stoves at Tralane.'

He prodded the girl's shoulder and reluctantly Caithleen got up to stand a moment with a fierce pout, then to leave the room in a huff with only, 'My thanks t' ye. Dr. Fraser. 'Twas kind of you to read t' me, seeing as I've neither th' knowledge nor th' art.'

'Robbie, go with her.'

'Hamish, Erich burned that book in his stove.'

'So Trant was telling me.'

'When?'

'Mary, why in God's name won't you tell me what's been going on? You're scared stiff. Even a daft old bugger like myself can see it.'

'Because I can't. Because nothing's been going on. Because Trant is overly suspicious of everyone and kept me waiting far longer than he should have.'

'Did you see Erich?'

'He isn't allowed to come to the library.'

Fraser set the book aside. It was just after 7.00 p.m. so she must have been somewhere other than that damned prison for at least an hour and a half unless, of course, Trant had really kept her waiting that long, but he'd best say nothing of it. 'Mary, the major has his worries. Apparently that bomb you found was only a small part of the five cases of gelignite that were taken from the Montrose Stone Quarry in the Mountains of the Mourne back of Kilkeel. God only knows why the place was left unguarded in a time of war, never mind the North of Ireland, but the IRA got away with sufficient fuse, blasting wire and caps to level a good portion of Tralane should they be so inclined.'

'I think I'll go and have my supper.'

'They even took one of the blasting machines—one of those plunger things that generates the electrical current needed to set off the blast.'

'Do you want some tea? I think I'll make myself some.'

'Jimmy Allanby was by. He's been out and about a good deal in the rough. He's been run off his feet.'

'That'll be good for him. I'm sure he'll have enjoyed beating up the natives and tearing their places apart. Now do you want some tea or not?'

'I do. Oh my, yes, but I do, lass.'

In the morning she went to see Parker. They had their chat about the cows and all, and only then did she timidly broach the subject that had brought her to him.

Parker waxed eloquent. 'Ah sure, and you could burn that stuff in the grate, you could, missus, and it'd not give you the twinkle of the tiniest star. You needs the cap and fuse, you does, or the cap, the wire and the electrical battery or the blasting machine—the plunger. Down with the one and up with the other, as they says, or the catching of the match head beneath the nail of your thumb and the burning of a few feet of black-powder fuse held so close the one catches light the moment the other does. But now why would a girl like you be wanting to know a thing like that?'

'Nolan left a bomb at the colonel's party.'

'And did he now?'

Parker would have heard of it—the whole of County Ar-magh would have. He'd know about the theft from the quarry too, but one had to go carefully.

'How many sticks was there now?' he asked, sucking on that fire of his while leaning on the handle of his pitchfork.

She wished he hadn't asked. 'I didn't count them. A lot, I think.'

Parker pitched out another clump of manure from the pony's stall. 'Twelve they was, missus, and there's the likes of Liam Nolan himself busting his britches to get a bomb inside the colonel's house but forgetting to wire the blessed thing up.'

He clucked his tongue, sucked on the fire and speared more

manure, his life a round of cows, their milking and the pony cart to the stop out by the road to wait for the dairy's wagon to come along and take the milk away.

'Captain Allanby was here, he was. A ginger man, missus. A man with vengeance in his heart, I be thinking, and purpose on his mind.'

'He didn't search this place, did he?'

'Now why would you be thinking the likes of that?'

'I'm not. I only . . . No, of course not, Parker. Not you.'

'And why not? Sure and it's as good a place as any to hide five cases of gelignite and some fuse and all, but the captain didn't search, missus. He has them dogs what's trained t' smell dynamite. All they got was manure.'

Dogs that had been trained—the shed at home! Oh damn, but she couldn't leave now, couldn't run from him, would just have to tough it out and take a chance things would be safe. 'Parker, what exactly do you mean by cap and fuse or wire?'

He stabbed the pitchfork into the heap and wiped his hands on the seat of his trousers. 'Well, it's been some time, missus. Was that dynamite sticky, do you think?'

'Sticky? No, not at all.'

Then she'd had her hands on it well enough, she had. 'And not leaking, thanks be t' God, otherwise you might have jarred it and we'd not be talking. Nitro doesn't like to be knocked about and that juice would have been nitro.'

A length of frayed halter rope served as the black-powder fuse, a bit of lead pipe no more than two hands long was the stick of gelignite, and a cigarette cadged from God knows whom for it had been ages in his pocket, was the blasting cap.

'You must crimp the black-powder fuse into the cap, missus, using a set of pliers. Then the cap be inserted into the end of the dynamite like so, after first cutting off the length of fuse you needs.'

Some fuses burned at a foot a minute; others were faster, and still others much slower. One had always to check the rate of burning first.

'You slits the other end of the fuse, missus. A good half-inch now, and no more, being careful not to spill the black powder out.'

Just like a trooper she was, attentive and all. 'The match must be at its hottest, so if you're wise you'll break the head off one and tuck it into the end of the fuse.'

'Which end?'

'Why, the one you lights. T' other's in the dynamite, for God's sake, and stop makin' me so blessed nervous with all this talk!'

So the blasting cap went into the stick of dynamite, the fuse into the cap, and the head of a match into the other end of the fuse.

'There'll be a spout of flame near two feet long when you lights it, missus, so don't be afraid. Just drop the *ould* soul and run like th' divil for cover.'

'And the electrical method?'

O'Shane had the notion to tell her to buzz off home and come back another day, but she didn't look as though she'd leave. 'Them electrical blasting caps are different. They has two wires sticking out of one end.'

'So you make a hole in the end of the stick of gelignite, fit the cap in and then wire it up to the battery?'

Well now . . . 'That you do, missus, that you do, but God help the poor sinner who has the stick in one hand and the battery in the other.'

'How much electrical wire would you need?'

'Enough to give you cover.'

'Five hundred feet?'

'And a wall or a house or a hill between you and them, but I doesn't know a thing of this, only what I's heard. I be but a poor farmer with a handful of cows.'

'Good ones, too. Mary still producing well?'

Jesus save us! 'As well as can be expected in these troubled times.'

'Do the dogs really sniff out the dynamite?'

O'Shane reached for the pitchfork. He'd suck on his pipe and try not to look at her, for she'd a powerful interest, she had, but then it wasn't every day that a girl found a dozen sticks at a party. 'Not if there's ripe manure about, missus, the riper th' better. Urine, too. A healthy good piss is always best even if you've the freshest to do your hiding.'

The faint but grateful smile she gave made him want to haul her aside and say, *Now listen here. Don't play where fools would play,* but he held his tongue, for she'd said, 'Thanks, Parker. Thanks a million. I'll be seeing you soon,' as one would to a friend.

'Lest you blows yourself up, or was you only asking for interest's sake?'

'For interest. I . . . I was just curious, that's all. Ever since I found that bomb, I've been asking myself what it should have looked like.'

'Bundles of six, with the primer in the middle.'

'The primer?' she bleated.

And wasn't she that dismayed you'd think the bloody Bank of England had foreclosed or she had accidentally swallowed one of them cyanide pills the Nazis keep hidden in their back teeth! 'The one stick that does it all, missus. The one with th' blasting cap.'

'Oh.'

She rode away on that bicycle of hers looking as fresh as a Michaelmas daisy but grim and thinking things no daisy should ever have thought. 'Manure,' he muttered. 'Manure's the only thing lest one pisses on it, too, and the dogs catch the scent and find they have t' piss themselves and are distracted and wander off elsewhere.'

'William, I need some manure for the roses.'

'The gardener will look after that, m'am. 'Tis early yet to bed the roses.'

'I can't wait for a gardener who never shows up. Just help me to fill this barrow and be quick about it.'

William was all of fifteen, a young man growing—spindly, sandy-haired, wild-eyed at times like this and ducking away to hide the truth. 'Well, what is it?' she demanded. 'Not more of your lies.'

'No, m'am. I doesn't lie. I doesn't. Now I doesn't.'

'All right, all right—good God, you've got me repeating myself!'

''Tis th' manure, missus. If you use this, you'll burn th' roses like they was in the fires of hell.'

'But manure is manure, isn't it?'

'No, missus. It has t' rot, it does. Th' doctor, he be putting it in three piles. This year's, last year's and th' year before that.'

The smell would have vanished by then but saying that she wanted to hide six sticks of gelignite would do no good. 'Just show me, and we'll do it together.'

They carted six loads to the rose garden and banked the manure up against the brick wall on which the red ramblers grew. 'Hamish loves these roses,' she said, working the spade in hard. 'He even enjoys looking at the rose hips in winter.'

'That he does, missus. That he does.'

It took them all of two hours and at the end of the digging and the heaving she was tired. Hamish and Robbie came out to see what they'd been up to. 'That's a bit rich,' was all he said, he like the Abbot Gregor Mendel in his Augustinian herb garden. Slippers and steamer robe of brown camel hair with tassels at the ends of the purple cord and Robbie giving the manure a good working over for beetles and worms and things.

'I'm trying, Hamish,' was all she could find to say, letting him think what he would.

Later, under cover of darkness, she buried the six sticks of dynamite next to the wall, using a Grant's shortbread tin she'd been saving up. The seal around the lid was carefully wrapped with electrician's black sticky tape to keep out any moisture. A last look under hand-blinkered torchlight seemed to satisfy, but the night was so silent, even the sound of her breath came easily now as the earth *and* ripe manure were softly spilled into the hole, but as she put the shovel away in the stables, there was a sound. 'Who's there? I know you're there,' Mary heard herself bleat, but would they think she had reached for the shovel to protect herself?

Nolan's voice came first, caught as she was under their torchlight. 'Mrs. Mary Fraser it is.' No laughter now, no teasing, not this time. Manure and earth on her boots, shovel still in hand . . .

Fay Darcy snorted, 'Out and about at this hour and suspecting the worst, is it?'

'What the hell do you people think you're doing by coming here like this?'

'It's yourself who should be answering why you're out and about in your nightdress and gown,' said Fay.

'I . . . I thought I heard someone.'

Fay switched off the torch and stepped closer. 'Not us. Most likely that husband of yours. Hears a lot more then he should, he does. Goes about looking where he shouldn't.'

The colonel's party . . . 'You didn't need to hit him so hard. He's got a concussion.'

'Oh and has he?'

The Darcy woman was now so close, the sour odour of endless nights and days on the run was evident. Mary felt her robe being touched and leapt. 'Where's Kevin?'

The Fraser woman was not even aware that Liam had removed himself and was watching out. 'Kevin, is it? You'd be feeling safe with him, now would you, Mrs. Fraser? Safe as an angel in his arms.'

'Look, it's crazy of you to have come here. If I hadn't been outside, what would you have done?'

The cord around her waist was now being fingered.

'Gone inside, I suppose,' said Fay. 'Liam's good at that sort of thing. Very quiet he is. Like a lady's slipper what falls on her lover's carpet.'

Had Nolan left them? 'What do you want?'

The cord came undone and the robe fell open of its own accord.

'Please don't touch me. I'll . . . I'll scream.'

'You do and you'll be getting the lesson of your life. We want the girl. You've not been to Dublin like you said you would and can go in there right now and bring her out. Now, I'm saying!'

'I can't. I won't. I refuse absolutely. She's suffered far too much.'

'Liam?'

'Fay, cut it out! You know what Kevin said. There's far too much at stake. It's not her fault Brenda was killed.'

'My sister, Mrs. Fraser. Shot up and some and heaving her guts out in the road while the bastard Garda laid them into her just for the fun of it. Kevin's in the South, having a look into things, seeing as no one should have known Brenda and me was having a meeting. No one.'

The woman stepped away. The pony snorted nervously in its stall, and from somewhere in the inky darkness came a click and then another, the cylinder of a revolver. 'Please, I . . . I didn't have anything to do with that. How could I? And as for taking Caithleen to Dublin . . .'

The sound wasn't that of a revolver. The Darcy woman was over by the car, and must be flicking a fingernail at it in the darkness. 'Look, I haven't met with Erich's superior officers yet, have only set that up. There simply hasn't been enough time.'

The pony was getting restless.

'Time? That's something only rich people have,' breathed Fay. 'You'll meet with them tomorrow and you'll tell them you need something solid to send over on that wireless, otherwise Caithleen O'Neill will be hanging from a tree and you yourself will come to an untidy end.'

'How can you talk like that to anyone?'

Nolan came back, saying they must be away. Mary had never heard him anxious before, but the Darcy woman gave no sign of wanting to leave.

'Your gallant Captain Allanby is out there a-raiding, Mrs. Fraser, with the tracking dogs and all. You wouldn't have told him where to look for us, now would you?'

'Dear God, I don't know where you've been hiding! How could I? I can't even see you now.' They were crazy, the two of them. Crazy!

Nolan crowded close. 'Fay, we've got to go.'

'Liam, shut yours. Allanby won't think to come here. It's too good a place. Dublin, Mrs. Fraser. On Sunday it is, with a message for them fellows in Berlin.'

'The colonel will refuse to let me take Caithleen. I . . . I haven't got any other excuse. Not now. It's . . . it's a dead give-away if I try to go there by myself.'

'Liam?'

'Fay, you know what Allanby's like. The horses . . .'

So they'd come on horseback. That must mean they had left them down the road a piece in a copse perhaps, or at the very back of the garden, in under the apple trees. The garden . . . . Had they heard her digging and decided not to say a thing of it? Had they? 'I'll tell the colonel that Franz Bauer was the one who hanged the Second Lieutenant Bachmann.'

Back to hangings was it? Leaving the car, Fay closed the gap between them.

'Bauer . . . Franz Bauer was involved, this much I do know, but . . . but if I tell the colonel, Bauer will try to kill me. I'm sure of it, in . . . in spite of their wanting Erich to escape.'

'Liam, take hold of the slut.'

'Fay . . .'

'Do it, damn you!'

Mary knew she'd choke as the nightgown was lifted, that she'd scream for help if she could and try to get away, but would be beaten down.

Fay's hands were cold but the muzzle of Nolan's pistol was being pressed behind her right ear, the woman breathing into her face as her nipples were pinched and held.

'You'll give the colonel that booger's name, you will, do you hear? Him that wants shall receive but only after the giving of his promise to let you take Caithleen on Sunday.'

'Fay . . .'

'Liam, there's a small matter we must discuss with this col-laborator of the Germans. That of the six sticks of gelignite that went missing.'

Her breasts were still being held but no answer was forthcoming. 'There were eighteen, Mrs. Fraser, and you took six of them. Now tell us why?'

'I didn't. Allanby said there were twelve. He . . . he must have wanted to downgrade the size of the bomb. Now get your filthy hands off me.'

'Filthy, are they?'

'Fay, leave her be. We haven't time for this.'

'A pity. Well, later then. So it's a meeting tomorrow, it is, a giving of a name, and then off to Dublin's fair city with you on Sunday.'

Nolan pressed two cartridges into her hand and said, 'Those are for good behaviour.'

Things had been speeded up.

Dropping the nightgown on the floor beside her bed, Mary tried to rub away the feel of Fay Darcy's hands but it was no use. She wished Erich hadn't lied to her, wished she'd never been unfaithful to Hamish, wished she had her wedding ring, wished so many things.

Nolan and Fay Darcy might well come to think she must have buried the dynamite in the garden. They would let her believe it safe, then would shove the evidence in her face, and that . . . why that would bring its punishment.

Wishing was, of course, of no earthly use, and she couldn't go out there now to see if they'd taken it. The truth was, she'd never know with them, but then that was also true of Trant and the others.

She could hear the colonel saying, 'Bauer . . . Oh yes, we rather thought he might have been involved. He's not the only one who put the noose around that chappie's neck, Mrs. Fraser. Oh my, no. There'd have been others. The Nazis never do a thing like that without a proper tribunal. At least three, I should say, perhaps even four or five. Find out for us. There's a good girl, hmm?'

'Caithleen . . .' she'd say.

'A bit of a bother, is she?'

'Colonel, the IRA might try to take her from the house.'

'Perhaps we'd best leave her there, then, Major?'

Trant would allow a brief, effacing little smile, and would say, 'We've been having the house watched round the clock for just such a thing.'

She'd have to beg. 'Please let me take her to Dublin on Sunday. It isn't fair. I've done what you wanted. Well, some of it anyway.'

The colonel would have none of it. 'Mrs. Fraser will have to go before the courts with this Bauer thing, eh, Major? It would be best then to have the names of all of them'.

Hans Schleiger and Erich Kramer—she knew that's what they would want her to say but was it true? If Bauer was one of them, and 'Franz' such a good man in a pinch, then hadn't he been acting under orders and wasn't that why Helmut Wolfganger had said, 'It's a good thing they hanged Bachmann when they did'?

'Mary . . . Mary, what is it?'

'Nothing! I . . . I couldn't sleep.'

She was caught in the passing moonlight of drifting clouds, was over by the windows, naked and so very lovely it hurt to look at her.

'Hamish, please leave. I . . . I just need to be alone.'

'Lass, for God's sake let me help. *Och*, I know you're in love with Erich. I canna fault you for that, but is there something else?'

They'd kill him if she said anything, and when he took hold of her, she pressed her forehead against him.

'I love you, lass. I always will.'

She mustn't cry. 'I wish I hadn't lost my wedding ring, Hamish. It did mean something very special.'

In words that were so hard to find she told him of the child she had had to leave behind in Canada—she owed him that much at least—and he told her he'd always known she had had a child but hadn't felt it his place to ask though had seen how terribly upset she'd been with herself and still was. 'The tears caught at an introspective moment when you'd be alone and looking out into the garden, Mary, the times I'd see you longingly linger over the dolls and toys in some shop. *Och*, if there'd been something I could have done to bring Louise back to you, I would have. I know you ache for her, but it's us we have to settle. Erich will be sent to Canada soon. He'll be out of our lives and wasn't meant for you in any case.'

They'd kill him. 'Get out. Get out of my room.'

'Mary, he doesn't care two pins for you.'

'Hamish, I know that. Now please go.'

'And have the house turned into a prison?'

'Yes. Yes, that's it exactly!'

7

Again at dawn the hills were wrapped in mist, and the green of them was like a dream, but then the sound of gunfire came. Three short bursts from a Thompson submachine gun, then a longer one, a whole clip that time, the singular flat reports of Lee Enfield rifles breaking through with the pop, popping of pistols and revolvers and then another long burst and more of the other.

Mary found she couldn't move. The patient gurgling of the Loughie beneath the bridge was as horrid laughter, but no more gunfire came and the silence went to a hush that hurt, she straining to listen.

The lolling toll of Parker O'Shane's lead milker returned, the cow tossing her head for some reason. Distant beyond the hills came the faraway honking of migrating geese, wanderers from the high Arctic: Brants or Canadas.

The gunfire had been over towards Parker's farm. Three short bursts and then a longer one. A confusion of singles with one final shot as if to finish things off.

Trembling, she shut her eyes, tried hard not to cry, hadn't

slept, had come out here to watch the sun climb over the hills to burn off the mist or be drowned in the rain. It was Thursday, the day of her meeting with Erich's superior officers, yet the dawn had brought something other than the peace of mind she'd so desperately needed, and it had come swiftly, unexpectedly.

'Mary, don't go near him.'

There was no memory of having ridden from the bridge to the farm, none whatsoever of dropping the bicycle in the road. No memory of the men, the sweat-lathered horses with their military saddles, the uniforms, the Sam Brown belts and guns, the guns.

Smoke from the turf fire in the thatched-roofed cottage trailed thinly into the air . . . *'Jimmy, let go of me!'*

The smell of him, that of his horse, of the hay, of cowpats, ragwort, Michaelmas daisies, rotting apples and hawthorn berries came to her. 'Parker . . . Parker, what happened?'

Mary shook Allanby off, but the men stood round watching her, some out in the adjacent fields, some over by the paddock gate, a cluster by the stables, one standing near the manure pile with a pitchfork in hand. A pitchfork!

There was blood on the road—blood melding with the grey of scant limestone gravel and the black centuries of spilled peat. Parker . . . Parker lay across the hump in its middle, his left leg thrown out, the right one bent up and in towards the stomach. His face had been smashed to pieces; his hands were broken. The stomach had been ripped open, his intestines protruded.

'Mary, he ran.'

Her voice when it came was shrill. 'Why shouldn't he have? You *jumped* him! He had nothing to do with anything. He wasn't one of them. He was just a friend. Just someone I could talk to.'

Kneeling in the road, she reached out to take Parker by the shoulder, to try to awaken him. Turning, she angrily looked up and Allanby heard her saying, 'What happened, Jimmy? Did you panic? Is that why the army sent you to Tralane?'

There was only hatred in her, no thought of compromise. 'Sergeant Stewart, see that Mrs. Fraser is shown the others, then take her to the cowshed and stable.'

Jimmy had been wounded and was holding his left shoulder. 'You broke under fire. You shouted at your men and they opened up on a poor old defenceless man.'

'Sergeant, I gave you an order. See to it.'

They took her out into the pasture and she saw the Lee Enfield rifle that had been pitched aside as the man had fallen.

'Thomas O'Grady, m'am.'

Mary had never seen him before. He was just a life expending its last moments twitching in the grass. 'Can't you help him?'

He wasn't old, wasn't young: a man with a parched throat, stubble on his sunken cheeks and wearing a black frieze stovepipe suit that had seen poteen and cigarette ashes and egg or colcannon and porter dribbled and spilled with lashings of pork dripping and all other such things including jam roll-up and milk too, for he must have been a farmer at one time.

They left that body and went over to another.

'Janet Duffy. Age twenty-two years, seven months and four days.'

This one was lying by the hedgerow that ran alongside the road. The girl's ash-blonde hair moved gently in the wind. She was on her back, and the whole of her blue pullover where the grey tweed jacket lay open, was soaked with blood.

There was a revolver lying not far from her left hand, and Mary had the thought then that the girl had been the last of them and that Jimmy hadn't felt she'd try to shoot him, that she'd been trapped against the furze and had lifted the gun after all.

It was mad; it was insane.

'A student, m'am, of divinity at the university in Dublin.'

There were still two bodies to come. Had Fay Darcy and Liam Nolan been caught? If they hadn't, she was in for it . . .

They were lying on the other side of the cottage, one of them in the chicken run, the other over by the cowshed. Two brothers—the red hair was the same, the freckles, too, the build, the height, the chubbiness, even the way they had clutched their rifles to the last and hadn't let go of them.

Questions would be of no use with them, torture neither, but then she was taken to the cowshed to see the reason why Jimmy had wanted her to view the others first. It wasn't Kevin O'Bannion but a haunting similarity was there in fast-fading eyes that squinted up into the half-light. The short, crinkly black hair was the same as were the facial clefts, which now drew in as a spasm came.

He'd been shot in the groin, was sitting slumped against a post, mired in cow shit. A Thompson submachine gun, obviously a gun of many killings, leaned against the far wall, having been picked up by one of Jimmy's men. Spent cartridge casings lay about.

'Brian Doherty,' said Sergeant Stewart. 'A cousin of Kevin O'Bannion's and one of the ringleaders of the Belfast organization.'

'Go fuck yourself, you tommy bastard.' Doherty winced but when the spasm passed, he swept stern grey, searching eyes over her just as his cousin would have done.

It was Stewart who, nudging Doherty's left boot with his own, snorted and said, 'You'll not be playing stud to the girls anymore, Brian. Tough luck.'

'Give me a gun and let me kill myself!'

His scream was shattering. Sunlight played on the hand that clutched the bloodied crotch.

'In the name of Jesus, have some compassion,' he cried. 'The pain's fair killing me.'

'Then suffer.'

Stewart turned away but Mary remained, for Doherty was begging her now yet could so easily have watched another die if the situation had been reversed. 'Let him die as he wants,' she heard herself say.

But that, of course, would not have done, and she was taken from the stables. Jimmy had had his shoulder bandaged. Four cases of dynamite had been dug out of the manure along with some sacks of fuse and things that had been wrapped in oilcloth. Fay Darcy and Liam Nolan had got clean away—that was all there was to it and she had best get used to it, but had they gone from the house last night to Parker's farm or had it been the other way around and had that been why Nolan had been so anxious, the rest of them waiting here for him and Fay to return? Certainly at some point, Fay and Liam had noticed that they weren't alone. Somehow they had slipped away because there was no sign of them and no one here was saying anything of them.

They would have muffled the hooves of their horses and muzzled them, would have led each one across the fields and back through Jimmy's line of men because that was the way Liam Nolan was.

He'd have let the others take the rap. Fay would have wanted to warn them at least, but in the end Fay would have had to tag along.

BETRAYAL

Of the five cases of dynamite that had been stolen from that quarry, one remained. There'd be fuse and caps enough and electrical wire, too, and the blasting machine.

As on the road at dawn, Mary had no memory of riding home, of putting the bike away, or even of going into the house to numbly tell them what had happened. Hamish had rushed off in anger at the stupidity of mankind but by then an hour or two had elapsed since Brian Doherty had been wounded. There would be no hope of saving him, the delay deliberate—a plan to crush the IRA in the North as well and drive the whole lot of them into the grave or the sea, but would Nolan and Kevin O'Bannion be forced to flee the country as the Earls of Tyronne and Tyrconnel had done, though in a German submarine?

Mrs. Haney, who hadn't had two good words for her half-brother, had keened like a wild banshee at the news. She and Bridget and William had rushed off home to attend to their grief and the grieving. Caithleen and herself had been left alone in the house, the girl not speaking, just sitting in her room as Parker's words kept coming back, 'Ah, and sure, isn't death an Irish pastime?'

Six lives in an instant and tears that came of their own in sudden rushes. Think, said Mary to herself. You must.

Out at the back of the garden, some of the windfalls had been crushed beneath the horses' hooves. Following their trail, she went after them, a hoofprint here, another there, a broken stem of grass. More by luck than skill she found the place where Jimmy and some of his men had waited. One of them had urinated close in and high up against the trunk of a tree so as to make no sound. Because of the shade and the damp, the stain had not yet dried.

They'd have been nervous, jittery—afraid for themselves, would have known that Fay Darcy and Liam Nolan had come to the house but for what reason?

To see her, of course.

There could now be no longer any doubt of it. Trant and Jimmy and the colonel must know the IRA had been black-mailing her, but did they know for certain that she'd been helping Erich to escape?

Caithleen was still in her room with the door closed and locked. Mary knew she ought to tell her she'd get her safely away before it was too late, but knew the girl would only turn her back on her and say nothing.

Putting on her gumboots, she went out to the stables to stand before the piles of manure that were heaped against the barn-board fence in the yard. Nolan and Fay Darcy wouldn't have had time to hide the rest of the dynamite here. They wouldn't have dared. Even so, she had to be certain. Taking up the pitchfork, she went to work—the fresh, of course, but then the not-so-fresh and well rotted. If anyone should come along, she'd have to tell them: Throwing the one into the other. Turning the bloody stuff over because . . . why because she'd had to do something, couldn't have stood or sat still a moment longer, was having enough trouble just stopping the tears. Parker had been her friend, *her friend!*

There was, of course, no sign of the dynamite. Nolan and the Darcy woman really wouldn't have had the time, yet they'd been in the stable.

Setting the pitchfork down, Mary glanced into the yard and along the drive, cleaned off her boots and, crossing to the loft ladder, removed them just in case.

The wooden powder box, looking not unlike a butter box, was under the hay at the very back against the wall. Its lid had been opened and then nailed loosely, and when pried off, there was a hollow in the regimented rows of waxed, stiff, brown paper-covered cartridge sticks, each of one inch in diameter and eight in length.

A label had been stencilled on the lid: GELIGNITE. NOBEL NUMBER ONE, 50 LBS, 110, 40%. One hundred and ten sticks, less the eighteen, all with 40 percent active ingredient, i.e., nitroglycerine, the words *dynamite* and *gelignite* often being used interchangeably, though there were differences.

There were blasting caps enough and fuses and coils of thin electrical wire and the plunger thing, all in three canvas sacks. Nolan was a bloody fool! The dogs, those tracking dogs . . .

Taking four sticks out, she gingerly brought them up to her nose, the smell rocketing sharply to her head as before, making her instantly dizzy and sick and lightheaded all at once, a smell like no other: aromatically clinging, heavily cloying and of ammonia yet still so hard to define. Not quite of bitter almonds but very much of them. Not sweet, but then of a sweetness.

Her head began to fiercely ache. The stiff paper covering wasn't sticky, so none of the nitroglycerine could have leaked through, but Nolan mustn't find out that she had discovered them. Putting the sticks back, she carefully refitted the lid, but couldn't remember exactly how it had been and had to hunt for the nail holes.

The lid had been banged on, then, with the heel of a hand—the nails had been loose. Yes, yes, that's how it had been. But she couldn't do that, not with her hand.

Finding a bit of wood, she wrapped it in a sleeve and gently tapped the nails back in so that the lid was still loose and could easily be pried off.

One thing seemed all but certain. Since Fay Darcy and Nolan had been busy up here, they might not know she had buried those six sticks in the garden, yet she hadn't heard them when she'd first come to get the spade, only when she'd brought it back, a worry.

'Fay would have had to keep watch while Nolan hid things here,' she muttered to herself. They'd been on the run from Parker's, with Jimmy probably close on their tail, but if Fay had seen her up to something, was she now planning to ask her about it later?

Knowing that she shouldn't, that they might well have counted the blasting caps but that there could be more than they'd ever need, Mary crawled over to the sacks.

The blasting caps were of two types just as Parker had said— pencil-thick cylinders an inch and a half long and of either aluminium or of copper. The type for the black-powder fuse was of aluminium and had a hole in one end into which the fuse was inserted. A row of tiny dents encircled the metal where the crimper was to be squeezed to bend the metal in and hold the fuse securely.

The copper fuses had two brown-covered electrical wires protruding from one end. The wires for each cap were looped over several times and secured with tape. Delays were of thirty ms, whatever that meant. It was dangerous to handle them, or so the labelling on the packets stated, but how many would she need and would they be missed?

It was a chance she'd have to take. Fortunately two of the packets had already been broken open, at the quarry probably, so the gamble wasn't all that much. Parker had said, 'In bundles of six, with the primer in the middle.'

Pocketing two of each type of blasting cap, Mary climbed back down to the stable floor and from there went into the shed to find both a small set of pliers and the pocketknife Hamish used to cut twine for the garden. With this last, she cut off two lengths of fuse, one of twelve feet, the other of twice that—delays, then, of eight and sixteen minutes according to the label on the roll. 'I mustn't let the black powder run out on to the floor,' she muttered, 'must blow away what has.'

Taking two coils of electrical wire as well, she covered up the sacks. With Bridget and Mrs. Haney absent, there was little chance of them discovering anything. Even so, she hid everything at the bottom of the cedar chest in her room, broke open a new box of mothballs and scattered them before locking the chest and hanging the key around her neck from a bit of string.

An hour passed, sitting by the window staring emptily into the garden—no chance of seeing the red ramblers, though, no chance of keeping an eye on the bomb—she'd have to call it that now, would need a dry-cell battery large enough to give a good, strong current, would need a packet of matches too.

No chance of knowing really what she'd do with the thing, once she had it assembled, nor of knowing yet exactly how to make it or even what method to use.

When Hamish didn't come back at noon, Mary told Caithleen that she would have to come with her to Tralane. 'I can't leave you here alone.' It would be best this way. Confronted by the girl, the colonel or Trant or both might just let her take Caithleen to Dublin, especially as she'd have to tell them about the rest of the dynamite—that hadn't been an easy thing to decide, but she'd win their confidence and cut down on the loss of life.

Besides, Jimmy would have figured out where the stuff was anyway. Better, then, to tell them than to have the stables and the shed torn apart and the garden all dug up.

Of course they'd want to leave it right where it was in hopes of catching Fay and Nolan, but there was a chance they'd let her take Caithleen to Dublin. After that, nothing else really mattered except for Hamish.

The dress was white, the hair shorn, and when Caithleen O'Neill was brought before his desk, Bannerman saw that she was comely.

So this was the girl who'd been stripped and tarred, this was the girl Jimmy had threatened to set alight for withholding information. He'd take his time mentally undressing her, for there was such hatred in those sea-green eyes, such fear it gave one pleasure. There had been a time when he'd have thought of indulging in such a pretty thing should the chance have allowed at Gwen's house in the Midlands, but that was now out. Both of the boys had been engaged to decent, lovable girls, one not quite five years older than this Irish wench. Big-breasted, high-breasted—did they breed them that way as they tried to breed their damned cows? She'd have screamed—by God, she would have shrieked that pretty head of hers off as they'd ripped the clothes from her.

'Cat got your tongue?' he asked.

'Colonel, I . . .'

'Mrs. Fraser, when I wish you to address me further, I will say so. For the moment, I want to hear what this one has to say about things.'

'Nothing, sir. The army will kill me, like she says, if I stay here much longer.'

The army . . . 'Caithleen, I have lost my two sons to German panzers. That is war, and I can stand it for I've been a soldier all my life, but what I cannot stand is this . . .'

'It's not my army, Colonel, sir. I was never a part of any-thing of theirs nor did I ever wish to be.'

'But you were born to it, girl. I daresay you were suckled on it, so I'll not have you interrupting me either.'

That lesson would never be learned. He could see it in the way the little thing tossed her head in defiance and straight-ened those shoulders of hers.

'Now as I was saying, what I cannot stand is the heartless meddling of this "army" of yours with the death notices of my two sons. I don't make deals, as Mrs. Fraser has had the gall to ask, nor does the British Army I represent.'

'You've informants, Colonel,' said Mary. 'Aren't deals made with them; doesn't money change hands?'

'By damn, how dare you interrupt me again?'

'Caithleen can tell you nothing. I've a far better reason than her for Liam Nolan and Fay Darcy coming to our house.'

'And what, pray tell, is that?' He'd say nothing of the fact that the O'Neill girl had been, and still was being used by the rebels to twist her arm!

'Colonel, on humanitarian grounds, if on no others . . .'

'Like bloody hell I will! They invade the sanctity of my house and terrify my good wife. You warn no one of the bomb they've planted until after you've carted it off and had a look? They steal enough explosive materiel to level a good portion of this castle and release all of our . . .'

Trant leapt to his feet. 'Colonel . . . Colonel, if I might in-tercede. Mrs. Fraser has come forward with an offer. Given the circumstances, would it not be wise of us to make some sort of an accommodation?'

Bannerman's look revealed doubt and the fear of having said too much, that they'd been afraid Nolan would, indeed, blast through the walls and let everyone escape, Erich especially.

'Are you quite done with the girl, Major?' he asked.

'She has served her usefulness, Colonel. We'll get nothing out of her, will we, Caithleen, even though Liam Nolan could just as easily murder you in your sleep as he did the two women who sheltered him in London when he killed that child?'

Trant had always had a way with him, sighed Bannerman. The O'Neill girl was shattered by the news, as was her guardian. 'Well, Mrs. Fraser, since the major thinks it best, I'll defer to him.'

It was now or never. 'Your promise first, in writing.'

'Mrs. Fraser, surely the colonel's word will be sufficient?'

'That of a gentleman—is that it, Major?' She'd never get it in writing, but had Nolan really murdered two innocent women in their sleep?

Trant gave her that little smile of his, but she'd have to continue regardless. 'Our stableboy often sleeps in the hayloft when he thinks he can get away with it. After I'd told Mrs. Haney and my husband what had happened at Parker's farm, I went to tell William he'd best go home. Parker was his uncle.'

'These damned people are all related,' said Bannerman, reaching for a glacier mint and slowly untwisting its cellophane.

'After William had left the loft, I noticed that something wasn't quite right.'

Oh and did you now? thought Trant, but he wouldn't press the issue. He'd watch the O'Neill girl who, with evident dismay had swiftly turned to hear what the Fraser woman was saying, since the stableboy had been implicated.

'I found the last of that dynamite, Major. I didn't touch the box. I left things exactly as they were.'

But you want us to know that you didn't touch anything, thought Trant. The O'Neill girl had gone quite pale, Mrs. Mary

Ellen Fraser having just signed her own death warrant should Nolan or any of the others find out they'd been given away.

'Look, I would have told you, Colonel. Hamish and I really want to see Caithleen safe. That's . . . that's why I tried to make a deal with you.'

It was Bannerman who, taking the mint from his mouth, said, 'Is there anything else, then, that you'd like to tell us, hmm?'

As if there had to be. 'No. No, there's nothing else.'

'Then might I make a suggestion, Mrs. Fraser? Bring us the names of all those who were involved in the hanging of Second Lieutenant Bachmann. Bauer was most certainly one of them—we've established that since we last saw you here, but there were others.'

'And Caithlcen?' asked Mary, seeing in his eyes an emptiness that haunted.

Bannerman let her have it as planned. 'The girl is to be taken by you to Dublin on Sunday.'

'Mrs. Fraser, if I might have a word.'

Trant caught up with her in the no-man's-land of the bailey. Above her the flag flapped mercilessly at half-mast. He had had Private McQuinn leave her at the side door to the southern of the eastern gate towers, had let her walk out here again, all on her own. 'Well, what is it, Major?'

She was trembling with indignation, knowing they were using her and not liking the choice of meeting place either. God alone knew who might be watching.

He'd affect an apologetic smile. 'I just thought I ought to warn you Franz Bauer's not been locked up.'

'But . . . but if he thinks I've . . .'

'Now steady on. I thought I detected a blitheness to your step. See that you keep it up. There's a good girl.'

Stung by this, anger leapt into her eyes.

'Major, don't patronize me. If Bauer suspects I've told you about his part in the hanging, he'll try to kill me.'

'Not in the library, surely, but just in case, I'll detail two of the men to stand watch if you wish.'

Mary knew that he had deliberately pinned her down. 'That wouldn't be wise, would it? I'd not find out what you want.'

'My thoughts exactly, but if there's the least sign of trouble just give a shout and my men will come running.'

'Bauer's not the type to allow a shout, is he?'

One had best let her have it gently. 'Nor are his *Kameraden*, Mrs. Fraser, a point you must never forget.'

Trant allowed her a few steps before calling after her, 'Oh by the way, there's been word of another escape tunnel. See what you can pick up on it, will you?'

There'd been no books today—forgotten of course, and left at the house, no doubt. It couldn't have been pleasant her seeing the dead and the wounded at dawn, but why in God's name had she been out on that bicycle of hers at such an hour?

Her back was still to him, she waiting with hands crammed into the pockets of her mack.

'You can go now, Mrs. Fraser. Go and do your stuff.'

Private Summers met her, he all smiles and holding the heavy door to the keep open for her while shouldering his rifle. There were armed guards in the halls, guards at every turning, the prisoners nowhere in sight, not even in the great hall.

'Special rules, m'am. Confined to quarters until fifteen hundred hours. You'll have an easy day of it.'

Alone in the library, waiting, trying to collect her thoughts and put reason to Trant's not having told her, Mary wondered if she would be allowed to meet with Erich's High Command, or if Trant had known all about it.

Bauer was among the first to enter and one look at him was enough. He'd kill her, if not today, then soon. *'Du kommen, ja,'* he said. *'Kommen.'*

Three candles glowed in the darkness of the little chapel that had been built into the warren of cellars beneath the castle. The race through corridors and up and down staircases was now over.

As Bauer stepped aside, Mary caught a breath. Five men stood waiting for her but only three of these could be the High Command. The tallest, she was quickly told, was Oberst Karl-Ernst Tatlinger of the Luftwaffe. Walter Storch, a Generalmajor, was from the army, a short, squat, fiercely tough and distrusting man.

Vizeadmiral Dietrich Huber was somewhere in between, but was he the only one who spoke English?

'Mrs. Fraser, our lack of time necessitates we dispense with formality. Kapitanleutnant Kramer, here, has told us much about you. Now, please, what is it the IRA are demanding?'

She would have to be straight with them. Even the slightest sign of weakness would be wrong. 'Proof that I've met the three of you, and something substantial to be sent over by wireless to Berlin.'

And a firm answer from one so gullible, thought Huber. 'Is it true that the British killed six of their members this morning?'

How had they found out so quickly? 'I was there just afterwards. Parker, the man at whose farm it happened, was my friend, but he wasn't one of them, hadn't been in years, I'm certain.'

And yet again that firmness. 'There was a quantity of explosives. Was it all recovered?'

Huber was the key to this whole thing. 'Some was left at my house, but . . .'

'But what, Mrs. Fraser?'

How quick he was to search for answers. 'But the British know about it. I had to tell them otherwise this meeting would never have taken place.'

The three of them conferred rapidly in *Deutsch*, Huber insisting that they note how resolute she seemed, circumstance having led them to believe otherwise of her. Each threw her glances from time to time while Erich remained indifferent—at attention over to the left of the altar, with Bauer standing directly behind her and . . .

Mary turned sideways to see Hans Schleiger looking at her, Erich's Number One.

Again it was Huber who did the talking. 'Please tell us what you meant by this meeting not being allowed to take place. Is it that the British are aware of your dealings with us?'

As quickly as she could, she told them how things were, that the IRA were insisting she take Caithleen to Dublin on Sunday, and that in order to gain permission she'd had to tell Bannerman and Trant about the explosives in the loft.

Huber knew he had to be impressed with this . . . this woman of the Kapitanleutnant's but did such a summoning of spirit on her part not spell trouble in the end? '*Ach*, you are playing such a dangerous game, aren't you, Frau Fraser? Let us hope it will soon be over.'

He had said it in *Deutsch* and she had given him nothing but a blank look.

Again the three of them went into a huddle. Again there were glances—Tatlinger flashing her a brief but encouraging smile. From Storch, there was only brutal suspicion. He clearly didn't trust her and didn't like their having to depend on her.

From Erich there was nothing. It was as if she no longer existed for him, as if he really had hanged Bachmann and that it had been his decision, and his alone.

'This Nolan, Mrs. Fraser. How far can we trust him?'

'Nolan's not their leader. Kevin O'Bannion is—he's quite different, far more reliable.'

'Cool-headed?'

'Definitely.'

'And this O'Bannion is in the South?'

Again Mary had to ask herself how they had learned of it. 'He was the last time I talked to the others. He may have come back. This I simply don't know.'

And again a directness that both troubled and puzzled. Had she sized him up so easily and intuitively known precisely how to answer, that her life could well depend on it? wondered Huber. 'And the British don't suspect you of helping us?'

He had known, too, that she had seen Nolan last night. 'They suspect it, of course. I did lose a button but . . .'

Huber gave a curt nod to Erich who stepped forward and held out a fist, didn't even smile, just let her see that he'd been the one . . .

'A measure of our trust,' said Huber. 'The British did not find it as I'm sure you must have feared.'

'But . . . but why wasn't it returned?'

And at last the forgetfulness of a spark of anger. 'To put you on your guard. To make you far more careful. Please do not be dismayed. The Kapitänleutnant has always been under our command and was ordered to do as he did. We must escape and you have been of such help, it is only proper that we should guarantee you safe passage to the Reich.'

Surprise was shown, the woman blurting, 'Safe passage . . .' before recovering control. 'They know about the other tunnel you've been digging, Vice Admiral.'

Had that caused her to think escape was now impossible? he wondered. Had she been relieved? She was hard to gauge, was entirely contrary to what they'd come to believe of her. 'It's a false one. You need have no worries. Tell this Nolan that when the time comes for us to place the charges, we will be ready.'

'And Berlin?' she asked.

'A simple message of five-letter groupings. The Kapitan-leutnant will give it to you after we have left. Memorize the groupings then destroy the message. Have Mrs. Tulford send them over. Berlin will agree to the IRA's demands.'

'But . . . but what about the last of the explosives?'

A logical concern she'd not avoided and he would acknowledge with a curt nod. 'Nolan's problem and yours.'

They had realized that Trant and Jimmy would leave the dynamite where it was in hopes of catching Nolan. Taking all but one of the candles, they left her with Erich and the others, none of whom said a thing. All just simply looked at her, Erich still over by the altar, Bauer still behind her, and Hans Schleiger by the side door from which the High Command had departed.

'Mary, have you brought us another bullet?'

Even now he still did not move. Reluctantly she unbuttoned her blouse and found them both. She mustn't let Erich and the others realize how terrified she really was and had been, yet mustn't let them think she was invulnerable—they'd want her to be just the opposite, would want always to believe they had the upper hand.

Only then did Erich grin. 'Still warm,' he said, glancing at each of the others before pinching out the candle.

Mary waited. She mustn't run, mustn't cry out, must just try to be still and yet . . . and yet none of them moved. 'If you harm me in any way, you'll get nowhere,' she quavered.

It was Erich who said, 'Why should we when you've been so useful?'

The patient dripping of water came from somewhere.

'Be careful what you say to the British from now on, Mary.'

Erich had moved to stand in front of her. As her blouse was unbuttoned by him, Bauer pinned her arms to her sides but he did not laugh at her, just held her in a vice for his captain who slid a small, folded bit of paper in and under her left breast before kissing her lightly on the lips and saying, '*Liebling*, there are no tears?' and buttoning her up.

'Nolan now has a man inside the British garrison, Mary. Don't try to betray us. Bachmann had to hang.'

There were seven five-letter groups in the message. They'd all been written in a line with slashes to separate them. It made no sense when read straight through, was simply a jumble of letters. Only twice was one repeated in sequence. There were two of the letter I and, at the end, two Cs. CCRMR—C-and-C U-boats Berlin? Was RMR some sort of code for Vice Admiral Huber? CCRMR did have that ring to it.

GBXLM/AKZOM/DORPT/FCJAU/SIIMN/VGDRQ/CCRMR . . . MOST URGENT YOU AGREE ALL DEMANDS RELEASE STOP HAVE DETAILS ENEMY RADAR NORTH ATLANTIC LOSSES FOR C-AND-C U-BOATS STOP HUBER.

That might be it—something substantial but far too many letters. By cutting, using a pencil and paper at her desk, she ended up with: MOST URGENT AGREE STOP DETAILS ENEMY RADAR STOP RMR, but if the British had recovered Erich's ciphers intact would Huber and the others, forced with mounting IRA losses, not have wanted to signal this as well, though in an entirely different code? One known only to C-and-C U-boats Berlin? Each letter might then be transcribed into two or even three others, or into numbers, thereby allowing a much longer message.

MOST URGENT YOU AGREE IRA DEMANDS ESCAPE PLAN TRALANE CASTLE EARLY NOVEMBER STOP U-121 CIPHERS RECOVERED BY BRITISH STOP CODES BROKEN REPEAT BROKEN STOP TOGETHER WITH DETAILS NEW ENEMY RADAR EXPLAINS INCREASED U-BOAT LOSSES NORTH ATLANTIC STOP HUBER.

Or simply: URGENT OFFICERS U-121 ESCAPE HANGING STOP HUBER.

She would never know the answer, never be able to memorize the groupings, not with the state her mind was in. Mary smoothed the tiny slip of paper out. Even when held up to the light, in reverse, the letters made no sense but gave a further possibility to the decoding.

Caithleen had gone to bed and had been looked in on hours ago. Hamish must have decided to stay over in Belfast where he'd gone to lodge a stiff protest over Brian Doherty's being denied immediate medical attention. The house felt strange without him and Robbie.

Leaving the light on, she went downstairs to his study, but left the room in darkness. He loved his books, his fishing and his dog. As always the books smelled musty at first. Tobacco smoke hung about for ages, especially if from a pipe. There was a warmth, though, to the room, a comfort.

She must have slept for an hour, not much longer. The afghan she'd pulled over herself had fallen to the floor—she'd become cold. That's why she had awakened, or was it?

BETRAYAL

The ashes in the grate had gone to dust through which ember cracks seemed all but lost and the caking grey of the peat crumbled as it fell.

The wind, never calm for long, was gusting fitfully in the beeches, the shutters were creaking.

When a mouse made its way across the hearth, Mary relaxed at its furtive progress, but when it scurried away, she sat up, sucking in a breath, her heart hammering as she looked for something with which to defend herself, but then . . . then the little fellow came back.

There were crumbs on the hearth. Toast had been made. Cinnamon toast. Mrs. Haney's precious cinnamon. Hamish *would* let Robbie lick the crumbs from his plate, but since some of them must have been missed, and the toast waved about a good bit, why that could only mean that Hamish had . . .

Running, moving swiftly, Mary went silently through the house and up to her room to hide the message and burn her attempts at decoding.

Lights off, the black-out curtains flung open, she looked out into the night, knowing he and Robbie must be out there, knowing, too, that so was Jimmy Allanby and several of the men.

This thing wasn't going to end easily, and she'd best get used to that.

Parker's body had been placed in an open coffin on the plain deal table in the centre of Mrs. Haney's house. White bedsheets had been wrapped around the coffin. Crosses, made from black crepe paper, had been scattered, each of their crosspieces twisted by deft motions of the woman's hands.

Mary knew she couldn't help but see those motions in memory. Several women in black, with lace shawls over their heads and tied tightly under their chins, sat around the body telling their beads and muttering prayers. There was no keening as such, no wailing now.

Men of all ages but mostly older, sat around the perimeter walls of this one room that constituted a house she'd never been in before, their black suits, boots and pinched collars only adding to the glum expressions, they trying to keep life in the clay pipes they'd been given.

A plate of cut shag lay on a chair by the hearth. Mrs. Haney got up and they embraced, the woman whispering, 'M'am, you shouldn't have.'

'I had to, Mrs. Haney. He was my friend.'

'He was indeed, that he was.'

A fine linen table napkin—a relic of some estate, their own perhaps—had been spread over Parker's bullet-shattered face.

'He died quick, he did,' whispered Ria, that lump still in her throat, she having taken the doctor's missus by the arm. 'And here is me that was always criti-cruelling him.'

'Now you didn't, Mrs. Haney. Not really. He always had a kind word for you.'

'He did. Now I know he did.'

There was a turf fire in the hearth, the kettle on the boil and the air reeking of tobacco smoke, the closeness of the crowd and the scent of poteen.

'Dr. Fraser, God bless him, was by th' morn, he was, missus.'

'And Robbie,' she said, grateful to know that Hamish was safe, though that hadn't been the reason she'd come. She had owed it to Parker.

Mrs. Haney's husband got up to welcome her, a man too tall for the doorway of his house, all bones, knees and elbows, and of a deep and weathered shyness. He offered her his chair and took it from the wall so that she could sit among the women, knowing as he must that she'd not been to church in years and wasn't even of their faith, but that neither mattered. She had come across the hills to be with them and that was enough.

Later the scones were passed. There was bramble jam and spiced crab-apple jelly, brown bread and good country butter, sponge cake, queen cakes and a bowl of barley sugar all of which had been favourites of the deceased at one time or another.

There were three bottles of sherry, too, and she had the thought that Hamish must have brought them.

'M'am, Bridget and I have found that button you was needing.'

'Oh good. I knew you would, Mrs. Haney. It's such a lovely blouse. I'd hate to have to change all the buttons.' This, too, had been said in a whisper, but Parker wouldn't have minded the lie of it. Not Parker.

Ria found more of the heart-shaped queen cakes that were stuffed with saved-up currants. Mrs. Fraser was that partial to them, she took another and then another. Eating for two she was. 'Will you be taking Caithleen to Dublin soon, m'am?'

'On Sunday, God willing.'

Folks came and went. At no time were there less than twenty in the house, the single candle fluttering at each disturbance, the husband getting up to greet them all, he saying exactly the same thing to each as he'd said to herself.

Crickets chirped on the hearth. Mrs. Haney gave her a nudge. 'William has gone away for a bit, m'am. To my sister's in Kilkenny. I've told th' doctor, I have.'

'I'm glad. It was good of you to think of William, Mrs. Haney.'

'Bridget is on her way to my brother who has a farm in

County Meath and is in need of help, he having a wife who is with her sixth and due at any moment.'

'Did Hamish ask you to send Bridget and William away?'

'That he did, m'am, and give them each a five-pound note. Back wages, he said. Back wages, says I? Ah and sure they was and that girl will spend it all before she ever gets there. Not a penny saved. Licorice most likely, and them movie magazines or Bing Crosby records if she can still find them, not that my brother has one of them machines on which to play them, as has the doctor.'

Walking back across the fields Mary felt a oneness with the place she hadn't felt before. It had been right of her to have stopped there awhile. No one had tried to contact her and she'd had the feeling, too, that they'd not have dared, and would not have been welcome. Nolan and Fay Darcy would be on the run for days perhaps. Somehow she would have to find a way to get the dynamite out of the stable loft without anyone realizing what she'd done, and somehow she was going to have to hide it somewhere else, and lastly, she admitted, somehow she was going to have to get Sunday over with.

After that she would see about the bomb. An alarm clock might do, but it would, perhaps, be too loud; then, too, thirty ms couldn't mean a delay of thirty seconds. Electricity was instantaneous. Millimetres? Milli . . . Milliseconds? Ms, yes, that was what the label on the packet must have meant. An electrical blasting cap with a thirty-millisecond delay.

It was as if Parker was smiling down at her, as if he'd told her exactly what to do.

At supper there was little talk and, in the evening, none at all until she could stand it no longer. The fly-tying lamp was on in a far corner, over the cluttered workbench that was jammed against the books. Robbie was at his feet and when Hamish thought he might need some hair, he spoke softly, asking permission before clipping off a bit.

Was it a Yellow Dog he was tying, a Hairy Mary or a Jock Scott? Hamish often experimented with concoctions of his own. He tied flies in winter for pleasure and relaxation but at times like this, she knew it was because he had to think things through for himself.

Neither he nor Robbie turned to look up as she came into the room. A knot in the silk thread was being teased. 'Mary, it's dangerous for a woman to interrupt a man while he's on important work like this.'

That 'work' being spelled *wurk*. 'Hamish, I've decided to take the train to Dublin this time. Will you drive us over in the car to the station at Scarva? I don't want to be late. I'd like to catch the morning mail.'*

Fraser warned himself to ignore the positive tone and improper use of the motor. 'I thought the colonel said Sunday?'

Why wouldn't he look at her? Had Bannerman and Trant told him everything? They must have.

'Sunday?' he asked again.

'Yes, but the shops will all be closed. We can't send Caithleen off without a winter coat and gloves. A new dress . . .'

'A full wardrobe, is it?' he arched, the frugal, parsimonious Scot he wasn't.

Peacock feathers were now being selected. 'Don't be so damned stubborn!'

'Jesus, woman, you've made me prick a finger!'

---

* Train service to Dublin and within the South soon began to lessen due to the ever-increasing shortage of coal, which was obtained from England.

He had *shouted* at her. 'Sorry.'

'How did you convince the colonel to let you go?'

Had they not talked to him? 'I gave them what they wanted.'

'Trant and the colonel?'

He had still not looked at her. 'Yes.'

'They'll want everything, lass. You know they'll stop at nothing.'

'Hamish, I had no choice.'

'And what did Erich have to say about it?'

He was being cruel now. 'Nothing. It's . . . it's finished between us. I . . . I never want to see him again.'

The chair was one of those office things but scrounged from some church jumble or flea. Fraser pivoted sharply round to face her, she finding that she couldn't force herself to look at him. Dear God, he ached to reach out to her, to put an end to it all and wrap his arms about her, but he mustn't do that, she had to decide for herself. 'They're using you, lass. *Och*, I've been the biggest fool, but I had to give you head. I thought . . .'

Mary wished he wouldn't make it harder for her. 'It was a bargain I made. I'm keeping my side of it.'

He arched his eyebrows. 'Let's hope the colonel keeps his. I'd no trust that man wi' my wallet were I dying in th' middle of the road.'

'Why "the road," Hamish? Why?'

It had hurt her deeply, but in for a penny, in for a pound. 'It's as good a place as any, isn't it? Parker saw fit to use it. He died quick, I gather.'

And cruel again! 'Look, I know you don't trust me. You think I'm up to things I'm not. That business at Parker's had nothing to do with me.'

256

Her voice had climbed again. 'Didn't it?' he shouted.

Cruel yet again! 'I *want* to help Caithleen. Is that wrong of me? Well, is it?'

'Don't you dare get haughty with me, my girl.'

'I'm not "your girl." Don't you ever patronize me!'

And clenching her fists, was it? 'You listen to me, my lass. Liam Nolan killed two women near Malvern before that bomb he set off. He murdered them in their sleep, Mary. The one because she was the mother of the other and would have given him away; the other because she'd been to bed with him that very night.'

Then he *had* been talking to Bannerman and . . . 'Trant told Caithleen and I that Nolan had done that. Well, not all of it, but enough.'

'And it doesn't matter? And you don't know why the major told you? Mary, for God's sake wake up! They're no blind. The IRA are using you. Trant and the colonel must know of it. Jimmy Allanby certainly does.'

'Yet none of them are saying so—is that what you've been thinking? Jimmy can believe what he wants. It just isn't true.'

Furious with her, he tossed a hand. 'Then go to Dublin by motor. Take the bloody thing and be gone.'

He couldn't mean that, he couldn't. 'Darling, don't be so stubborn. Just help me by playing dumb. Drive us to the station and . . . and kiss us each good-bye.'

'Mary, what in God's name have you got yourself into?'

His voice had leapt; hers wouldn't. 'A game in which there can be no winners.'

'Has it come to that?'

He'd been subdued by the thought. 'It has, and now you know.'

'*Och*, I wish you'd let me help.'

All the fight had suddenly gone out of him. 'Then do exactly as I've asked. Keep out of things. Just trust me.'

He reached for Robbie and took him into his lap. 'Fool that I've been, I thought the war would pass us by.'

Robbie licked Hamish's chin; he rubbing Robbie's throat. 'Admit it, you wanted to escape all the rest, not just the war.'

'But find there is no escape, not even in the bottle—is that what you're thinking?'

'Yes, that's it exactly. Get drunk, if you can find a drop left. Go on a bender and stay the hell out of my life!'

The rain . . . always there was a rain some place in Ireland. Every minute of every day some place was getting a damned good soaking.

She thought it the most drenched place in the world next to the rain forests of the Amazon.

The wheels of the train never let up either. Caithleen was trying to look at the pictures in the magazines she had brought along for the girl. The compartment was jammed—the old, the young, all morose, all staring at her in that mindless way cattle would. No manners. None at all! 'She's not my daughter, and she's not my sister either,' she said to the brat whose scruffy shoes had kicked her own one last time, his grey school cap askew.

The boy stuck out his tongue and was slapped on the wrist by the mother. 'He's going to have braces put on his teeth,' said the woman. 'It being wartime and all, it's cheaper in the South, I'm sure.'

'You'd better be,' said Mary tartly, knowing it would shut the woman up and hating herself all the more. It had been cruel of her to have said what she had to Hamish last night. He'd never forgive her, poor darling, but she'd had to stop him somehow, couldn't have him lying in some road.

'Look, I'm sorry I said that, Mrs. . . .'

'Fitzpatrick.'

'I'm Dr. Fraser's wife.'

'Oh and are you? Robin, if you fidget about again, I'll take your drawers down and paddle that bum of yours!'

The rheumy eyes of an old man found delight in the exchange, but when she smiled back at him, Mary knew she was being held by that look of his. He'd got on with them at the station. There'd been six or seven others, though she couldn't remember the faces, hadn't really paid much attention.

Unsettled by his continued staring, she turned away. Sooty smoke and steam from the engine billowed against the compartment windows, and for a time the landscape was blotted out. They'd not catch a glimpse of the sea until well south of Drogheda. Miles and miles yet. Hamish had been right, of course. The IRA would kill her. Once they had the message from the Germans, she'd be of no further use. Hadn't Erich warned her that Nolan had a man inside the castle? One of the garrison, he'd said.

She wasn't to betray the Nazis—yes, she had best be calling them that now, would have to face right up to what she'd been doing.

She wasn't to betray the IRA either, yet they'd get rid of her just as soon as they could.

And she wasn't to betray the British Army and her country, or they'd have her up for being a traitor and shoot her down with pleasure.

The Vice Admiral Huber had said she was to tell Nolan that when the time came for them to place the charges, they'd be ready, but would it be the last thing she ever said?

Somehow the Germans had learned of the dynamite. That could only have been from the man Nolan had inside the castle. But why put someone in there unless they no longer trusted her or thought, perhaps, she'd be removed?

The plan must be to break them all out of Tralane in hopes that a select few would manage to escape. No wonder Trant and the colonel were worried. Jimmy Allanby would watch the stable like a hawk, but would Nolan and the others really need her anymore?

The explosives would have to be moved—she'd already thought of that. She was the only one who could do it, but would that be enough and how could she possibly do so without Jimmy finding out?

'M'am?' Her left shoulder was being nudged. 'M'am?' It was the old man, and he was teetering over her as the coach rocked sideways at a bend.

'Yes . . . ? Well, what is it, please?' Must he lean so closely?

'A barley sugar from the wake of an *ould* friend for you and the girl.'

The train nearly threw him off balance, but he managed to grab the strap that hung by the door and, with the help of a sailor going south on leave, to lean over her again.

There was a small but crumpled white paper bag in his hand. Embarrassed and in confusion, she thanked him.

'Go you first,' he said, indicating the bag as he let himself be flung back into his seat.

Alongside a single paper twist of barley sugar, her fingers touched two cartridges, and for perhaps ten seconds, Mary couldn't move. 'Nolan . . . ?' she blurted, looking up at the man.

'Two others in me pocket, missus. Ah, and I'm sure there are.'

He squeezed himself sideways, pushing the Fitzpatrick woman with him as he retrieved the things and then got up again. Twists of barley sugar were hesitantly extended, not bullets, thank God. Again he was very nearly thrown off his feet; again sooty smoke and steam rushed past the windows, blotting out everything else.

'Two,' he said with a wink when the Fraser woman had turned back to look at him with wounded eyes. 'A tall one with the humour of a rake handle and the temper of a Mother Superior's broom. He'll be the easiest for you to spot.'

Again he allowed himself to be flung back into his seat but Caithleen, on hearing all that had been said, had panicked, burst into tears and was about to make a run for it if she could. 'Caithleen, don't!'

The girl sat down. The rheumy eyes of the old man took her impassively in, and Caithleen turned swiftly away to stare out the window and hide her tears.

Puzzled as to what was going on, and sensing trouble, the boy took to glancing from one to another of them while the Belfast draper buried his face in his sample book.

''Tis t' other one I'd be watching, missus,' said the old man. 'You being on your own like and with the girl.'

Mrs. Fitzpatrick had long since taken notice but would have to be ignored. 'Who?' asked Mary. 'What does he look like?'

'The backside of an Angus bull and every bit as tiresome. Two coaches back. Go have a look. The rest of you keep shut or you'll feel the end of my pistol.'

Only the sailor, a tow-haired boy of twenty or so, showed any sign of objecting. The woman and her son would say nothing until they got to where they were staying. The draper would simply be glad to get off the train in one piece.

As she left the compartment, Mary reached out to the sailor and, finding a firmness that puzzled, said, 'Please do as he says. We'll be all right. You mustn't worry.'

The train hit a smooth stretch along the canal near Poyntz-pass. A bridge came up, a lock, the lockkeeper's house in ruins, a legacy of the Troubles which had destroyed so much of Newry.

Then they were by and the train was running, running, and the passengers were all sitting, some smoking cigarettes, some looking up at her as she passed by their compartments, others engrossed in a book, a newspaper, or studying the ends of their fingers and wanting the trip to be over. British soldiers, too, British sailors, British airmen . . . Loud laughter, the not-too-secret roll of dice and the *clickety-clack* of the wheels. It all seemed so ordinary, but Trant had been one step ahead of her and had had them followed, and of course Fay Darcy and Liam Nolan or Kevin O'Bannion—yes, it would have been him—had made sure they, too, were on to everything.

Caithleen had been terrified she'd be gunned down. Seventeen years old and her legs twitching on that cramped floor, the Fitzpatrick woman in hysterics . . .

She had reached the second coach. Now she'd have to take her time, would have to walk slowly along the thing until she saw the tall, thin one—he did look as if he'd such a temper.

The other one, the one she was to watch, had caught sight of her. Oh damn, it was Hamish and he was about to greet her as the wife he'd lost but never forgotten.

The washroom was cramped, the train in motion—no room to move. Hamish, his overcoat open, had pressed his hands flat against the door on either side of her, and she couldn't help loving him. He smelled so good, of tweed, pipe tobacco and whiskey, but just a little, and of himself too, himself.

'Darling, you shouldn't have come.'

'*Och*, I couldn't leave things between us like that. Besides, Caithleen won't be sent to the colonel's sister, not while I've a say in the matter. My brother Andrew and his Jean will take her in and welcome. Edinburgh's the place she needs, Mary. Warmth now, and a home she'll know is hers.'

Fraser released one hand from barricading the door long enough to brush it tenderly across her brow. 'Lass, I love you. I can't let you face this thing alone.'

There was that look of his, so hard to describe. One of great sadness but of warmth for her, of sincerity and commitment, of so many things. Trembling, Mary wrapped her arms around his waist. The train rocked, he bracing the door shut, she hesitating and uncertain still until, at last they kissed, and when they had parted a little, he said, '*Och*, I like it when you do that,' and she flung herself at him, said, 'Hold me. Please don't ever let me go.'

The train stopped, but instantly started up again as someone banged fiercely on the door. Squeezing round, Mary managed to open it a crack, only to see that it was the brat from her compartment. His twisted face was a mass of freckles and suspicion, two plum-blue eyes, a pug nose and a mouth that opened. 'Me mam says to tell ye that Paddy bastard with the gun has boogered off.'

Hamish slammed the door in his face. Mary pressed her forehead against it, but when he took her by the shoulders, she said sharply, 'Go away, please! You don't understand. You can't! They'll kill you if you interfere.'

'The Shelbourne on Saint Stephen's Green, please.' She wouldn't go to the White Horse Inn on Wilton Terrace, not this time, not if she was being followed.

'Right you are, m'am. Just wrap that fine blanket about your knees and we'll be off.'

Trant had anticipated things and had called ahead. A car had been waiting at the station, and before either she or Hamish could object, the three of them had been driven to the dockside.

Hamish and Caithleen had been sent on their way—there'd been no question of it, he saying at the last, 'No, we mustn't kiss good-bye, lass. We must let them think what we want them to believe.' He grim and unforgiving, or so it must have seemed, she knowing it would be best that way and extending a hand.

Even though she had wanted it, the separation had come too soon, too suddenly, too unexpectedly. A loss she had felt deeply and still did. Trant hadn't wanted Hamish around any more than had the IRA. There'd be questions now, and she'd have to keep saying Hamish and she had parted for good.

One had to sit sideways in these horse-drawn cabs. It gave good views of the streets and let her watch both behind and in front. Dublin was, as always, bustling in its quiet, dignified way. Not like London or Paris or New York before the war but more like Toronto used to be. There was lots of traffic around Tara Station and on Pearse Street. A lovely city. Georgian to its core. Fanlights above the painted doors, green letter boxes, green call boxes, Gaelic signs to mark the streets.

When another cab pulled out from the kerb, Mary knew she really was being followed, but the worst thing was, she couldn't get a good look at the person. A woman, this much she knew. Young, too. Not Fay Darcy, though. It couldn't be Fay.

It wasn't. It was some British agent, someone from MI6 or MI5.

Cyclists swarmed past, all going to their appointed destinations to the clip, clopping of the horse.

Hamish hadn't given her back her wedding ring, though she'd known he had wanted to desperately. He had left that to Caithleen. It was still clenched in a fist. One of the cabs passed by, a man in a bowler hat in that one, he touching its brim in salute and smiling.

A Guinness lorry came next, it honking loudly as if they'd collide, the ring falling to the blanket to roll away, its gold catching the light as she made a desperate grab for it and stuffed it into her coat pocket to lie there safely with the bullets.

She would wear it around her neck on the string that held the key to her cedar chest. She wouldn't put it back on her finger, not yet, but it was good to know Hamish still loved her. It made her feel warm inside and able to face things better. He'd be out of the way for a while and safe, and when it was all over, would forgive her even if no one else did.

8

'Will there be just yourself, m'am?' asked the waiter.

'Yes, thanks. Would you bring me a gin sling, the prawn soup followed by the smoked salmon and then a salad, please?'

'And for the main course?' Gin at the supper table and she not English, Irish or from any of those parts. An American, was it?

'The beef Wellington,* I think, and an iced sherbet, and coffee if you still have it. Yes, coffee.'

'You'll be wanting a brandy, then, to top it all off, will you?' Was she away to the races in the middle of the night?

'A double, but . . . but let me have it in this.'

Jesus, Mary and Joseph, a bloody flask and silver, no less, from the Highlands! 'That I will, m'am. That I will.'

The main dining room at the Shelbourne was all a-glitter.

---

* While there were, even in England, vast differences from area to area in what was and was not available, a reference to a Dublin visit in February 1942 gave the peace of lighted streets and consuming all the butter, meat and alcohol wanted. Even in 1944, a hotel menu taken back to London produced tears. There were shortages but in general these were never as harsh as in England. Fuel was the major concern and it became desperate.

A last bastion of British rule, the hotel had been done over in the late 1880s. Life-size statues of bare-breasted Nubian princesses stood outside the entrance in all weathers, holding the lamp standards: turbaned ebony and gold, wrought iron and gas lamps. The foyer was grand and very Victorian, the ceilings high and done with exquisite plasterwork in swirls of leaves and roses, doves and cherubs.

The chandeliers were of Waterford crystal. The grand piano gleamed. The tables, with their silver, crystal, candles and starched white linen, were all occupied now, the men in dinner jackets and black bow ties, the ladies dressed to the nines and off to the Abbey Theatre. All very elegant and unlike the war and the North, but Dublin, she knew, was a city of much beauty and great poverty. From Saint Stephen's Green to Trinity College Park, and from that line stretching to the southeast right to the Grand Canal and beyond it some, there was one of the finest residential districts anywhere. Once outside of this area, in the adjacent Irishtown or Belleville or over further west into the industrial area of Dolphin's Barn and up north, across the Liffey into the heart of old Dublin and watch out.

There were huge and depressingly poor areas of what had been loosely called 'decayed housing.' Gorgeous old Georgian houses gone to rack and ruin, their fanlights broken out, the paintwork chipped and the red bricks of someone's former delight now scrawled in chalk with all manner of trash. Garbage reeked, cats and people squalled, fought, kicked, punched, swore like blue murder, the kids with runny noses and their clothes hanging out each way, the adults not much different. Young women with the faces of the old, the men a shambles of crumpled stovepipe suits, hats, boots and cigarettes, most of them out of work and hating it but knowing there was little they could do but one thing, that being to join someone else's war.*

She didn't want to have to go into any of those districts tonight. They'd not understand why she was there in the fog, would think her lost perhaps, or simply try to rob her.

This afternoon, after finally getting rid of the people Trant had tailing her—the man and the girl at the station—she had telephoned Mrs. Tulford from a call box only to find that the woman no longer worked at the White Horse Inn. 'Was you the lady from up North, missus?' the man on the reception desk had asked.

He had told her to ring back at 10.00 tonight. Ten, and a fog rolling in from Dublin Bay with the stench of soot and sewage.

'Your gin sling, m'am.'

'Oh, thanks. I'd forgotten about it. Look, could I ask a favour? Would you bring me a large Bushmills instead? I'll pay for the two of them.'

'A large whiskey it is, m'am.' And was she going out a-whoring tonight with them melting eyes of hers? Canadian, be Gad. From Orillia, no less, and where th' divil would that be? Among the savages?

She was dressed fine enough for the whoring, though more for the likes of this place. A russet suit of good cloth and exceptional fit, a cameo at the throat and a jerkin of soft yellow mohair with buttons down the front and her hair pulled back into one of them ponytails as if she really was going off to the races and had just come in from a jaunt.

The dogfights? he wondered. One saw all types even in the fanciest of hotels. An attractive woman, this Mrs. Mary Ellen

---

* By the war's end, those who had left to work in factories in Britain had all but cured Southern Ireland's unemployment.

Fraser and she claiming the sanctity of marriage but without the wearing of her wedding ring.

A Protestant. She'd have to be one of them. It being Sunday tomorrow, she'd sleep in heavy.

When he brought the whiskey, she asked for a pencil and paper, and he thought that she'd give him the room number of her gentleman friend and ask that the note be passed along but she just set the bloody things off to her left for later, and took to sipping her whiskey. A little water was added, then a dollop more.

Mary set the gold pocket watch she'd bought this afternoon in a shop on Grafton Street beside the silver-plated candlestick. Hamish and Caithleen would be in Holyhead. There had been nothing on the news to say there'd been an attack by submarines or enemy aircraft over the Irish Sea, but still it was a worry. They'd probably have to take the train to Birmingham and change over there. Birmingham had been hit severely. London got so much of it, but other places did too.

She hoped they'd make it, hoped things would all be over by the time Hamish got back. The change to whiskey hadn't just been because of what lay ahead of her tonight, but as a salute to the man she'd married and deceived and now loved again with all her heart. How could she ever have strayed from that?

It wasn't the time to ask such questions nor to anguish over guilt. The pocket watch was a Longines whose gold case had been made in Canada but whose jewelled movement was Swiss. Not a new watch but one that had been brought in for repairs and never collected. She had wanted a Longines especially because her wristwatch had never let her down and she couldn't have that happen. No she couldn't.

The hands were Big Ben-ish, with the minute hand nearly a quarter of an inch longer than the hour. The sweep second was enclosed in its own circle towards the hinge, so well below the centre and well out of the way of what she needed. Undisturbed progress.

Moving the watch, Mary brought it a little closer to the candlestick, knew that people would be looking at her and wondering why she was alone, knew that Trant's people would be waiting in the foyer probably or chatting up the desk. The redhead, with her lovely long legs, would be in the Horseshoe Bar having a gin sling or tonic. The one with the black bowler hat, the manner and the smile, would be the go-between, now to the desk, then to have another peep into the dining room to see how the dinner was being taken, then off to the bar for a visit with Miss Long Legs or up to Mrs. Mary Fraser's room to search through her things, such as they were.

They'd find nothing. The watch was here, the bullets and the message safely tucked away, but she really was playing a very dangerous game.

The prawn soup arrived though she hardly tasted it. The Longines was ticking, the second hand sweeping round while the minute hand moved much slower and much more decisively.

Hamish had given her one of his mother's diamond rings but she had never worn it much, believing it far too valuable. She would use it when she got home to drill a small hole in the watch crystal up near the number ten. That would give her fifty minutes if both of the hands were set at the twelve.

Gold was a good electrical conductor but when silver was added, in an amalgam, this did tend to slow the passage of electrical currents—she'd found that out in the library and had probably baffled Trant's people by poring over a handful of metallurgical tomes and would have to think what to say to them. Trant would want a reason, and she'd have to have something good unless he was too busy with other matters.

Yet if the candlestick represented the dry cell battery she'd purchased from a shop in Henry Street, one wire must run from a terminal to one of the wires of the blasting cap that had been pushed into the end of the primer stick.

All well and good. The other wire was the problem.

She set her soup aside to make room for her hands only to have the waiter whip the smoked salmon in front of her with its dainty wedges of toast, she not even looking up. A woman, then, he'd think, whose mind was so fixed on the time, she had set the watch in front of her! And what was she doing staring at a man's pocket watch? he'd be wondering.

The watch must be the break in the circuit, she silently said. From the other terminal of the battery, a wire would have to run to the watch and be fastened securely to the fob loop. Good electrical contacts, then. Battery all wired up and placed back in the shortbread tin next to the dynamite.

Now for the tricky part. The other wire from the blasting cap must run to the watch but never touch the face or any other part except for the crystal, since glass was a nonconductor, an insulator.

That meant fixing the bare, cleaned-off end of the wire down into the watch through the hole so that it didn't touch the face. Then when the minute hand came round to the ten, it would come up against the bare wire to complete the circuit and set off the bomb.

'Is the salmon not to your taste, m'am?'

'Did I finish the soup?' she asked, blinking up at grey mutton chops and severe blue eyes that were full of puzzlement, the cheeks flushed by the liquor he'd taken, namely one discarded gin sling.

'The soup?' she reminded him.

'That you did, m'am. Well, the most of it.' Now what the

devil was the matter with her? Had that bloody pocket watch of hers stopped?

'Just let me take my time,' she said. 'I've lots of it.'

Two timepieces of it, the other on her wrist!

'I bought this for my husband,' she said, all dreamy like and looking like Dierdre of the Lost Sorrows herself. 'I was testing it.'

Oh and were you now? 'Enjoy the salmon, m'am. Would a glass of the white not suit?'

'Instead of the whiskey? No, the whiskey's fine, thanks.'

The thought of walking alone through Dublin's back streets frightened her. She had found a set of stairs that had led down to a service entrance and from there to a lane. She would telephone the White Horse Inn from a bar, but not from here.

Nibbling at the salmon, Mary used the pencil and paper to sketch the battery, the primer stick, blasting cap and watch. It would have to work. There would be the smell, though, and she would have to worry about that later, but would wiping down the inside of the tin with vanilla help?

Twisting the paper, she burned it in the candle flame, tossed off the rest of the whiskey and laid into the salmon so much, she had to ask for another portion and if they had any capers to go with it.

Capers and lemon and stuffed baked tomatoes, potatoes, onions, cauliflower with a cheese sauce, bags of buns with butter, and a beef Wellington that would melt in the mouth. Then the lemon ice and the coffee, and more of the latter and another brandy, she being forced to fill the flask herself in front of everyone.

The room was small and squalid, the tenement to the north of Tyrone House near Summer Hill, she thought, but the trouble was, she really had no firmer idea. Two men had picked her up near the southwest corner of Saint Stephen's Green, the fog so thick the car had appeared as if out of nowhere.

There had been drunks in the street outside the tenement, drunks in its doorway and some even on the staircase sleeping it off. The stench of rotting garbage and urine had been everywhere, still was, for that matter, the wallpaper hanging in long strips and curls, or absent entirely.

O'Bannion raised a tired hand in salute but wouldn't smile. 'You find us on the run, I'm afraid, and not staying in any one place for more than a night. How have you been?'

A chair, a small suitcase, an iron cot without a mattress, a stoneware chamber pot, washstand and basin seemed to be it—he could see this in the glance around she gave. There were two blankets on the cot and a filthy pillow without a slip, the feathers sticking through, and for as long as she lived, she'd remember panicking at the thought of lice, and he could see this passing through that mind of hers like lightning. A fancy woman after all and petrified by the sight of life as it really was.

He'd indicate the chair; she'd refuse it and did, had seen the revolver lying beside him and would have to be told. 'You're being followed everywhere you go, Mrs. Fraser. What are the major and the captain up to?'

'I don't know. My husband put me on to them. I . . .'

'That husband of yours has been making a nuisance of himself.'

'He's gone with Caithleen to Edinburgh. He'll give you no more trouble.'

'Let's hope so, but a correction is needed, I think. The doctor was forcibly exited from the scene. Am I right?'

'Why make me say it?'

'I won't, but what are Trant and Allanby up to, not to mention Bannerman?'

'They . . . they must know I intend to meet with you.'

The truth at last, but pulled from her. He'd take out a cigarette but decide not to light it, would keep himself sitting on the edge of the bed in his undershirt, trousers and boots. She'd notice that his hair was wet, would know he'd been out and about himself, and would wonder where the devil he'd been. 'Oh they know you'll be meeting me, but even I'm not what they want. That'd only be the half of it, now wouldn't it?'

The carousing, the whoring and the crying all seemed to reverberate through the tenement. Mary knew that he had wanted her to experience it, that he'd had to give her reasons for what he did. He looked grey and gaunt and not at all like she'd remembered from the ruins near the school on the outskirts of Ballylurgen.

When she didn't answer, he said, 'You see it's this way. De Valera and his government don't want us dealing with the Nazis for fear the Brits will step in and occupy the country, having first bombed the hell out of it—what they don't want of it, that is. They also think we're a threat to their precious government in other ways, so they've had a talk with the major, they have. Let us keep an eye on Mrs. Mary Ellen Fraser and see where she goes. Let us cooperate with you. Send in MI5 and we'll turn a blind eye for a bit so long as you let us in on it. Have you gone over to the other side, I wonder?'

'Of course not. How could I?'

'Then why did you let Mr. Morgan Davies follow you from that fancy hotel of yours?'

'But . . . but no one followed me. I was certain of it!'

Her dismay was clear enough. 'The point is, they're on to you. Oh they'll not tell you this and we'll play the game too, so long as it suits us, but Morgan Davies was not to be messed with, and you've made me do the messing.'

Forgetting the threat of lice, she went to sit in the chair. 'Who was this Davies?'

All choked up, she was. 'One of Eire's Secret Service who'll be pushing up the daffodils come spring. Now let us have it. You've a message for Mrs. Tulford.'

Had she served her purpose? wondered Mary. Would he kill her just as he'd killed this man Davies? Nolan did have someone inside Tralane—he must have. Once the deal with Berlin was on its way, she'd be of no more use, would have to be firm then, couldn't let fear get the better of her, would have to lie a little, too, and not show it. 'The message is in code and I've had to memorize it. The German High Command at Tralane will ask for proof I've met with Mrs. Tulford and given her the message myself.'

'Or else they'll rot in that castle? Come on, Mrs. Fraser, who the hell do you think I am?'

Instantly she got up and went back to lean against the wall by the door, getting ready to run. 'Well?' he asked.

'A man who's afraid and on the run. A man whose organization here is in a shambles and whose people in the North have just been cut to ribbons. You're in no position to argue, Kevin, and neither am I.'

And tough now, was she? Mary could see him thinking this, and yes, he must have appreciated her spirit, for he smiled in that distant way a man does who has had his fancy momentarily tickled.

She'd want a little something, decided O'Bannion. 'It's a queer state we find ourselves in, now isn't it? We need the Nazis like we've never needed anyone for centuries, and they need us, yet think we're an undisciplined mob and totally ignorant of how to go about things, and we really don't give a damn what they think or stand for. Is it like it was with the Spaniards at Kinsale, I wonder?'

That battle with the English had taken place in 1601.

'Mrs. Fraser, the Irish Secret Service and the British MI5 want Mrs. Tulford and her wireless very badly. They want Liam, too, and everything else they can get, myself as well, but Ursula is high up there on the agenda, otherwise they'd have had you in for a session and that husband of yours would have found you in the Garda's report of the day. Beaten—knocked about like you wouldn't believe—raped, they'd have that done too. Mugged, robbed, murdered and left to lie starko on the bank of the Grand Canal which has to be one of Dublin's rankest sewers no matter the quality of the residences it passes.'

As she blanched and swallowed tightly, O'Bannion let her have it. 'You're an embarrassment to them. A traitor. Don't ever forget what I've just said, because that is exactly what they will do to you.'

He asked what had happened at Parker's farm and at Tralane, and in a halting voice, Mary told him as best she could, and he saw that the killings had upset her a good deal and that what he'd said about Trant and MI5 and the Irish Secret Service had rattled her all the more.

'What will you do with the rest of the dynamite?' he asked, and she knew that she would have to answer.

'Take it stick by stick into the house and hide it.'

'They'll be watching for just such a thing.'

'Not if I make dummy sticks out of bread dough and wrap them in heavy, greased brown paper to look like the real thing. I mustn't take all of it anyway. Some will have to be left on top so as to give the smell and hide what's happened to the rest. It's the plunger thing that worries me. That and the sacks of fuse and the blasting caps.'

She had thought about it well enough, she had, but was her

spirit building with the knowledge—did he detect a newfound resilience, a toughness she, herself, was not yet aware of?

To lead her on a bit really wouldn't be fair of him, but he'd have to do just that. 'Take only one coil of the black-powder fuse—that'll give Liam fifty feet. Take a packet of each type of blasting cap.'

'How much of the wire?'

O'Bannion gave her a queer look, wondering perhaps how she had known so much or had such an interest, but fortunately he didn't question this, just lost himself in thought again.

'The wire, yes. Two coils—no leave that. I'll tell Liam to find his own and the battery from a motorcar. Forget about the plunger. Just the dynamite. Paxo's no good.'

'Paxo?'

She was that curious it was a puzzle. 'Sodium chlorate and paraffin wax. It's highly volatile but not what we need for this job.'

'Will you try to blow a hole in the castle walls and let them all escape?'

She'd been thinking about it, all right, had been going over and over it in that head of hers. 'God willing, we'll do just that and don't you ever repeat it.'

He lost himself in thought again. At some point in the distant past he'd been wounded twice—once high up on the left part of the chest; and once, a long and ugly scar across the right arm, near the shoulder. The skin over both wounds was glazed and of a deep, dark bluish red.

O'Bannion glanced at his wristwatch. She was studying him, she was. He'd light the cigarette now, then, would let her look at him all she wanted. A pretty woman who would use that body of hers to escape—was that what she was thinking, or had she something else in mind?

'They'll be watching that stable of yours, Mrs. Fraser, but did you think to warn Liam or Fay?'

'How could I have? There wasn't time. They're still on the run for all I know.'

She was still afraid of him, thought O'Bannion, and this she couldn't have hidden. 'Is it that you're hoping, as you must have at Parker's, that they had both been among the dead?'

She would never know where she stood with any of them, but would have to be convincing, mustn't waver, not now. 'I want Erich out of Tralane, Kevin. I'm going to leave my husband and go to Germany—that's all I've got, isn't it, seeing as I'm carrying his child? Look, I know you think Erich's promise hollow, but Hamish isn't coming back. He knows I've deceived him because I've told him.'

'Oh and does he now? Lies, is it? Lies upon lies? We've a traitor in our midst down here in the South, Mrs. Fraser. A man so trusted we worshipped him yet he sold us out for silver and the promise of a better life in America. That man has now been apprehended and will be put on trial—we're not like the Black and Tans. We do give them a fair hearing. He'll be court-martialled. Is it that you're wanting to witness the execution?'

'All right, then yes. I did hope they'd have been killed at Parker's. Wouldn't you have felt the same had you been me?'

'So you didn't warn them Jimmy Allanby would be keeping that stable of yours under surveillance?'

'Like I've just said, I couldn't.'

He'd pick up his gun now and get to his feet, thought O'Bannion. He'd let her have it. 'Take off your coat, woman.'

When she didn't, he shrieked it at her. Quivering, she laid it over the back of the chair, but would she strip if asked—was that all the guts she really had in spite of that newfound toughness? 'Let's have the message. Let's not have any more of this damned business about your needing to see Ursula.'

Was he going to kill her? wondered Mary. Would she kneel and start to cry—beg him not to do it? Somehow she had to stop him. 'I . . . I've only the two bullets I was given on the train.'

Two was it and more lies? 'Let's see them, then.'

Mary turned away. She couldn't have him seeing her wedding ring and the key to the cedar chest that hung about her neck—if he found those, he would kill her. Again he shrieked, the noise of him and those of the tenement suddenly coming from everywhere only to die away to weeping.

Opening her jerkin, she unbuttoned the blouse only enough to awkwardly remove the bullets.

He took no interest in her predicament. He hefted the bullets, took two others out of that revolver of his and compared the weights.

Satisfied, he said, 'Liam ought to have been more careful. You won't be needing these until you're back in the North.'

He wasn't going to kill her yet, but when he returned them, he forced her to look into the emptiness of his eyes, said only, 'God, I hope you're not lying.'

Unbuttoning her blouse further, Mrs. Mary Ellen Fraser found the message right enough but made no attempt to dart away in fear for that life of hers. Instead, she looked steadily back at him.

It was now 2.10 a.m. 'Put the bullets away,' he said, and as he watched her, 'You lied to me.'

'The message was too long. I . . . I was afraid I'd forget something or . . . or get muddled.'

As she swallowed under scrutiny, O'Bannion knew that if forced, she would yield readily enough, but what then would be her ultimate game? To set the dogs of lust among them? She could probably do that well enough should Liam take a notion to get free with her at Fay's prompting, but was there not something else? A death wish of her own? She had that look about her and he knew he was troubled by it.

'Button up and I'll take you to Ursula.'

The drunks were settling down, and when she was shoved into the car, the slamming of its doors was overly loud in the fog. O'Bannion pushed her to the floor in the backseat and held her face-down as the car took off and they drove through the night for perhaps fifteen minutes, it was hard to tell, she trying to plot the route.

Let out some place—a lane, Mary thought—she was by then blindfolded and he had to lead her, his steps cautious, his grip telegraphing the anxiety he felt. He'd have drawn his gun, would shoot her if he had to.

But then they took some stairs—a short flight in at a tradesman's entrance, she thought. The landing was cramped. He removed the blindfold and whispered that she was to go on up to the fourth floor. 'Ursula will be waiting. Pacing about like blazes probably. I'll just have a look around.'

Mrs. Tulford had left the back door unlocked but was nowhere in sight, not in the spotless kitchen, nor in the dining room with all its silver out on the sideboard. The flat was Edwardian. There were gorgeous oils, the portrait of a woman in a fabulous gown with a choker of exquisite pearls; one of a thoroughbred and three times winner of the Grand National, for the cups and ribbons were there to one side of the clock. Other paintings were of the hunt, of foxhounds on the run and grouse and pheasant on the wing. The carpets were Afghan— there were two rifles leaning against a far corner, a pith helmet much like the one Hamish had in his study . . .

BETRAYAL

The Tulford woman hadn't been pacing about at all. She'd been up on the roof stringing her wireless aerial.

'Mrs. Fraser, you're late. Please write out the message for me at once.'

The woman was tall, thin, severe, iron-grey, blue-eyed behind wire-rimmed spectacles and when she saw the blouse being unbuttoned, scathing.

'These people are fools. They send their men and women in without the least security or training and then don't wonder why they get apprehended or killed, only that there must be a traitor among them!'

Ursula Telford was in her sixties. The hair was pinned back in a bun whose severity matched the stern and unyielding manner of a *Kindermädchen.*

'They let you people carry messages like that. *Ach*, you stupid, stupid girl. Did you think the British or the Irish Secret Service wouldn't strip you naked to find this?'

'What does it mean?'

'It does not matter to me and is of no consequence to you.'

'But you must know?'

'Why should I? It's simply a sequence of letters broken into groupings. If they had wanted me to know the contents they'd have written it in clear. This way is best and far more secure, though I still must re-encode it.'

Mary knew she would never get another chance to ask. 'Does O'Bannion know how to transmit?'

'Why do you ask such a thing?'

The suspicion had been instant. 'No reason. I . . . I just wondered.'

'Erich Kramer has asked it of you?'

---

* A nanny.

'Why, yes. Yes, he did. They're . . .' Mary glanced towards the back door. 'Worried the IRA might . . .'

'Kill me? Don't be silly. Without me, these people are nothing.'

Kevin O'Bannion would be on his way up the stairs. 'What is it they want from Berlin, Mrs. Tulford? The Vice Admiral Huber asked me to find out.'

'Money, what else? A million pounds sterling in one- and five-pound notes.' Again the Fraser woman glanced towards the door . . .

'And guns?' asked Mary.

What a strange person you are, thought Ursula. So pretty and yet so foolish. 'One hundred Luger pistols, ten thousand rounds of ammunition for those, a dozen MG42 machine-guns, forty Schmeissers and another one hundred thousand rounds. Incendiaries, mines and grenades, most of which I cannot possibly see them getting since a submarine has far too little room to spare when outward bound. Are you really in love with this Kramer?'

'Very much. He's . . . he's going to take me with him.'

Was she really so gullible? 'Then we'll be together and can get to know one another better. Now I must get back to the wireless. Tell Kevin there is some beer and other things in the kitchen.'

Kevin . . . 'Whose place is this?'

'That is not for you to know and you should not ask it.'

'Has he been staying here with you?'

'He comes and goes. I was lucky to get away from the White Horse, and lucky he was here in Dublin to help me.'

'Then it's one of their safe houses?'

Such an interest could only mean trouble. Kevin would have to be warned of it. 'As safe as anything of theirs can be in a country where everyone else learns only too quickly what they're up to. By himself, Kevin is . . . How should I say it? Special. But in trying to lead the others he'll be lost unless he's very careful. Their best men nearly always are. These people talk far too much. Now that is all, and you would be wise not to repeat what I've said.'

Alone again, Mary moved about the flat. There were some fine pieces of porcelain in a superb mahogany vitrine. Dover pillow lace lay under Derby and Coalport cups and saucers, French biscuit porcelain figurines and lovely Meissen ones. A handful of Roman and Etruscan coins—nothing too valuable, not of gold, but things picked up on archaeological digs, lay scattered between the figurines, forcing her to ask again whose place it was and to wonder why its owner would have let them use it.

The woman whose portrait hung above the mantelpiece must have been the owner's mother. Beautiful, regal—the very epitome of the English aristocracy, and there was Mrs. Ursula Tulford huddled somewhere over her wireless, tapping out the message in dots and dashes at 3.02 a.m. Did she always transmit in the small hours of the morning?

A million pounds. Enough to finance such a campaign of terror, but also guns and ammunition enough to start a second front. No wonder de Valera and his government were worried; no wonder Trant and Jimmy and the colonel would do all they could to stop it.

O'Bannion watched her from the doorway. He had the thought that she was equal in beauty to the woman into whose portrait she seemed to have retreated, and he didn't like the thought of his thinking this. 'Where's Ursula?'

Startled, Mrs. Mary Ellen Fraser gripped the mantelpiece but didn't turn, exuding a fear he found worrying.

She told him plainly enough, but just what the bloody hell had she been thinking? 'Don't get to wondering whose place this is. Forget what you've seen of it. The owner's away, that's all, and we're using it in his absence.'

'You've been staying here with her. That . . . that tenement room was only for show and my benefit.'

She still hadn't turned to face him, was still hanging on to that mantelpiece as if it were the rack. 'Lying's become a pastime with us.'

He would have smiled at the thought had he known, but she wished he'd not used that term, for death really was the Irish pastime. 'Did you have to shoot that Secret Service man?'

Had she hoped it not possible of him? 'Davies got in the way. Look, we're fighting a war. I couldn't have you leading him to us, now could I?'

'So you had to check everything out and take me halfway across the city only to bring me back?'

O'Bannion felt the curse rise in his gullet but forced it down even though she was being far too smart for her own good and still stood with her back to him, gripping the mantelpiece like that. 'Davies is the one in the canal, Mrs. Fraser. Be thankful it's not yourself. Now hopefully no one will know you've been out and about the night, and you'll be away first thing in the morning.'

'Right after breakfast?'

At last she had turned to face him. 'I didn't think you were eating that these days.'

'In your own way you're just as cruel as Liam, aren't you?'

He didn't answer. He simply took out a cigarette and, pausing to look at her again, lit it.

The Tulford woman didn't come back into the room until 4.27 a.m. Berlin couldn't have been pleased with the contents of the message. There must have been argument, discussion—others to contact, orders from above, so many things, and then the wording of a reply and its encoding and sending, but when Kevin asked its meaning, the woman said, 'That is only for the High Command at Tralane and you know this. In any case, it is not in the code I use.'

'Try it and see,' he said.

'I already have.'

'Then bloody well try it again!'

'Kevin, it will do no good. I can't go back. I've closed off the set and shut down and taken in the aerial. If I were to try to reach them, they would automatically think the wireless compromised. In any case, the code . . .'

'They don't just go by the day, Ursula. I'm not a bloody fool. Sometimes the code is used for several days.'

The woman reached out to him. 'But it would not matter. As I've already told you, the vice admiral must be using a code that is known only to C-and-C U-boats and himself.'

'Then she'll have to take the message back into Tralane for us.'

Had he been disappointed? wondered Mary, only to hear the woman saying, 'But must memorize it now.'

'Ursula, there isn't time!'

'Make it! Don't be foolish. Why waste everything when you have the answer you want right in your hand?'

For an instant they looked at each other, then he said, 'All right. Have your things packed and ready to go. I don't like your staying here any longer. We'll find you some place else when I come back from delivering this one to her hotel.'

'By then it will be daylight.'

He nodded acceptance of the fact, reached for his coat, and Mary knew then that she had just witnessed the bond that was between two vastly different people who must live in constant danger. Though Ursula Tulford might think little of the IRA as a group, she both liked and respected Kevin O'Bannion.

The Shelbourne was just around the corner and he didn't even bother to try to hide the fact, for there really wasn't much he could have done about it. They went in at the tradesman's entrance and climbed the back stairs to her floor. Following her into the room, he put the lock on just in case there might be trouble, and only then switched on the bedside lamp.

'Don't pay any mind to what Ursula might have said about us, Mrs. Fraser. The Germans are a funny lot of people.'

'She's right, though, about my memorizing this.'

'Tuck it away for now. Leave first thing as I've said, but be sure to lie down here and not drift off, or you'll miss your train.'

'I couldn't sleep anyway.'

'Get out of those things of yours in any case or else the chambermaid will know it soon enough when she brings your tea.'

He watched as Mary took off her coat and went over to the closet to hang it up, watched as she began to unbutton the jerkin, gave no sign of leaving.

The jerkin went on to its hanger. Unfastening her skirt, this lover of a U-boat captain, stepped out of it and took the time to carefully smooth it down, knowing every second that she was still being watched but was she wondering what did he really see in her? A badly frightened woman, a traitor or nothing but a beautiful woman?

'You'd best go, hadn't you,' she said, her voice strange-sounding in the half-light.

The blouse came off, and she stood there with it in hand, her back to him. O'Bannion knew he had to wonder why she'd not objected but had she a purpose of her own?

Unfastening her hair, she shook it out and ran the fingers of both hands through it, tilting back that head of hers, the slip white, no lace at all, just slender straps of satin across her shoulders, overtop those of her brassiere.

Still with her back to him, she began to take off her stockings, to reach up and under the slip to unhook the bloody things, knowing he was still watching her.

Switching off the light, he stepped quickly over to the windows to part the curtains and peer down at the street below. 'A car,' was all he said. Mary hadn't even heard it, but somewhere now a lift door opened, he turning from the windows to swiftly say, 'Get into bed. Look as if you've been asleep for hours but switch that light back on.'

The steps came soon enough and with them a panic she could not fight down. There were two men rushing along the corridor: the night clerk objecting to the intrusion, the other one having none of it.

O'Bannion had flattened himself against the wall so as not to be behind the door when it opened, but rather a little ways from it and still out of sight—a clear shot then at whoever it was, that person being distracted by her and by the bedside lamp.

Knocking shattered the silence. 'Mrs. Fraser . . . ? Mrs. Mary Ellen Fraser?'

Was she to be arrested? 'Yes . . . Yes, what is it, please?'

'The Garda, m'am. Detective Inspector Hanlan.'

Had something happened to Hamish? she wondered, panicking all the more and stumbling blindly into a chair, O'Bannion grabbing her by an arm. 'Your dressing gown,' he whispered. 'For Christ's sake, woman, look as though you've been asleep!'

He tussled her hair and nudged her with the gown before going back to stand with his back to the wall.

'Mrs. Fraser, m'am, I must ask you to open this door.'

Mary tried to think what would be best. 'I'm coming, Inspector. You've awakened me.'

Blinking at the supposedly unaccustomed light, she looked out into the corridor. Hanlan was in his late fifties, a big man with a wide moustache, black bowler hat and no patience.

'Are you all right, m'am?' he asked. She'd been asleep, she had, and was clutching the dressing gown about herself.

'Is it my husband?' she asked. 'Has something happened to him? Well, has it? Please, you must tell me.'

Hanlan was genuinely baffled, 'No, m'am. I just thought . . . That is . . . Ah th' divil take it. I must have been mistaken.'

He had thought she wouldn't have been in the room at all, or certainly not alone and not asleep, but she knew then, too, that they must have found Davies's body and had come looking for answers. And yes, she had just let Kevin O'Bannion know she must still be very much in love with Hamish.

They didn't stop her at the border, didn't even bother to go through her luggage, just asked a few routine questions. The dry cell battery and pocket watch had been in her handbag with their respective proofs of purchase but she'd not even had to open it or mention them. There'd been no questions either from Trant or Jimmy or any of their men, no sign at all of them, and she'd not been followed home, she was as certain of this as she could be.

The murder of Davies must be hanging over them. Certainly they would suspect her of having met with the IRA, but they'd have no proof as yet, none either in so far as Mrs. Tulford was concerned, but Mary knew she was getting in deeper and deeper. This thing was not going to stop, and would only become far worse.

Unsettled, she lit the stove in the kitchen and then the copper boiler. It would take a good hour to heat water for a bath. Pulling on her gumboots and the old raincoat she wore for rough work, she went out to the stable to see to the pony, couldn't help but think of having to move the dynamite, but O'Bannion had said they'd not need the blasting machine—had he tried to make things easier for her?

Finding two apples, Mary fed them to the pony, rubbed his muzzle and scratched behind his ears. 'I think we should re-name you Cuchulain or Brian Boru at least. You're a dear, dear thing, and I know I love you very much.'

She fed him properly, brushed him down, mucked out the stall and listened to the rain. Standing in the doorway, she watched the puddles in the yard, the concentric rings the hammering droplets made and just as instantly destroyed. Would she have that fifty minutes? she wondered. Would the bomb even work?

At 4.30 p.m., and with the doors and windows all locked and Robbie over at Mrs. Haney's, she went upstairs to the bath. Steam fogged the mahogany oval of the mirror that hung be-hind the sink. Large bronze hooks protruded from either side of it, but there were others on the back of the panelled door—that, too, was locked, though it wouldn't keep anyone out if they re-ally wanted to get at her.

The two bullets and the message lay on a corner of the sink. She would never be able to memorize the thing, would never be able to destroy it. 'DKYBI,' she began. 'MZTUH . . .'

Forcing herself not to look, she tried printing it out on the fogged glass of the mirror, each of the letters giving slices of herself. The ring and the key were still around her neck, their string now soaked through and clinging to her. 'DKYBI slash MZTUH slash VT . . . VTLIQ—yes, that's it, I think.'

She would have to memorize it. Trant or Jimmy would have her thoroughly searched this time. And what about the bullets? Was she to leave them behind, and take them in only on a last visit?

'DKYBI slash MZTUH slash VTLIQ slash BGZRO . . .' Ducking her head, she hurriedly read the rest. 'MWBSP slash RYWJE slash BYAPV slash YUBKJ slash CCRMR.'

There it was again at the end of the message. Deftly she printed it all out across the mirror, the condensation running down the glass beneath each stroke.

CCRMR couldn't have meant Huber then, but rather their code name for the escape. Five letters out of forty-five this time, the message perhaps to read: HAVE AGREED TO IRA DEMANDS STOP ARRANGE ESCAPE NIGHT 7 NOVEMBER—would that be too soon? Wouldn't the tenth be better, or even the fifteenth, somewhere closer to the full moon?

An island . . . would they use one as the rendezvous? There were lots of them off the west and northwest coasts and many of them were uninhabited.

HAVE AGREED TO IRA DEMANDS STOP ARRANGE 13 NOVEMBER STOP KRAMER AND OTHERS OF U-121 TO BE TAKEN OFF WITH HUBER TATLINGER STORCH AND TULFORD. Signed . . . ? What would their code name be for the operation? Tory Island? No mention of Nolan, none of Kevin, and none of herself either, but still far too many letters. Then what about: AGREE DEMANDS RENDEZVOUS 13 NOVEMBER AT 0100 HOURS STOP KRAMER TO BE TAKEN OFF WITH TULFORD?

There were still too many letters, and why, please, a code that wasn't being used for normal clandestine transmissions unless the British really *had* broken the German naval codes or there was fear of this?

'M'am, there's a powerful lot of flour missing from this here bin. Was you baking bread and not letting it rise?'

'Bread . . . ? Why, yes, I was, Mrs. Haney. I did spoil it. I should have waited for you to come back. I'm sorry if I've run you short. I . . . I fed it to the swans and the Brants down at Lough Loughie.'

And her looking across th' water like Guinevere at King Arthur's Camelot! 'Parker's wake was hard, m'am. With Bridget away the while, I shall have to take things easy.'

'I wish you'd just stay at home and rest up. Hamish won't be back for a week at least. I can manage on my own.'

And make mischief, was it, behind the dear doctor's back, and him the saint he was? 'Ah, and sure you can, but 'twill take my mind off the loss of my dear departed brother and give me something to do. Now it will, I say. It will.'

To argue would not be wise. 'Let's have a cup of one of your teas, then. The blackberry, I think. The scones I made are not nearly as good as your own, but all the same I'd like you to try them.'

The swans and the Brants hadn't seen a particle of that flour. All of it had gone into making fake sticks of dynamite, but making the exchange would be the hardest part, though with William away, her caring for the pony would be excuse enough to visit the stable.

'M'am, are there soldiers watching the house?'

'Not that I know of. Why should there be?'

''Tis what I've asked myself.'

'Did you see any of them?'

'That I did. Robbie, being the dog he is, found them out and they told me, now they did, I do declare, that I was to keep that dog locked up.'

'I see.'

The breath had gone right from Mrs. Fraser. 'The doctor mustn't stay away m'am. He must come back.'

They had their tea, with Robbie choosing to lie at Mrs. Haney's feet.

'M'am, is there something you would like to tell me? I'm not of them. I never was, nor my mother and father or my brothers. Parker . . . now Parker was, but that was over and done with long before they ever came to leave that blessed gel-ignite at his farm.'

'He was a good man, Mrs. Haney. I liked him very much.'

'That you did, now you did, and given time, I'm certain you'd have come to know us all.'

'Mrs. Haney, tell me whatever you can about the O'Bannions.'

Kevin, was it? 'Two strapping boys up to no good under the hand of a drunken, rebellious father near twice the age of his poor young wife, and she so swollen up with them, she died in the cowshed and left those boys to him.'

'Did they have relatives in the west, in Donegal perhaps?'

Donegal was it now? 'Who among us haven't kin in the far corners of the earth? Ireland is the leaving-us country of them all.'

'But Donegal, Mrs. Haney? An island perhaps?'

Islands was it now and herself being led by the nose yet letting it happen as two sisters would? 'I mind there was one sprig of that family living in the northwest, I do. Inishtrahull it was, and them scratching what living they could from the stones and the sea, but they was all moved out years ago. In 1928 it was, and the place a terrible ruin by then.'

'Did Kevin ever go there for a visit?'

And her using that one's first name while fingering the rim of her saucer as a young girl would under watchful eyes. Caution would be best. 'That I wouldn't know. Now I surely wouldn't.'

'But it had a harbour?'

'A cove of sorts, with a loading boom to snatch the little boats out for fear of them being dashed to pieces on the rocks.'

'It's very stormy there, is it?'

Lord save us but she had a powerful interest. 'M'am, you're not thinking of going there, are you?'

'No. No, I . . . I just wondered.'

About storms and seas and places to land a boat. 'Sure and it's the worst of places for mean weather I ever did know, save for that Tory Island which is off to the west of it. But I was only a girl then. Just a slip of a thing, I was, me hugging my china doll and everyone so terrified the ship would go to pieces on them rocks and we'd all be drowned to death, we would.'

'I didn't know your family had once thought of emigrating?'

'Haven't all of us thought of getting out? Mother would have none of it after us fetching up on that blessed island. Sick, she was so sick we saw the inside of her toenails. Ship's biscuit and all.'

'So you came back home.'

'And my father died of a broken back the very next year to the day, it was. The day, m'am, and me only ten years old. Ten, I was. You'll have me crying, you will. Me who thought I was wrung dry of it all them years ago.'

And didn't Mrs. Fraser reach across the table now to lay a hand on her own? Ria blinked away the tears of forgotten times. 'Them scones are quite satisfactory, m'am. Now they are, I say.'

'Be the friend that Parker was to me.'

She had meant it too. 'Friend it is, for surely this old house must be a lonely place for a young woman like yourself.'

The sun came out in midafternoon and Mary took Robbie for a walk on the leash. From the road atop Caitlyn Murphy's Hill there were breathtaking views all round but nowhere was there a sight of Jimmy and his men.

It had been good to get things straight with Mrs. Haney. One felt one had overcome a major difficulty and had acquired God on one's side, if that was ever possible. Good, too, to know that Kevin O'Bannion must be thinking of Inishtrahull as a rendezvous.

Good just to be out walking with Robbie. The wind ruffled his fur. Shelties were such handsome dogs, so perfectly proportioned, but Robbie was something extra special even then. No wonder Hamish loved him.

'What is it, Robbie? Can you smell them?'

He barked three times in quick succession, short, sharp barks as a sheepdog would, he facing intently off to the north-northeast, to a copse on the side of a lesser hill, down among the hedgerows and the green, green fields.

'They can't want you around, can they?' she asked, saddened that it could only be true. 'No one will try to contact me as long as you are here to give them away.'

Jimmy would have men hidden everywhere he could. Starting across country in the opposite direction, she had the thought they'd run into others and that it would be best to avoid them if possible. Jimmy'd be cursing Robbie and wishing he'd been kept at Mrs. Haney's or had gone away with Hamish and Caithleen, custom's regulations or no; the war, or no.

As always the fields accepted her. There'd been flax grown here, and in summer the blue of its flowers had been like no other. A good farm with rights of passage for herself and Hamish because it was land they had leased to Mr. Makepiece O'Fenlan.

And there it was: Thackeray again. *The Virginians*, then the Shelbourne where the great writer had once stayed, and now another connection she'd entirely forgotten: William Makepiece Thackeray. Had it meaning for her?

The leash tightened as they approached the far corner of the field. There were fieldstones in the lowland wall, bramble bushes along it, and hawthorn, and there it was again. Another coincidence—was that it only? Kevin O'Bannion and herself meeting in the ruins near the school, red berries and thorns, the same things here?

Robbie barked. 'Robbie, *sh*!' She yanked on the leash. Pointing, he stiffened. '*Hush*, do you hear me?'

Following the hedgerow, they soon came to where it cornered at the road. She could see the stable quite clearly now, could see the top of Caitlyn Murphy's Hill.

'Mrs. Fraser, get that bloody dog out of here.'

Robbie didn't just bark. He let the world know about it, she yanking on the leash and pulling him back on to his hindquarters as Jimmy stepped from cover, the leash slipping from her. 'Robbie, no!'

He darted in to nip at Jimmy's heels and leap for the crotch, got a good hold of the trousers, snarled, pulled . . .

'Sergeant, see to this bloody dog!'

A savage kick was given, Robbie bending almost in half only to land on his feet and go right back into the fight, she yelling, 'ROBBIE, NO! IT'S ALL RIGHT. HE WON'T HURT ME.'

A bayonet flashed. He yelped, squealed, quivered—lay there in the grass panting, not knowing what had happened to him.

'Mary, I'm sorry. The dog . . .'

'You bastard!' she screamed as she fell to her knees to take him up and hold him. Blood had gushed out as the bayonet had been withdrawn, and no matter how much she tried to wipe it from his fur, it wouldn't stop. 'Robbie . . . Robbie, please don't die. Hamish will come home. He'll need you then more than ever.'

'Mary, leave him. Sergeant, see that she's taken back to the house.'

'NO! Don't you dare have anyone "see to me." I'll take him home myself.'

After dark she moved the dynamite and buried Robbie in the garden where she'd first hidden it. She built the bomb, and when that was done, vomited into the bathroom sink, partly from the nausea the gelignite brought, partly from fear.

Wiping her mouth on the back of her hand, she forced herself to look in the mirror, but could see only a person she loathed—threw her head forward, smashed it and the glass not once but twice, said, 'Forgive me, darling,' the blood spattering the basin and her hands. 'Oh God, I've been such a stupid fool.'

'You've hurt yourself,' said Trant.

'I walked blindly into a door. I was drunk. Look, I don't give a damn what you think of me, Major. Your people killed my husband's dog.'

Best, then, to affect a deferential air. 'He got away all right? He and the girl?'

She faced him across the desk, hadn't yet been told to sit down. 'You know damned well they did. We didn't even have a decent chance to say good-bye.'

'Then I think I should tell you, that your husband will be staying in Scotland for a while.'

'What's that supposed to mean?'

She was furious with them. 'Make of it what you will. That more books?' he asked, distracting her as one must now and then, and she was distracted, oh my yes.

'Of course it is.'

But not wary enough. The books would be clean. No hidden messages, not today. 'Like your library work here, do you?' he asked.

'If you wish me to stop, I will.'

'No. No, nothing like that. The colonel would most certainly wish you to continue your valuable work.'

'Then may I get on with it?' Trant wasn't looking directly at her, but concentrating on her bandaged forehead. He touched his lips as if in thought.

'In a moment, yes. Please sit down. What I have to say won't take long.'

A girl, a young woman in uniform, came in with some papers for him to sign. After he'd done this, Trant glanced up at her. 'Ask Miss Sanderson to come in, would you, please, Corporal Bridgewood. She'll want to be present.'

The Sanderson woman had been waiting out in the foyer: a thoroughly brutal looking forty-year-old who'd been taking a last drag at a cigarette and had then pinched the thing out, the build of less than medium height and chunky, the hair a tired shade of disinterested brown.

'Mrs. Fraser, this is Miss Maureen Sanderson. Maureen, Mrs. Mary Ellen Fraser.'

The grip was that of a man, the eyes not blue, not grey.

'Maureen's one of ours, Mrs. Fraser. As I was only just saying, Maureen, we won't keep her long, will we?'

'Not long, Major. A matter of a few minutes.'

'Good. Now, Mrs. Fraser, events have taken a turning here. You know, of course, that certain members of the IRA are still on the loose and haven't yet attempted to collect the explosives they parked in the stable loft of yours.'

Could he please just get to it?

'We have reason to believe they have made contact with some of the prisoners.'

'Not through me.'

Could she lie so fiercely and still be brash about it? That cut on her forehead showed abrasions all around the bandage—a good three inches across and two in width. A nasty, nasty thing. Bulged a bit, too. 'Our informants tell us there is another tunnel. The prisoners do have a plan to escape and have expended considerable effort in this regard.'

Their informants . . . 'If so, I've overheard nothing of it.'

'Oh? We rather thought you had, didn't we, Maureen?'

The woman had found another cigarette and was lighting it. 'Major, I know nothing more of any tunnel than the rumour you told me the last time I was here. The men wouldn't talk about a thing like that in my presence. They'd be . . .'

'But they talked about Bauer and the others, didn't they?'

Letting him fluster her would do no good. 'Major, I told you about them.'

'About Bauer, yes, but not about the others.'

It had to be asked and he'd forced her to. 'Is Bauer still allowed to walk around in there?'

'Of course. Is there something the matter, Mrs. Fraser? I thought I told you we needed the names of all of those who were responsible for the hanging of that man?'

'Hans Schleiger.'

'Don't tell me you've been holding out on us?'

'I *don't* want to be killed, Major.'

'Then cease to go in. Stop if you wish and I'll tell the colonel it's all off.'

He wouldn't, not really, and she could see this, was sickened by the thought. 'Look, I really don't know if Schleiger was involved. I . . . I shouldn't have said that.'

'Mrs. Fraser, are you carrying anything into Tralane that you shouldn't?'

'Of course not. Why would I?'

'That would constitute an act of treason, would it not?'

Did he have to hear her answer? 'Yes. Yes, of course it would.'

He'd not even sigh, would just let her have it. 'Then you'll have no objections if we look a little further. Corporal Bridgewood will accompany you and Miss Sanderson. That is all for now.'

'Major . . .'

'I said that was all, Mrs. Fraser. Please try to understand there's a war on.'

The room was just across the foyer and one that he must use for interrogations. A plain table, two wooden fold-up chairs, a brown metal wastebasket, an ashtray and a window . . .

It was the Sanderson woman who said, 'Please empty your bag on the table.'

'And if I don't?'

'We'll do it for you.'

For the life of her, Mary couldn't remember why she'd snatched her handbag at the last and brought it along. She seldom did unless she was having her period, hadn't had that in a while . . .

The woman flicked her gaze over the lipstick that was never worn on visits to the castle. The change purse was gone through, her handkerchief opened and shaken out, that last letter from home perused.

'You can leave these here. Now your shoes.'

'Look, I've done nothing wrong. I *won't* be subjected to this sort of treatment.'

Corporal Bridgewood turned away to lock the door, then stood in front of it, a bright young thing who was obviously uncomfortable about her duty but would do as ordered.

'If you don't do as you're told, Mrs. Fraser,' said Maureen, 'we will have to strip you ourselves and can't vouch for not tearing things if you should resist.'

This couldn't be happening to her, yet was. Mary took off her shoes. The Sanderson woman went over them thoroughly.

She took off her overcoat, scarf and tam, and the woman examined everything, saying only, 'You can pick these up afterwards when you get your bag.'

The jacket came next, its dark brown velvet crushed in those meaty fists. Then the jerkin Hamish had bought for her birthday, and the blouse he had liked so much, the skirt, the seldom-worn silk stockings and garter belt, each item being examined in turn.

'Now are you satisfied?' Mary heard herself ask.

The woman shook her head.

Off came the slip and she threw it at the bitch only to hear her say, 'Now the rest.'

'I won't! I refuse! You've gone far en . . .'

Seized from behind, she was forced over the edge of the table and held down by the younger one. Rubber gloves were found, Mary struggling, kicking out as best she could and crying, 'Don't you dare put your filthy hands on me!'

The step-ins were yanked down, her legs spread, she stiffening as something hard was rammed into her vagina, then into her rectum.

The brassier was taken off, its padding slit.

The Fraser woman hadn't like it one bit, was hanging her head in shame. 'Get dressed.'

'I have to go to the toilet.'

'Then go on the floor and clean it up. From now on you'll do exactly as we say.'

Bannerman gave her a moment to compose herself in the chair he'd placed directly in front of his desk. Signalling that the others, except for Roger Trant, should leave the office, he came round to stand in front of the woman. It couldn't have been pleasant being searched like that. She was pale and shaken and badly frightened, her refusal to look up but a further indication of the humiliation she must be feeling.

But no matter. 'My dear young woman, we have been keeping track of your progress for some time. Let me assure you that hanging is a very unpleasant business and that in your case it would be made far worse by a good deal of publicity and the presence of your husband. Now what's it to be, *hmm*?'

Still she could not look at him.

'I have nothing to say to any of you.'

'My dear, we . . .'

'I'm not "your dear," Colonel. My name is Mrs. Mary Ellen Fraser.'

'My dear, we are sorry for what has happened to you but war is war and from time to time certain things are necessary.'

'Colonel, might I suggest . . .'

'Roger, I will thank you kindly not to interrupt me.'

'Of course, sir. It's only that Mrs. Fraser was not completely searched.'

'What was that? Goddamn it, I gave you strict orders. Oh blast it, man, you've made me tell her who was responsible!'

Trant stepped into view but she wouldn't look at either of them, not yet.

'That cut on her forehead, Colonel. Miss Sanderson neglected to remove the bandage.'

'All right, all right! It's true the IRA have been using me, but I don't know much of what's up, not really.'

The two of them must have exchanged glances, for Trant quickly stepped from view. She heard him strike a match, knew he must be lighting a cigarette, but it was Bannerman who said, 'Let's try Dublin for starters, *hmm*?'

Dear God, she wished he wouldn't *hmm* at her! 'I met no

one. I did a bit of shopping, went to the library for Hamish, and had dinner at my hotel, then went to bed early and left first thing in the morning.'

All cut and dried, that it, and she still not able to face them? He'd fold his arms across his chest and settle back against the edge of the desk, thought Bannerman. He hadn't wanted to order the body search, not with a woman like this whose husband, if he got word of it, would raise the bloody roof, but Roger had been adamant—they had had to strike while they could. 'Please don't be difficult, Mrs. Fraser. An inspector in the Irish Secret Service was murdered on the night you were "asleep," as you say, in that hotel of yours. Morgan Davies was the father of seven children, all of whom are under the age of fifteen.'

'I'm sorry to hear that, Colonel, but know nothing of this man.'

Even now, was it that she could continue to lie? 'Of course you don't. It's the slug that killed him which is of interest. Markings on the bullet match those from two other brutal murders.'

'I still don't understand why you're telling me this?'

By God, he wished she would look at him! A damned good thrashing was what she needed, bare backside and all! 'Kevin O'Bannion, Mrs. Fraser. The gun was his. The Garda have the proof.'

Trant stepped in to keep the pressure up. Mary knew he was going to rip the bandage away. 'Liam Nolan did murder the two women with whom he was staying in London, Mrs. Fraser. Jauncy Gilmore is the son of one of them and just happens to have a flat in Saint Stephen's Green. Perhaps you know of it? Young Gilmore is acting as a purchasing agent for His Majesty's Government. Travels a good deal in Eire and Ulster. Leaves his flat empty.'

He paused, must still be looking at the bandage.

'But knows, Mrs. Fraser, that it might well be used when he's absent and turns a blind eye because he has to, his rebellious sister Janet having a crush on a certain Liam Nolan.'

'The girl, I should add,' said Bannerman, 'whose father had Nolan, but an urchin then, stripped and tied to the pump standard in his stable yard until Lady Prudence prevailed upon his lordship to have the boy cut down and taken to her bed.'

They were like priest and bishop at the trial of a wilful girl, both despising her and enjoying what they were doing. It would now be Trant's turn.

'Nolan has had a running, if shabby and intermittent love affair for years with Lord Gilmore's daughter. No doubt he first seduced her at a very young age, though there is some doubt as to which of them seduced the other.'

'Janet Gilmore was a headstrong girl. The hand that fed the urchin and nursed him back to health was rather badly bitten, I should say,' said Bannerman, affecting the tired, rather bored air of the bishop.

'Nolan murdered Lady Gilmore and her daughter, Mrs. Fraser. Before he killed them, I'm sure he told them what he thought of them.'

'You said they had died in their sleep.'

'Did I?' exclaimed Trant. 'A correction, then. You see, he did awaken one of them—couldn't have done otherwise, not a man with a grudge like that. Lady Prudence made it half out of bed, and was found with her throat slit and her head twisted sideways against the carpet. Can't have been pleasant, her hearing him saying such things. I gather there was a great deal of blood. Corpses do tend to drain when they're left like that, and Nolan has been known to butcher hogs and game from time to time.'

She would have to find the will to look up at him. 'And Janet?' she asked.

'Janet, yes. The girl was found stark naked and spread-eagled on her bed, Mrs. Fraser, but before he killed her, Nolan and she had sex. Then, and only then, did he go for the mother, so guess what he told that one had just happened?'

Bannerman could hardly wait. 'On the night you were at that hotel, MI5's Listeners in Dublin, Wexford, Cork and Dundalk picked up the clandestine signals of an enemy transmitter. Others in Holyhead, Aberystwyth and Milford Haven also found the sending very fast, even for a good Morse operator. There was considerable traffic at that hour, a lot of interference due to bad weather over the Continent, the result of which was that, though they recorded what Mrs. Ursula Tulford sent over to Berlin, they got only a portion of what was sent back. We absolutely must have the rest of it.'

It was Trant who, setting his cigarette aside, said, 'You have a very clear choice in this matter. You can either cooperate, in which case you will be forgiven certain, shall we say, "indiscretions," and perhaps even given a medal and a suitable rank in one of the services, or you will be taken from this office and placed under arrest for treason.'

She mustn't cry, must just try to face them. 'What is it you want of me?'

'The message, of course,' said Bannerman.

'Liam Nolan, the Darcy woman, and Kevin O'Bannion,' said Trant.

'The confessions of Erich Kramer, Franz Bauer, and the other officers of Kramer's U-boat. They hanged the Second Lieutenant Bachmann. That lover of yours put the rope around his neck, Mrs. Fraser. Kramer kicked the chair out from under him. Kramer, damn you!'

'Stop it! Please stop it.'

They gave her a moment. It was Trant who said, 'GHQ and

the prime minister are demanding that an example be made of you. The colonel and I are giving you the opportunity to clear your name.'

'Mrs. Fraser, we really must have the location of this tunnel they've been digging. We must have the rest of that message the Tulford woman received from Berlin.'

Could she not simply force herself to look up at them? wondered Mary. 'My husband is never to know of this.'

Trant glanced at the colonel who indicated that he should take it from here. 'Hamish won't be allowed back into Ireland until it's over. You have my word on this as an officer and a gentleman. He'll be kept right out of it.'

Mary knew she couldn't stop the tears but must she disgrace herself further? 'I'll be shot, won't I? It'll be a lot easier that way. Look, I know that's what you people have in mind. No problem, Major. No need for all this talk of medals and commissions in some branch of the services. Just a bullet in the face or back and an end to the problem. Admit I'm right.'

'What did you do to your forehead?'

'I hit it against our bathroom mirror. I was angry with myself for having inadvertently caused Robbie's death.' Trant would tear the bandage from her now and would force Hamish to watch her hang. 'Do I have your guarantee I'll be killed, Major? Shot accidentally?'

Visibly shaken, he said, 'There's no need for that. We're not inhuman. We do have our good side.'

'Oh? Caithleen would have been set afire, Major. Parker was shot to pieces though I'm certain Jimmy knew he had been held to ransom and had taken no part in things. And Robbie . . . Why, Robbie was just a dog. A dog!'

'My dear young woman, you have no other choice,' said Bannerman quietly.

'Then let me have a piece of paper and a pencil. They made me memorize it this time.'

Trant swept uncertain eyes over the bandage and nodded, though intuition warned him to look behind it.

'Which part of the message did they pick up?' she asked.

He let an exasperated breath escape. 'Just write the whole of it down.'

And gamble, was that it? Gamble that if she lied, they'd not pick her up on it? 'Mrs. Tulford did say the code wasn't the one she was using.'

It was Trant who sighed and said, 'Then neither she nor the IRA will know of its contents.'

'The Nazis won't tell me what it means, Major. You must know that as well as I.'

'Then you must let them know the deal's off unless they do.'

Shaking her head, she went back to getting the message down. 'They'd only suspect that I was working for you.'

'Convince them otherwise. Find out its contents.'

When handed the sheet of paper, Trant quickly scanned it, then gave her a look that could mean so many things. Triumph or doubt, praise or anger, even hatred, for he must despise her as would the colonel.

'Now go and do your stuff,' he said. 'There's a good girl. You're one of us.'

'And if Franz Bauer should suspect it?'

'Then we must take our chances, mustn't we?'

9

From the gatehouse and the barbican, the rampart walk ran westwards for a good three hundred feet to the cantling tower. Buffeted by the wind, Mary stood alone, first looking uncertainly towards the tower and then back at the door through which she had just come.

When she tried to return, she found that door locked. There were no sentries in evidence, no machine-gun emplacements, just the rampart walk with its crenellated battlements, the wind gusting and, in the near distance atop the tower, a ragged flock of rooks tearing across a cloud-riven sky.

Trant had washed his hands of her. He must have had a note delivered straight to the German High Command: *Have Kramer and the other officers of U-121 sent to his office immediately.* No time for her to figure out what to do or say, none even to try to hide. There'd be no bullet in the back or messy trial, simply another murder in a prison full of German officers some of whom had already done in one of their own.

It would stick all right because she could have named them as the killers of Bachmann. Trant wouldn't want the High

Command to hear the complete message nor the prisoners to get their hands on the rest of the dynamite, would have to let them kill her.

The castle's warren began with a corridor that was far too wide and a drawing room that was huge, barren of every last stick of furnishings and so cold and empty, her steps sounded hollowly as she ran. She would try to reach the great hall, would try to barricade herself in the library. Helmut Wolfganger would help her. Helmut wasn't like the others and neither was Philip Werner. They wouldn't let Bauer get near her . . .

At the sound of rushing steps on one of the stone staircases, she darted into a room and threw her back against its innermost wall.

The steps ran past—there were several of them. Prying off her shoes, she started out again but in the hush there was nothing but the terror of knowing she alone stood between Bauer and the others and the hangman's noose. Never mind their orders. Never mind the escape or that Nolan had someone else inside the castle. She was now simply too much of a threat and Trant had seen to this.

Room fell upon room and she realized, as she slipped into each, that the mustiness of disuse and the high and ornately plastered ceilings of the derelict meant that this section of the castle had never been open to the prisoners.

Coming to what must once have been the main ballroom, she saw that there were murals on the walls and ceilings. Scenes of the hunt, stags being torn to pieces, medieval times . . .

Mary hesitated as she put her shoes back on. There were four doorways leading into corridors. Five men were watching her. Five! Hans Schleiger and Erich . . . Erich was just staring at her from across the room, she not knowing if she could make it to the emptiest of those doorways.

'Franz!' The rest of what he shouted was in *Deutsch* and she couldn't understand all of it and raced for that one doorway, heard them all coming after her, darted down a staircase, hit the door at the bottom, found it open, and raced out into the bailey, knew then that Trant would be watching for just such a thing.

Dragging in a breath, she ran past the main entrance and up the steps of the keep and in at that door. She had to make it to the great hall, had to get into the library but now there were men everywhere. They filled the corridors, turned their backs on her and when she tried to get through, sometimes stood in her way. 'Please, you don't understand. I had to tell Trant and the colonel. I had to!'

When Bauer broke through to cut her off, she darted into the stairwell that was just beside the washroom—took the stairs two and three at a time, climbing, spiralling up and up, then went along the corridor to her right, he so close behind she tripped and cried out as he gave her a brutal shove and sent her stumbling blindly up the last flight of stairs to burst into the room at the top.

The room where she and Erich had made love.

Bauer slammed the door behind himself. There was a knife in his right hand and he gripped it as if she had one too. Forced up against the far wall, she began to edge her way towards the window . . .

'Bauer, stop this at once.'

The words had been in *Deutsch*, the lifeless eyes blinking as the knife clattered on the floor.

'Herr Vizeadmiral . . .'

'Silence! Now get out of here.'

Huber had had only the bearing of command as his defence, yet Bauer had instantly stood to attention.

'Mrs. Fraser, you must forgive what has just happened. Events here have moved far too quickly even for us. Please sit on the floor and rest yourself. What I have to say won't take long. Major Trant is using us against you and that we cannot have. But . . . but you have hurt yourself.'

Shutting her eyes, Mary gingerly probed her forehead. Blood came away. 'It's nothing. The bandage is still there. He . . . he could have removed it but didn't.'

'Please, you are in no further danger from any of us. Franz Bauer will be punished.'

Going over to the window, Huber looked out over the bailey, taking a moment to gather his thoughts. 'After what has happened, we can't expect you to help us anymore. This I regret very much and apologize profusely. Bauer will be made to face the charges against him but not the others. Not Erich Kramer. Did you know he has a wife and little boy?'

'It doesn't matter.'

Had that newfound resilience and toughness he'd experienced in her before been but a passing moment of defiance? 'But it does matter. It was unkind of us to have used you, and now I am wondering what we can do to get you out of this mess we have created.'

'Trant had me strip-searched. I can't bring anything more in to you people. I'll be up for treason in any case.'

His nod was grim. 'Then they'll have found the bullets and will now turn the castle upside down for the gun.'

She shook her head. 'Not yet. In here. It . . . it was the only place they didn't look.'

Crouching in front of her, Huber gently teased a corner of the bandage away. Two cartridges were embedded in a wound from which splinters of glass glistened. How had she stood the pain and the threat of Trant's finding them?

'*Ach*, that cut must be cleaned and stitched. Dr. Conner is in the infirmary and while he won't do the job your husband would, it will suffice.'

'Wait, please. I . . . I didn't give Trant all of the message Mrs. Tulford received from Berlin.'

Liebe Zeit, was that toughness of spirit still with her? 'For now just come with me and I will take you to the infirmary. There will be time enough later.'

Huber helped her to her feet but she refused to leave until he had written down the message. 'The CCRMR is the same ending as before, Vice Admiral. The major didn't ask me about the message you had given me for her, only about this one, but I think he must know of it as well.'

Did she really feel the only way out for her was to cooperate? 'CCRMR is a code within a code. Since it is one that is not regularly used by our forces, the British may not yet have had a chance to break it, especially as repeated use is one of the very reasons codes are broken.'

'Trant will only ask me what it means and if I don't tell him something, I'll be sent straight to prison. The CCRMR is what made him send for Erich and the others. I . . . I fudged it and some of the other groupings, and he . . . well, he realized I had.'

To have memorized the groupings alone had been one task, to deliberately and quickly 'fudge' them in the face of such a threat, quite another. 'The CCRMR means Heidi, which is the code name for the escape and for yourself.'

Heidi. 'What does it say?'

She had not averted her gaze, but could he trust her after what had just happened to her? The message would take about five minutes to decode.

Mary waited. Huber exuded a confidence that was comforting, but she knew that at the first sign of weakness she would be forgotten. He struck a match and burned what he'd written.

'In essence, it means, Terms agreed. Fix rendezvous zero one hundred hours, twenty-three November.'

Again he paused, and she had the thought then that he must be deciding whether to tell her something or not.

'Kill Heidi,' he said, not averting his gaze. 'It ends with that, and for this I am sorry.'

The woman didn't flinch. Perhaps she was simply beyond this. If so, she would now need encouragement. '*Ach*, Berlin are so distant from this little place of ours, Mrs. Fraser, it is an order I can only rescind. On this you have my word.'

'And what of the charges Trant will bring?'

'Franz Bauer will be told he must hang for the murder of Bachmann, but the others must be allowed to go free. You will therefore tell the major that only Bauer was involved and that this is all you will swear to in court.'

'Is Erich that important?'

This one was being very direct. 'For what we need, he is by far the best. Now come. That forehead of yours must be attended to.'

Mary reached out to stop him. 'I . . . Look, I don't want anyone to be killed, Vice Admiral. I . . . I couldn't bear it.'

To have a conscience at such a time was, in itself, a warning that he could not overlook but something would have to be said. 'Then rest assured the gun will only be used if necessary.'

'And the explosives? I managed to get most of what was in the box out of the loft of our stable.'

'But will tell this Nolan only when necessary, and that if harm should come to you, he will have to answer to me.'

Again Mary stopped him. 'Trant will force me to give him the complete message and will demand to know what it means, so I must give him something so close to the truth, he won't question it.'

This was no ordinary woman and they had best not forget it. 'We will have to use the code again—perhaps two or even three times . . .'

'He'll have to be satisfied, Vice Admiral. He may even decide simply to have me arrested. I really don't know. One never does with him.'

'Then tell him, Terms agreed. Fix rendezvous. Forward via Heidi.'

As the needle went in again, Mary lay on the makeshift operating table with her head tilted back. Dr. Connor had removed all of the glass but had said she'd have a scar and that this could not be helped.

He pulled the suture tight; she heard the scissors snip it off. 'There now. Back in four or five days and right as rain.'

The lamp was switched off. Blinking, she looked up to see him grinning down at her. 'Liam said I was to take good care of you, and by God I have, even if I do say so myself.'

It was Huber who laid a hand on her arm to stop her from sitting up, Connor flicking a glance at him before saying, 'You weren't to know, but under the circumstances, the vice admiral here thought it best.'

'You're Nolan's other contact.'

'That I am. It's your husband's misfortune to have received a rap on the head for misbehaving at the colonel's party, and mine for being his replacement.'

'Did Nolan threaten you?'

'Ah and sure you're not to worry yourself.'

'Your wife and children?'

'Look, let's just do as we've been told and pray t' God we get out of this.'

Connor had the pudgy grey and lined face of the heavy drinker. The eyes were grave, blue, tired and watery, the hair all but gone. A bit of sticking plaster clung to his chin, another to the left cheek. A man of perhaps forty-five but looking near to sixty.

'If you're finished with that scrutiny of yours, the vice admiral would like a word.'

He turned away. She sat up. 'Doctor . . .'

'M'am?'

'Thanks.'

'Ah think nothing of it. I'll just see to my bag.'

Huber told her to rest. 'The major will be along at any moment.'

Waiting, Mary lay there not knowing what would happen, but all too soon Trant barged in and she had the two of them standing over her, one on either side.

'Well, what the devil's been going on, eh?' demanded Trant. There were three armed men with him.

'Major, regrettably Mrs. Fraser was attacked on her way to the library and suffered a fall that reopened a cut on her forehead and required a few stitches.'

'Rubbish. Where are Kramer and the others? I specifically asked that they be sent to my office.'

'They are in the other room. Major . . .'

'Well, what is it now?'

'Franz Bauer went after Mrs. Fraser. Erich Kramer and the others had to restrain him. Bauer will confess to the hanging.'

Trant swiftly took him in and snorted derisively. 'Bauer wasn't alone. All five of them were in on it.'

'But he will confess, Major,' said Huber.

A fait accompli, that it? 'Then bring the bastard in and let's hear what he has to say.' They'd get precious little out of Bauer. Sweating him would do no earthly good but he might yet have his use. There was a dungeon in the cellars below the cantling tower. Bauer could be held there pending trial and would be well away from the others. *And Mrs. Fraser?* he demanded of himself. He'd have to hear what she had to say, but later.

As Bauer was led in by Erich and Hans Schleiger, Mary knew at once that he'd kill her if ever the chance arose and that Trant, who never missed a thing, had seen this and would use him if necessary.

'Major, you wanted them to kill me.'

'My dear young woman, I wanted you to see how tenuous is your position here. Those men are Nazis—Huber, Bauer, Kramer, even Wolfganger. Bauer will put his neck in the noose and gladly for that Führer of his. He's been *ordered* to, God damn it!'

'There's no need to shout. I understand perfectly.'

She hadn't flinched at the sound of his voice but was looking rather pale. 'Admit that you've been taking things into Tralane.'

'Books, that's all. And . . . and messages, of course.'

And still trying to be tough about it—was that it, eh? 'Treason, damn you. Treason! Need I say more?'

'Look, I'm sorry I lied to you about the message but I was afraid and very angry about what you and the colonel had ordered that woman to do to me.'

'Then let's have it, and while you're at it, write down whatever it was Huber told you it meant, and he must have done, mustn't he, otherwise you'd have nothing to give O'Bannion and the others.'

Snatching up a pad and pencil, he thrust them at her and watched as she quickly jotted the five-letter groupings down and then wrote out their meaning.

'Terms agreed. Fix rendezvous. Forward via Heidi.'

Mary forced herself to gaze steadily at him. 'That is what I was told it meant, Major. I think the vice admiral wanted me to know I was trusted and essential to the escape.'

Correction, thought Trant. He wanted O'Bannion and the others to know this. 'What sort of terms?'

'I've no idea.'

'Safe passage to the Reich for Nolan, that it?'

When she didn't avert her gaze or respond, he raised his voice a little. 'Guns, Mrs. Fraser? Ammunition and money—enough to open a second front in Ireland? Where, by God, is this rendezvous?'

'In the South, I think. Perhaps near Kinsale—that's where I met Fay Darcy's sister.'

Trant compared the coded message with the bits and pieces MI5's Listeners had picked up. An invaluable group of dedicated ham operators scattered throughout the British Isles, the Listeners had been recruited by counterintelligence in the winter of 1938, then welded into a listening network at the outbreak of hostilities. Two further reports had come in, one from as far north as Tigharry on the west coast of North Uist in the Outer Hebrides, and the other from the lighthouse on Tory Island some 170 miles to the south-southwest of there and off the north coast of Ireland. Tory was right smack against one of the busiest shipping lanes, a convoy beacon that could not have been extinguished, but like Inishtrahull it was not a part of Ulster and not under British rule. Odd, though, that they should have responded, having picked up the Tulford woman's exchange of signals, but then they constantly scanned the airwaves for German U-boat traffic as well as for Allied shipping.

Huber could have twisted the message sufficiently to mislead, but it was a chance he'd have to take. 'Mrs. Fraser, if this message is as you've stated, we have no choice but to also use you as our contact. You will therefore meet with the Darcy woman and the others, assuming we haven't apprehended them first, and you will find out the time and location of this rendezvous. We'd like that U-boat intact. Yes, indeed, we would.'

And everything else they could get. As she got to her feet, he stepped aside, but when a hand was extended, he was forced to shake it. 'Of course I'll do all I can, Major. I wouldn't think of doing anything else, not now.'

Surprisingly her grip was firm. A last shred of dignity then, or one of stiffening resistance and rebellion? 'Well, just in case you don't, let me remind you that Bauer is now housed in the dungeon. Cross me once more and you will join him.'

'Major, you needn't have been so brutal. Will Jimmy still keep the house under surveillance?'

Was she being coy? 'We mustn't let our end down, now must we?'

She was at the door when he asked, 'This tunnel they've been digging. Where is it located?'

Mary shrugged but wouldn't turn. 'We didn't talk of it, Major. There simply wasn't time.'

Connor drove her home, having tied the bicycle to the back of the car, she silent, lost in thought, and wondering what to do. 'It's a fine state we find ourselves in, now isn't it?' he said. 'If this gets out, I'm finished. The Brits will have me shot.'

'Me too, but it's already finished for me.'

'Sure and I can imagine what the major must have said, but will the Nazis take you with them?'

'I hope so. You see, I'm carrying Erich Kramer's child.'

'You're not!' Why hadn't Nolan told him? 'That does put another spin on things, now doesn't it?'

'Listen, we haven't much time unless I were to ask you in. There's no whiskey, but . . . now wait, there is some brandy.'

'Is Liam Nolan aware of your condition?'

'They dragged that out of me weeks ago. Look, tell them not to come anywhere near the house.'

'Sure and they must already know that.'

'Tell them to look for my bike in Ballylurgen. They can leave a message in the carrier basket. I'll . . . I'll come as soon as I can.'

'They'll want to know what transpired between you and that Huber fellow.'

'I'll tell them myself. Look, I'm sorry, but it's best you know only what is necessary.'

And she sounding like a regular little cadre herself!

They went in at the drive and coasted to a stop before the house. Mary listened for Robbie, only to remind herself of what had happened. 'Please leave your bag in the foyer and go in to see Mrs. Haney, Doctor. Keep her busy while I go upstairs.'

'For what?' he asked, alarmed.

She would have to tell him. 'For some of the dynamite you'll be carrying in to Tralane.'

'Lord have mercy on us, who the hell is it you're wanting to work for?'

'Myself. I've had enough of being pushed around. You can tell Nolan that, too, if you like. The prisoners will have to wire the dynamite up themselves, so I'll give you some of the blasting caps and fuse.'

'I can't take much.'

'You'll take everything I give you and you'll spill ether in your bag to dampen the smell if you have to, and you'll come back for more using the excuse of the cut on my forehead. Now let's get at it, shall we?'

The late news over the wireless from the BBC London was particularly grim. Mary wished she'd not switched it on but had felt desperately alone—not brave or tough as she'd been with Dr. Connor, just damned scared. The British aircraft carrier *Ark Royal* had been torpedoed off Gibraltar. In Russia, a railhead near Leningrad had been taken by the Germans, tightening their hold about the city. Allied shipping losses for October had been among the worst. The U-boat threat was a menace everyone would hate. Her hands had shaken at the thought.

The dry cell battery and its leads lay nestled in cotton wool, well separated from the metal of the shortbread tin. There'd be no stray electrical currents, no shorts she couldn't afford. The six sticks of gelignite lay diagonally across the tin with the battery to one side, she having used one of them as the primer and, finding the gelignite surprisingly soft, had pushed the blasting cap in and tied the wires around the stick so as to secure them.

One lead ran from the blasting cap to the battery—she'd not wired that up yet, nor had she done the others, the links from the battery to the watch and from its crystal to the blasting cap.

The second hand swept around, the minute hand moved. Men would be killed during the prison break—there wasn't much she could do about it, though she'd try if opportunity arose, assuming that she would be made exactly aware of where the charges were to be placed and the time of their detonation.

Somehow she'd have to find out. There were so many things

to do, so many questions still. Answers . . . she'd have to have answers ready.

The bomb was complete—Nolan wouldn't know of it and neither would Fay Darcy or Trant or Erich or any of them. She'd keep it all to herself, but they must be made to take her with them.

Terms agreed. Fix rendezvous 0100 hours 23 November. Kill Heidi.

Once Erich was out from Huber's command, her life wouldn't be worth much, so she would have to hold something back, have to make certain of this.

A heavy woollen pullover went into the rucksack she'd brought from the mudroom. Hamish and she had spent days hiking in the Highlands. It had pleased him to see her so well prepared. Good hiking boots, knee socks, trousers and flannel shirts, even binoculars.

Mary added two pairs of heavy socks, putting these on either side of the tin, then a spare pair of trousers and another pullover. Making room for the rucksack, she squeezed it down into the cedar chest and laid a couple of blankets over it before spreading more mothballs.

There was a calendar hanging from a nail in the study. It was now the night of Tuesday, 11 November 1941. The twenty-third fell on a Sunday. There were twelve days left, then, in which to contact Berlin, fix the rendezvous, break the prisoners out, and cross into Donegal before finding their way to Inishtrahull.

She was certain Kevin would use that island. Deep down inside him, he was still of his family and roots. He'd want somewhere hidden and out of the way, would want to choose a place he knew and this last would probably govern everything else.

Inishtrahull, it had that ring to it. Hamish had maps, but when she'd located the island, Mary found herself sick with dread. It sat right out in the shipping lane that led to the North Channel, was right under Londonderry's thumb and subject to the RAF bases there and to its coastal patrols. It also had its own lighthouse, so wasn't completely uninhabited or undefended either.

Nolan stepped from behind the forge at the old Darcy place. Caught in the half-light, Mary glanced past him to the corner where the shafts of the pony trap stood on end. 'Where's Fay?' she asked.

Still he did not move. 'Look, it's crazy of us to meet here. Jimmy Allanby knows it far too well. He'll . . .'

'Have followed you, is that it?"

'I didn't tell him, if that's what you're thinking. I did exactly as your note said. I left my bike outside the shop in Ballylurgen, went through to the back to hitch a ride in Joe Kivelehan's lorry, then walked in from the road, walked right up that lane, or what's left of it. I . . . I seem always to be meeting you people in ruins of some kind.'

She'd not moved a muscle, still stood beneath that gap in the slates knowing now, though, that the fond slash of morning would touch those dark brown, velvet eyes of hers and the turned-up collar of a camel-hair overcoat. 'How is the captain these days, Allanby that is?'

'I've hardly spoken to him of late. Look, I *don't* like him. I never have. He had our Robbie killed.'

'And the major, what of him, then?'

Quickly Mary told him where things stood. 'I've arranged with Dr. Connor to move the rest of the dynamite into the castle. Huber said to tell you Berlin have agreed to your terms. You're to fix the rendezvous for zero one hundred hours on the twenty-third and to relay everything back through me.'

She still hadn't moved. 'Made yourself essential to us, have you?'

He had come to stand in front of her. 'Please don't touch me.'

Unbuttoning the top of her coat, Nolan brushed the lapels as a tailor might before using the soft yellow mohair scarf as a halter. 'I'll touch if I want.'

'Kevin won't like it.'

'Still fancying him, are you?' He wished that Fay had come inside. Fay would have made sure they pried the truth out of the woman, but Fay was still pissed off about what had happened at O'Shane's farm and was watching out for Allanby.

'Got the bullets to that lover of yours, did you?' he asked.

There was no laughter in him now, no mischief, not even suspicion, just an emptiness that frightened because she could not know what it might mean for her. 'You killed those women.'

'That what the major and the colonel said?'

'You know it is.'

'Then maybe they should have told you that the mother didn't just save me from the pump standard in their stable yard but took me to her bed. She was a stupid cow with talcum powder all over her—I used to dust her down after the bath. She got what she deserved.'

'And the daughter?'

She'd been shocked all right. 'The daughter was the punishment. After all, I was only seven when the mother first made me put my head between those dusty bags of hers. The rest came later when I was ten and twelve and she found she enjoyed my tongue and other things.'

And shocked again. 'Didn't the daughter love you?' he heard her ask, innocence itself.

'Janet Gilmore? Christ, the girl was a slut. She knew I was poling the mother and wanted a bit for herself, so I obliged the two of them. I had to, didn't I?'

'That's still no reason to have murdered them.'

'Worried, are you?'

'Yes.'

'Don't much like the truth, then, do you, but that was the way of it. My da would have lost his job had I not done what those two wanted of me. His lordship knew it, of course, and thought it a riot, since it freed him up with the housemaids.'

Nolan let go of the scarf. Now his arms hung loosely at his sides. 'If you harm me, the Germans will kill you.'

'That what Huber said to pass on?'

When she didn't answer, he came quickly to a decision, but was it one he didn't like?

'Tell the Nazis the break is for the night of the eighteenth. That'll give us five days to reach the rendezvous.'

The eighteenth. 'What time of night?'

Interested, was she? Fifteen minutes past midnight. We'll use the north gate—it's been bricked up—but they're to set all but two of the charges under the barbican and the main gate-house to make it look as if the break is to be there.'

Had he really decided to trust her, or would he simply give the correct information to Dr. Connor?

'I'll need three dozen sticks of that gelignite of yours, two hundred and fifty feet of the safety fuse and sixteen blasting caps—eight of the electrical ones, the same of the others. Set those aside for me. See that Connor gets the rest into the castle as soon as possible—we'll make sure that he has something else to carry in as well so as to make the job easier. We may have to move the date up, though, if the major gets wind of things.'

'Huber wants to know where the rendezvous is. He's insisting that you tell me.'

Ah, and was he now? 'Tell him he'll know soon enough. Just say there's a meeting place he won't forget.'

Tucking her scarf back in, he chucked her under the chin, then said, 'Remember we've means and ways if you spill it all to Trant.'

She jerked her head away. 'I won't. I'm coming with you. I . . . I don't want to hang.'

So they'd put it to her right enough, the major and the colonel and she was smart enough to know they'd do it even if she did tell them everything. 'Just keep that motorcar of yours in readiness.'

'But . . . but they'll know it's my husband's?'

She was so tense, so wanting to have him say she'd be allowed to go with them. 'It'll be dark. It'll be all right. We'll ditch the motor where they'll never find it.'

The car . . . Had Nolan lied to her? Unsettled by the thought, Mary leaned the bike against the arbour. The pony would still be out in the paddock. She could go into the stable to get the halter—that would be excuse enough should Jimmy and the men be watching, as they would be, but they'd not see her walk over to the car.

Nolan wasn't going to let her come with them. She had had that feeling ever since leaving him, had it now as she took the halter down.

Setting it on the bonnet, she crouched to peer beneath the car, located the drive shaft, transmission casing, brake cables and exhaust pipe, then the muffler at the back and the fuel line which ran from here to there.

Opening the bonnet, she ran her eyes uncertainly over the engine, didn't know the first thing about it, would be lost—entirely lost.

When she reached the pony, Mary slipped the halter on him but didn't cinch it too tightly. 'We'll take the trap down to Lough Loughie,' she said, giving him a hug. 'I need time to think things out. I wish, though, that Hamish was here to tell me what to do, but am glad he isn't.'

Nolan was going to kill her and she had the thought then that she knew exactly how he'd do it.

Hitching the pony to the trap hadn't been easy—memories of Orillia had had to be dredged, things she hadn't thought of in ages, things like the barn after a Sunday's dinner, the house asleep, and Frank Thomas. Frank who was to become a young lawyer, but who had been killed in North Africa just like the colonel's sons. Frank fondling her breasts and pushing her underwear down in spite of her objections, the blood pounding in her head, the door deliberately locked, she trying to get it open. Frank and herself in the backseat of a brand-new Chev that had been parked in that barn not far from where the horse had stood patiently in its stall, the new and the old side by side just as they were in Ireland. Would her last flash of thought be one of what had happened, of sex, or merely the smell of new upholstery?

She had been confused, uncertain—thinking all those things a girl would at such a time—but he had just wanted to have fun, had been handsome, well-to-do. 'A lush,' some had said, 'a rake'—small towns were always like that, and yes, she had ignored those whispers, had thought they might really have been in love.

He'd been with another girl in the boathouse at the Thomas cottage on Lake Couchiching when she'd found them like that, herself six months pregnant and coming home from Trinity College in Toronto to tell him they'd best get married.

She hadn't said a thing, hadn't stuck around, had gone off to Montreal, hadn't written, hadn't let anyone know, least of all Frank, had taught herself French, if Parisian French, and found a job teaching in a Catholic day school after Louise had been born. Louise . . . but then word had got out and the job had ended. An unmarried girl with a child was no example to anyone, and now here she was with another child, another horse—well, just a pony—and another car. A last ride, the turn of the ignition key? Was that how it was to be? Death in milliseconds at the hand of the Mad Bomber of London?

Louise had been three years old—long enough for them to have come to love each other entirely. 'I betrayed her. I know I did. If I could make it right, I would.'

The light had almost gone as she rubbed the pony down. The rain had started up again and she could hear it on the roof.

Nolan wanted 250 feet of safety fuse. She would have to get it for him now. Four more coils, then, each of fifty feet. To the sack, she knew where the fuse was kept. Reaching for the wooden pitchfork William had left up in the loft, she dug it into the hay, would not go near the sacks yet, would do what she should first, lest someone come looking.

Pitching the hay down brought back its memories—laughing, exploring, doing all those things young girls will in barns and stables, but was life one round of things? Was it always like this before one's death? Being pregnant and unmarried had been the greatest of sins, never mind who the father, or that Frank had been no good and wouldn't have cared a damn had he known.

The coils of safety fuse came on fifty-foot spools, two to a packet and tightly wrapped in waxed brown paper to which white labels with black lettering had been attached. Jimmy would have made a tally of things but that would have been done right after she had told them of the cache, yet if he should check, what then? He'd discover what she'd done, would find that nearly all of the dynamite was missing.

Lies, lies and more of them. Threading a length of cord through each of the four coils, she tied them tightly around her waist beneath her overcoat, had reached the floor below, had just turned from the ladder when Jimmy stepped in out of the rain.

For a moment she clung to the ladder, and he caught sight of her, wondering what she'd been up to.

Without a word, Mary dug the pitchfork into the hay, was glad she had had the presence of mind to have thrown so much down. He let her fork it into the pony's stall and watched as she spread it around, and she knew then that he must think or know she had met with Nolan this morning, yet had waited until now to confront her.

Rainwater dripped from the camouflaged slicker he wore and from the glossy black peak of his cap.

'What were you doing up in the loft?'

His voice made her start. Momentarily the pitchfork stopped, then she threw more hay into the stall. 'Isn't it obvious?'

'Mary, put that thing down and open your coat.'

'Why should I?'

'Because I ask it of you.'

'Orders, Jimmy? Is that how it's to be?'

Leaning the pitchfork against the wall, she waited for him to say she'd met with Nolan, and when he didn't, said,

'Am I to be strip-searched again, Captain? Does the thought excite you?'

The rain hammered on the roof, the pony tossed its tail. Allanby knew she was hiding something. 'Just open your bloody coat.'

He was perhaps ten feet from her, would see the coils of fuse, would take her to Tralane. 'I'm pregnant,' she said, giving him a fleeting smile that was, she knew, both cruel and introspective. 'Erich's child, Jimmy. The bastard of a Nazi U-boat captain. It's . . . unfortunately it's beginning to show.'

She brushed hands down over her front, stood waiting for the storm that was in him, but it never came. 'Does he know?' he asked.

Mary fingered the shaft of the pitchfork. 'Of course he doesn't. Nor does Hamish, and I'd ask that if you really did once feel anything for me, you will keep it to yourself. Erich and I are finished. It . . . it could never have amounted to anything.'

'Finished.' Allanby shook the rain from his cape before flinging it back over his shoulders. 'Sodding country,' he said. 'Bastard place. You know how much I hate it.' She had said the reverse about Kramer to the major and must have lied about it only being Bauer who'd been after her. Huber must have had to step in to save her. 'Wait here while I have a look in the loft.'

With a start, Mary realized what she'd done. It took him an age to come back.

'You're just saying you're pregnant.'

She shook her head. 'I wish I wasn't, but am.'

Somehow the evening passed, somehow she pulled herself together. Jimmy was letting her sweat it out. He *must* know what she'd done; he was watching the house to see what she'd do.

Outside there was only darkness. Trant and the colonel would expect her to be at the castle tomorrow at 2.00 p.m. sharp. She would have to do exactly as they said, and while she was away they'd have the house searched. Jimmy'd find the rest of the dynamite, the fuse and blasting caps, the bomb she'd made. It would all have been for nothing.

Hamish hadn't understood her loneliness, how could he have? His bedroom was empty, the sheets like ice. When sleep wouldn't come, she did what she had never done before but had often, in her doubting moments, tried to find the courage.

He had a steamer trunk in the attic, a thing from that other war. Perhaps he'd oiled its leather countless times, but since finding her and coming to Ireland he'd put it up here out of the way.

The attic was all but empty—they'd not had time to collect the passing memories of a long and happily married life, nor had he brought much from the days with his first wife.

There were dormers—chances for Jimmy to catch a glimpse of light, if she was so foolish. The trunk was at the far end, near one of the chimneys—great stalwart things of brick these were. Mould clung to her fingers. The leather straps were stiff, the buckles tight.

Setting the torch she'd brought down on the floor, Mary struggled to turn the trunk so that when the lid was opened and left up, it would shield the light.

A strong smell of camphor came, the coarse feel of khaki. Under a sliver of light it all looked so neat and tidy. Hamish had belonged to one of the Highland regiments. His dress tartan, with dirk and sporran, were to her left, the uniforms to the right. He'd once owned a motorcycle and at first she thought the goggles that lay buried between the two must have come from that, but it was his gas mask.

Try as she did, she found it hard to imagine him as a young man in that other war. Far from bringing her closer to him, the contents put distance between them. It was something private, something from another life, and she but an intruder.

When she found photographs of the French girl he'd been in love with, that girl stared out of the past with accusation and a sense of being violated, of horror at what she was doing. Pretty, very French and not quite twenty by the look, with large dark, dusky eyes and the sharpness of feature the Midi-French so often have, the hair thick, dark and worn long just like her own.

Marie . . . her name had been Marie-Louise but was it meaningful or just coincidence that half her name should have been the same as that of the daughter she'd had to leave behind?

A portrait photograph revealed that the girl had had a lovely expression but had the eyes been just like her own? Had Hamish seen this girl in herself when they'd first met—had that been why he'd sought her out?

There was nothing to indicate why the two had parted. A handkerchief that had lost all trace of its scent, seemed the only bit of evidence, but his gun lay beneath it. Had he had it out for some reason—that bridge they'd had to cross on their way to find Caithleen?

It was a Webley service revolver and just like the one she'd taken into Tralane. There was a box of cartridges. Breaking the cylinder open, revealed that he'd not reloaded it, not since he'd had to shoot one of the enemy in a shell crater during that other war. Hamish had been finished with war then, had not even removed the spent cartridge or unloaded the rest, had simply hated what he'd had to do and himself.

Knowing this, Mary put the gun back exactly as found. It was now the night of Wednesday, 12 November. There were exactly six days left to the prison break and a further five to the rendezvous.

In the morning there was a letter from him. They'd had a good crossing. Caithleen was settling in. He had tried to book passage back but with the war, every avenue had been blocked which meant, of course, that he'd been prevented from returning.

At noon she left the house to watch the swans, and at 2.00 p.m. was at the castle. Trant was busy at his desk and didn't look up or offer a greeting of any kind. Unbuttoning her coat, Mary waited for him to speak but nothing came from him, not even when Dr. Connor was shown in, he nodding self-consciously and giving her the shallow grin of the deceitful.

They'd got to him then—Trant and Jimmy and the colonel. Connor had told them about the dynamite. He had that whipped, hangdog expression.

'You've met with Nolan?' asked Trant suddenly, but still not bothering to look up.

Had he had enough of her lies? she wondered, glancing uncertainly at Dr. Connor. 'The rendezvous . . .' she began, only to hesitate.

Still not looking up, Trant indicated that she was to continue. 'There are to be no secrets from the doctor, Mrs. Fraser. He's in one everything, or didn't we inform you of this?'

Must she be forced to carry on?

'Well?' he demanded.

'Major, the rendezvous is . . . is to be on the night of the twenty-seventh of this month.' There, she'd got that much out.

'So late?' he asked, looking up at her now in doubt.

She mustn't waver, mustn't give herself away—must play it out no matter what Dr. Connor had told them. 'The break is scheduled for the night of the twenty-third at just past midnight. Twelve fifteen.'

Trant shoved the sketch he'd been perusing across the desk towards her. 'Have a look at this and tell me where that tunnel is.'

'Major, if I knew, I'd have told you already.'

'Then take a guess.'

He ignored Dr. Connor. The sketch was a plan of the cellars. Passageways ran beneath the rampart walls to each of the towers. There was a dungeon beneath the cantling tower, then the brewhouse and the tunnel that had already been discovered. Beyond this tunnel, there were the kitchens and storerooms, a warren of passageways, some of which led to the chapel where she had met the High Command.

There were sewers and 'latrine pit holes,' water wells and 'grottoes,' even a catacomb. It was possible to walk from the barbican and south gate right around the bailey without ever seeing the light of day.

'I don't know, Major. I can't even guess. I would only mislead you.'

'Dr. Connor, enlighten Mrs. Fraser.'

'Surely, Major, but I wish to God you'd not brought the two of us together.'

'Oh, and why is that?'

Ignoring the giving of such an obvious answer, Connor ducked his head and tapped the sketch with a forefinger. 'The tunnel runs from the foot of these stairs to the barbican and main gatehouse.'

Just beyond the kitchens and the first of the storerooms there was a square stairwell. Mary tried to visualize the castle above it. There'd be an entrance to what had once been the owner's private apartments. There was an arched entrance . . . yes . . . yes, she had it now: well to the south of the keep. The staircase would be just inside that entrance and on the ground floor below the southwestern corner of the great hall and not far from the library. How had they managed to dig such a tunnel in secret? It must be at least two hundred yards in length. Totally unexpected because it ran not from the castle walls to freedom, but under the inner courtyard.

'Just what have they got planned for this?' asked Trant, 'now that the dynamite's been taken care of?'

Connor . . . she mustn't look at him, he having definitely given her away. 'I . . . I haven't the slightest idea, Major.'

'It leads to a blind wall, a footing beneath the barbican,' he said, lost to it, or seemingly so, but was it the fake tunnel Huber had said they wanted the British to find? she wondered. Nolan had said to tell the Nazis to use most of the dynamite beneath the barbican and the main gatehouse so as to make it look like the breakout would occur there. This tunnel led straight to them.

With a sinking feeling, she realized they had found the real tunnel, but had Dr. Connor been the one to tell Trant of it or had he shown Connor where it was?

'What did Nolan say they would do with this tunnel, Mrs. Fraser?'

Mary thought to run, thought how foolish that would be.

'The truth,' he said, 'or else.'

Jimmy had found she'd taken the dynamite from the stable; Dr. Connor had been caught with some of it and had betrayed her. A tunnel . . . explosives placed under the barbican and the gatehouse; 12.15 a.m., 18 November, not the twenty-third as she'd only just told him. 'I guess Nolan planned to use the explosives there.'

'You guess,' snorted Trant. 'Did you think I wouldn't realize the two of you were working together?'

'We're not. I . . .'

'It's the God's truth, Major. Don't be daft, man. Mrs. Fraser may be doing what you want with the prisoners but as for my-self, I . . .'

'Uphold the law and the rights of the British Crown, that it?'

'You know it is. Now if you don't mind, I'll be away to my rounds.'

'Just don't let the bastards know we've discovered their tun-nel. I'm warning you.'

'Warn all you like, but leave me to do my job.'

Connor reached for his bag which he'd set on a chair. He was at the door when Trant said, 'Take Mrs. Fraser with you, then. She and I are finished for now.'

Once again the walls closed about her. As the wind gusted across the bailey, Trant's parting words clung until at last she said, 'I thought you'd given me away.'

'And there was me thinking the same of yourself. Sure and the major's a tricky devil, but if he's so suspicious, why is he giving us a chance to talk?'

The wind lifted a corner of her coat, forcing her to hold it down. 'Because if we're working together, we'll now doubt each other, and because he likes to put people out here all on their own so that he can take the long view of them from that office of his.'

'Right-oh, then, we'll give him the thumbs up. I've got that dynamite you gave me in this bag of mine.'

He hadn't! 'I just wish you had the rest of it. They've got dogs that can smell that stuff. Dogs!'

'You're getting to be quite an expert, aren't you? God it's a marvel what necessity makes a person do.'

'Like this latest tunnel we're walking over,' she shouted. 'What will Huber and the others do now that Trant's discov-ered it?'

They'd be above the thing, they would, and she with the

eye of a coal miner! 'Dig another,' he shouted back. 'Prisoners have but one task; jailers another.'

At the door to the keep, Mary told him there wouldn't be time. Though worried and afraid, Connor found the will to grin. 'You've played the lark with the major, you have. See that you play it with the others in here and maybe the two of us will come out of this alive.'

He left her then, left her all on her own. Empty halls, not a soul about and the prisoners confined to their quarters—of course they'd be. No chance to meet with them, no chance to tell them anything.

They were punishing the men again. Trant . . . Trant had let her come in here thinking she'd be able to meet with Huber.

Mary started to cross the great hall, but it was so like that time before, she had to stop in its centre. Waiting, she looked up to each of the stone balustrades, expecting to find Trant looking down at her. When he didn't come, she went on to the library but now everything was tumbling in on her, the lies, the deceit, the betrayal of Hamish and her country, the need to tell Huber she hadn't had the ghost of an idea where their tunnel had been, that Trant had tried to pin the blame for its discovery on her.

Erich . . . there'd be no escape because there never could be. There'd be no new tunnel, no explosives under the barbican and the main gatehouse, no breakout on Tuesday, 18 November.

No rendezvous. Nothing.

'M'am, will you not eat a thing?'

'I'm afraid I couldn't, Mrs. Haney. It . . . it looks lovely. Shepherd's pie has always been a favourite of mine.'

'It's them goings on at the castle. Tunnels was it? And them

Nazis burying themselves like moles of a Sunday, burrowing holes t' get them all out of that place and under them walls.'

'Mrs. Haney . . .'

'M'am?'

'Nothing. No, never mind. I . . . I just don't want to talk about it.'

'If only the doctor would come home, he'd put things to rights, he would.'

'He mustn't, Mrs. Haney. For his sake and for my own.'

Had it come to that? Sure and there'd be no good come of all these goings-on, and her looking like the Shroud of Turin wrapped round the very Lamb of God. 'Is it that you're in trouble, m'am, and if so, could I not be of some assistance, seeing as the good doctor is away?'

'I can't have you mixed up in things. It . . . it wouldn't be right of me.'

Ria ladled out a healthy portion of the shepherd's pie. Adding steamed sprouts and chopped carrots, she set the plate in front of the missus, then took a slice of the whole wheat bread she had baked that very day, and buttered it. 'Now you eat something solid and you listen. Trouble comes when it's never wanted. It has to be turned and the only way for a body to do that, is to face it with trouble of your own.'

Mary wanted to reach out to her. Mrs. Haney was such a big, strong, dependable, kindhearted woman, but she couldn't involve her in things, mustn't do so no matter how desperate.

'Liam Nolan and Fay Darcy are over the hills a piece, m'am. If it's wanting to send a message to them, I could find a way.'

Tears that hadn't been able to come for some time, came suddenly. Ria watched in compassionate silence as they ran down those fair cheeks the good doctor loved. 'M'am?' she asked, stern and insistent now.

'Tell Nolan they've found the tunnel. Tell him I wasn't allowed to see the Germans.'

'Is the house still under surveillance?'

'Of course it is.'

'And by preventing you from meeting with them Nazis, does the major not wish to force you into seeking a meeting with the others?'

'Yes . . . Yes, I suppose he could have had that in mind. I hadn't thought of it, though.'

'Then Liam's not the one to tell, else he'll come traipsing in here of a dark night and he so reckless he'd break eggs before ever they was laid.'

Friday came and went with no sign of Mrs. Haney, no word at all. Saturday came and then Sunday. Mary leapt when there was a knock at the front door, a pounding. Trant . . . was it Trant or Jimmy Allanby?

But it was only Dr. Connor. 'I've come to pull those stitches. Now I've not forgotten.'

Led through to the kitchen, it was clear that she was in a state—he could see this at a glance. 'I'll just wash my hands,' he said. She didn't look well. No, indeed, she did not. 'You weren't at the castle yesterday. The major was asking after you.'

Connor was taking his time at the sink. 'I . . . I didn't feel well. I . . . If you must know, Doctor, I couldn't face it.'

'Small wonder.'

He took one of Mrs. Haney's tea towels and proceeded to do the unpardonable by drying his hands on it, then set his bag down on the big deal table where the cares of the world had been rolled to smithereens more times than one. Using tweezers and surgical scissors, he first tugged at each suture, then snipped it off and pulled it free before at last brushing a thumb over the cut. 'A small scar, but nothing, though you've a slight allergy to catgut. Best to keep it in mind.'

For what? And why wouldn't he tell her what had happened at the castle?

When Trant stepped into the kitchen, she felt her stomach wrench.

Outside the house, and wearing a black beret and battle fatigues, Jimmy Allanby strode quickly past the window. He had a Thompson submachine gun cradled in his arms, was fiercely grim. She heard him trying the door to the mudroom.

Trant told Dr. Connor to go and open it. 'The house is surrounded. There's nothing either of you can do.'

Forever that moment would remain fixed in memory. The stove, the copper boiler, the shamrocks on the biscuit-work plates that hung on the wall next to the plaster cross to which had been nailed a pitifully thin, unshaven and sorrowful Christ in lime green, pearly, iridescent, aquatint tones with a god-awful frame to which a dried yellow rose had been fastened. The clock above it . . .

Trant's black brogue was planted firmly on the seat of Mrs. Haney's favourite chair. Jimmy came into the room, still cradling the ugliness of that gun. 'Stable and outbuildings swept, sir. Gardens being searched. House secured.'

He'd not a glance for her, not a thought, and she knew then that if she ran for it, he'd cut her to pieces with that thing.

'Mrs. Haney . . . ?' began Trant, the suspicion all too clear. 'Gone South, I take it?'

Jimmy hadn't moved from the mudroom's inner door but stood to one side of it. Dr. Connor looked oddly foolish, caught out perhaps, pilloried beneath the single, unlighted electric bulb that hung from the ceiling in its shade of Edwardian glass.

'Gone South?' she heard herself asking.

Trant lifted his shoe from the chair. 'Oh, sorry about that,' he said of the mud he'd left on the cushion. 'Gone South, yes, to County Meath, to see her brother at his farm near Kilmessan. Paid the Hill of Tara a pilgrimage. Did all the things a penitent should.'

'Bridget, our kitchen girl, is helping Mrs. Haney's brother and his wife. Ria's very religious.'

'So I gather, but in November, in an icy rain?' he all but shouted, startling her and Dr. Connor.

Jimmy still hadn't moved.

Trant set his cap and gloves on the table. 'The point is, Mrs. Fraser, your cook was hoping to meet someone.'

'And did she?' Jimmy had finally thought to watch her— she being the closer of them to the front entrance and freedom.

Again there was that dryness of Trant's. 'We were rather hoping you'd be able to shed a little light on the matter.'

Dr. Connor flicked an anxious glance from one to the other of them. To distract him from trying to make a run for it, Mary heard herself saying, 'Doctor, doesn't this cut of mine need a bandage?' but her voice must have been too high, for he leapt at the sound of it.

'Your cut? Ah no, m'am. No, indeed. Th' redness will soon pass and you'll have the fine brush of the morn in no time.'

'Tea, Major?' asked Mary. 'I was just about to make some. Dandelion if you would prefer, or the black currant.'

Dandelion . . . Just what the hell else had she been up to? he wondered. 'With your permission, Mrs. Fraser, Captain Allanby will search the premises. Captain, see to it.'

They'd find the bomb, find the dynamite . . .

Warming the Brown Betty Mrs. Haney always used, she set out a plate of scones, pots of raspberry jam and a little honey, the cups and things, the saccharin, too, and margarine automatically following, she moving now just to give herself something to do. 'Doctor, I'll take your coat and bag through to the foyer, but would you see to the kettle for me?'

The two of them had been caught out—they gave every indication of this, thought Trant, nodding to indicate that she could momentarily leave. 'There's no escape,' he said.

From the hall, Mary could hear them upstairs. They were going through the bedrooms. There was mud from their boots on the carpet, more of it on the stairs.

Covering Connor's bag with his overcoat, she set both on the bench across from the foyer's mirror. When she reached the staircase that led to the attic, she hesitated. Jimmy would have found everything by now, would know she and Connor had already moved some of the dynamite into Tralane.

'Where is he, Mary?'

The timbers in the attic and the brick chimneys framed him. 'Who?' she asked, genuinely puzzled—had he not found the dynamite?

'You know bloody well who. Kevin O'Bannion.'

They'd thought him hiding in the house. 'I've no idea. Look, he certainly wouldn't have come here with you constantly watching the place.'

As in the kitchen, Jimmy didn't move, but stood just waiting for her to do something. 'What about Nolan and the Darcy woman?' he asked. 'Admit that you've met with them.'

'I haven't left the house since I came back here from Tralane on Thursday. No one, except for the postman and Dr. Connor, have been to see me and he's only just arrived as you must surely know.'

She had come up the last of the stairs to finally stand before him. 'What about that husband of yours?'

'Hamish? You know very well he's in Scotland. I had a letter from him the other day. If you like, I'll show it to you.'

Allanby noted how worry furrowed the cut on her brow as doubt about the husband crept in. He saw her thinking that Fraser might well have found passage across the North Channel, saw her eyes moistening at the thought.

Glad that he had hurt her, he stepped brusquely past and went down the stairs.

Mary heard him barking orders to his men. They'd search the ground floor now and then the cellar. She hesitated, said, *Hamish?* to herself, and went along to the steamer trunk to hesitate yet again. She'd have heard Hamish if he'd come home. He'd not have had time to get his revolver but she knew then that he'd try to do so if . . . if ever he did manage to make it back.

Leaving the trunk, she uncovered the dynamite which lay between the floor joists beneath a wicker hamper in a far corner and under an ample dusting of moth crystals with splashings of turpentine on covering rags. Taking a half-dozen sticks—gathering them quickly into her arms as one would sticks for the fire—she bundled them into her apron and headed for the stairs. It was crazy of her to do this. Crazy!

Running down the stairs, she reached for Connor's bag, fought to open it and found so little room it caused her to drop one stick on the floor. One! Would have to kick it under the bench and hope for the best. Shoving the rest down into the bag, she left it unfastened under the coat and raced for the kitchen.

It was Trant who, startled by her sudden reappearance, said jovially, 'Ah, here she is. The doctor and I were just having a chat. You've been playing quite a double game with us, haven't you?'

She couldn't look at Connor. She mustn't! 'Only what you've told me to do.'

'Then why did that cook of yours tell us . . .'

'Major, if you've harmed Mrs. Haney . . .'

'Harm her? Good gracious me. Most cooperative. Said you had wanted her to contact Kevin O'Bannion and that she'd done so. Oh come now, Mrs. Fraser, your cook's not in the Kilimain Jail or in Mountjoy. Nothing like that. Your Mrs. Haney's a realist. Given the circumstances, she caught the drift and readily agreed to assist us. I daresay she'll be home tomorrow.'

Again the moment would remain fixed in memory. The major sitting with his elbows on the table, Dr. Connor still holding the teapot, the crumbs of a broken scone strewn across the table in front of Trant. 'They haven't come to see me, Major. No one's hiding here. I . . . I just couldn't face going to Tralane anymore.'

'But you will on Tuesday as usual. That right?'

'Yes. Yes, I'll be there then.'

Unable to sleep—how could she after what had happened today?—Mary lay on her side in bed, hugging the pillows and staring at the electric heater whose coils crackled as the thing warmed up and then as it cooled.

There'd be no need for her to go to Tralane. Nolan had wanted the break to take place very early on that Tuesday; she'd have arrived hours after it had occurred. Hours, but by then Jimmy would have come for her and she'd have run out across the fields here, have run until . . .

Dr. Connor had taken the dynamite with him and not given a hint of anything untoward when he'd picked up that bag of his. The stray stick had been recovered, but it was never going to happen. There'd be no break at all and Trant had known this, no chance for them to reach the rendezvous. How could there be?

The heater reached its maximum and automatically began to cool, the cherry red of its coils waning to yellow and then to amber. All night it would repeat this cycle. Hamish had bought it for her in Armagh, had been so pleased with himself. The automatic safety feature was both 'economical and prudent.' She loved him dearly but knew it was too late for this.

Just when the heater started up again, she'd never know. Even at its peak, the thing threw only the dullest of lights, but had she drifted off, had something awakened her? 'Who's there?' she asked, her voice that of another person.

The coils began to crackle as she got out of bed. Reaching for her dressing gown, she began to pull it on only to hesitate. She wasn't alone. There *was* someone else in the room. Nolan . . . was it Nolan?

He was standing against the far wall, beside her bureau and had been there for quite some time. Had he been listening to see if she'd been asleep? Had he thought to murder her in bed?

Letting the dressing gown slip from her fingers, she heard it crumple to the floor, heard this against the crackling of the heater and the loneliness of the wind outside.

He stepped from the wall; she thought to run but when he took hold of her by the shoulders, she heard him saying, 'I got here as soon as I could. Your Mrs. Haney did a fine job of leading them astray.'

He was holding her up. Her knees felt as though they would buckle. 'Kevin, you've got to take me with you. Trant knows everything.'

He let a breath escape but didn't remove his hands, would feel how nervous she was, how very afraid.

'Trant doesn't know what he needs to know. The break's still on.'

She stepped away from him and he wondered if she was

done with all notion of him and reasoned that she was. 'Why haven't they stopped you?' she asked. 'Did you have to kill one of them out there?'

She had turned sideways to him and he saw that her hair was loose and knew she must wear it that way every time she went to bed. 'The Brits won't know I've been and gone unless you tell them.'

Briefly, and as quickly as she could, this contact person of theirs told him what had happened. The fact that Trant had discovered the tunnel wasn't good, and she'd been only too aware of this, but he'd best remain calm and decisive. 'The Germans will have to make some other arrangements. Liam will be ready in any case. Perhaps we'll handle the whole thing from outside.'

He had meant it too. 'Nolan told me to have the car ready.'

O'Bannion gave her a nod. He'd let her think what she would. So much depended on the element of surprise. A massive detonation directly beneath the garrison's barracks with half the men asleep would have been perfect. Absolute chaos had been crucial to the plan, so much so he wondered now if they really shouldn't call it all off. 'Does Trant think you lied to him about the date of the breakout?'

Her head was shaken, she having lost some of her wariness.

'I don't think so, but he . . . he does expect me to be there on Tuesday.'

'What have you done with the rest of the dynamite?'

'It's in the attic. I . . . I didn't have time to give Dr. Connor any more blasting caps. I . . . I can get it for you now.'

He asked for a bag to carry it in and she couldn't help wondering if there was safety in helping him but said, 'A canvas hamper for the firewood. It's . . . it's in the kitchen.'

'Get it and the rest.' She was gone in a flash, that little woman. Suddenly exhausted, for he'd been on the run for days and had more of them to come, O'Bannion went over to the bed and sat on its edge, warming his hands at her electric fire. Christ, there'd been one damn thing after another with this caper. The sooner it was over and done, the better. And the Fraser woman? he asked. Just what the bloody hell had she really been up to on her own? She was not a woman to take orders for long. Not that one.

When she brought him bread and cheese and the last of a brandy bottle, she left him again to get the explosives, but left him with the trembling touch of a hand. Had it been one of friendship after all, of 'Thank God it was you, Kevin'; or had she reasoned that a certain element of closeness would suit her purposes best?

'You have to take me with you,' she said.

Startled, for he'd not heard her return, O'Bannion looked up from the heater, still couldn't see her, but had she read his mind?

Watching him, her back to the closet door, for she'd come into the room so silently he'd not seen her even yet, Mary wondered at his gazing so deeply into the electric fire. Had it been the look of a man who knew in his heart of hearts that the battle before him had already been lost?

He longed for a cigarette, but she'd none and he didn't want her going downstairs again to look for one. 'I've a good twenty miles to cover before dawn,' he said, the weariness suddenly there so strongly she'd wonder at it and have to feel a particle of sympathy for him. 'If you do get through to Huber and the others, for God's sake tell them the rendezvous has been arranged. Tell them we'll do all we can and that it'll have to be enough, but that they must be ready at a moment's notice. The north gate as before. Don't be forgetting that and having them go to some other place.'

She would sit on the floor now, Mary told herself, would hug her knees as she looked up at him. What light there was would give shadows to the clefts in his face, and the deepness of those shadows would only grow as the coils cooled.

He was looking at her now, was wondering what she'd do and thinking she'd try something.

'You really do have to take me with you, Kevin. You can't leave me behind to face things on my own, not after all I've done.'

Dear God but she was a beautiful thing, but what the hell had she in mind?

'The rendezvous is on Inishtrahull,' she said. 'If anything should happen to me, I've left a message with someone I trust implicitly.'

Startled, alarmed, he let the ghost of a sad smile momentarily lighten the grim grey darkness he felt. 'You were not to know, but we'll take you with us, never fear.' It had to be the husband she'd left the damned thing with.

Mary knew that the nightgown clung to her thighs well enough. She'd a good figure and he'd been only too aware of it, couldn't seem to stop those sad grey eyes of his from slipping over the length of her. 'Why does Nolan need our car when he knows the British will only recognize it, if by no other means than its licence number, the shortage of petrol and the need for ration coupons?'

She was playing with him, was using that body of hers to tempt him. 'He must have some place in mind to ditch it.' Had she really sent a note to that husband of hers? Ria had said the two of them were very much in love and that the doctor would lay down his life for his young wife, she her own for him.

He'd take another pull at the bottle, would give her time to sort out any such thoughts. Liam would have taken care of things by now. They'd have to kill the husband as well if he got in the road again, but Fraser really was in Scotland. The censors would have got at that 'message' of hers and she'd have damned well known this but had been bluffing anyways. 'Don't leave the house until midnight,' he said, 'then drive like the blazes for Tralane and have the motor waiting for us at that clearing by the lake. We'll meet up with you there.'

He had said it as if he had really meant it and she told him she was glad he was back. 'It'll make all the difference, Kevin. I know it will.'

As he reached for the canvas bag she'd stuffed, light from the heater caught in the gold that was around that pretty neck of hers and hanging with a key from a bit of string. She'd been kissing that ring when he'd first come upon her and hadn't yet realized she'd not tucked it out of sight.

When she said 'You'd best go. I think I heard something,' he left her without another word, left her standing beside the bed, she fingering the ring now and knowing that she had betrayed herself.

At dawn, she watched the drive and the road beyond. There were now some eighteen hours left, but was it meaningful that the remaining time and the date of the breakout should be the same?

At noon a milk cart turned in, its driver, one of the local farmers, touching a turf-stained cap in salute to his passenger. Bundled in an ankle-length muskrat coat that must reek of moth crystals, that fedora of his tilted well back, Hamish gazed fondly up at the house he loved, and when she opened the door to stand gaping at him, he said, 'Mary, lass, are you no glad t' see me?'

There were two suitcases, the one of books, for it was the heavier, he clutching both by the handles as if just back from America.

'Well, lass, do I not warrant a word, let alone the kiss of welcome?'

'But . . . but how did you . . . ?'

Trapped she was and looking pale and anxious and not glad to see him at all. '*Och*, I found a passage of my own. Where's Robbie? I don't hear his welcome. Has something . . .'

Stricken by the news, he fought for words. 'Dead? My wee dog? Ah, say it isn't so.'

When she didn't answer, he set the cases down and asked if there was petrol in the car.

'No! No, it . . . The tank was drained.'

'And me a doctor?'

'By Jimmy. They . . . they've been watching the house and were afraid someone might try to use it.'

'Then I'll have to take the pony trap. Aye, I will. The colonel and I'll have words on this. My Robbie taken from me while my back was turned and me not here t' see it would na happen!'

'Darling, wait. Please come in. Let me fix you something to eat. You must be starved.'

And she like a Jezebel! 'I've eaten well enough. I'll away to Tralane, I will.'

Nothing would stop him, and there was nothing for it but to close the door. His suitcases sat out there for hours until at last she could stand it no longer and had carried them in. Then she went upstairs to the attic, to his steamer trunk to get the revolver and its box of cartridges before he did. She couldn't have him lying dead in the road like Parker, couldn't come upon him that way.

The gun and the cartridges went into her rucksack, shoved well down and hidden as best she could, everything left in the shed now, for if she had to use her bike, she would. She'd never touch the car, but Hamish might and she couldn't have that either. No, she couldn't.

At 5.00 p.m. he still hadn't returned, nor at 6.00. Dreading what she had to do, Mary went out to the stable, to the car. The smell of petrol seemed everywhere when she opened the bonnet and shone the torch over the engine, but she'd never find the bomb. Never.

Lying under the car, she shone the torch up into the engine and right away found it fastened to a pipe: three sticks of gel-ignite wrapped tightly together with electrician's sticky black tape. One primer stick and two wires that ran from the blasting cap but all too soon disappeared up into the engine.

Kevin had known Nolan had been out here wiring it up while the two of them had been in her room. Though she had suspected as much, it was still a terrible letdown.

Slowly, with infinite patience, she ran her fingers gingerly along the wires. Could they safely be cut?

'Mary, lass, what are you doing under there?'

'Hamish, *don't* touch anything! Darling, please don't.' He was looking down at her through the engine. 'Just . . . just let me deal with it. The wires must be connected to the ignition switch and the battery. I'll just have to disconnect them at the blasting cap. Could you hold the light for me?'

When the thing was done and laid out on the workbench, Fraser fingered the pieces. She'd known exactly what to do, had been calm about it, so much so he had to stand in awe of her.

'What time is it?' she asked, not finding the will to look at him.

'Ten past nine.'

At midnight she went outside to listen and he caught her standing in the rain looking off towards Tralane. 'Lass, there'll be no breakout. Dr. Connor simply handed all that dynamite you sent in there over to the major.'

10

From the top of Caitlyn Murphy's Hill, the land stretched down and away in fields and woods to breaking rays of sunshine and the Loughie black among the folds. Mary stood alone, a last walk of a morn, a last look back to where so much had happened. She remembered that first day Hamish and she had looked at the house. They had had such hopes, the two of them, but did such things matter now?

Hamish would not be allowed to accompany her to Tralane. She had packed a small suitcase, a few personal things. Jimmy Allanby would come for her at 0900 hours and that would be it. On trial for treason, sent over to the Old Bailey to be made a spectacle of.

A Nazi lover. Would they shave her head? Women who'd had that done to them had always looked diseased.

Would they hang her in public and take photographs afterwards?

Idly she kicked a stone and watched as it rolled away. She ought, really, to try to escape but it'd be of no use, and when the black Rover the major used, and then an army lorry roared past her to turn in at the drive, Mary gave a last look round before starting down the hill to meet them.

Hamish had come outside to stand on the doorstep and close the door behind him. Jimmy, now dressed in parade-ground drill, was impatient. There were guns everywhere—guns to collect one lone woman.

'Jimmy, I want the morning with my husband.'

'You've had enough time.'

'Mary, don't. It'll do no good.'

'Then at least a walk round the drive? Look, I can't run away, can I?'

Allanby wished she'd try. 'All right, a walk. Doctor, get your coat.'

'I don't need my bloody coat. The lass and I have things to say.'

Unable to say those things, they had all but reached the road in silence when Mary took him by the hand and pulled him to a stop. 'Darling, listen to me. As God is my witness, I love you very much. I've done all the wrong things, Hamish. I'm pregnant with Erich's child—I would have cheated on you and lied about it if I could, but I do love you. I know that now.'

'Lass, I'll find a way to help.'

'You mustn't. For your sake and mine, let me think of you as before this happened. Try not to forget me. Know that if I could change things, I would.'

He was shivering, and when she tried to warm him by stepping closer, he was embarrassed, knowing Jimmy and the men were watching.

At the end, she couldn't bring herself to let go of him and was forced to make a spectacle of herself. Shoved into the car, her wrists handcuffed, the door was slammed on her, slamming out the last glimpses of freedom. She should have tried to make a run for it, should have let them cut her down.

Bannerman kept her waiting all morning in one of the interrogation rooms. Only at 11.50 a.m. did he deign to see her. 'Mrs. Mary Ellen Fraser?' he asked—was she now to be a nonperson?

'You know that's my name, Colonel.'

'Please just answer the questions.'

The girl, Corporal Bridgewood, typed things down. The Sanderson woman had come into the room with Major Trant—wasn't humiliation what jailers did to prisoners they wished to break?

The colonel still waited for her answer, Corporal Bridgewood's fingers were poised over the keys. 'Yes, my name is Mrs. Mary Ellen Fraser and I . . .'

'You will address me only as directed,' said Bannerman.

'Colonel, is it all to be a matter of form?'

'Really, Mrs. Fraser, I would have thought you'd be willing to cooperate at this point.'

Trant had said that. There was no sign of Jimmy.

'Did you willingly attempt to supply explosives to the prisoners through Dr. Connor?'

'Of course I did, but not willingly. You know very well that I was being . . .'

'Mrs. Fraser, must I remind you to simply say "yes" or "no"?'

'Then no! I didn't. Make of that what you will. You'll get nothing further from me. I want a lawyer.'

It was Trant who told her she had no rights. 'The prime minister and the chiefs of staff are demanding a signed confession. Let's keep it simple, shall we?'

Did it really matter that she'd been blackmailed into helping the IRA, that Erich had used her? 'All right, then yes, I willingly did so.'

'You do realize the severity of the charges against you?'

Bannerman had said that. The Sanderson woman hadn't taken her eyes off her for a moment. 'Yes, I know I'll be tried and found guilty.'

'You'll hang.'

That had been Trant, but must they keep on at it?

'Did you take anything into Tralane other than those books of yours and sundry messages?'

Trant again, but was it that they still didn't know about the revolver? 'I want a lawyer, Major. Even when charged with treason, under British law a person has the right to a fair trial and that means a counsel for the defence.'

'You're full of it, aren't you? You betray that husband of yours, betray your king and country, and yet have the unmitigated gall to take up our time with talk of a lawyer? Colonel, have her placed in the dungeons with Bauer. I'm sure that will clear her head of any further nonsense.'

Bannerman glanced at his wristwatch. 'Confound it, Roger, I'm expecting a call from GHQ Belfast at any moment. I need that paper signed by her now. You know she's to leave with Kramer and the others at fourteen hundred hours.'

'Then allow me to take her for a little walk. We'll soon straighten her out.'

'She's pregnant, Major.'

'That is the least of our concerns, Colonel.'

'Very well, see that it's done.'

It was now 12.03 p.m. They would take the rampart walk which ran but a short three hundred feet from the barbican to the cantling tower. Once there, it would be the staircase, she held between the two women, Trant a step ahead of them and down, down, down. Guards with bayonets fixed, guards both behind and ahead of them.

The wind hit her as they stepped out on to the rampart. At

once the crenellated, machicollated parapets of the cantling tower's defences rose high above her, with slits for arrows, quicklime, hot stones and boiling oil. Forced to hurry, Mary almost ran, but would it be four or five minutes after 12.00 p.m.? Why should it matter? They'd be taking her in an armoured van to Belfast with Erich and the other officers of U-121 at 2.00 p.m. In chains, to be shipped off to London, the rope coarse— would they slip a black cloth bag over her head just before they put the noose around her . . .

For some reason Trant had stopped. Flinging out an arm, he indicated the bailey far below them. All the prisoners had been assembled; all stood perfectly to attention, their lines so straight and equally spaced it defied reason.

'Sod the bastards, Mrs. Fraser. Sod them. They're out there where we can keep an eye on them, and the sooner you and that lover of yours are gone from us, the better.'

A last glimpse of the battlements revealed machine guns; another of the bailey, the same.

'Think they'll blow their way out of here, do they?' shouted Trant. 'Well, we'll see about that, won't we?'

Seven . . . would it be seven or eight minutes past noon? she wondered, again asking, Why should it matter? As their steps pounded on the stairs, they spiralled down now, almost at a run to the clashing of bolts at the bottom, the image of an iron portcullis's spearlike points being raised as they hurried underneath, only to come to a crowded halt.

The whole of the floor beneath her was an open grillwork of iron bars, and under this, standing in the dingiest of light and gazing up at her, Franz Bauer waited.

He was grinning at her and must have known they'd do this. A litter of straw and a wooden bench were all he'd been allowed. He was still in chains.

'A nasty man, Mrs. Fraser. So what's it to be?' asked Trant.

There was a hole in the floor below, a drain of some sort, the latrine.

When she didn't answer, he told the guards to open the trapdoor and lower the ladder. 'You'll be asked to climb down there, Mrs. Fraser. If you don't do so willingly, we will force you to. You'll be left alone with that animal, and I don't give one sweet damn if you come out of there alive.'

He thrust a paper at her; she took the pen he offered. 'I . . . I'd best use the wall or the floor back there. Look, I'm sorry for what I did, Major, but I really had no other choice. Erich and the others would have told Hamish I'd betrayed him; Fay Darcy would have made certain Nolan killed not just myself but my husband.'

'Madam, that is of no consequence. Sergeant Malcolmson has a table in the guardroom. See that you use it and sign that thing properly. I daresay there'll be time enough for written confessions of your own later on.'

He glanced at his wristwatch. 'Not quite twelve thirteen,' he muttered to himself. He was afraid and she wondered at this as she was taken to the guardroom.

'Sign it here, m'am.' Malcolmson stabbed a blunt forefinger at the last line as she took up the pen.

'Shall I date it?' she asked, surprised at how calm she felt now that it was all over.

'Best to do so, I guess. They've forgotten to type it in.'

So they had. They must all be afraid of something. That was why the prisoners had been put on parade . . .

The nib was dry. Before opening the lever on the barrel, Mary held the pen to one side so as not to get ink on her coat— to think that she'd even worry about such a thing at such a time. 'It's empty,' she said. 'Have you got an ink bot . . .'

Flung back against the wall, dazed and bleeding from the

nose and ears, she fought to clear her head. Dust filled the room—blinding, choking masses of it and splinters of stone, a hail of them, a constant rain. Mary tried to shield herself, tried to make sense of what was happening. The walls and floor reverberated, shaking again and again as blocks of stone fell. She must get up, must try to save herself, was numb, in shock and terrified as a hand groped for her through the darkness. Bauer . . . was it Bauer?

A rush of rubble fell and she could feel the blocks bouncing about yet there was now no sound, only a constant roaring in her head. Her head . . . she was going to pass out, but that hand had closed more firmly about the front of her coat. Deaf . . . were they all deaf?

Aching everywhere, she struggled to pull herself up into a sitting position only to bang her head on the table and realize that it must have helped to save her. Was that a light? she wondered, yelling, 'Here! There are two of us!' but hearing nothing, just the roaring in her head. Her ears—were they bleeding?

Later, much, much later, a distant shout came. Much closer there was a gasp. 'My legs. I was just on my way in to you.'

Another rush of rubble came, and then someone distant yelled, 'WATCH OUT, YOU BLOODY FOOLS!'

Then there was nothing, not another word, just more of the falling rubble, the choking clouds of dust and yes, the squeaking and sighing of blocks of stone as they moved against one another and finally came to a precarious rest.

'Let go of me,' she heard herself saying. 'Major, I . . . I think I'm all right.'

'Nolan. It was that bastard Nolan.'

Another rush of rubble came and then a scream, after which there was only a silence that grew and said that those who were searching had found it far too unsafe to continue.

Trant had passed out or died. Prying his hand away, Mary squeezed to one side and set his head gently down. There was hardly room to move. She knew she was badly bruised and that there were lots of little cuts, but nothing seemed to be broken. 'Major . . . Major, are you still alive?' she asked. His legs, he'd said.

With difficulty, she got to her knees. 'HELP!' she cried out. 'CAN'T SOMEONE PLEASE HELP US? IT'S MAJOR TRANT.'

He would need tourniquets. Hurrying as best she could, she managed to pull off her stockings, couldn't let him die, mustn't. Later . . . how much later? she found a passageway off to their right and began to drag him inch by inch along it, but there were often tumbled blocks of stone and heaps of rubble to be got round. Avalanches continued. 'Don't die,' she said. 'Please don't.'

Leaving him, for she could go no further with him, she crawled upwards over the rubble towards the light to drink in the cool, sweet air and call back, 'Major, I think everything's going to be all right. Just hang on a little longer. Hamish will be here. Hamish will know what to do.'

Rescue crews were feverishly at work on the battlements, Jimmy among them, Jimmy who when he noticed her, snatched up a rifle and aimed it at her, she now waiting for him to shoot her.

Mary told him she had the major, Allanby lowering the rifle to rap out a string of orders. Taking several of the men, he raced along the battlement and she caught sight of them now and then, was resting Trant's head in her lap when they reached her.

'Twelve fifteen, that it?' managed Trant.

'Please don't try to talk. Just rest.'

He asked for a cigarette and one was lit and handed to her, she holding it to his lips. 'Stupid of me,' he managed. 'Knew they would try something. Kramer . . . did Kramer get away?'

Jimmy had come to crouch beside them. 'He and a lot of the others, Major. They bolted through a gap in the north wall just after the tower went up.'

'But you'll get them for us, that right?'

'Major, *please* . . .'

'Of course we'll get them, sir. Derry's been alerted. Colonel's been on to them and to Belfast and Newry as well.'

'Dublin? Best to let them know.'

'Major, please just try to rest.'

Trant took another small drag. 'You tried to save me. What did you do a thing like that for?'

'Jimmy, can't you do something? Hamish . . . Where is he?'

Someone lifted her from the major; someone else helped her to walk away. The tower's walls had tumbled in on one another. Men were still crawling over the blocks of stone, trying to free the trapped. Bodies that had been pulled out, were being placed in a row. The Sanderson woman's head had been crushed; the Bridgewood girl had lost all of her clothes and now stared emptily at the sky. 'Please just leave me. I can walk. I must try to find my husband. Hamish should be here—why isn't he?'

Put into a car, she was driven to the house and told that they'd come for her in a day or two, and that until they did, she would be left on her honour. Too worried to care, she stood in the drive wondering why Hamish hadn't gone to Tralane. He would have heard the blast—everyone would have. Even now, though, he didn't come out of the house, didn't come to her. 'Darling . . .'

The car wasn't in the stables; the pony was in the paddock.

Spilling the cartridges from his revolver on to the kitchen table, Mary stood under the light and took aim before pulling the trigger. The gun was heavy but if held with both hands, this helped to steady it. Though time was precious, she had best force herself to repeat the process and only when satisfied would break it open and reload it.

The night was dark, the garden quiet. Thumbing back the hammer, she shattered that silence, did so again and again, but if one simply pulled the trigger, all pressure on it had then to be released before the next round could be fired. It was something she would have to remember.

Going back into the kitchen, she reloaded and went outside to empty the gun at the stars. There were some eighty miles, as the crow flies, to the mainland off Inishtrahull, far more by road, for not only were Irish roads like no others, every road sign that might have been of use to invading Germans had been removed in May of 1940. By morning the whole country, North and South, would have been placed on full alert. The Royal Ulster Constabulary would be out in force in the North, the Garda in the South and in Donegal, too, and the British Army's four divisions swarming everywhere and especially close in around Tralane. Every border crossing would be under surveillance. A lone woman on a bicycle, with a rucksack on her back, stood no chance of getting through.

Night would be best—this one. A good ten hours of darkness still lay ahead. Hamish . . . she had to try to save him. Having heard the explosions, he would have rushed off to Tralane, would have been so worried about her, but must have been stopped on the road—she was certain of this now. Erich Kramer, Liam Nolan—others perhaps, it did not really matter which of them—had forced him to pull the car over and then had made him drive across country. A stroke of luck for them, a disaster for Hamish and all those he could have helped.

'A meeting place,' O'Bannion had said; Nolan, 'A place Huber would never forget.' Somewhere up in the wilds of Inishowen, near Malin or Malin Head probably, far up in the north, in Donegal anyway. There'd be a border crossing to get through—it would have to be faced.

Sliding Hamish's revolver into the breast pocket of her anorak, she added the box of cartridges, then twice tried the revolver and found that by leaving the top button undone, she could get it into hand easily enough.

Gumboots, heavy woollen socks, long john's, grey tweed trousers, a flannel shirt and a cable-stitch pullover completed her attire—gloves of course, a woollen scarf and a knitted toque. Inishtrahull would be no picnic, not in mid-November, not living in the rough. She would have to add a few things for Hamish, couldn't have him getting wet and cold. And how was she to make the crossing once she got to the coast? Five and a half miles of open water lay between there and the island.

One would have to deal with that later. For now there was the problem of cutting O'Bannion and the others off. Hamish would be killed if she didn't. Nothing else mattered. Somehow she had to get transport to Inishowen, and somehow she had to be within hiking distance of the coast near Malin Head by dawn.

The map went into a side pocket of the rucksack. Drawing in a breath, Mary took a last look around the kitchen, was suddenly filled with remorse as she reached for a few of the shortbreads in the tin Mrs. Haney always kept to hand.

The shortbreads were loosely laid on top of everything and the straps securely fastened. At 8.17 p.m. she had reached the clearing by the lake. Tucking the bike away behind some fir trees, she listened to the night, heard no sound at all at first and then . . . then the distant murmuring of voices that rose steadily from beyond the castle walls, becoming louder and louder until bursting into shouts and ragged cheering, all of which suddenly died away as at a football match.

Puzzled—deeply troubled—she strained to listen. The night sky above the castle glowed. Floodlights? she wondered as the hush settled around her. For perhaps ten or fifteen minutes there wasn't a sound, but when a lorry reached the crest of Caitlyn Murphy's Hill, it accelerated. Soon it roared past on the road behind her and the beam from its headlights cut through the trees at a bend to spill over the road again.

Fifteen or twenty minutes later, another murmuring grew into that same ragged cheering, but this time the sound didn't die away and was abruptly silenced by a burst of firing from a machine gun.

They were bringing the escapees back and each time a new group arrived, those within the castle welcomed them.

As the sentry paced back and forth in front of the barrier bar, floodlights, mounted high on poles, shone to the right and left of the guardhouse, revealing the coils of barbed wire that had been strung around the perimeter of the castle.

There were lights on in the guardhouse, and from where she was standing, hidden in a copse of alders, Mary could see the sergeant on duty inside the hut. A half-dozen others were with him, the guard that had been detailed to accompany the incoming prisoners. For some time now, though, there had been no new arrivals, and she wondered if the remaining ones had managed to get away.

On more than one occasion the stillness brought mention that Colonel Bannerman was in disgrace—he'd be 'chequered out.' The prime minister had even called. GHQ Belfast had been on the line near half the frigging night.

Some fifty yards of clearing separated her from the barricade. Beyond this clearing, floodlights lit up the road to the gatehouse for perhaps another one hundred yards. Then there was a patch of semidarkness, but beyond it another pool of light bathed the road as it ran in under the portcullis of the gatehouse.

Herded by rifle butts and sharp commands, each batch of escapees had refused to give the sergeant their names, ranks and serial numbers. As they were marched away, the murmuring had become a steady hum and, as always, this had risen to break into cheering. Her only hope lay in using one of these batches as a screen. Distracted by them, the sergeant and his men mustn't see her. It was a chance she'd have to take. There was so little time. By dawn she must be far away from here, the car well hidden and no chance of its ever being found.

When another lorry arrived, there were perhaps twenty prisoners who jeered and laughed at the sergeant and his men. As they milled about the barricade, she ran for the back of the lorry to hug its shadows and wait for the barrier to be raised . . .

The sergeant was shouting orders, the men were being bunched up. Run . . . she'd have to run but mustn't, must just walk in behind them and keep on going even when someone shouted, 'Hey, you can't go in there like that without first checking in with us.'

The anorak's hood was up. They'd see this and the boots and rucksack, the height of her as well. Throwing up her hands, Mary kept on walking. 'Well, at least that Kraut's shown a bit of sense and come back of his own accord,' shouted one of the sergeant's men with a laugh. She couldn't believe they'd let her continue, kept on walking, went in under the floodlights of the gatehouse unchallenged now, for there was no one here on guard.

Shaking in the darkness of the doorway, she heard still others approaching the barrier. Soon there'd be the cheering, perhaps another firing of a machine gun.

Opening the door, she went quickly up the stairs. No one yet. Not a soul. All too busy. Great comings and goings out in the bailey.

Bannerman was standing at the windows in the darkness of his office and alone—Mary was certain of this, and when the telephone on his desk rang, she stepped away from the door to stand with her back to the wall, watching him move about against the light from the bailey.

'Bannerman, here. Yes, yes, I know it's a proper balls-up, General. Look, man, for God's sake be reasonable. We're doing everything that's humanly possible. Another lot have just arrived. Allanby's out there having a parley with the Nazi High Command. They've had the infernal cheek to present us with a series of demands. Better food, coal for their bloody stoves instead of peat, more exercise. You can be damned certain we'll tell them where to . . .

'Huber? He's not back yet. Kramer, neither. He and the rest of U-121's officers are still unaccounted for. Bauer died in the explosion. Bastard must have placed the charges himself. They'll have used the ventilation shaft to pass them to him.

'Nolan? General, we'll get them all. I can promise you . . .'

The general must have said something sharp, for the colonel set the receiver down without a word. Lost in thought, he reached for the whiskey bottle that was open on the desk but in his agitation knocked it over, he crying out, 'Oh blast it! Damnation, why the . . .'

Jamming the muzzle of the revolver into his back, she said, 'Easy, Colonel. It's loaded and I'll kill you if I have to.'

'What in blazes do you think you're doing?' She was to his left, had come round the desk from that side.

'Just put your hands on top of your head. Yes, that's it. Now listen to me.'

'Why the bloody hell should I? If it hadn't been for you, none of this would have happened.'

'Walk over to the windows. Please don't try anything. They've taken Hamish with them, so I've come to make a deal with you.'

'You've nothing to offer.'

Prodding him with the gun, Mary said, 'I've this and the location of the rendezvous. Now do we talk, or don't we?'

The prisoners had been herded into a barbed-wire compound in the centre of the bailey. Floodlights lit up everything. Machine guns faced the four corners; there were guards with dogs on the leash. Some of the prisoners sat on the ground, though most milled about and, as the latest group were let in, there were renewed shouts and cheers.

'A game . . . They're treating it as if it was some cheap game of theirs!' said Bannerman.

'I really do know where O'Bannion and the others plan to meet that submarine, Colonel. All I want in return is for Hamish to be unharmed.'

He jerked his head back. 'Nothing else?' he asked. 'Not planning to join Kramer, are you?'

'Not unless I have to.'

'Where is it, then? You hold back information like that and I'll . . .'

'You'll do nothing, Colonel, or I'll kill you. Hamish means everything to me. Why not try to see it my way? You'll get what you want out of it, and when it's over, I'll willingly let you send me off to stand trial.'

The bitch had meant it too, but what she'd not realized was that Allanby was heading for the office. Seven minutes at most and then they'd take that weapon from her.

'Put on your overcoat and cap, Colonel, and stand to one

side of the door with me. Try to warn him and I really will shoot you both. I would have to, wouldn't I? Nolan was always one step ahead of everyone and we'll need to be if we're to succeed with what I've in mind.'

The road was narrow and for a time it had passed through farmlands with apple orchards whose bare branches had been etched against the darkness of the night, but now it ran through peat land and Mary knew they must be somewhere just to the south of Lough Neagh and to the east of Dungannon.

Jimmy was driving; the colonel and she in the back—it was best this way, she to his far left so as to keep an eye on both, the gun in her lap and pointed halfway between.

'Bloody road peters out, Colonel. We'll have to double back.'

Her voice leapt. 'Wait! It . . . it must continue. They've been working this bog for hundreds of years.'

'Have they?' snorted Bannerman. 'Perhaps you'd best let the lady drive, Captain.'

It had all been so easy up to now, the getting into the castle, the drive out past the barrier—had they managed to signal to someone that they were in trouble? Jimmy had suggested the main roads, knowing they'd be watched, but must have known she would demand they take the back ones.

The car came to a stop. Ahead of them a kind of corduroy road passed through half-frozen ooze with walls of cut peat stacked on either side. 'Drive on, Jimmy. I'm warning you. Don't get stuck.'

'Got your boots on, have you?' scoffed Allanby. The rear wheels spun on the alder poles that lay across the roadbed. Though thrown about, Mary jammed the gun against the colonel's neck.

'Back up, Captain. Give it a bit of a run. She means it.'

Bannerman was surprised at how calm he felt, now that the chips were down. It was as if the years had been stripped away. It made him feel good, this taste of a past London had overlooked for far too long. 'You've done us both a favour, Mrs. Fraser. Dead, I become a hero overnight, Captain Allanby as well.'

The clutch was let out, the handbrake released, the accelerator touched, but as the rear wheels began again to slip, Mary shouted, 'Floor it, damn you!'

'Not losing your nerve, are you?' asked Allanby, laughing now as the car rocked from side to side and she was thrown about. 'We'll stall,' he said.

'Captain, just do as she says.'

Bannerman had always believed he knew what was best, thought Allanby. Seldom if ever, would this 'Colonel' of theirs ever listen, but one would have to try. 'It'll be dark out there in that bog, Mary. The headlamps won't last because I'll pull the ignition wires before I go to ground. Have you ever been lost in a bog with someone after you?'

Whipping the gun away from the colonel, she fired it at the front windscreen. At once there was panic, the sound of shattering glass, the stench of cordite, and suddenly a scream of terror that frightened.

'Sod it you stupid cow,' said Bannerman. 'Captain . . . Captain, we're not in France. Just do as she says. There'll be another time.'

Jimmy sat up, but for a moment didn't otherwise move. Shattered, the windscreen would give little protection from the weather and would have to be broken out completely.

'Damned thoughtless of you, Mary,' he managed, having got a grip on himself. 'It would have been far better had you put a hole in the roof.'

Jamming the gearshift into neutral and yanking on the handbrake, he reached for his gloves and began to smash out the rest of the glass. 'Couldn't see a bloody thing for the cracks. Nolan's going to kill us. You do know that, don't you?'

Cold on the wind, the air rushed in and with it, the first fitful droplets of rain.

Near Stewartstown there was higher ground and Mary made him drive westward towards Omagh. Each time Jimmy speeded up, the wind stung her eyes; each time he slowed, she knew it was only a matter of time until he tried something else. He was terrified.

Bundled in his greatcoat, with collar up and scarf about the throat and ears, Bannerman feigned sleep and smiled inwardly at the tightness of her silence. Stripped of its location and with a change of sex and skin, the whole thing was not unlike that brief little dust-up in Afghanistan, the year 1919 and he still a captain at the ripe age of forty-four. Married long since. Dotty and the boys in Kabul with Nanny Price. Dear old Nanny. A kidnapping then, another one now; some bloody wog fanatic with a Mannlicher rifle and nerves at the breaking point. Feigned sleep then and now this slut of a doctor's wife.

The wog had died with a shot from the Webley service revolver he'd had the audacity to purloin and hold in his frigging lap, but Mrs. Mary Fraser wouldn't die that way—he'd see to that. And Jimmy . . . why Jimmy Allanby had a lot to learn about the bumbling old fart of a colonel who'd been washed up in Ireland at that infernal castle he hated so much.

She'd think he was asleep and when she least expected it, he'd take that weapon from her. Still as a mouse, she had eased her mind a good deal. Jimmy was the stud she had always feared and now must realize he had broken under prolonged fire, that the wounds had only been a part of the captain's having been sent to Ireland, and that Jimmy knew it most of all himself.

But things wouldn't go wrong. They'd get that gun and then would make her tell them everything. A deserted hut, a bit of ruins, a field in the middle of nowhere if necessary. 'Petrol stations simply aren't available in rural Ireland, Mrs. Fraser. Omagh might have one that is still open, though I very much doubt it.'

'I didn't think you were asleep, Colonel, but lest you worry too much, there'll be jerry cans in the boot. Even I know the British Army always carries extra.'

Some three miles to the north of Omagh, she made Jimmy turn off the main road on to a secondary one. The map she clutched was soaking wet, the torch fast losing power each time it was switched on. 'We'll cut across country to Castlederg,' she said.

The car began to climb into some hills. As before, as nearly always, there were glimpses of farmhouses, of hedgerows . . . never much for it was far too dark. Once a fox paused in its run to stand in the middle of the road and stare at their approach. Cows, sheep, horses . . . they caught glimpses of these now and then. There were more hills, bits of woods, hawthorns, gorse and brambles. Jimmy geared down. The road into the hills seemed to be taking forever. Had she been wrong to have come this way?

'You'll never do it,' sighed Bannerman. 'Sod it, woman, if Hamish is with them, the last thing you want is for us to run into them.'

'Mary, if we come upon them, they'll only think we've come in force.'

'Tell us where that blessed meeting place is and we'll agree to let bygones be bygones, won't we, Captain? No one else need know you've told us, certainly not Nolan or the Darcy woman. Now what about it, eh? It's a decent offer. You're in no position to refuse.'

Far from good, the roads became quagmires in the valleys, rivulets of mud and stone on the hill slopes. They could see so little through the rain now, it was frightening. Permitted crossings would be no good anyway.

'Turn off on to that track, Jimmy,' she shouted.

'Which one?'

'Back there. You just passed it.'

'That's some farmer's lane, for God's sake!' snorted Bannerman. They'd get her now. He'd have to hit her two or three times, but damn it, the car had stopped. Ahead of them the lights had found the rear of what looked to be a butcher's van. It's doors were wide open . . .

'Colonel, we're too exposed,' managed Allanby.

'Captain, control it.'

The van had skidded off into a bog, the bonnet down, the front wheels having sunk into the ooze. 'Go on past it,' said Mary.

'I won't!' cried Allanby.

'DO IT!' she shrieked.

Bannerman told her not to yell, and for a few moments spoke softly to Allanby and then, 'Mrs. Fraser, surely you must be able to see how things are. If there's any shooting, do the sensible thing and hand me that revolver of your husband's. You will be absolutely no match for any of them, and they will be certain to kill you.'

The car began to inch forward. Never good, the visibility became worse, and when they reached the van, Bannerman asked for the torch, and reluctantly Mary set it on the seat between them.

'Tooley's of Armagh,' he snorted, shining the light over it. 'They'll have more than one vehicle. We'd best get out and walk.'

'Colonel, just put my torch back where you found it.'

The road turned to the left and they followed the gully of a stream for perhaps a quarter of a mile until coming to a hastily built bridge of heavy timbers. This was not a forbidden crossing as such, for there were no concrete obstructions, no barbed wire or torn-up roadbed, the crossing having been judged impossible probably, the banks too high and steep.

With difficulty Jimmy took the car across. A muddy track paralleled the gully on this other side, leading them further away from the crossing.

When they reached a proper road, Mary told him to turn north and then to go west at the first chance. 'Stay well away from Strabane. We're in Donegal now. We've made it!'

The cottage lay among hills and fields whose hedgerows of bracken, gorse and stone stretched away until lost in the fog. The booming of the surf came from some place distant, though, from cliffs that were among the highest in Ireland. Sheep dotted the nearest of the fields; cattle grazed the next, while turf smoke struggled up from the loneliest of chimneys.

Mary knew she would have to do as they said, that it was senseless to continue. They were all but out of petrol. The thatched roof of the cottage was crossed by ropes that were tied to pegs in the walls just below the eaves. The half-door had been painted yellow years and years ago; the stucco and trim were white, or what was left of it.

No dog barked. At 8.37 a.m. the yard looked deserted. Malin Village was now well behind them, the road unclassified as had been all of them since then.

'All right,' she said, 'we'll go in and ask to warm ourselves by the fire.'

Irritably Bannerman flung his cigarette aside. The cottage was both a blessing and a curse. There would be witnesses to what was to come, but there'd be a moment when whomever was inside the place would see the gun and realize something was up, thereby distracting Mrs. Mary Ellen Fraser long enough.

He'd jump her, would throw the slut against a wall, kick her, hit her, knock that bloody firearm from her no matter what.

Peat smouldered in the blackened hearth, the kettle was on the hob, the table still laid with the ruins of a hasty breakfast for more than one, though the bed in a far corner behind its open screen hadn't been slept in, a puzzle, but Allanby headed straight for the hearth as he should have done and was yanking off his gloves. He'd crouch and prod that fire to life. Now more than afraid, the Fraser woman hesitantly closed the door behind her.

Bannerman shook the water from his cap. 'May I?' he asked.

Setting the rucksack on the floor next to the door, she gave him a nod, he unbuttoning his greatcoat as Jimmy smashed a reed basket into pieces with which to feed the fire, its light now coming in bursts which all too soon died away to nothing.

'Mind that hearthrug, Captain,' said Bannerman. 'We are but guests, are we not?'

He had pulled off his coat.

'Blessed thing is soaked right through and weighs a ton, Captain.'

More of the basket was thrown into the fire. Again there was light but then a pall of heavy smoke!

Blinded, fighting, stumbling backwards against the weight of the coat, Mary pulled the trigger, firing once, only once. She couldn't understand why she couldn't fire any more as she hit the floor, was lifted up, smashed down again and again, couldn't get free of the coat, couldn't see a thing, tried to hit back, and was smashed again against the floor.

'Out . . . The cunt's bloody well out, Captain, and it's about time!' shouted Bannerman. He'd not lost the touch. No, by God, he hadn't! 'Get her up. Tie the slut into that chair and I'll teach her some lessons. The sooner she talks the better.'

They were burning the spinning wheel, piece by piece, but they'd not yet seen that she'd awakened. Jimmy was getting ready to leave. He'd take the car and try to reach Malin Village, would telephone Derry from there, leaving her alone with the colonel. They had removed her coat, boots and pullover, had opened her blouse and bared her breasts. A poker had been jammed deeply into the embers. 'What time is it?' she asked, startling them both.

'Well, well now,' said Bannerman. 'Awake at last, are we? It's nearly noon. We thought you might have been in a coma.'

'Mary, tell us where their meeting place is. You know you've lost, that it's over for you.'

'I never did know where it was, only that it was a place Huber would never forget.'

'And the rendezvous with this submarine?' asked Bannerman. She'd a nice pair of tits and would be worrying about them. The hill tribes had had many ways of making the recalcitrant talk. Fire had only been one of them and she knew what he was on about—oh my yes, but she did, knew, too, that she'd scream her heart out when touched.

'It . . . it must be somewhere along the coast,' she said.

'In spite of all the cliffs?' scoffed Bannerman. 'That's not good enough, is it, Captain?'

'Colonel, I don't think we should . . .'

'Shut it, Captain. Please just shut it.'

'Colonel, if I knew, I'd tell you. Hamish has been my only

concern in this.' He was going to touch her with that poker—
he had that look about him.

'The doctor, yes. Hold her, will you, Captain, and that is an
order.'

Her scream must have filled the cottage but she had no
memory of it. Someone was gently slapping her into conscious-
ness. Laughter sounded.

Again she felt herself slipping away. They'd get nothing
from her. Hamish would be in danger if she told them where
the rendezvous was. Hamish . . .

'Mary . . . Mary, lass, it's me. Wake up.'

It *was* Hamish, and behind him, holding a gun to the colonel's head, was Nolan.

The cliffs ran out to sea, the land lay shrouded in dense fog,
and everywhere now there was the booming of the surf and the
cries of hidden gulls and solitary ravens, a mad torment too,
as masses of boulders were thrown against the base of the cliffs
some eight hundred feet below.

Fay Darcy was in the lead, Nolan brought up the rear. One
other, their guide when he chose, walked at the middle of the
column: Dermid Galway.

The three of them were well armed. The colonel and
Hamish were tied by the wrists and roped between Fay and
Galway; then came herself and Jimmy. Galway had the broad,
blunt, bony features of the Celt, the shoulders too, and lack of
height. His beard was shaggy, the mass of dark brown hair left
long and free to blow about were it not for the grease of too
little washing. He did not speak much, was guttural, taciturn,
secretive, intent on seeing this thing through, and totally without fear. It was odd, though, the things one discovered simply

by walking behind a person. Galway loved water. If a rivulet or pool were there, he'd step in it rather than avoid the thing. It cleaned off his boots, made him master of all he crossed, made the well-worn Lee Enfield he carried seem as if of a man long-accustomed to doing so.

He also stank of sweat, urine, raw wool and sheep dung.

The column had stopped.

'Give us a fag, Liam.'

Fay Darcy's voice sounded very near yet she was perhaps twenty-five feet away.

'Later. We're too exposed up here.'

'It can do no harm,' snorted Bannerman. 'Good God, man, who in their right mind would . . .'

Fay smashed him in the mouth with her gun. Blood streamed from battered lips as shock registered.

'Fay . . .'

'Liam, you're not the high king himself. He needed that. Fat tub of lard. You're going to die, Colonel. *Die*, do you understand? We're going to fling you off them bloody cliffs.'

'Let me see to him. Come, come, Miss Darcy, cut me loose. You've broken his teeth,' said Hamish, doing nothing to disguise the outrage he felt.

'Have I now,' taunted Fay. 'And was you wanting the same?' She yanked on the rope, trying to pull Hamish off his feet.

'The Nazis will want the colonel in one piece,' he said, having braced himself. '*Och,* they'll want to take him and Captain Allanby back to Germany as prisoners of war. Think of the propaganda value to them, if you must.'

'Says who?'

'Says Dr. Goebbels.'

'They might and they might not,' countered Fay, tossing her head. 'If I were you, Doctor, sir, I'd be worrying about that missus of yours, I would. Didn't the colonel brand her with the mark of a slut?'

'Fay, cut it out! Let's get a move on. The others will be wondering where we've got to.'

The woman gave Nolan a dark look but did as asked. Yanking savagely on the rope, she pulled Bannerman's arms straight out in front of him and he was forced to stumble among the hummocks where Sphagnum moss, leatherleaf, Arctic willow and Arctic tea grew with cranberry and other stunted shrubs. The smell of the bog, that stench of rotten eggs, came with every step. Between the hummocks there were pools of water or springy patches of moss that leaked. Fay deliberately led them through the wet places. Bannerman wore only shoes; Hamish also, and Jimmy. Their feet must be freezing. Mary was glad of her gumboots and the dry socks Nolan had let Hamish take from her rucksack at the cottage.

All too soon, though, they left the hill and headed down into a long valley that ran under the fog and out towards the cliffs. There were boulders here, sedges, rushes, geese and ducks taking wing at their approach, feather mosses and tall grasses whose tussocks had been twisted together by the wind. More than once someone tripped on these last. Fay never let up. Galway seemed to spur her on.

Then there it was, the very edge of the cliffs vanishing suddenly into the clinging fog. They came across a sheep track and followed this into the rain the salt spray and the fog produced. Miserable, it was cold and wet, the burns on her left breast chaffing and stinging with each step even though under gauze and the Glasgow Cream* Hamish had used, he having said, 'Mary, it is yourself who should be forgiving me. It was all my fault.'

---

* Number 9 Glasgow, with sulphanilamide antiseptic and cetavalon cleansing cream.

After another hour of mostly slogging it uphill, they took shelter in the lee of a ragged ledge of rock. Nolan offered cigarettes, lighting them for those whose hands were tied. Fay sat apart; Galway silently having gone off to keep a lookout.

'You really ought to let me attend to the colonel,' said Hamish to Nolan. 'The Nazis will want him. I'd also like to look at those burns of my wife's.'

Suspicion registered, since an element of privacy would be demanded for the latter.

'We're not far from the meeting place. You can do it then.'

Another hour brought them on to a plateau to which the fog clung thickly. In places the ground was bare of soil and they walked across a land scraped clean by glaciers of long ago but littered with boulders of all sizes. In places there was stunted grass, then tufts of it and sedges, patches of wetland, but on the plateau and reaching up into the fog, the long, low shape of a hill rose incongruously off to their left. Since leaving their rest stop, Galway had changed places with Fay. God only knew how he found his way across the terrain, but he seemed to know every rock outcropping and boulder.

The hill grew steadily. There were no boulders on its slopes or crest, simply turf, but it wasn't until they had come much closer that Mary realized with a start just why Nolan had said the vice admiral would never forget the meeting place.

'It's a Neolithic passage grave, a long barrow, Hamish. Those portal stones must each weigh several tons.'

He had no liking for it, nor had the colonel and Jimmy, for it had but one entrance, its exit.

At some point in the night Mary awoke to hear the endless crashing and booming of the surf against the cliffs and then, as a higher whistling, sighing series of sounds, the wind. The fire had gone down but trails of peat smoke continued to make her eyes water. The burns on her left breast constantly stung.

Across from her, the Darcy woman sat alone with Hamish's revolver clutched in one hand and a pistol in the other. Above them, above the central chamber, the roof was corbelled, large slabs of grey soot-stained stone lying in layers, one atop the half of another to bridge the span like the underside of an ancient staircase. The main chamber was perhaps no more than twelve feet across but nearly twenty in height. Giant stones formed the base of the wall, large upright ones having been inset into the four corners so that the encircling of the wall passed through them.

Fay was now looking at Bannerman and Jimmy who feigned sleep but not well enough. Perhaps Nolan and Galway had gone off to find Kevin, perhaps the woman felt she had her hands full—they'd never know for sure, but when the wind stirred the powdery ashes to life, her expression softened only to tighten at some other sound.

At last she could stand the waiting no longer and, leaving them, backed away and down the central passage on her hands and knees. There were two lesser chambers, the central passageway being nearly eighty feet in length. Burial vaults with their own cremation pits opened off each chamber. More than once Fay had threatened to shut them all into them. Dear God, what were they to do?

'Mary, try not to let the blisters break,' whispered Hamish . 'The longer they're kept, the better. Infection's the thing we must watch for. Even if the gauze gets wet and dirty, it's better than nothing. We must keep the air away for as long as possible.'

Was he thinking she would be left behind while he and the others were taken to Inishtrahull, or did he sense he'd be the one to be left?

'They're agitated, lass. They're not in command of themselves. Something must have happened to O'Bannion and the others.'

Bannerman pulled himself into a sitting position. 'Captain, see if you can get this rope off me.'

Fraser knew the time for such could never be better. 'Kramer has a flesh wound in the right shoulder, Colonel. That shouldn't have held them back but are there others in worse shape?'

'Just you and that wife of yours keep talking. You're the ones that bitch will first see when she comes back through that portal. I'm going to bash her bloody brains in.'

He had a boulder of granite in mind. Jimmy's fingers were stiff, but at last he managed to free him and then be freed himself. Fay still hadn't come back. Had Kevin and the others run into an ambush?

Mary felt her hands come free, Hamish having untied her, but still they had to wait, still there was only the constant sound of the surf and the wind . . .

'Put the fire out!' hissed Bannerman. The toes of someone's boots or shoes were scraping the floor of the passageway, now to brace themselves, now to be dragged forward.

'It's not the Darcy woman,' said Mary, her disappointment all too clear.

The scraping took nearly a half-hour, and only then, did they hear the laboured breathing. Bannerman lowered the boulder and, reaching well into the passageway, said, 'Come on, man. I've got you now. There's a good chap. Just hang on a bit longer. Dr. Fraser's here and will attend to you.'

Jimmy struck a match. Hans Schleiger lay in the colonel's arms, the whole front of his turtleneck pullover soaked with blood.

Hamish knew there was no hope. By degrees they got the

fire going, but by then Schleiger had died and they were left to wonder what had happened to the others and why Fay Darcy had not returned.

'I'm going out,' whispered Allanby. 'Cover me, Colonel.'

Bannerman's look was one of, 'Do you really mean it?'

'Someone has to,' he said. 'It had best be myself.'

As they disappeared into the passageway, Hamish drew her close. Perhaps twenty minutes passed, perhaps a little more, then Bannerman returned, grim and silent. Blood streamed down the right side of Jimmy's face and neck. In shock, he was right back at Dunkirk, had that look about him.

'She'll have his balls next,' breathed Bannerman. 'Lay in wait for us. Placed that revolver of yours against his forehead. He froze, poor bastard. Pissed himself and I can't say that I blame him.'

Fay had cut off Jimmy's right ear and had tightly closed his hand about it. Hamish did what he could for him, but two others soon came. Both had been badly shot up and were grey with fatigue and pain, the one having been carried for miles. His name was Horst Laggerfeld and he was one of Erich's other officers. Helmut Wolfganger, though, was with him, a bullet in the left lung. Philosophical about it, he gave her a wan smile and managed to say, 'So we meet again.'

'Helmut, why did you have to come with them?' She was clearly distressed.

'Why not? We all knew it was a chance.'

'But you must have been ordered not to join them?'

Again he gave her that smile, causing her to wonder what he was thinking.

'Someone had to take home the truth about Bachmann, Mrs. Fraser. He was one of the best and they had no right to do that to him. Bachmann's wife and family need to know this.'

'Did Philip Werner escape?'

'On crutches? But of course. I . . . I was helping him. The dogs . . .'

Wolfganger choked. Hamish warned him not to talk, but Helmut raised a hand. 'It is all right, Doctor. This lady and I have things to discuss.'

A British Army lorry had been commandeered and that's when the shooting had happened. Erich hadn't been with them but two others had. Philip had had to be left behind, but had managed to walk away. Outside of Omagh, they had run into Kevin O'Bannion, Vice Admiral Huber and some others in a stolen butcher's van. Kevin had got them across the border and had delegated one of his men to guide them. Huber hadn't been wounded. Erich had, as Hamish had said, and was with them now, but Kevin had not been seen since.

'They are very worried,' managed Wolfganger. 'It appears to have all been for nothing.'

Telling him to rest, Mary thanked him for having been kind to her at Tralane. Things were now so crowded, she offered to crawl into one of the burial vaults, and when Helmut said he'd not mind joining her if that were possible, she did her best to make him comfortable, he holding her with a look.

'They'll kill you, Mrs. Fraser. The vice admiral will not be able to stop them. Too much is at stake.'

'Won't they take us to the island?' she asked in barely a whisper.

He took her by the hand. 'I don't see how they can. There are at least seven of them in addition to Huber, Erich and the others. You'll be taken out and shot. The *Genickschuss*. The back of the neck. It's the way of this lousy war, or so I've heard my own have been doing in Poland and other places, the camps, too, that no one wishes to speak of.'

'But Hamish . . .'

'The others are either not wounded or not so badly. The doctor is of no further use once Horst and myself are gone.'

'But Kevin . . .'

Had she some thought O'Bannion might have sympathy for her and the husband? 'O'Bannion gave the order before he left us.'

Releasing his hand, Mary turned swiftly away. The roof of the burial vault was just above her, the walls with their carved spirals close, shadows flickering over them from the one candle she had brought with her from home and had lighted.

Crouching, she removed everything from her rucksack but the bomb. Shielding it from Helmut, she knelt looking at it for the longest time. In spite of knowing that they'd all be killed, she checked to see that the hands of the watch were where she'd set them. All that was really needed, then, was for her to push the stem in. Hopefully Kevin and Mrs. Tulford would soon arrive, but she'd have to wait until they did, would have to force herself to say nothing of this to Hamish, but just to be with him when it went off.

Putting the lid loosely back on the shortbread tin, she carefully repacked the rucksack, but left the straps undone.

Wolfganger wondered what she was up to and when he asked, she said, 'Just some photographs and letters from home. I was going to take them out but decided not to. Memories, Helmut. I once had a child of my own. Louise . . . Her name was Louise.' The smell . . . had he noticed it?

Awakening with a start, she tried to swallow but couldn't. Hamish was gently shaking her. 'It's time, isn't it?' she asked, her stomach in a knot. 'Will they blindfold us?'

Fraser dropped his hands in defeat. Wolfganger must have told her what was to happen. 'O'Bannion's here, Mary, with a German woman.'

'Mrs. Tulford. . . . Has she her wireless set?'

He nodded. 'They're trying to get through to Berlin.'

It would be late then. 'What time is it?'

'Nearly two a.m. Nolan's broken an ankle. Is there any surgical tape in your rucksack?'

She shook her head, wanted so much to hold him tightly but the burns were hurting terribly.

'Lass, O'Bannion thinks you must have let someone know the location of the rendezvous. Was it Ria? Apparently the British Army have swarmed into Donegal; Dublin's calling it an act of war.'

'Is Erich here now?'

'Does it still matter?'

'I need Huber, too. Darling, listen to me, please. I love you very much, that's all that counts.' Breaking away from him, she went in to the rucksack, felt for the watch and pushed in its stem, waited, but could not possibly have heard its ticking, said only, 'Use this shirt of mine, Hamish. Tear it into strips.' Save Nolan, but only for a little.

O'Bannion was waiting for her in one of the lesser chambers. An arsenal of guns leaned against the far wall; two Irishmen she had never seen before were busy cleaning and oiling them and didn't even bother to look up.

Behind Kevin, Erich Kramer, Vice Admiral Huber and one other man stood in a tight circle about Ursula Tulford who was on her knees in front of the open suitcase that held her wireless set. There were numerous dials and switches. The set must weigh a lot, for the suitcase wasn't small. Again and again the woman sent a signal, pausing each time to listen intently through the earphones. An aerial wire had been strung along the roof of the passageway. O'Bannion told her to leave it alone or else. 'Fay's out there with some others. I'll be along in a moment.'

Somehow she had to stall for time. Ten minutes . . . had ten passed since she had left Hamish? 'Isn't Berlin receiving her signal?'

He pointed to the passageway and reluctantly Mary got down on all fours and crawled into it. Hamish wouldn't know what happened. The poor darling would be dead in an instant.

The night was cold, the wind bitter. There were stars in plenty, and the booming of the surf was much louder than before.

Fay saw her standing just beyond the portal stones. Things hadn't gone well. Liam had been out looking for Kevin and the others when he'd taken a wrong step. They'd be lucky to get him off, lucky to get to the island at all. Kevin hadn't liked what she'd done to Jimmy Allanby and had knocked her down and threatened her with dismissal. Never mind that she and Brian Doherty had been lovers, or that Brian had been his cousin. Never mind, too, that Liam, if he'd had an ounce of guts, could have saved the lot of them at Parker O'Shane's and killed Allanby into the bargain. Never mind that everything counted on the Jerries bringing in that submarine. More guns and ammo than they'd ever had before and a million pounds sterling. Kevin was just too soft on this one and had told her never to touch the woman again.

'So it's you who are to get it first, is it?' she said. 'God knows I'll be listening.'

'Fay, take off. I want to talk to her alone.'

'Fancy her, do you, Kevin? Soiled goods I should think.'

'There's no sense in getting her back up. She has to cooperate. We've got to know if the island's clear.'

'I'll tell you nothing, Kevin, unless you let my husband go free.'

Fay sucked in a breath but O'Bannion knew he would have to ignore her. 'You know I can't do that, Mrs. Fraser. Both of you know too much.'

'Then take your chances on Inishtrahull!' she yelled as she ran from them. She would lead them on a chase, lead them back and round the barrow before coming out on top of it. Forty minutes . . . would it take that long? Thirty-five? God give her the strength. She had to do it for Hamish's sake; had to for herself.

Huddled in a crevice, Mary listened to the waves. She knew she couldn't help but hear them break and be filled with terror, for as they hit the cliffs below, a hail of boulders both large and small smashed against the rocks. Then the waves would drag everything back, only to fling it again while in between, the boulders and pebbles would roll about and bash each other, and everywhere about her the rocks were slippery, the wind like ice and blinding.

Fay Darcy, Kevin and some others had chased her out to the very edge. More than once she had had to go to ground, their torches searching for her only to pass overhead. Hounded by their shouts, she had been forced far from the barrow, one fold or furrow much like another until at last she'd reached the very edge and known it instinctively, she dropping to her knees to reach out and feel the emptiness ahead.

Only darkness was out there; behind her, the land in silhouette with dark shadows outlining the more prominent. But nothing had moved for some time and the problem was she had no idea of how long she'd been on the run. Fifty minutes—had it been that long? Shouldn't she have heard the bomb go off?

When a figure darted across the rocks at a crouch, another took its place. When Fay Darcy stood not six feet from her, Mary knew it was the end. Flashes of fire shot out of the Thompson gun the woman held, herself hugging the crevice and crying out for mercy.

Fay's boot nudged a shoulder. 'Up you get, sweetheart. Kevin and the others have gone back so there's only the two of us and you to answer to me. He's seen the light, he has. Your running away's what did it. Disappointed in you, he was, but settled now.'

The muzzle of the gun prodded the slut in the backside. 'Who'd you tell about Inishtrahull?'

Clawing for purchase, Mary found a rock and waited as the question was repeated. There'd be no sense in lying, none whatsoever in telling her anything.

Dragged by the hair, she was forced to stand. As Fay set the gun down, it began to slide away and the woman had to use a foot to stop it. 'How's the baby?' she asked. 'Not jarred the little bastard loose, have you?'

Swinging the rock, brought only a laugh and, 'A fight, is that what you're wanting?'

The rock fell. The two of them rolled over and over. Fay was far too heavy, far too strong. Lifted up, Mary was bashed down against the rocks only to be yanked up again and swatted several times until, dazed and bleeding, she began to crawl away only to be caught and dragged back across the moss. A rock . . . she had to find another.

Shrieking as she was bitten by the bitch, Fay hugged her tightly and rolled the two of them over and over towards the edge. She'd toss the fucker into the air, would kick her if she could.

A rock . . . a rock . . . Mary found one and swung it hard against the woman's head, felt spittle and blood fling themselves into her face, mustn't shut her eyes, must kill her, kill her!

They went down together and Fay jerked away to grab the slut and throw her from the cliffs but teetered on the brink herself. 'Ah Jesus . . . Dear Jesus . . .'

With a piercing shriek, the dark silhouette of her disappeared.

At dawn a Bristol Beaufort flew low in along the coast and Mary heard its engines long before they had drowned out the sound of the waves and the boulders, but then the aircraft passed swiftly on to lose itself in the west over Malin Head.

Easing her cramped limbs, she slowly dragged herself up into a sitting position and, leaning against the rocks at the very edge, took to searching the awakening land.

A tooth was loose, there was a split in her lower lip and a cut above her right eye. The blisters had each broken. The breast was red and swollen, its ruined nipple stinging even more with the salt spray.

Not a thing moved but the tussocks. There was not even a gull. Satisfied, she got shakily to her feet and when she reached the Thompson gun, flung it into the abyss. She had as much as killed the woman and they'd not forgive her, but the barrow would be gone, blown to pieces. Hamish would be dead.

When O'Bannion came upon her, she had tripped in her haste to get back to them. At first he thought her crazed by being lost and afraid of this more than what they'd do to her, but then he realized she was terrified of something else, for when he made her stand still, she continually looked away towards the long barrow.

'Where's Fay?' he asked at last. Vacantly she blinked and he shook her sharply.

'Fay?' she blurted. 'How should I know?'

The Beaufort came back and they heard it long before they saw it as a dark shape on the western horizon. The plane, flying traverses at regular intervals, came closer and closer and went on out to sea off Glengad Head.

She seemed as much in fear of discovery as himself, and he couldn't understand this, was alarmed by it. 'Mrs. Fraser, what the hell happened? Did you fight with Fay? We tried to bring you back. We thought you'd fallen.'

Stubble bristled the clefts that lined his cheeks. The grey eyes were not hard and unforgiving but full of concern, though not for herself, never that, not now. 'Fay's dead.' She knew the loss would hurt him deeply and when this registered, knew it was all over for herself, but then he said, 'Come on, and we'll make a run for it.'

Mary let him take her by the hand and ran with him over the hills and down into the valleys, through the shallows, through anything until, still some distance from it, she saw the barrow and stopped suddenly—couldn't understand why there wasn't a gaping hole in it; looked questioningly at him, only to see that he was at a loss to know what was the matter with her.

'Who did you tell about Inishtrahull?' he asked.

He'd shoot her now. 'Ria. I asked if you had relatives up here someplace.' The bomb . . . why hadn't it gone off?

O'Bannion nodded. Looking away in the direction the Beaufort had taken, he said, 'That's why they're searching for us up here then.'

For all the world they were like two people cast upon an empty land, but she still couldn't understand what had gone wrong.

'Does your Mrs. Haney know the date and time of the rendezvous?'

'No, I . . . I didn't tell her that.'

'Even so, the lighthouse crew will have been notified. The Brits will be waiting for us.'

'Not if the Royal Navy want to capture that submarine. Trant did tell me that was what they'd in mind. If so, they'd leave the island to you and the others, probably wouldn't even notify the lightkeepers. Besides, you could always leave some of your people here to make the British think they had caught up with you.'

She had meant it, and he couldn't understand her desire to cooperate, was suspicious of it and silently cursed himself for not having killed her. Yet if the Royal Navy really did want that sub, they'd do as she'd said, and there might just be a chance.

Again he wondered about her, for she couldn't seem to take her gaze from the barrow, kept searching the very length and height of it. 'What is it with you?' he asked.

Starting out again, she told him. 'I want my husband freed. That's all. Do that for me and I'll help you all I can.'

11

Inishtrahull . . . in Gaelic, Mary knew it meant 'the big strand,' but when viewed from the sanctuary of its lighthouse not a thing moved but the windswept grass, the waves and an occasional herring gull. Here and there a small cottage stood out among fields whose bleakness matched the emptiness. All had long since lost their thatched roofs. Caved in, blown away, they had but rafters, chimneys and crumbling walls of island stone.

The lighthouse was on the bleak, low summit of the hill at the eastern end of the island, perhaps one hundred feet above the sea. From here, the land fell into a flat, grassy saddle which—never more than six hundred yards across—stretched for about a mile to the west before rising to the fog station on the other summit. All around the island there were rocks, much gullied and often stripped bare of turf. The 'strand' wasn't at water level but formed the rim of the saddle where an ancient beach had been left high and dry by rebound of the land since the last Ice Age. Now that cliff, some fifty feet high and steep, faced the fiercest gales but left the rocky shores and present beaches to meet the sea at all other times.

They had come across from Culdaff, the small fishing and farming village just to the south of Glengad Head. Kevin had had a trawler waiting there. The crossing, after all that had come before it, had been rather uneventful: pitching seas, an absolute drenching—six or seven miles of it, Jimmy Allanby silent and withdrawn.

The bomb had not gone off because Helmut Wolfganger, having smelled the gelignite, had stopped the watch with only four and a half minutes remaining. He had even managed to replace the lid and to repack some of her things before he'd died, but hadn't tried to dismantle the bomb and could not have told anyone of it, not even Hamish, leaving her to puzzle over his reasons. Would she ever know?

In a tiny cove just below the lighthouse and facing north, there was a small concrete and stone wharf, and she remembered how calm it had suddenly become once they'd passed in under the light. Fine if the wind was from the west as it had been, not good if from the north.

A boom hoist serviced this wharf. Nearby there was a stack of steel forty-five-gallon oil drums and a shed where the lighthouse crew must keep the hoist's donkey engine. Not far from the pier, the raised strand ran its edge round to the ruined cottage where they had taken shelter after leaving the trawler. There had been no shooting, no killing—Kevin, Dermid Galway and some others had simply rushed the lighthouse to seize it. Now the light's crew did as they were told. Now, at least, she and Hamish, and the colonel and Jimmy, were warm and dry, and for the first time in ages, had had something to eat.

When Fraser found her, she was looking out a small window on the narrow staircase between the second floor and the light above. 'What were you thinking?' he asked.

Mary leaned back against him. 'Only that I seem always to

be finding myself among ruins with these people. If not a Neo-lithic long barrow, then an empty smithy or the walls of some ancient abbey. How could people have lived continuously here for over five thousand years? It's horrible, so isolated and hard, it's cruel.'

'But safe,' he said, his hands now on her hips.

Two curraghs lay side by side behind the low stone wall that surrounded the lighthouse on three sides, the sea being at its fourth. Each of the boats was perhaps fourteen feet in length, and both were higher in the prow and blunter in the stern, the whole made of tarred canvas that had been stretched over a lathed frame, but lying there like that, they looked like strange, shiny black sea creatures that had crawled up to feed voraciously on the windblown turf.

Hamish pointed to the fog station at the far end of the island. Smoke rose from its chimney to be quickly caught by the wind. 'There's a man in that hut, Mary. O'Bannion was asking the others where he was, and they told him he'd been taken off last week with stomach cramps. That man must have heard or seen us come in last night and has decided to stay put. If I could get to him . . .'

Alarmed, she turned to face him. 'We're not to go outside. Someone's always guarding the door. There's no place for you to hide . . .'

'But there *is*, lass. Once I'm below the edge of that elevated strand, I can make my way around the shore and out of sight until I reach the far end of the island.'

It might be possible, but from there he would have to run across empty fields in full sight, then up the other hill to the station and without a stone wall to hide behind as here.

Depressed at the thought of his attempting such a thing, she said, 'Darling, even if you did manage it, what then?'

Fraser knew that something had to be done, and that he couldn't lose her now. 'They'll have a flare pistol in that hut. It's our only hope. Bannerman thinks Derry are on to things and is certain that is why they've left us alone. They must really want that sub.'

'And Jimmy?'

He'd have to tell her. 'Is terrified. *Och*, I've seen too many break. Nolan's aware of it too, but if he goad's him one more time, the captain may well do something we'll all regret. Let me get to that hut and get us some help. Distract the guard. O'Bannion and the others are busy discussing things, but when chance allows, he'll want to check it himself. With luck I won't be missed and can get back before he does.'

'And if you're missed?'

He held her from him. 'Then find a way of putting a hole in each of those boats. That sub won't be able to come right into that wharf, not at night.'

Kevin had six others, not counting Nolan. There was Erich, too, and Huber and Mrs. Tulford. 'They're bound to see you, Hamish.'

'And we've four days to wait, lass. Four! Berlin couldn't move the rendezvous up as Huber wanted. They've had to set things back.'

At the entrance to the lighthouse there was a mudroom with oilskins, boots, sou'westers, lanterns and other gear. This inner door opened on to a short length of corridor whose brown linoleum led past the staircase to the light and came to a T-junction, on the left side of which was the wireless room, while to the right, another short length took one to the spacious kitchen, coal-fired stove, table and chairs.

Beyond the kitchen, there were floor-to-ceiling lockers for the men and finally the sleeping quarters: two small rooms with bunks and dressers, the last of these being where Jimmy was now being held.

Mary reached the corridor. The guard had been changed but Galway now stood at the far end with his back to her, Hamish being directly behind her. If only the door to the mudroom wouldn't squeak, if only Galway wouldn't turn—he mustn't see her, not until she had darted outside, slamming the outer door behind her to run across the yard towards the outhouse that stood against a far corner of the wall.

She was halfway there when he thrust the barrel of his rifle between her legs causing her to hit the ground with a shriek as he roared at her, 'Just what the bloody hell do you think you're on about?'

Wild . . . he had the look of a madman. She tried to yell but his boot was pressed under her chin, hard against her throat, and the muzzle of his rifle was at her forehead. 'I . . . I'm sick of using that bucket!'

As he yanked her to her feet and propelled her towards the lighthouse, she shouted at him, 'There aren't any aircraft today. No one else could have possibly seen me!'

'Woman, you were told not to go outside. By Gad, don't you ever cross me again!'

'Dermid, leave her. I'll deal with it.'

O'Bannion indicated that she could use the outhouse. He said he hoped she'd not been hurt, and when she was inside, closed the door and put the hook on. Then he started after Hamish, and Mary watched him through a crack between the boards until he suddenly disappeared from view and must have gone over the edge of the raised strand. She couldn't let him get to Hamish . . .

Scrambling up on to the seat, she braced herself and booted the door next to its hook. Bolting across the yard, racing for the stone wall, she went over this and down the embankment near the ruins of the first cottage, a sheer fifty feet of gravel and sand that ended against the wave-washed rocks, no time to think, just over and down, sliding, slipping, crying out and falling to skid the rest of the way on her back.

Now the shore stretched before her in wave-washed ridges of rock that were strewn with boulders, tangled masses of netting, driftwood and kelp. She had to stop Kevin, couldn't have him killing Hamish, was terrified of this and stumbled as she ran.

O'Bannion caught her by the shoulders and shook her hard. Above the wind Mary heard him shouting, 'Why, for Christ's sake, why? Did you think I'd not be watching?'

The foghorns began to shriek. With a curse, he ran from her, she hurrying now to follow and crying out, 'Please don't hurt him, Kevin. Please don't. I'll do anything you want.'

The wind blew her words away. Stumbling blindly, at times falling, Mary hugged the face of the cliff which towered above her. Boulders and gravel were thrown about by the waves and as always now the cliff gave way beneath her when she tried to climb it. 'HAMISH . . . DARLING, I'M COMING. KEVIN, DON'T!'

It was no use. The sound of shots came to her and for an instant she cringed, only to then tear at the cliff face, to scramble up and up over the loose sand and gravel only to slide back down and try again until, dragging herself over the edge of the cliff, she lay there a moment unable to move.

Dermid Galway and two others had raced from the light-house and were now halfway to the fog station. Kevin had gone inside the building . . .

As she ran up the hill towards it, Mary felt her boots dragging at the ground. More than once she stumbled, the image of Galway firing his rifle at her so clear, she couldn't understand why her legs wouldn't move faster. The blasts from the foghorns were deafening as she burst inside the door.

A harpoon was leaning against the wall among coils of rope and grappling irons, she thinking to take it up, to run at Kevin with it, since the cabinet that had held the flare pistol was empty. 'Hamish . . . Darling, I . . .'

Seized from behind, she was dragged from the building, and as the foghorns were silenced, drunkenly pitched across the turf. Still reeling, she saw them take hold of a little man whose face was grizzled, the dark eyes filled with uncertainty.

Kevin placed the muzzle of his revolver to the back of the man's head and fired. Jimmy was next, and when he was dragged from the lighthouse, he screamed.

Alone, huddled on the rough-hewn planking, propped against one of the massive, timbered posts that supported the light, Mary waited for them to decide what to do with her. For some time now there had only been the sounds of the wind outside and the endless turning of the antiquated gear wheels whose interlocking teeth swung the Inishtrahull light around and around above her.

Poor Jimmy had been absolutely terrified and had had to be held by two of the others. Bannerman, Hamish and herself and the lightkeepers had been forced to watch. There would be no more trouble. Kevin had made sure of this. Nolan had wanted him to shoot her, too, but had been told to leave it, and would bide his time.

Now, no matter how hard she thought about things, it all seemed utterly hopeless. Eventually Kevin would have to kill them, but would spare the others since there would be no advantage in the murder of those men, but had Bannerman been right? Would the Royal Navy and the RAF leave them alone long enough for that submarine to come in? Was there nothing she could do?

Again Mary let her mind drift back to the fog station. There had been that narrow corridor but surely there should have been a room of some sort, with a switch or something to operate the foghorns?

'The smoke, the boiler,' she muttered. 'Of course, that's what was on the other side of the corridor's partition, that's why the man was there. He must have been servicing it.'

A routine the crew would have to perform every day and night, the boiler would supply the steam that made the foghorns sound. There would be a lever one pulled down to lock the system open, after which the timing of each blast would be automatic, the steam building up and being released, only to repeat the cycle again and again.

There would be pressure gauges, the boiler itself, sacks of coal and a firebox, a glass to indicate the level of water in the boiler. Surely someone on the mainland or on some ship would have heard the warning and understood it for what it had been, the day having been clear? But if she could manage to get back there, if . . . Would they let her live that long?

Kevin would have to send men with the crew member each time the station was serviced, but that would still leave far too many of them here, and of course they would now be wary of just such a thing.

From one of the windows, Mary watched as the sun went down behind lead-grey clouds. Well offshore, the tops of the waves curled over in masses of foam. Inishtrahull's light would be seen from a distance of at least five miles, a beacon to the passing convoys that sought the North Channel into the Irish Sea, but a beacon also for German U-boats which would use it as a directional fix. There was no way the Royal Navy could have avoided such a thing. The rocks were far too menacing to have the light extinguished. Inishtrahull stood right out in that shipping lane.

Faint traces of sooty smoke came to her from the west as she lay down on the floor next to her rucksack. She had to sleep, was exhausted.

Through the pitch-darkness of the night, the sounds from the meshing gear wheels above her came, and beyond these, those of the breaking waves and the wind. Each time the beam of the light passed above one of the little windows on the staircase to it, she would see the darkness being pierced out there, the beam also giving brief glimpses of the room and its timbers. Then the light would pass on, the gear wheels would creak, there would be a moment of utter darkness and again the light, and again.

No voices filtered up from below, and when she pressed an ear to the floor, it was as if they'd all been taken off and she'd slept right through everything.

The light came around again. There were two beams, their source the same, they at 180 degrees to each other, so there wasn't much time between. A pale pinkish glow touched the glass, but died away and was taken over by the brilliance of the light. She must have been awakened by something . . .

Stealthily Mary reached for the rucksack to close her fingers about its straps. She would only have time to touch the loose wire to its battery terminal and push the heel of her hand down against the one that ran through the crystal of the watch.

'I've awakened you, Mrs. Fraser. Please accept my apologies.'

It was Huber and he was standing just to the left of one of the windows.

'Come and have a look at this.'

'What time is it?'

'0120 hours.' One twenty a.m.

Still clutching the rucksack by its straps, she made her way over to him. The light came round and Mary saw how intently he watched the sea. He was smoking a cigarette and might not smell the gelignite . . .

'Now, I think,' he said.

Flames erupted on the horizon. The billowing pillar of fire was brilliant, the night sky instantly lit up, giving but a glimpse of a tanker, Huber telling her the ship must be at least ten kilometres away.

The beam of the light passed overhead. As quickly as it had come, the light departed and in three massive flashes of fire, the tanker rose up at its bow to slip beneath the waves.

Huber caught the cry she gave and gripped her by an arm. There was a further explosion some distance to the north. As the torpedoes struck this tanker, the whole thing flashed into view, much closer than before. Huge detonations seemed to rock the surrounding seas as the light came round again and his hold on her tightened. Men would be spilling from that burning ship, the seas on fire. There'd be flames in their hair, a face would glisten in the heat, a hand thrown up.

'Please don't make me watch. I . . . I know what I've done. I've had nightmares about it and can only hate myself.'

The flat and distant sounds of three massive explosions reached them.

'So now we wait,' was all he'd say, thought Huber, but had she lost that newfound resilience, that toughness? he wondered. Had she seen that for her and the husband there really was no longer any hope?

Another ball of fire erupted on the horizon, a munitions

ship this time, no chance for the men to escape—she'd know this—just a brief glow and then total darkness.

'Why have you come up here?' she asked, unable to hide the bitterness.

He would not even bother to look at her. 'Because from here there is a better view.'

In the morning there were bodies washed up along the shore and an oil slick that stretched far out to sea; in the afternoon the overturned remains of a lifeboat. At 5.00 p.m., a destroyer of the Royal Navy stood off about a mile and Mary knew there would be an exchange of wireless signals. O'Bannion and the Tulford woman would have to watch the operator closely. If only the ship would come in and send a boat ashore, if only . . .

But it turned away in the continuing search for survivors and she knew then that its captain had been told none had reached the island.

At suppertime Huber brought her a mug of broth, four sea biscuits and a plate of stew. 'Now do you see how things are?' he asked. He wasn't an unkindly man, not that she knew of anyway. He was simply a man at war, under orders and with a duty to fulfil.

'Mrs. Fraser, it is time we had a little talk. Please eat, though, while it's hot. Your husband has turned himself into an excellent cook but is worried and has asked that, your having seen how things are, you be told not to do anything foolish. Because of our position here, O'Bannion and as many of the others as possible will have to accompany us. We will, of course, put them ashore off the west or southwest coast, if at all possible, since of them only Nolan is to accompany us as agreed. If we can't do that, however, they will all have to accompany us to the Reich, and we will then have to find some way of returning them.'

'Why is it you're telling me this?'

'Because, my dear young woman, surprising as it may seem, we do not wish to see any further harm come to you or your husband. O'Bannion understands this clearly, but . . .' Huber gave it pause. 'For the moment has the upper hand, of course.'

'Then what you're saying is that if we behave, you'll let us stay here. Is that it?'

'And leave you to face British justice instead of a heroine's welcome?'

'Vice Admiral, you know very well what I mean?'

A realist, was that it? 'You, your husband and Colonel Bannerman will, I assure you, be taken to the Reich. Now please, eat while it's hot. The first duty of any prisoner is always to fill one's stomach.'

'I thought that duty was to escape?'

'Even though for yourself there can be none if we leave you behind?'

Mary took a sip of the broth, then reached for the spoon. The stew was excellent and suddenly she found herself famished.

Huber watched her eat. She was very thorough and that was a good sign. 'Nothing further must happen. Just let us get off this island. I can assure you things will not be nearly so bad as imagined.'

'Aren't submarines cramped for space? Look, I know there won't be much room.'

'But, my dear lady, what you witnessed last night has a direct bearing on things. U-397* has used its torpedoes and can now afford us all the room we need.'

Could it be that simple? 'When . . . when is it to come in?'

The woman felt quite sick at the thought and had let him

---

* Scuttled in May 1945.

see this, so must believe emphatically that he had been lying to her and that she and the doctor would be shot. 'In two nights and not before then, so please remember what I said. No trouble, and a secure future.'

When he reached the ground floor, Mary overheard him telling Galway, 'She clings to that rucksack as a drowning person does to a life preserver. Let her settle down and then find out what's in it.'

Galway hung the lantern from one of the beams as Nolan grinned and hobbled across the floor on makeshift crutches. 'Surprised to see me up and about, are you? Ah and sure that husband of yours set this ankle of mine in plaster like a magician and gave me something to numb the pain.'

Dragging the rucksack into her lap, Mary slid her hand inside it. 'I want to see Hamish.'

And wasn't that voice of hers tight? 'Thought you had us there for a while, didn't you?'

Did he mean the fog station or the barrow? 'My burns are infected. Hamish had best look at them.'

And wary as a little mouse. 'Dermid, would you say the lady's been hiding something in that sack of hers?'

Gripping it tightly, she leaned away from them. 'There's nothing in this but my clothes.'

Yanked to her feet by Galway, Mary reluctantly let them take it from her. A pair of woollen socks were tossed out, a flannel shirt, pullover, hiking boots, underwear, a forgotten packet of dried soup . . . When they came to the shortbread tin, Nolan glanced questioningly at her, for there were two loose biscuits lying on top of the thing with a scattering of crumbs.

'I was hungry. I had to eat something, didn't I?'

'A whole tin of shortbread?' Fay would have sorted the woman out, but Fay was no longer with them.

Black electrical tape had been placed around the tin to seal it, but this had been removed and now only its stickiness remained.

'I wouldn't open it, if I were you,' she said. 'You see, if you listen closely you'll hear something sloshing about in there and know soon enough if you . . .'

'Jesus, Liam, the slut's pissed in it!'

Galway flung the tin away, but the electrical tape was something they weren't about to forget.

It was Nolan who said, 'You dismantled the bomb I fixed to that motorcar of your husband's, or so he's been generous enough to have told everyone. Full of praise he was, but that's something of a puzzle, now isn't it?'

She would have to gaze steadily at them. 'I wouldn't know, now would I, my being held here alone?'

They looked behind her, looked up into the timbers above, looked everywhere they could, she ready to dodge and run if possible.

'Take off that coat,' said Nolan. What the devil was she hiding? Above them the gear wheels meshed, the light came around, but she'd not have chanced a hand up there, would have lost it for sure.

'It's too cold to take off my coat.'

'Do it!

They were afraid, all right, afraid that she might just be able to stop them from getting away but couldn't know of the bomb.

Reluctantly Mary removed her coat and then, gently pulling up her things, let the sight of her breasts unsettle them. 'Will I ever be able to suckle a child, Nolan, should you people let me live?'

'Why the bloody electrician's black tape?'

'Ria. Mrs. Haney was simply determined to keep our girl Bridget from getting at the shortbreads she kept for my husband.'

At 9.00 p.m. she was taken downstairs to see Hamish. Everyone was crowded into the wireless room. The BBC news broadcast had just started. Though security negated one's completely trusting the accuracy of such reports, the War Office had had to admit something. Seven ships had been sunk in the raid, with a total loss of 32,000 tonnes of supplies and materiel, and 217 men. At least three U-boats had been involved, perhaps even four. Mr. Churchill's comments were particularly vitriolic, the prime minister vowing to bring all those responsible to British justice no matter how long the war should last.

As Hamish attended to her burns in a far corner, he managed to tell her that the Germans had used the attack to bring U-397 close in to the island but that the sub was now lying low. 'The Tulford woman made contact during the raid, Mary. *Och*, there was so much wireless traffic, I greatly fear the signals went unnoticed.'

'Why isn't she using her own set?'

It was against the wall by the door. 'There's no need. Apart from her codebooks, the station's wireless has everything she could possibly want.'

As he applied more of the Glasgow Cream, the news broadcast went on to events in North Africa. One of the fiercest battles of the desert war was now raging at some strange-sounding place in Libya. In Russia, units of the Waffen SS had reached to within twenty kilometres of the Kremlin but were being held up by the intense cold of winter. The battleship *Barham* had been sunk in the Mediterranean by a U-boat. Off the west coast of Australia, the cruiser *Sydney* had encountered an enemy raider and, after a stiff exchange of fire, had gone down with the loss of all hands.

When the broadcast came to an end, there was some discussion among Huber and the others; little but disgruntlement amongst Bannerman and the three remaining crew members, one of whom was older than the other two of middle age and all of whom must surely be wondering what must happen to them.

It was Erich who came to escort her back upstairs. As he set the lantern on the floor next to her rucksack, he seemed at a loss for words, the light serving only to etch his uncertainty further.

'Mary, where is whatever you've been hiding from us? Nolan and Galway won't have looked thoroughly enough. The Irish are fools and will never be rid of the British, not in a thousand years.'

'Nolan's cleverer than you think. If I were you, I'd make sure they have the money and the weapons aboard that submarine. If not, you and the others will never get off this island. Now if you don't mind, I'd like to get some sleep.'

She must hate him. 'Are you really carrying our child?'

'Would it have made the slightest difference?'

'*Ach*, be sensible. The vice admiral is determined to take you and Hamish and the colonel with us, no matter what O'Bannion and the others say. There are places in the Reich, Mary, homes for such children. I would be only too willing to . . .'

'To what, Erich? See that it is raised as a good Nazi?'

She would never listen. 'I would have thought that after the raid last night you'd have seen the sense in what I'm saying?'

'If you mean the cruelty, then yes, I witnessed it.'

The vice admiral had insisted that when he'd first met her at Tralane, he had been certain she had found a new strength in herself, a determination that could well make trouble for them. 'The Reich will win, Mary. It's stupid of you to think you can hide things from us. Now where is it?'

'Or you will burn my other breast?'

'Please, you know what I mean.'

'Then understand that I've hidden nothing. Nolan and Galway were very thorough and are a lot smarter than you think.'

Kramer picked up the lantern and, walking past her to the light's mechanism, held it high. She really couldn't have hidden anything up there. To do so would have been to risk losing a hand or arm. Like all lighthouses, though, even those with the most antiquated of systems, there was a spare mechanism in case of breakdown. Here the reserve mechanism lay directly below the one in use and right at floor level and thus much easier and safer for her to get at. All that was needed, when the mechanisms were to be changed, was to swing the one above out of the way as it was lowered, and then to hoist this one up and into place.

He began to search in earnest. Silently Mary moved away. She couldn't let him find the bomb. By a stroke of luck there had been a flange in among those turning gear wheels, one just big enough to hold it, but she had had to let the watch dangle from the wires.

Stumbling on the stairs, she saw him swing the lantern round, she now running up the rest of the way to push on the trapdoor as he yelled, 'Mary, don't! It isn't safe!'

Around the light, both inside and outside the building, there were iron catwalks. Erich had to follow her. He must be made to think that she'd come up here and tossed whatever it was away or hidden it.

The light was huge, the reflectors brilliant, the hiss of the lamp blotting out all other sounds. Throwing her shoulder against the door, Mary tried to budge the thing but it was no use. The wind was far too strong. The light was coming around. Hot . . . it was so hot. She must cover her eyes, mustn't look . . .

Bursting through the door, she stumbled out on to the cat-walk to frantically grab its iron railing as the wind hit her.

'MARY, COME BACK!'

'I'M GOING TO JUMP!'

He must have heard her, for he gripped the edge of the door and the railing as if to launch himself after her. Then the door smashed shut behind him, shattering its window as he stumbled forward and the light came around. There were eighty, ninety . . . one hundred and ten feet to the rocks below but he would be far more used to heights and to the wind than herself, would know exactly what to do.

Grabbing her by the coat, Kramer shouted into her left ear, 'Get back inside!' but she broke away and ran from him, bouncing between railing and the outermost glass of the light. He couldn't let her do this. 'MARY!' he shouted. Salt spray stung his eyes. 'MARY!' he called again.

She was over by the door. Ducking his head, Kramer threw up an arm to shield himself. Again he caught her by the coat, again she pulled away but this time the wind threw them both against the glass as the light came round and he pulled her down, shielding her from it, and let her bury her face against his chest.

Butted sharply under the chin, his head was thrown up, he unable to stop it. The light . . .

He screamed in agony and released his grip to tear at his eyes and stumble blindly away as she ran from him, ran for the door and tried to get it open.

Round and round the catwalk they went, Erich grabbing at the railing and trying to reach her until falling to claw at the iron decking.

Lifted away, she shielding her eyes, Mary was passed from hand to hand and taken down the stairs but again and again Erich screamed. Shuddering at what she'd done, horrified by it, she knew she hadn't meant it to happen, not until that very last moment. They'd kill her now, they'd have no other choice and would force Hamish to witness it, but then the screams abruptly ceased, and only the sound of the light's mechanism came to her above those of the wind and the breaking waves.

Later it was Huber who came to see her. 'Erich has told us you tried to kill yourself and that he went after you. One hundred and eighty-six thousand candle power, Mrs. Fraser. You have destroyed his sight. Now where is it, please? We know you've been hiding something.'

'The pocketknife Helmut Wolfganger had with him. You'll find it outside on the ground.'

It would do no good to shriek at her in anger. What had been done could not be undone.

Rejoining the others, he drew O'Bannion aside and told him to have someone search for it in the morning. 'It will have the eagle and swastika on it. I only hope for her sake she's telling the truth. From now on she had best stay down here with the rest of us.'

'Inishtrahull . . . Inishtrahull, are you reading us? Over.'

'Inishtrahull here, Beaufort CC Derry zero-four-two, roger. Over.'

'Lifeboat sighted to the north of you and drifting towards you, Inishtrahull. Can you do anything for them? They look half-frozen. Over.'

Again the wireless operator, one of the lightkeepers, pushed the key in. 'Will try to assist. Estimate time of arrival. Over.'

The key was pulled back. 'Snow's icing us up, Inishtrahull. Should estimate three-quarters of an hour at most. Looks to be bearing straight down on you. Rudder must be lashed in place.'

Key in again. 'Can you signal help is near? Over.'

Key out. 'Am wagging wings, Inishtrahull, but there's no response. Will advise Derry of sighting but ask them to maintain contact with you. Do what you can. You'll need all the luck you can get. Over and out, chaps.'

Key in again. Black Bakelite switch to the left of it turned hard to the left, full stop. Set now down—frequency dials having fallen to zero. Earphones being removed, though these hadn't been needed. *Why?* wondered Mary.

The switch below the amplifier was thumbed up and off as an afterthought, but could she operate the set on her own?

Tensely she watched everything. With the overflight of the Beaufort, the others had all crowded anxiously into what she'd now learned was called the watch room. It was here that the men on duty wrote up the log, looked out to sea or manned the wireless set. From here they had also gone at dawn to draw the black curtains over the light, protecting its lamp from the converging rays of the sun—what sun? At evening, they'd pull those curtains aside and give the lenses a final polish before lighting the lamp. They had also gone out to the fog station, and in weather like this, both the foghorns and soon the light would be kept on all the time. No one had been able to find the pocketknife she'd said she had thrown, a piece of luck for her, since snow was sheeting across the bits of pasture and scattered ruins, even blotting out the fog station at times, and sweeping over the seven bodies that had been carried up from the rocks to be laid under weighted canvas. Huber had not been satisfied, of course, and cursed the weather, Bannerman telling him he couldn't refuse to give assistance to the lifeboat, not a navy man.

Stung by such a reminder, the vice admiral turned from the windows. 'Seaboots and oilskins, Colonel, and your word not to try anything. Do I have it?'

'Have you line rockets?' Bannerman asked of the man who had operated the wireless.

'Sure and we have, Colonel, but they'll be of little use.'

His name was Dan Flaherty. Plucking at the frayed left sleeve of his pullover, he gathered a handful to wipe his nose only to see her watching him and, thinking better of it, drag out the handkerchief he should have used.

In doubt as to what to do, Kevin O'Bannion glanced swiftly at Mrs. Tulford, then to Nolan and lastly herself. One of the lightkeepers had gone to the fog station with two of the men, the other one was still upstairs servicing the light with Dermid Galway.

'All right, we'll go,' said O'Bannion. 'The colonel, Dr. Fraser, myself and . . .'

'You'll need all that can be spared,' said Flaherty, 'myself included.'

'Ursula will stay by the wireless, then,' he said.

'She's a woman, for God's sake!' snorted Bannerman. 'How the devil will she explain that to Base Derry when they contact us again, as they surely will?'

'Liam will stay with her.'

'Then tell him to tone down that Oxford accent or they'll think they've rung up the reading room!'

Bannerman was enjoying their predicament. Hamish started to say something about hypothermia, but decided not to. They'd know the worst soon enough.

After the others had filed out of the room, Nolan sat down and leaned his crutches against the wireless bench. Erich was in one of the bedrooms. When Galway came downstairs with that lightkeeper, both would also have to join the others. Running everything through her mind, Mary watched the cove from the windows and tried to see the fog station through the snow. Ursula Tulford had set her pistol just to the left of the station's Morse key. The suitcase set was still where the woman had left it, Nolan's crutches the nearest to it. Somehow they would have to be distracted long enough for her to race upstairs, recover the bomb and then try to fit it into that suitcase.

'So, it is only the three of us alone at last, Mrs. Fraser,' said the woman.

'Base Derry will be on to you, Mrs. Tulford. They know about us being here.'

'That is not possible. For some time now they have been searching elsewhere. The raid the other night will only have confused things further. That Beaufort contact was merely routine.'

Nolan watched the two of them closely. Mrs. Mary Ellen Fraser had betrayed herself by glancing again at the pistol. 'What she means, my dear Ursula, is that the Brits have been trying to pull the wool over our eyes but that the storm has forced them to contact us.'

'You'll never get away with it,' said Mary, turning from the windows. 'They want that submarine, Mrs. Tulford, and are not about to let it go if you bring it in here.'

'Kevin should have killed you in Dublin.'

'But couldn't force himself to.'

'Is it that you still don't bloody well know him?' snorted Nolan.

'That money they'll be bringing from Berlin won't be any good. It'll be counterfeit. The Nazis . . .'

'Stop it, this instant!'

The woman had snatched up the pistol. 'Go on and shoot me, then. Erich called you a pack of fools, Nolan. Ask her if that's not what she and Huber also think.'

'Sure and they think us that, but the feeling's mutual, so you see, we're even.'

'I'd still make sure I checked that money and counted it if I were . . .'

'Oh I will. Now what's up out there? Give us the benefit of a running commentary.'

'See for yourself.' Nolan didn't bother to get up, nor did the Tulford woman, but it wasn't good. Ten of them were out there, all bundled in whatever they could find, some in oilskins, all with life jackets. Hamish wore his overcoat, he having acquired gloves with gauntlets. Galway was beside him, the others huddled out of the wind behind the ruined chimney and wall of the cottage nearest the pier.

They had several coils of rope, line rockets by the look, and grappling irons but they'd never be able to fight their way out along the pier. Cold . . . it must be bitterly cold.

'I'd best help them,' said Mary.

'You'll go nowhere unless told to,' said the woman.

'Ah let her go,' said Nolan. 'It's only the more for us to watch.'

Ursula Tulford stepped away from the wireless to stop her. Nolan laughed, but the set gave a flash of green, and the woman was forced to turn back.

Outside, the storm was rapidly building and in the distance, always evident now, there was the sound of the foghorns.

Hugging the innermost wall of the corridor, Mary went back along it until she could hear the two of them quite clearly at the wireless. Both were occupied. She'd never get another chance. Darting in, only to find the suitcase set both heavy and awkward, she managed to lug it upstairs and lay it on the floor. Yanking up an arm of her pullover, she reached well into the light's mechanism . . .

The bomb came away. Nothing seemed to be missing. In the cove below, they'd formed a human chain to fight their way out along the pier. There was still no sign of the lifeboat. It could come in at any place or miss the island completely.

Springing the catches on the suitcase, the impossibility of what she had to do presented itself. The face of the wireless was an ordered mass of dials and switches with instructions in *Deutsch*, the one side for transmission, the other for receiving. There was simply no place for the bomb, none even for its battery.

Then she saw it and told herself to hurry. A catch, when opened, revealed a compartment for accessories—the earphones, Morse key, aerial wire on a spool and supply of cord with socket adapter if household electricity negated using the set's battery, extra radio tubes in a protected case, even pliers, a screwdriver and a roll of electrical tape.

Though the sticks of dynamite were too long, their smell would be sure to give her away and she'd have to do something about that.

The light came round, the gear wheels meshed, the fog station let out another blast . . .

Unravelling the tape she had used to hold the sticks together, Mary peeled back the waxed brown paper and broke an end off each, allowing the rest to be tucked into the compartment. So far so good. Now for the battery—she could have used the set's but there would be no time for this, and the other fit but just. Now she must wire it up. Never mind that Nolan or the Tulford woman could come looking for her, never mind that they would kill her if they found out.

The smell . . .

Shutting her eyes, she forced herself to be calm. Taking the bare end of the wire, she found the hole in the crystal of the watch and slid it through until positioned just above the face. The resin she had used had hardened. A torn corner of electrical tape would have to do.

The gelignite was pliable—really like bread dough. Kneading each leftover piece, she packed the compartment, using them to securely hold the watch and dry cell battery, before taking off her scarf and wadding it carefully down on top of everything. Now all she needed to do was to push the stem in to start the watch, take care of the smell somehow, and dispose of what she'd had to remove from the compartment.

These last items she took up the stairs and hid them out on the catwalk. Closing the suitcase, she carried it downstairs only to find there was no one in the room. Nolan's crutches were gone.

Setting the suitcase against the wall by the door, her head aching terribly from the smell, Mary noticed that some of the gelignite clung to her fingers and went through to the kitchen to clean it off before it was too late. With the smell, though, she could as yet do nothing.

Back in the watch room and still alone, she went over to the station's wireless. Nolan and Mrs. Tulford must have gone outside to look for her. The keeper had had to tune things in using the central dial and then the one next to it. She mustn't forget the key that would let her talk.

'Derry . . . CC Derry, do you read me? Over.'

Nothing happened, not even static. In a panic, she ran her eyes over the set but there were so many dials and switches.

Her thumb nudged the switch on the handle of the microphone and at first she didn't realize what it was.

Pushing it up, she said, 'Derry . . . CC Derry. This is Inishtrahull calling. Do you read me? Over.'

Again there was nothing, not even static, she realizing that she'd forgotten to flip the out switch so that they could come in. At once there was static and then, 'Derry here,' Inishtrahull. Over.'

Suspicion was in that voice but she'd have to continue. 'Germans and IRA have us hostage. Repeat hostage. Bannerman alive; Allanby dead. U-397 lying in wait. Contact to be made at zero one hundred hours this evening. Over.'

'Derry here, Inishtrahull. Are you the folks from Tralane?'

Did they not yet know this? 'Of course we are. Over.'

'How many of them are there?'

'Ten and . . . and six of us. Three lightkeepers, Dr. Fraser, myself, and . . . and Colonel Bannerman. Look, I've got to hurry. None of them know I'm doing this.'

'Message understood, Inishtrahull. Weather negates our getting relief to you next forty-eight hours.'

'But . . . but we can't wait that long! They'll kill us.' She depressed the key and did it again and again. 'Derry . . . Derry, are you still there?'

No further response came from them. Switching off the set, she sat a moment, felt so lonely now as the foghorns gave another blast and the wind kept buffeting the lighthouse. The surf, when she looked, was boiling into the cove. Hamish . . .

Erich had heard her and was standing in the doorway. An arm stretched out in front of him, he started forward, his eyes so very blue. 'Mary, what have you done?' he asked as if he still couldn't believe it of her but would know it anyway.

'Contacted Derry. Told them we're here.'

He did not swear at her, did not even cry out, just took another step and another, felt for things, stumbled when he came up against a stool, he spreading his arms widely now as if to grab her if he could, she backing away until finally he had come too close and she had ducked under his arm and run.

The lifeboat was lifted up by the seas, its bow rising higher and higher as the rocket line trailed across the canvas tarpaulin that had been fastened down over the entire length of the boat. But the line slid off into the sea and another was soon fired, it passing uselessly over the stern which had pitched down into the trough of the waves.

The chain of men, each linked by an arm, stretched out along the icy pier whose boom and rigging threatened to snap free at any moment. Bannerman was fourth; Hamish two from the near-shore end. Kevin . . . Huber . . . Galway . . . Mary picked each out, then tried to search the surrounding terrain for Nolan and the Tulford woman. The snow was blinding but now and then there would be a pause and she would have a view of perhaps one hundred yards.

Huddled in the ruins of the cottage nearest the pier and without her coat, hat or mittens, she was freezing. Ten minutes . . . fifteen . . . Would it take much longer? Already she felt a lethargy that was hard to resist. To have run from Erich had been foolish, but to have told him what she'd done, far worse. They would kill her now, no matter what. Kevin would have to, and if he refused, Liam Nolan would shame him into it until he did.

The lifeboat surged high on a wave. There was a collective cry of anguish from the men as the boat settled back, only to then be dragged far down in a trough, the grey seas roaring into the cove, the boat now gathering momentum as it shot towards the shore.

Mary caught sight of someone on the cliff in front of her. It wasn't Nolan or Mrs. Tulford. 'Erich,' she gasped.

He was stumbling along the very edge, had been making his way downhill towards the ruins of the cottage, guided only by the briefest of memory from the night they'd landed.

Again he appeared through the driving snow and the spray. The boat was dragged back only to be lifted and flung harder this time at the shore. A man sat in its stern, clinging to the tiller and grey with ice, frozen stiff. A man . . .

Erich was facing towards the sound of voices from the pier. He stretched out an arm in front of him, seemed to teeter on the brink, wasn't even conscious of what was happening to the lifeboat.

Again the sound of the surf came to her, the sight of the men all clinging to one another as the wind tore at the tops of the waves and the lifeboat was plucked up. 'ERICH!' she cried.

He took a step and disappeared as the boat came down and was dashed to pieces. The men on the pier began to run, to slip and fall and try to scramble back up on to their feet.

'Erich . . .'

'So he is dead, and you will die for it. Now move. There is nothing you can do for any of them.'

Ursula Tulford caught hold of her. Jamming the muzzle of her pistol into Mary's back, they left the ruins to walk along the edge of the cliff.

The chain had formed again. The men were attempting to reach Erich who lay face down on the rocks. There were bodies in the water—men in life jackets, dead men, frozen men. Pieces of the lifeboat were being sucked away or tossed about by the exploding waves. O'Bannion and the others couldn't reach Erich. The waves took him. Suddenly he was gone. Mary couldn't understand why she felt the loss. Dismayed by the thought, she shook her head, must have felt remorse because of what she'd done.

They started for the lighthouse and she went meekly enough, was resigned to having lost everything, but would they allow her a few moments with Hamish? Would they? Suddenly she had to see him, had to say so many things to him.

As the others clambered up from the shore, she caught sight of the colonel. He had a fire axe held close in against his right leg, half-hidden by the slicker he wore. He mustn't do anything, not now, couldn't know that she would be dead in a few minutes, that her death might give him and Hamish a small reprieve.

A first scattering of the men caught up with her and Mrs. Tulford. Each of them was trying to shelter himself from the wind and the spray. Suddenly there were ragged, gaunt faces around her—half-frozen eyes that numbly sought her out, wondering what she'd done and why she'd no coat, hat or mittens.

They were all exhausted, all in a state of shock at what had happened. In ones and twos they passed through the gap in the low stone wall and made their way wearily up the path towards the lighthouse, the ground webbed with wet snow which lay thickly among the tussocks, the two curraghs lying there, black like ebony, their rib lines showing through the tarred canvas. Old boats? she wondered.

A figure plodded past her and Mrs. Tulford. The axe was raised, Bannerman giving a grunt of triumph as he dashed it down into the first of the boats.

The sound must have startled everyone. He tugged at the axe, let out a curse—roared at it as another and another of the men rushed past her and he savagely swung the axe at the nearest of them. There was a shot, she turning to grab the gun in Mrs. Tulford's hand as the colonel smashed the axe into the other boat.

The gun went off again. The woman was too strong. Grimacing as someone grabbed her from behind, Mary fought to get the woman's gun but was dragged screaming from her as another shot and another followed and Hamish . . . Hamish had placed himself between Bannerman and the woman.

Dashing the axe into the other boat, Bannerman tried to tug it out. Perhaps there was a split second when he realized he'd never do it, but then a sudden burst from a Thompson gun tore into him and he turned towards it to lift the axe up, blood rushing from his nose and mouth.

Flinging the axe at Nolan who had fired that thing, he pitched forward. Mary tried to reach Hamish and finally, at a word from O'Bannion, was allowed to crouch over him.

'Lass, I'm not hurt. It's only a graze.'

'Inishtrahull . . . Inishtrahull . . . CC Derry here. Do you read us? Over.'

No one moved. No one said a word. They were all crowded into the watch room, everyone still freezing, still wet to the skin and tense.

Hamish was holding a wad of gauze to his forehead, the Tulford woman looking questioningly from Kevin to Huber as static crackled and the call sign was repeated.

Derry wouldn't let up, not now. 'Go on. Do it,' said O'Bannion to Flaherty, the lightkeeper.

'Or else what, lad?'

'Don't be stupid.'

Flaherty knew that Sean Harvey had gone to tend the foghorns and Angus was up winding the light mechanism.

'Inishtrahull . . . Inishtrahull . . .'

Turning his back on O'Bannion, he reached for the microphone. 'CC Derry, we are reading you loud and clear. Winds from the north-northwest gusting to forty-eight knots and gale force ten, repeat ten. Visibility less than one hundred yards. Over.'

Gale force ten . . . his voice had been so matter-of-fact.

'Inishtrahull, have you sighted that lifeboat? Over.'

Would Derry now ask where she was? wondered Mary.

'All hands frozen stiff,' said Flaherty.

'Can you give us the name of their ship?'

Static crackled. Kevin placed the muzzle of his revolver against the man's head, Flaherty using a finger to push the barrel aside. 'I don't need t' be reminded, son,' he said quietly. 'Now see that you give me a chance t' talk to them.'

A gnarled forefinger and thumb closed over one of the switches, a tuning dial was turned, then turned back a little, the lightkeeper listening intently until satisfied he'd done the best he could. 'Inishtrahull calling CC Derry. Have we lost you? Over.'

'We read you, Inishtrahull.'

'Roger, Derry. Lifeboat from the *Grand Manan* out of Halifax, Nova Scotia. There were at least five in her, Derry, but no bodies could be recovered due to heavy seas. Over.'

It was coming now, and she could almost hear Derry asking, *What's happened to the woman who contacted us?*

'Storm should reach its peak around midnight, Inishtrahull. Expect hurricane force winds will abate slightly as dawn approaches. Will attempt overflight and sea search then, if possible. Over.'

'Derry, supplies are very low. Could they drop us something?'

Flaherty hadn't wanted them to break off contact; Kevin had again nudged his revolver against the lightkeeper's head.

'Will ask Beaufort CC Derry zero-four-two if it's possible, Inishtrahull, but doubt it. Maintain contact, report on winds. There's a disabled tanker listing badly to her larboard some sixty-eight miles to the north-northwest of you.'

'Are you still in contact with her, Derry?'

'Contact with the *Island Fogo* out of Saint John's, Newfoundland, was broken off at zero nine hundred hours. Over.'

Nearly an hour ago . . .

Almost too eager to reply, Flaherty said, 'Will attempt to contact her, Derry. Hope she picks up our radio beacons. That fog signal may not be of much use in this weather, nor the light. How's her steering gear?'

'Gear jammed, repeat jammed. If she comes in close enough, will advise abandon ship. Over.'

'Not on your bloody life, Derry! Them seas be far too murderous!'

'Roger, Inishtrahull. Will advise accordingly. Request you stand by twelve hundred hours. Over.'

Reluctantly Flaherty signed off but then the green light flashed and he had to turn back to the set.

'Tanker contact resumed, Inishtrahull. Position: latitude fifty-five degrees, fifty-three minutes north; longitude eight degrees, fifteen minutes west. Speed eight knots and drifting. Wind fifty-six knots and rising rapidly. Seas breaking over entire vessel. Will notify all stations Donegal Coast to be on full alert, repeat full alert.'

'How many hands, Derry?'

'Twenty-seven, but there's a woman passenger. Have advised not to abandon ship. Request stand by, further notice. Over.'

A woman . . . 'Roger, Derry. Over and out.'

'A woman,' said Huber. 'For a woman to take passage on a tanker is almost unheard of unless Russian.'

'Does the tanker even exist—is this what you're saying?' asked O'Bannion.

Huber reached for a towel. 'I am merely suggesting that you should tell that man to attempt to raise this tanker. That should let us know the truth soon enough.'

Flaherty hesitated. 'I'm supposed to stand by. I can't . . .' He felt the gun nudge the back of his head.

The static was impossible, he turning the volume up, adjusting dial after dial and even trying other frequencies until at last faint snatches came through. 'Radio mast broken . . . Jury rigged . . . Attempting to repair steering gear . . .'

The voice faded but then it came loudly, was crystal clear. 'Cargo of aviation fuel leaking. Have had to shut down diesel power plant. Am on emergency lighting . . .'

Contact ceased. Flaherty tried desperately to raise the ship. The seas would be piling over the tanker. Her bow would rise up with each towering wave, the ship plunging into the troughs and breaking into the next wave only to be lifted up.

'Inishtrahull . . . *Island Fogo*, calling Inishtrahull . . .'

'Roger, *Island Fogo*. Go ahead. Over.'

The static was too much. A tense half-hour later contact was reestablished. By then two of Kevin's men had passed mugs of tea around.

'Inishtrahull, we require urgent medical assistance. Request you relay CC Derry who will over to us. Have badly injured man . . .'

'*Island Fogo*, we have a . . .'

Kevin's gun came down. Flaherty threw out his hands, his head hitting the wireless bench before he slid slackly to the floor.

Cringing, Mary stared blankly at the mug in her hands. It had all happened so fast.

'Inishtrahull . . . Inishtrahull, are you receiving us? Over.'

The Tulford woman switched off the set, the wind shrieked, and in that moment of comparative silence, each of them heard it.

Then the foghorns sounded and, after their six seconds had passed, Huber resigned himself to things and grimly said, 'Re-establish contact. We mustn't leave them without help.'

'But, Herr Vizeadmiral . . .' began the woman, only to be silenced, Kevin reaching for the microphone and setting it upright.

As one of the others dragged the lightkeeper aside, Hamish started after them only to be stopped by Huber. 'They will want your advice, Doctor. That one will have a sore head, nothing else.'

It began again, everyone watching as Kevin familiarized himself with the set, having laid his revolver to one side. Hamish moved closer to him but Mary could no longer see the gun. 'Inishtrahull, *Island Fogo* here . . .' Static broke things up and all they caught was, 'Nurse Ellen Simpson will relay injuries . . .'

'Roger, *Island Fogo*. Go ahead with nurse. We are standing by.'

Contact was lost. Its thin thread had been broken and now no matter how hard they tried, they couldn't raise the ship.

Nolan's hand had closed over Kevin's revolver. Hamish hadn't had a chance.

'Nurse Ellen Simpson,' said Huber, giving her a look that said much and made her wish her middle name hadn't been Ellen and he'd not remembered.

The smell of molten tar, tobacco smoke, sweat, too many men and burning coal made the kitchen stuffy and close. Outside, the wind shrieked. Snow whipped across the island or was plastered to the bleak, ruined walls and chimneys of the isolated cottages.

Huber finished the cigarette he'd been budgeting. Lost in thought, he ground out the butt as Hamish said, 'How many men must die, Vice Admiral? You know you can't get off this island. That submarine . . .'

'U-397 is hardly feeling a thing at a depth of ten fathoms, Doctor, so we wait, yes, and we each keep to ourselves.'

'*Och*, don't be daft, man. She has to come up for air and to recharge her batteries. She can't run on diesels below the bloody surface!'

'If she has to, she will lie on the bottom, to the lee of the island.'

'And if my memory serves me, there are very strong tidal currents sweeping in and out of the North Channel and through Inishtrahull Sound. Aye, there are, and you know it too.'

'Perhaps, then, you would give me your word there'll be no further interference from yourself and that wife of yours.'

'The lass must speak for herself. As for myself, I ask again that you give up. Let one of the lightkeepers contact Derry. There's no sense in this waiting. For God's sake, listen to reason. You can't continue.'

'You'll never get Nolan into one of those curraghs,' said Mary. The boats had been carried into the shed that lay below the lighthouse. More tar was being heated, its smell permeating everything, thank fortune.

'The curragh is a most seaworthy craft, Mrs. Fraser. These people . . . The Irish understand the sea. Those boats have been in use for centuries.'

Was Huber beginning to enjoy their little chat?

Gruffly Hamish said, 'No doubt they've been in use for thousands, Vice Admiral. Aye, they'll repair them soon enough, and worse for it, will attempt the impossible.'

'This business with the *Island Fogo* was all a *Funkspiel*, wasn't it, Mrs. Fraser? A wireless game.'

'I . . . I don't know what you mean?'

'My dear lady, you most certainly do. I admire your courage, but of necessity must have the truth. Erich Kramer would not have come after you like that had you not done something he had failed to prevent. You contacted Derry and Erich heard you at it.'

Nolan got up from his chair and was now resting on his crutches, she tearing her gaze from him to the corridor where Galway stood.

'Doctor, I have to know if she advised the British of our presence,' said Huber.

With difficulty, she found her voice. 'That's just not possible. I know nothing of wireless sets.'

Nolan flicked a glance beyond her to Galway. There were two other IRA in the room—young men with several days' growth of beard, though this didn't make them look more menacing, simply exhausted and afraid.

'There has been no contact with the other lighthouses along the coast, Mrs. Fraser,' said Huber. 'In a storm such as this, lightkeepers the world over like to maintain contact with each other if only to brace their courage.'

'Not in wartime,' said Hamish. He had moved himself closer to her.

'Especially in wartime, Doctor. We have it on record, yes? Our U-boat captains log observations that might even seem trivial. Inishtrahull, as with the light on Tory Island, does keep in touch with the others. They relay chitchat back and forth all along the coast—Eire's not in the war. These men are not under

Base Derry's command. In any case, it helps our boats to get a navigational fix, and so we record it. With a tanker in distress, a major storm, and a convoy that has been scattered by our boats, there is only more reason for them to do so, yet . . .' He would give them a moment. 'Yet, there is none of this.'

If Hamish could have done so without being seen, she knew he would have reached out to take her reassuringly by the hand. 'It is wartime, Vice Admiral. Perhaps there are special orders in effect that negate such traffic.'

'Even though I have said this can't be so?'

'Yes.'

She was lying—Huber was certain. They had, then, perhaps forty-eight hours left at most. The storm might abate slightly by morning but he doubted it. U-397 would have to surface several times in exceedingly rough weather. 'I can't call off the operation, Doctor. Far too much is at stake. I must ask again, Mrs. Fraser, did you contact Base Derry and is that not why Erich Kramer came after you and went to his death?'

'I've nothing more to say, Vice Admiral, than that I could not possibly have done it. Erich came after me but only because of what I'd done to him. I . . . I was terrified he'd . . .'

Struck hard, stung by the blow, she was all but thrown off her feet, her eyes instantly smarting as she clutched her cheek half in shock at what he'd done, half in pain. 'Hamish, DON'T! Darling, please! I'm all right.'

Nolan had closed the gap between them; Galway had levelled his rifle at Hamish after having jammed him against the wall. The smell of melting tar came back, the foghorns sounded, the wind shrieked.

'You leave this to us, Vice Admiral. We'll soon loosen that tongue of hers. Have we any feather pillows, Dermid? Of course we have.'

'They'll not be taking you with them,' shouted Hamish, 'not with that ankle of yours!'

The revolver was lifted, she screaming as the gun was fired, Hamish shouting, 'You'll hang, you bastard! Hang!'

The hammer was being thumbed back again. 'Nolan, please don't. Just take me to Kevin and I'll tell him. I will, I promise.'

'Mary, lass . . .'

'Hamish, please just trust me.'

'Come on, Dermid. Let's take the slut into one of the other rooms and put an end to her. Kevin's too soft.'

The two young men came with them and they took her through to the kitchen and then into the farthest of the bedrooms, closing its door behind them. At a nod from Nolan, they began to pull and push her, then to fling her from one to the other, Mary trying to keep her balance and fight them off, but they were too fast for her, there were too many of them. Round and round she bounced, faster, faster, all of them laughing at her now, all of them shouting, 'You take her. No, you can have her first!'

'Stop it! Stop it!' she shrieked. Someone punched her hard, another grabbed her from behind, they all rushing in on her and trying to yank her trousers down as she shrieked at them to leave her alone and fought back but was grabbed again and forced to kneel shouting, 'Please don't. I'll tell you everything.'

'LIAM!'

'KEVIN, YOU KEEP OUT OF THIS!'

'LET HER ALONE, THE LOT OF YOU!'

'THE DEVIL SAYS WE WILL. THE SLUT'S BEEN HIDING FAR TOO MUCH!'

The voices ceased. There was a soft, metallic click. Her chest heaving, Mary felt the hands that had been gripping her begin to lessen their hold and finally to slip away.

The bolt of a Thompson submachine gun had slid into place.

'Kevin, don't. It's what she wants,' said Nolan.

'Then leave her be, Liam, and come and help us with the boats. Once they're repaired, we'll try to move one of them over to the lee shore.'

'You'll never do it.'

'Not without the lot of you.'

As the Fraser woman got unsteadily to her feet, her gaze locked on his. By rights, he ought to kill her and the husband and get it over with and she knew this, knew he was arguing with himself.

'Go back to the wireless and stay there with Ursula and Flaherty. Don't try anything stupid.'

'I haven't hidden anything.'

'Go on, damn you, woman! Just do as I'm telling you.'

The gun was still trained on Nolan and two of the others; a third man was to her left. As she stepped into the corridor, the gun went off. Cringing at the sound of it, she tried to duck and huddled on the floor.

As rapidly as it had started, the shooting ceased and again Mary heard the sound of the waves as they broke against the shore.

'What . . . what has happened?'

It was Mrs. Tulford. The pistol she had held on the lightkeeper was in her hand, but there was no sign of Flaherty.

Pushing past her, the woman went into the room, Mary hesitantly following. Kevin still held the Thompson gun. The two men who were with Nolan were afraid to move, he leaning on his crutches but a few feet from them.

In a pool of blood that still spread, the other man lay shabbily on the floor. His legs and arms had been flung out. He still clutched the revolver he had tried to use against Kevin, who now said, 'Cover him, Liam, and that's an end to it.'

'Not until she's dead.'

'DAMN IT, DO AS I SAY!'

'You'll not kill me, Kevin. Not after all we've been through and not when Belfast has charged you with bringing this all off and getting me safely away.'

'For the love of Jesus, Liam, I'm begging you!'

'And I'm waiting.'

O'Bannion swung the gun at hip level, Mary shrieking at him not to, but there was a burst of firing that smashed all sense of being. Cringing at the sound of the gun, she managed to turn away at last, but the firing seemed to go on forever, only to then abruptly stop.

Cartridge casings littered the floor; the stench of cordite filled the room as she waited for him to kill her.

Nolan had been flung back and now sat on the floor slumped against the wall. Blood rushed from between the fingers of the hand that gripped his stomach. Baffled by what had happened, he looked up at Kevin but even as he did, the light faded from his eyes. He tried to say something. Kevin started towards him but held himself back.

The gun was lowered. 'Now cover them, the two of you, then come and give us a hand with the boats.'

Through a trapdoor in the kitchen, a steep and narrow set of stairs led down into the shed at ground level below. The last to follow him, Mary was in shock and held herself by the shoulders, Hamish looking up at her, he standing beside one of the curraghs with a tarbrush in hand and one of the lanterns hanging from a rafter nearby.

Bannerman had died in vain. So much had happened since, so many killed, and now this: men frozen into inactivity by doubt and fear, by the sound of gunfire from above and by the task that still lay ahead of them.

They'd never do it, but Kevin would force them to try, because he would have to. Nolan who had always done the unexpected, had known he'd never get off the island and that Kevin would have to leave him behind. He had defied that leadership in order to strengthen it, having given himself both to cheat British justice and to ensure that Kevin did what had to be done.

There were coils of rope, cans of paint, turpentined rags with tar on them—lots of these last. Clutching as many as she could when no one was watching, Mary carried them up the stairs and laid them on the floor next to the suitcase that held the Tulford woman's wireless and the bomb.

12

'Inishtrahull . . . CC Derry calling Inishtrahull Light. Over.'

Again everyone was crowded into the watch room, everyone listening intently, Mary standing to one side. A day had passed, the storm showing no sign yet of abating. Dan Flaherty was at the wireless, and after a minute's hesitation, he said, 'Roger, CC Derry, we are reading you. Over.'

It all seemed so distant. 'High frequency signals indicate enemy U-boat in distress, repeat distress Inishtrahull Sound. Contact using 7,782 kilocycles, report situation.'

Huber cursed the weather. Never had he experienced a storm such as this.

'Are you still reading us, Inishtrahull?' Had there been a hint of mockery in the Derry wireless operator's voice? Uncertain of what to do, Flaherty looked to Huber for instructions but the vice admiral remained lost in thought.

'Believe U-boat is sinking, Inishtrahull. Over.'

There were murmurs of consternation, barely breathed curses.

'Tell them we'll make contact,' said Huberresignedly.

Was the situation hopeless? she wondered, only to see Kevin O'Bannion snatch the microphone from the lightkeeper.

'They could be lying, Vice Admiral.'

Grimly Huber acknowledged this. 'What do you suggest?'

'That we wait. That they may have located the sub, but that it may not be in distress.'

'Switch to 7,782 kilocycles.'

Mrs. Tulford, who was keeping a close eye on things, was sitting right next to the lightkeeper. Flaherty did as asked, Kevin turning up the volume, they all hearing the S-O-S very faintly through the static, each of them knowing the sub must be on the surface. The S-O-S was being repeated every two minutes with an urgency that brought only dread and could not be avoided.

Huber knew he would have to contact Berlin, but first . . . 'Get through to the boat. Request normal transmission in clear. I will talk to them.'

'Is that wise?' asked the Tulford woman.

'Wise or not, we must know their situation. If all is lost, we must negotiate a surrender and try our best to save as many as possible.'

'I will kill myself.'

'You will do no such thing, and that is an order.'

'Then the British will hang me. Would you wish this?'

Huber knew that what she had said was true. 'Just contact them, Ursula. Let us see what we must do.'

At first there was no response but then a voice in thickly accented *Deutsch* came faintly through. 'Something has jammed their starboard propeller,' said Huber. 'They think this may have been a gill net and are barely keeping their position against the wind and the seas. Once their batteries have been recharged, they will again submerge.'

Twice each day there would be a high tide, every six hours or so, the change from high to low or low to high, the two tides alternating, the currents sweeping strongly around the Irish Coast and into or out of Inishtrahull Sound and the North Channel.

It was Hamish who said, 'They've another hour and a half to wait before the tide changes, Vice Admiral. They must know they're too bloody close to the coast here, otherwise they would never have sent that signal.'

Huber said something in *Deutsch* into the microphone, the exchange too brief for her to catch.

'When and if they can, Doctor, they will go down to the bottom and wait.'

'*Och*, don't be daft, man. The tidal currents are far too strong. The mud . . .'

'They have no other choice.'

'One hundred fathoms* of water, Vice Admiral. Are you mad? Order them to continue with their S-O-S.'

'I can't.'

'But . . . but there must be fifty or more men in that boat?' Hamish was genuinely concerned for the welfare of men he did not even know, the enemy.

Lying on the bottom, anything could happen.

There had once been as many as ten cottages on the island, the ruins widely scattered, each family having had land of their own, such as it was. Below the hill on which the lighthouse stood, a road of sorts curved by the cove but ran on across the flat saddle of windswept terrain. It gave no ease of access to any

---

* One hundred fathoms equals 640 feet.

of the cottages but simply went westward along the north coast from the gap in the outer wall round the lighthouse to the base of the rocky hill on which the fog station stood. In good weather a blindfolded person could have found his way between the two; in a storm like this, only when the wind abated considerably could one chance it, but at night that road would be something to follow, and once she and Hamish were inside the fog station, what then? she had to ask. Could they barricade the door and defend themselves long enough for help to reach them?

'So you have noticed it too.'

Startled, Mary found Ursula Tulford standing beside her at the window. 'The weather,' said the woman. 'It is clearing, yes? We can now see the other end of the island.'

The snow had stopped, the night had all but come down. 'Why aren't you at the wireless set?'

'You jump too much, Mrs. Fraser. You betray your innermost thoughts. Escape for you and your husband is just not possible. U-397 is now out of danger and safely submerged. All wireless contact has ceased until the appropriate time.'

Unbidden, tears began to trickle down her cheeks and, though she wanted desperately to stop them, Mary found she couldn't.

Ursula Tulford was unmoved. 'I shall be glad to be home where I can be of greater use.'

The ruins of the cottages lay dotted over the saddle of the island. Mary saw them as giant stepping-stones to the fog station, but could she memorize their locations, could she and Hamish find their way across the island in the dark?

'You will not get a chance to escape, Mrs. Fraser. If Kevin doesn't kill you, I will.'

'And Huber? What . . . what has he to say about it?'

'That even though you are carrying Erich's child, there can be no room for you and your husband.'

'He promised there would be.'

'Perhaps out of necessity the vice admiral thought to ease your mind, but U-397 must lighten itself considerably. Her starboard propeller shaft has seized and is bent. She can carry only so many.'

They would have to dump the guns and ammunition overboard as soon as the weather permitted. Men had died for those and Kevin wasn't going to like it when told. 'You're not off the island yet, Mrs. Tulford. As soon as the wind drops, the RAF will start hunting for that sub again and when they find it, they'll sink it.'

The woman left her. The two IRA who had witnessed the exchange averted their eyes. Flaherty and Angus, a man well into his seventies, continued to look at her. Then Angus, who was not a Scot and had the accent of the southwest, said, 'This girl of ours is in need of comfort, Dan, and one of those biscuits.'

The tea was black, from an equally hidden store, and when she grimaced, Flaherty found the four precious sugar cubes he'd been saving for those times when the loneliness got to a body and one just had to have a little something.

Lint clung to them, but it was good pocket lint. 'Thanks, you're both being awfully kind.'

'Sure and it's not your fault we're in this.'

'But it *is*. All of it, and if I could make it right, I would.'

Flaherty handed her a clean white handkerchief, she taking it to wipe those lovely eyes of hers and wonder now at the six fat, snub-nosed .455 calibre bullets it held.

At midnight the wind had dropped sufficiently for one of the lightkeepers to venture out to the fog station. Galway and one other man went with him but when, nearly an hour later and half-frozen, they returned, it was to shake their heads. Only as the grey light of dawn finally came up did the spray no longer fly so far, and when, in between gusts, the tussocks had all but ceased their moving, it was as if the island could be at peace again and now there were but a few hours left.

'I want my wedding ring, Kevin. It was in my rucksack.'

O'Bannion led her upstairs and she saw again the mechanism which drove the light, saw that it had stopped.

The ring wasn't in her rucksack. She insisted on searching for it. O'Bannion knew he oughtn't to let her, that she was just stalling for time, but when the ring couldn't be found, he went downstairs to ask Dermid for it, and reluctantly that one gave it up and she slipped it on her finger.

Galway had his rifle but there was a Thompson gun leaning against the wall just beyond the open door to the mudroom. By this and other things, Mary realized that they had all taken up defensive positions.

At noon a Beaufort flew near the island. It made three passes but kept well offshore. Continuing on out to sea, the plane was soon lost from view.

Huber had armed himself with Nolan's revolver; Mrs. Tulford had her pistol. Always now when any of the lightkeepers went about their duties, two men went with them. The fog station was serviced, though its foghorns had long since ceased and were no longer necessary.

Mary knew it was coming soon. Whenever she could, she tried to catch a glimpse of Hamish. Once they were able to touch hands but only in passing, she to whisper, 'The fog station. Take the wireless suitcase,' his gaze one of puzzlement. 'Do it, darling. Please!'

O'Bannion knew he had to kill the two of them, that for him there could be no other choice, and when she said, 'It's almost time, isn't it?' he saw that there was no longer any sadness in her, only a quietude he found unsettling. Was she like Queen Maev or Dierdre or Etain, he wondered, all three of whom had been slain either by others or by themselves?

Etain had been changed into a beautiful butterfly by the fairies and had been blown by the tempest into the drinking cup of Etar's wife. The woman had swallowed the butterfly whole, and the thing had landed in her womb and become a mortal child, a beautiful girl with no knowledge of her past. Ah well . . .

'There's time enough,' he heard himself saying. 'I'll try to give you all I can of it.'

'Did they tell you they've had to dump the arms and ammunition?'

Was it that she wanted to provoke him? 'There's still the money. With that, we'll buy all the guns we need.'

'The Nazis will only cheat you, Kevin. The money won't be any good. They've counterfeited before just as they've continually broken their word. No one should trust them.'

Sadly he said, 'I could have wished for better times.'

'When will that sub come in?'

There could be no harm in telling her. 'With luck, tonight. By midnight, or at one a.m. as agreed.'

'Nolan wanted you to kill him, didn't he?'

She wouldn't turn away, was demanding an answer. 'Yes, Liam wanted that but didn't think I would. Look, I don't want to see you hurt, and that's the God's truth, but . . .'

'But you have no other choice, have you, Kevin?'

He wished she wouldn't say his name like that. It both accused and expected better of him, was as if the two of them were back in that room of hers, he staring at her electric fire, not knowing she was watching him.

'It's cold in here,' she said. 'Has the fire gone out?'

As she shivered, she clasped herself by the shoulders, and he said, 'I'm sorry for what Liam and the others tried to do to you, Mary. There was no need for that.'

He would use her first name now and she knew he must have some reason. 'It doesn't matter. It's over. I'm not glad he's dead, Kevin. That's odd of me, I know, but I feel nothing for or about him, no remorse, no sense of loss either or of fear, just an emptiness.'

'Would you like me to ask your husband to kill you?'

'Hamish? No . . . no, I . . . I'd prefer he didn't see me die. You must separate us, Kevin. Take us each someplace different when the other doesn't know of it.'

O'Bannion nodded. Before she could say anything further, he turned from her and Mary watched in dismay as he left the kitchen, she not knowing if he'd take Hamish outside now, not knowing if she'd ever see Hamish alive again.

Retreating to the stove to sit huddled before it, she tried not to blame herself for inadvertently having said the wrong thing and, when she could stand the uncertainty no longer, got up to open the firebox door. One of the IRA told her to leave the stove, that he'd attend to it soon enough.

'What harm can there be in my adding another shovelful of coal?'

He was standing across the room from her, was leaning against the wall by the entrance to the corridor. Reaching for the shovel, she took up a half of coal and showed it to him before throwing it into the firebox. Using the shovel as a poker, she threw the cartridges in and covered them as best she could before quickly shutting the door, but didn't put the shovel down. The man was now trying to cadge a couple of puffs from the cigarette Flaherty had cadged from Angus, she to walk towards them, but would Galway still be on guard at the outer door? Would that Thompson gun still be leaning against that wall? Where was Mrs. Tulford's wireless set—where was Hamish?

There was one other of the IRA in the kitchen, slouched in a chair and trying to catch a bit of sleep. A Lee Enfield was across his lap . . .

Still nothing happened in the stove and she couldn't understand this, had now all but reached Flaherty who was rebelling at the loss of his only cigarette but had taken a last deep drag and given it again to the man.

In all but simultaneous bangs the cartridges exploded, the bullets pinging around inside the firebox as she swung the shovel hard and saw the cigarette disintegrate in a rush of crimson froth.

Flaherty leapt for the man in the chair and snatched the rifle away. Using its butt, he silenced him then turned the gun on the one she had hit with the shovel.

Steps came from the corridor, Mary flattening herself against the inner wall as Galway burst into the kitchen firing from the hip. Flaherty never had a chance. The rifle's stock was splintered, his hands and face smashed as Angus tried to turn away and was hit several times.

She couldn't seem to move. Pinned against the wall by the sound of that gun, she watched in horror as Angus fell into the counter by the sink, then hit the table which flew to pieces under another burst from that thing. Wanting to scream, wanting only to cower, Mary darted into the corridor and down it even as he swung the gun towards her. She would never make it, never get away . . .

There was a rifle leaning against the wall just inside the mudroom, she snatching it up as she ran outside, the wall nearest to her being shot to pieces. Run . . . she must run. The wind hit her as she raced for the gap in the stone wall. She had to get through it, had to put as much distance behind her as she could. He would fire at her again, would cut her to pieces.

When she reached the ruins of the cottage nearest the cove, Mary saw him and two of the others standing outside the lighthouse. The Thompson gun had jammed. He was fighting to free it, was trying to fit another clip into it.

Kevin came out but there was still no sign of Hamish. Had he already been killed?

Huber joined Kevin. One of them must have shouted something to Galway for he started after her.

She raised the rifle, had to get him in the sights, had to hold the gun steady but its barrel kept dipping . . . The gun was too heavy for her, too awkward.

In despair, Mary lowered the rifle to rest her aching arms only to see Hamish and find again that she couldn't bring herself to move. Somehow he had managed to get down the stairs into the shed below the lighthouse. He was carrying Mrs. Tulford's suitcase wireless, was walking away towards the stone wall. None of them had seen him yet. None of them.

Raising the rifle, Mary fired at Galway, the gun leaping and kicking her shoulder, he just continuing to stride steadily towards her.

Tearing her gaze from him, she searched the land behind her but there was no cover anywhere close. She would have to run for the edge of the cliff, would have to go down it and along the shore, but the waves . . . they'd still be far too high.

At a run, she started out for the road, carrying the rifle in her right hand. The fog station was impossible. Galway had only to spray the road with that thing and she was done for. She would go down in a hail of bullets, would lose the child just as she had imagined at the border crossing, only Jimmy wouldn't be the one to have done it. Jimmy . . .

Mary turned and, after struggling frantically with it, managed to work the bolt action and slide another cartridge into the chamber. Galway hit the ground, she having pulled the trigger, but everyone was running now. Firing again, firing wildly, she turned and ran for the next set of ruins which lay well out in the fields, lay too far from her, too far . . .

The Thompson gun tore up the ground, she screaming and throwing herself down to bury her face in the soggy turf and beg him to stop.

Another burst came and then another. Knowing she mustn't, she dragged herself up and ran. One hundred yards, fifty . . . With a shriek, she tripped and fell and the Thompson gun burst all around her, she cringing from it to hug the ground again.

The ruins weren't that far now. If only she could get to them, if only that gun of his would jam again. Starting out, she saw that there was a chimney, a bit of wall, one window frame, a steel forty-five-gallon drum, a litter of rubbish, a soot-blackened hearth with an iron hook . . .

Throwing herself down behind the wall, Mary tried to see if Hamish was out there and wondered if he'd made it to the lee shore and the cover of the cliff.

There wasn't a sign of Galway, nor of anyone else. Working another cartridge into the chamber, she tried to swallow, was still out of breath. Where had they all gone?

Only then did she realize that she'd chosen to fight on their terms and that they were far better at it than herself. In a place where there was nothing much to hide behind, they had automatically gone to ground.

Her pulse easing, she searched the barren, windswept terrain for them. Details she would never have noticed before came into focus and were sharpened. A low ridge of round boulders, a thing no more than a foot high and more often not of the same height, curved from the bend in the road at the foot of the lighthouse hill, around and across the fields. It would form an adequate cover for someone used to such and would lead them almost to her.

This ridge was to her right, to the east and southeast, whereas the ruins of the cottage nearest to the cove below the light were to the northeast and to her left. Galway could perhaps have taken cover there. The wall nearest to her was badly crumbled and she could see much of its chimney, including a good deal of the hearth.

The ruins were empty. Not a thing moved and yet there was this feeling that every minute she waited they would be creeping closer and closer.

There were furrows in places behind her, the deep ruts upon whose humps of sand and seaweed, potatoes had been grown down through the centuries. These places, these plots were isolated and not everywhere apparent, but they, too, could be used as cover.

Flattening herself against the ground, Mary crawled through a gap in the rear wall of the cottage and when she felt she could, raised herself up a little on her elbows to search behind.

The ruins of another cottage lay off to her left perhaps a further three hundred yards. The fog station was still too far away. She mustn't think of it, must save what bullets she had and make each of them count.

Perhaps a third of the way between her and the ruins of that cottage there was another curving ridge of boulders and she realized then that the islanders must have used these ridges as boundary markers.

Just beyond the ridge, there were the furrows of an old potato patch. Crawling back into the ruins of the first cottage, she again searched for Kevin and the others but there wasn't a sight of anyone and only the sound of the wind and the waves. Even the seabirds had deserted the place.

Worming her way across the land wasn't easy. Her burns hurt constantly. The tussocky surface was rough, soggy and freezing, but by setting the rifle aside and grasping the tussocks with both hands, she could speed things up a little. Still, it was too slow a process. The urge to get up and run was almost more than she could bear but she had yielded to that sort of thing once by throwing the bullets into the stove when Hamish couldn't possibly have known of it.

Reaching the low stone ridge at last, she slithered over it to lie pressed to the ground behind its meagre cover. All Galway or any of the others had to do was to stand or climb one of the ruined walls. They'd see her soon enough.

When she looked behind her, nothing moved but the tussocks. The furrows of the potato patch proved less than adequate. They were also drowned in meltwater and full of mud but she knew she had to go on, had no other choice. Again the urge to get up and run was almost more than she could bear.

When she reached the next set of ruins, Mary didn't get up at all but wormed her way around and back, to then crawl stealthily into them through the strewn rubble.

Cleaning off the rifle, she forced herself to take time with the front sight which had become clogged with mud. Again there wasn't a sound but that of the wind and the waves, and she thought then that Inishtrahull must be the loneliest of places.

It would be a test of wills, she to wait, they to wait, each to hunt for the other. The fog station was now perhaps a half-mile to the west, its hill somewhat higher than that of the light-house and more exposed. The absence of a low stone wall surrounding it made reaching it seem impossible. Even the road had given up at the base of the hill, yet she'd been up there before, could still remember the narrow corridor inside the door, the harpoon that had leaned against the wall . . .

A Bristol Beaufort was fighting its way into the wind, Mary hearing the distant drone of its engines as Kevin and the others would but telling herself not to stand and try to wave for help. Galway and the others would be watching for just such a thing.

The plane came in low over the island, she refusing even to look at it, but a head and shoulders, thinking her distracted, rose up to search for her. She took aim . . . Steady . . . She must hold the rifle steady, mustn't miss.

As the sound of the shot came to her, she worked another cartridge into the breech. The man now lay slumped over the low ridge of boulders behind which he had been hiding. The rifle he had once held was lying on the ground.

'I've killed him,' she said, saddened by the thought, 'but must somehow keep going.'

The Beaufort circled, the sound of its engines heavy. When the plane was upwind of the island, it released bundle after bundle of white leaflets and these were caught by the wind and blown like confetti. The RAF could have offered covering fire but instead had scattered these, each of them no more than five or six inches square. 'GIVE YOURSELVES UP. NO HARM WILL COME TO YOU. ALL RULES OF THE GENEVA CONVENTION WILL BE OBSERVED.'

It was signed: Brigadier-General Martin Quigley, DSO and bar, MBE, QC, Acting Head, Joint Chiefs of Staff, Base Londonderry.

Mary let the wind have it. Kevin still had Galway and three

others with him. Then, too, there were Huber and Mrs. Tulford, and soon, some of the men from U-397 should they be able to land and think the matter of her death necessary.

The confetti did one thing. As it blew about, it gave a brief, if new dimension to the land, helping her to focus better on the minute changes of relief.

When she saw a man hugging the ground in a hollow not thirty yards from her, a surge of sickness came. If he was that close, were there not others, and why hadn't she seen him before this? Why hadn't he tried to kill her while she'd been preoccupied shooting the other one?

He'd been afraid she would see him.

Letting the sights line up with the top of his head, she fired, he flipping over and back and dropping his rifle. Now there were only two others besides Galway and Kevin, *and* Huber, *and* Mrs. Tulford, and she had killed again.

The wasteland behind the cottage held one shallow depression and then another of the low ridges. The next set of ruins was well off to her right and she wondered if one of them hadn't managed to get byher. Could he now be hiding in those ruins? Had she reloaded?

Struggling with the bolt action, lying as flat to the ground as possible, she finally got it to work but stopped herself from closing the breech long enough to peer into it. There was at least one other cartridge left in the clip. Galway would have kept this rifle of his fully loaded—she was certain of it, but had as yet no idea of how many bullets that would mean.

Worming her way across the ground, she wondered if the Beaufort's leaflets would only help the others to spot her. The ruins of the next cottage were never near, always far. From time to time she tried to search the ground behind and in front but the tussocks often prevented this, the blowing leaflets a little more.

BETRAYAL

When at last she reached the ruins, Mary intuitively knew someone was waiting for her. The place was desolate. Roof rafters stared blindly up at the sky while a china Jesus, having lost its head, lay on the floor near the soot-blackened hearth, the hands clasped in prayer.

There was no one inside the ruins, and when she stood up gradually to lean against the wall, still not a sight of anyone, yet she felt certain someone was near.

The tattered remains of an armchair revealed its springs and stuffing. A gumboot stood upright nearby and she wondered why it hadn't been blown over by the wind during the storm, wondered why there wasn't any water in it, she spinning round and trying to raise the rifle, trying to point it. Where was he?

The cottage was very small—just a single room and smaller even than Mrs. Haney's house, but here the walls were better than most on the island and, with the rafters above, she judged it to have been among the last to have been abandoned, but hadn't they all left in 1928, all except those who would come to man the light?

Mary knew there was someone nearby. By not knowing where he was but by letting her sense his presence, he was both preventing her from watching for the others and allowing them to get closer should something happen to himself. All this and more she understood.

Easing her head through the gap of the only small window in the place, she saw that there was a steel forty-five-gallon drum at the far end of the ruins. The man was behind it. He was waiting for her to start out again. It wasn't Galway but the man's back was to the barrel, so the thing must be full of water and he had thought it would stop a .303 bullet or slow it down enough not to kill.

Worming her way out through the front doorway, she saw

that there was perhaps ten feet of wall she would have to cover. After this, she must go around the corner and along a further fifteen feet of wall. By then there would be his boots, for the one he'd left upright hadn't been his own. There would be the better part of his legs visible to her and the barrel of that Lee Enfield he held.

Was it Kevin? she wondered. Had it all come to this?

Turning away, Mary did what none of them would ever have thought possible. She started back towards the lighthouse but worked her way nearer to the road and as a result, well around the ruins, and when she reached the furrows of another potato patch, slid down into one of the muddy troughs and went along it and back to those same ruins.

The leaflets blew about, the grey skies boiled, the surf beat against the shore.

It wasn't Kevin. It was one of the others but there was no moment of elation, no feeling of triumph. The stain was crimson before she heard the sound of the rifle in her hands.

Mary started towards him. Even as the Thompson gun sprayed the ground, the wall, the body, smashing everything in sight, she knew she should have anticipated this. Galway had used the man as a decoy. Racing for the ruins, she saw him standing out in the field, saw him swing that thing towards her. Frantically she tried to reload the rifle. His legs were spread, the wind was in his hair and beard. He'd not had enough rounds to fill the Lee Enfield's box clip. She was out of ammo and he knew it!

Pulling the trigger, the rifle went off in her hands, he stumbling back. Grabbing his right thigh, he looked towards her in disbelief, cursed her and then lifted the Thompson gun . . .

She threw herself down. Bullets tore into the wall above her. Stone chips flew everywhere, she forcing herself not to panic but to crawl away on her stomach.

He had toppled over but again was reloading that thing, had a satchel of ammunition over one shoulder but was having difficulty getting at it. There was blood on the fingers of his left hand, blood where he had gripped his thigh.

Scrambling over the dead man and yanking the rifle from him, Mary stood up and fired at Galway. Nothing happened. The trigger wouldn't squeeze. Frantically thumbing the safety off, she pulled the bolt back and slid another cartridge into the breech. Galway had now reloaded.

Darting inside the ruins, she threw her back against the wall. The rifle's safety catch had been on and the only thing she could think of was that the young man she had just killed had not been aware of it either.

Above the wind she heard a metallic click, a curse. Galway's gun had jammed again. She stood and fired, hit him in the shoulder and, starting out at a run, didn't look back, couldn't do so now, had to reach the fog station, had to get away.

The door was open. Someone was standing there with the harpoon. 'Hamish . . .'

Fraser dragged her inside.

The wind . . . always she would hear it in these last few moments. An hour had passed in which she had found herself unable to move. Hamish had lain on the floor of the corridor all that time, with only chance glimpses round the corner to search the slender slice of terrain that was visible from there.

Mary knew it was hopeless. Kevin and the others could rush the station at any moment. There were no windows—there was only that single door. During construction of the station, the boiler and its firebox had been bolted to the concrete floor, the foghorns installed and only then had the clapboard building been erected around them. Hamish would be cut down in the rush, herself forced back along the corridor to wait for the inevitable.

Besides the boiler and its firebox, there were some sacks of coal, two shovels and the foghorns which were silent. The short bit of corridor simply came straight in from the front door before abruptly turning to the right to pass the entrance to the boiler, the bulk of the building, such as it was, being crammed with its antiquated Victorian apparatus. There was a glass gauge that showed the level of water and a lever one pulled down, it looking more like the handbrake of a steam tractor.

Hoses piped steam to the foghorns; valves closed these off, allowing the steam to pass into the chimney when the horns were not in use and the handbrake up, but once this last was pulled down and locked into place with an iron cotter pin as thick as her little finger, the pressure in the boiler would build until automatically released through the horns every two minutes.

It was all very simple, but of little use, the absence of windows drastically limiting visibility.

Hamish had tried to reassure her but he'd known something very fundamental had happened to her and this was troubling him. To kill so ruthlessly was not an easy talent to acquire, not for a man and seldom for a woman. He had been humbled by what he had had to witness and was still frightened by it, afraid now, too, more than ever that he had lost her and would never understand.

And myself? she wondered, but had no time for introspection. The wooden shaft of the harpoon across her lap was driftwood grey, the iron shaft as thick as the heel of her thumb, its teeth barbed, their points, and that of the end, exceedingly sharp. The blade itself would cut through the thick hide of a whale and could be used, in a pinch, to slice up the blubber.

When Hamish said, 'We've company,' Mary gripped the harpoon and got to her feet to stand behind him. 'It's Huber, lass. He's come alone.'

'He's a decoy. They'll have worked their way up here and will be waiting right outside the door on either side. Galway . . .'

'I thought you said he'd been wounded twice?'

'That won't matter, not with him. He'll get up and . . .'

'Lass . . .'

'Hamish, we can't trust any of them. I . . .'

He touched her cheek, then turned away before she could say anything further. Huber had come a little closer, but was still a good two hundred yards from them. Bareheaded, he had his coat buttoned up under the chin. A torn square of white cloth in his hand was tugged at by the wind, but would its release be the signal for the others to rush the station?

When he was about fifty yards away, Hamish told him to stop. Not for a moment did Huber's gaze waver. 'We want the wireless set, Doctor. Let us get off the island and we'll agree to leave you in peace.'

'What's happened to the last of the lightkeepers?'

'He's safe with Ursula, but I must warn you that if you persist, he will be brought to the base of this hill and executed.'

They were going to rush them—Mary was certain of it. Kevin and the others must be standing just out of sight.

'Please, this is not a trick, Doctor. The wireless set must not fall into British hands.'

'The RAF and the Royal Navy won't let you leave.'

Huber still held the white flag but was he now to let go of it? she wondered.

'That is a chance we must take. U-397 can't repair her damaged propeller shaft and must run on a single engine, but can still take us off the island and back to the Reich.'

'What about O'Bannion and the rest of them?' asked Hamish.

'All but Galway will come with us. He's badly wounded and not expected to live.'

'*He's lying!*' hissed Mary. 'Hamish, I know he is! They're right outside the door. They're going to rush us, darling. Please . . .'

'*Och*, the vice admiral wouldn't risk his life like this, and that's the truth of it.'

'Why must you argue? Why not listen to me for once? I've had to fight them, Hamish, have had to kill them.'

'Lass, I know that.'

'Then tell him he's to be our hostage.'

Reluctantly Huber agreed, but asked to inform the others. Mary knew they would have to let him leave. Waiting for a rush that didn't come, she wondered if his visit hadn't been but a part of some larger scheme. Darkness would soon be here—would they set fire to the fog station?

When she told Hamish this, he said, '*Och*, I greatly fear they've something else in mind.'

Carrying a canister of tea, Huber soon returned. The last of the biscuits that had been in Angus's tin were wrapped in the white cloth. To search him thoroughly, Hamish even had him empty his pockets and take off his boots.

'So, Mrs. Fraser, our places are now to be reversed but we Germans cannot let your bravery go unacknowledged. Please . . .' He indicated the tin mug he had just filled.

'You first,' she said.

He would grin and give her a shrug. 'With pleasure then, and I salute you both, yourself especially, though I must say you do surprise me. To shoot so well and then to worry over a little poison or sleeping drug from that bag of your husband's is rather odd, is it not?'

'I simply don't trust any of you. I've had no reason to.'

This one had changed. 'Then let me tell you both that U-397 is equipped with an eighty-eight millimetre cannon as well as two antiaircraft guns. There are also MG42 machine guns and various other light weapons should an assault on this lonely refuge of yours be necessary. Now please, you do not look well. The tea will help you to regain your strength for the long wait ahead.'

At dusk the wind had fallen to a whisper. By then the RAF had flown more than ten sorties over the island and had repeatedly swept the surrounding sea for the U-boat. A ship, most probably a destroyer, was steaming towards the island. As yet, though, word of its having been sighted hadn't come to Huber but he'd been warned of its presence by the wireless traffic he'd been given and knew that they'd not be allowed to leave so easily.

Not until 2100 hours did the ship begin to fire star shells into the air near the island, confirming that indeed it was a destroyer. The glow from the star shells, their myriad rain of flares, lit up the darkness, then their light would vanish and the island would again wrap solitude about itself.

When Kevin came up the hill, alone and unarmed, his hands on his head, Mary saw him first against the bursting of another star shell, and as the spluttering flares descended over the fields behind him, the ruined cottages stood out as stark reminders of all she'd been through.

He spoke not to herself, though, but to Huber. 'One of the curraghs is down at the cove with the Aldis lamp. By midnight the seas will have calmed enough for us to be quit of this place. Dermid's gone.'

Huber acknowledged the loss. 'He was a good man. I had hoped we could get him away to safety.'

'My little band of followers has been reduced to myself and young Kenneth McGrath.'

A boy of eighteen. 'There'll be others. You'll be back, you'll see.'

Kevin would be thinking of the Flight of the Earls and saying to himself that their cause had been as futile as his own.

Another star shell burst over the island. Both he and Huber knew they had very little time, that the destroyer would come in close with landing parties, yet they had to wait it out. U-397 had to maintain absolute wireless silence, nor could it signal to them by any other means.

'She still has three torpedoes,' said Huber. 'All things are possible, and the British will be only too well aware of this.'

Even as he said it, and Mary thought him lying, there was a tremendous detonation out to sea, to the northeast of them. In spite of having to hold the rifle on them, Hamish and she left the building. A wall of flame, brilliant in the darkness, flashed twice, outlining the lighthouse and the destroyer clearly.

Smoke billowed from the ship, alarm buzzers sounded, and they could hear these from a distance of what must be nearly five miles.

'So, the tide has turned in our favour once again,' said Huber. 'Always we keep a little something as a surprise.'

Near midnight the distant drone of engines was caught on the air and then lost. Huber was the first to notice them and to recognize their significance. Instantly he turned to look questioningly through the darkness at Hamish who said, '*Och*, man, go and raise that boat of yours and see if you can get off the island now.'

'I want the wireless set.'

'You'll have it when we're ready and not before then. Send Kevin to us when that U-boat of yours is in the cove. You'll find the curragh to be of little use.'

Huber stood a moment facing them. Neither would know

what was in store for them until it was too late. 'Then it's good-bye, Doctor, Mrs. Fraser. *Auf Wiedersehen. Heil Hitler.*'

Together, they watched him walk away into the night. All too soon they were alone, for he'd begun to run for the light-house.

Hamish tightened his arm about her shoulders. He didn't say anything but Mary felt the sadness that was in him.

Then the sound came again. 'It's as if something is fighting its way towards us,' she said, 'but is still too far for us to hear it clearly.'

'They're motor torpedo boats out of Derry, lass, and there are two of them. The sub will have to come in, and Huber will have to tell it to do so.'

The drone of the engines steadily increased but soon others were added and a Bristol Beaufort or a Wellington flew over the island to drop parachute flares which lit up everything as they slowly fell. Some canisters were then pitched out—tumbling, black drumlike things. One hit the rocks near the lighthouse and bounced before exploding. Others fell into the sea to sink below the heaving waves and then erupt in fountains whose flat detonations made her cringe.

The aircraft came round again, flying so low she thought it would hit the lighthouse, but it lumbered over the length of the island and they saw the dark silhouette of it against the night sky above. More depth charges were dropped, this time farther out to sea. The plane jerked higher, the drone of its engines increasing as it climbed and banked towards the southeast.

As the last of the flares fell and explosions ripped the water, it headed off towards Derry and they listened to the dwindling sound of it with a sense of loss even as the drone of the motor torpedo boats increased.

Then another plane flew over and the pattern was repeated: first the flares—released from much higher this time—then the depth charges, but only after a sweep far out to sea. Everything was now etched in silhouette, the ruins, the road, the pier—Kevin and the others putting the curragh into the water. Even from a distance of three-quarters of a mile, Hamish and she could see them clearly. The sea was still too rough. More than once they had to drag the little boat back. A flare was falling directly over top. Mrs. Tulford had gone to join them. Had she killed the last of the lightkeepers?

There was no sign of him.

Suddenly everything began to happen at once, Hamish and herself to run from the fog station, trying to find a bit of cover as tracers marked the path of gunfire from the motor torpedo boats and arcs of light raked the island to concentrate on the lighthouse first. In a steady but undulating sweep, streams of bullets progressed towards the pier. Kevin ran. The others threw themselves down. Bullets ripped and pinged, hit the concrete, the oil drums, passed across the island and up the hill towards the fog station. Again the sound of the Thompson gun came to her, but now there was no longer the fear she'd experienced among the ruins, the terror. The sound was recognized for what it was, and she knew this and did not cry out to Hamish.

As abruptly as it had begun, the curtain of fire was silenced. The last of the flares had gone out.

Warily she began to pick herself up. Against the steady throb of diesels, there were the sounds of breaking waves and those of the wind.

'Hamish . . . Hamish, where are you?'

The firing started up. Streams of tracers jerked and jumped and cut their swaths, only to suddenly cease, Mary scrambling towards the fog station. 'Hamish . . . Darling, where are you?'

Had he gone down the hill to kill as many as he could? Had she forced him into such a thing?

The motor torpedo boats continued to circle the island. The steady throb of their engines was always there in the darkness but well offshore. They were taking no chances, must be biding their time and waiting for the aircraft to return. The boats would use their sonar and radar to locate the sub. Besides their torpedoes, they would carry depth charges of their own.

The fog station wasn't far now, and when she got there, her foot struck something on the floor. 'Hamish!' she cried out and gingerly felt for him only to find the harpoon and take it up.

Making her way along the corridor, she went deeper into the building, would have to have the firebox door open, would need its light in order to reset the bomb, but would Kevin really come back for it?

Light flickered from gaps in the firebox door, making the dusty, open throats of the burlap sacks of coal seem as if standing sentinel while the pipes threw their shadows. Setting the harpoon down, she dragged the suitcase into the light. She would have to do it but could she really?

Putting the scarf back, Mary closed the compartment and the suitcase. It wasn't Kevin who came. It was Dermid Galway and as he fired that thing in his hands, it shattered the silence, ripped apart the walls of the corridor, splintered the boards and made her shriek in terror and try to hide.

As she backed away, she heard him reloading. Sacks of coal were now in front of her, the suitcase and the boiler's firebox door to her right, the armature for the foghorns to the left. Even as she got hesitantly to her feet and waited for him to kill her, Mary knew it would be best this way for there would be no questions to answer, no excuses to make, no thoughts of ever being brought to trial and made a spectacle of.

As a single shot rang out, a stab of pain gripped her middle. There was a curse, another burst of firing. 'Hamish!' she cried as she snatched up the harpoon and Galway came at her out of the shadows but he'd been hit. Hamish had been waiting for him. Hamish . . .

The Thompson gun was being dragged along the wall and, as the Irishman rose up to steady himself, he said, 'God's curse upon you, woman!' his voice breaking all about her now as blood trickled from a corner of his mouth and he fell to his knees before her. 'DO IT!' he yelled. 'DON'T KEEP ME WAITING!'

Coughing blood, he tried to drag the Thompson gun into position. The point of the harpoon was levelled at his chest. 'Do it, damn you,' he muttered.

'Mary, step away from him.'

Galway tried to reach the gun that had fallen from him as Hamish placed the muzzle of the rifle to his back and fired.

U-397 had surfaced but was still some distance to the north of the island. The brief flashing of Aldis signals gave their position; Huber signalling back from the ruins of the cottage nearest the pier. Against the deeper darkness of the waves and that of the night, the silhouette of the submarine momentarily appeared, only to vanish just as suddenly.

Its crew would be racing to uncover the deck guns. Mary knew there'd be a battle and that the sub could well be sunk, for the motor torpedo boats hovered somewhere off in the darkness, the throb of their engines coming and going against the deeper pulse of U-397's diesel.

When a flare, lingering long in the sky, arced through the night to hang floating brightly above the submarine, men swung the eighty-eight-millimetre gun on her forward deck while others raced to help them and a deafening explosion was followed by the whip crack of the gun. Again and again the sub fired. Tracers were now pouring from one of the torpedo boats, the sound of its engines increasing steadily as it closed the gap between them, becoming louder and louder until she caught a glimpse of the boat's silhouette as it leapt across the waves pouring its hail of bullets at the sub. The boat would hit the submarine with its torpedoes. They'd sink it.

There was firing from the northeast and from the east, another flare, another crash of the eighty-eight-millimetre gun, the *pom-pom* thudding of its antiaircraft guns.

Instinctively Hamish pulled her down as the torpedoes came on and she knew they'd hit the sub that she and Hamish would have to fight Kevin and the others.

In rapid sequence, two thunderous explosions rocked the shore as the torpedoes struck the island. 'The other boat must have missed the sub too,' shouted Hamish. Uncertain still, he got to his feet and reached to help her up. 'They'll retreat and wait for the RAF now, lass. Huber and the others will try to get off before they come back.'

The motor torpedo boats had lost themselves in the darkness. The submarine was out there some place too. An Aldis lamp flashed from its conning tower, rapidly winking in the night. Huber answered from the ruins.

'They'll want the wireless set, Hamish.'

Fraser caught the sadness in her voice but before he could say anything, Mary had started down the hill with it. Carrying the rifle at the ready, he followed at a distance.

Mary knew that Hamish could not know that for them things could never be the same again, and when Kevin met her on the road halfway to the cove, he was carrying a Lee Enfield, and she knew that he had come alone and that he hadn't expected to find her here at all.

'Where's Dermid?' he asked as if he still couldn't believe it was her with the suitcase.

'He's dead, Kevin.'

The emptiness in her voice told him she still thought him worthy of more than lying.

'Just put the rifle down on the road,' shouted Hamish from behind her.

'All right, I will,' said O'Bannion, no doubt reminding her of Liam but knowing, too, that the bloody Thompson guns were good at times and a curse at others because they were always needing a bit of oil and sand grains could do things to them even then.

Out to sea, the firing had started up again.

'The Nazis will only cheat you, Kevin. It will all have been for nothing.'

The wind tugged at her hair, blowing it about. Having set the suitcase down, her hands were now in the pockets of her anorak. 'We should have known each other in better times,' he said.

Though he'd not see it, she would shrug at this.

'Ireland will be free some day, Mary.'

'The border should never have been put there in the first place.'

'And we'll never stop fighting until it's gone.'

'Do you think I don't know that? I can't condone the killing, the things you people did to Caithleen, Kevin, any more than I can this war. It's all so stupid. Life's the greatest gift we have. We shouldn't take it from others, nor should others force us into situations where we have to.'

'You're still too soft. The Brits will never leave until we've driven them out.'

'I agree they have to leave, but the trouble is they won't until you people stop, and by then the whole of Ireland will be empty. It'll lift up its silence on the altar of its ruins just as this island has. No God will be listening, Kevin, because there will be no one to speak to Him.'

'What's to prevent the two of you from trying to stop us from getting off the island?'

'Only our word. There's been enough killing. We're done with it unless you come after us.'

Fraser, who had remained all but out of sight behind her, had said so little it had to make one wonder if he wasn't in awe of her himself. 'Then it's good-bye to you, and I'm off.'

She would say nothing further, Mary told herself, would simply let him walk away into the night because it had to be left this way. In his heart of hearts Kevin had always known it would all be for nothing and that for him the cause was over, yet she could not help but remember the ruins by the school and knew that he had been the only thing that had stood between Fay Darcy, Liam Nolan and herself.

'You've no harsh words?' asked Hamish.

'The time for them has passed.'

They didn't retreat to the hill. Taking him by the hand, she led him well out into the fields to stand alone, he no longer questioning her reasons, simply letting her lean back against him as he held her.

The RAF came back. Curtains of fire streamed from each of the motor torpedo boats, the sub answering them as parachute flares lazily drifted down, lighting up everything with a brilliance that frightened. The curragh was in the water. Kevin and the young man called Kenneth McGrath were at the oars, Huber in the stern, Mrs. Tulford near the bow. Cockleshell to the waves, it rose and fell as the two sets of oars rhythmically skimmed the water. They still had too far to go, would never reach the sub, would be shot to pieces.

With a deafening crash, the sub's eighty-eight-millimetre cannon hit one of the torpedo boats. There was a flash of burning diesel fuel. Parts of the boat—whole sections of it—flew into the air, disintegrating as they tumbled over and over.

One of the planes dropped its depth charges. Detonation after detonation threw fountains into the air around U-397. Kevin and the others had now left the cove. They were pulling strongly at the oars. The sub had seen them and was giving covering fire. More flares were dropping. Now the sea was illuminated and everywhere there was a ghostly light and more and more firing. They would never get away, never do it.

Another plane began to drop its depth charges. As the drums pitched out, the sub fired up at them with its antiaircraft guns. The eighty-eight-millimetre cannon flashed fire at the pinpoint of the streams of tracer shells that were pouring from the last of the torpedo boats. Again there was a tremendous detonation, shreds of debris spinning through flashes of fire to hit the waves and disintegrate. There'd be bodies, men blown to pieces . . .

In tears, Mary wanted to tell them to stop, but the planes came over again, this time one after the other to rake the sea with cannon fire. The curragh hadn't a chance. It was lifted up on a wave, only to drop away to nothing yet Kevin kept rowing. Again the little boat lifted, again the oars dipped. Splash points raced across the water as the boat hit the side of the submarine. The flares were still falling, men rushing now to throw ropes and secure the curragh. Mrs. Tulford tried to scramble up the side of the sub but slipped and fell into the water. The curragh was thrown towards her—Huber was leaning over, trying to reach out to the woman as Kevin . . . Kevin slung the suitcase up and it was taken and passed from hand to hand to disappear inside the conning tower.

The RAF, having given them all they had, were heading back to Derry as fast as they could.

'Darling . . .'

'Hush, lass. Let's just hope and pray we've seen the last of them.'

Mrs. Tulford had been dragged from the water. Kevin was climbing the ladder of the conning tower. Reaching back, he caught the woman by the arm. Huber was helping her, too. Kenneth McGrath had clambered aboard . . .

The bomb went off. It flashed so brilliantly, Mary ducked and buried her face against Hamish.

'That suitcase . . . ' he began. 'Their scuttling charges have detonated. Lass, what the hell have you done?'

He made her turn, made her look at it. A huge hole had been ripped in the sub; the eighty-eight-millimetre cannon had been knocked askew. Men hung limply over the gun mounts and the top of the shattered conning tower. Men . . .

They began to slip and fall away into the sea. The sub dipped down into the waves, was filling with water, was sinking. There was now no sign of the curragh, not even a bit of its wreckage. No sign of Kevin, nor of Huber or of either of the other two.

As the last of the flares went out, great geysers of water lifted but there was no longer any sight of the submarine. Then in one final detonation, its bow rose up suddenly as if to come back at them before the jagged teeth if its net cutter slid silently beneath the waves.

At dawn they walked among the bodies. Some of the men were very young, others not even of middle age.

There was no sign of Kevin, nor of Mrs. Tulford. Alone among the Nazi dead, the body of Kenneth McGraw lay with strands of kelp across his broken chest. Thousands of one- and five-pound notes floated about or clung to the oil-slicked rocks and the bodies.

'Come away, lass. There is nothing you or anyone else can do for them.'

Did Hamish despise her for what she'd done and become, a woman who could kill with a vengeance—had there ever been vengeance?

Crouching, she picked up one of the notes. The face of King George VI was very clear and sharp.

Sodden, the bill fell from her fingers to cling to the rocks.

'Lass, I'm sorry it had to end this way. *Och*, you know I'll stand by you.'

There would be an inquest, a trial and then a hanging, and nothing she or Hamish could ever say or do would stop them.

The man who sat across the desk from her in the bunker below 10 Downing Street was angry.

Winston Spencer Churchill thumbed through the dossier and the signed statement of thirty pages she had given at the inquest. Everything that had happened in what was now being dubbed 'The Tralane Affair' had been documented in the neatest and most precise of handwritings. The damnable inquest had gone on for weeks and it hadn't entirely been hushed up.

'Just what the devil am I to do with you?' he asked, chewing on his cigar. 'The Royal Navy and the RAF, in spite of repeated attempts, *fail* to sink this Nazi submarine but you . . . you, Mrs. . . . Oh damn it, what was it?'

'Fraser . . . Mrs. Mary Ellen Fraser.'

'Scottish! The Scots have always been trouble!'

He hunkered forward to fix her with a piercing gaze. 'Do you know what's happened? The Irish press has had the un-mitigated gall to release stories of this sordid affair. Fleet Street was never cosy with them but by God, the *Times* and the *Daily Mail* are suggesting I step down!'

Those bluest of eyes bulged in anger. 'From being labelled another Mata Hari, you've become a heroine, Mrs. Fraser. Con-demned to hang by the neck while myself and His Majesty are left with the decision of what to do with you.'

Mr. Churchill reached for his glass, the bulldog of the war lacking all patience. 'London . . . Dear old London,' he said with sudden sentiment that only set those eyes to watering, 'is being bombed to pieces, Mrs Fraser!'

She wished he'd not blame her for the Luftwaffe's raids.

'That husband of yours has given a lengthy interview to the *Times* and the *Daily Mail*. I have it on good authority that the *Manchester Guardian* and others have also received this "inter-view" but we do have censorship laws in effect, so I will say no more of it.'

He flipped through the pages. She had sunk this U-397, had learned on her own to use explosives and to shoot with the best. Instinctively she had handled herself remarkably well in very tight situations. 'There was mention of a child, I believe?' he said with sudden rancour.

'Yes, I . . . I lost it shortly after we left the island. On the boat, actually.'

That couldn't have been pleasant for her. 'Did you love this Nazi?'

How could you—Mary knew that was what he'd implied. 'I thought I did at the time but soon learned not to and . . . and in the end, caused his death.'

'And that of more than sixty others!' jibed Churchill only to see the tears he'd caused and to say with all sincerity, 'My dear, you must forgive me. This business has not been easy. Taken alone, it was a war on our very shores. We won it only by the dogged determination and spirit of will of one of our citizens. Can you begin to imagine what the nation wants of you in these deeply troubled times? You are a heroine, Mrs. Fraser, a British citizen who . . .'

'I . . . I'm a Canadian, Prime Minister. Though I'm married to a Scot, I've not yet . . .'

'A Canadian—from the Dominions, eh?' he accused as if that explained everything. 'Damned fine people, the Canadians. Damned good fighters.'

Drawing on his cigar, he paused to give her a moment. 'How is it that you have learned to speak and write French?'

Alarmed, puzzled by the question, she threw those big brown eyes of hers up at him in doubt and hesitation.

Her voice a whisper in the hush of the bunker, Mary briefly told him of the little girl she had had to leave behind in Montreal. 'My French is Parisian, but my accent Canadian, Prime Minister.'

'That could be ironed out, I should think. French was never a gift I'd have chosen for myself, though I speak it well enough.'

'I learned it against all opposition in a city where the English didn't bother to speak it. I needed friends, Prime Minister. I wanted to get to know my neighbours and the woman who looked after my little girl when I went out to work. I lived with French Canadians, not with the English. It was a lot cheaper and far friendlier.'

Churchill knew he was impressed, that this wasn't just anyone sitting so properly in front of him in that beige suit of hers, but a very resourceful young woman. She was tired and thin, and terribly worried but not afraid to pay for what she'd done.

'What has happened to that husband of yours?' he asked, adopting a rather bland and disinterested tone.

'He's here in London, staying with friends. He . . . he comes to see me every day.'

And talks to the press! 'Why isn't he in the services? Good, qualified surgeons are desperately needed.'

'Hamish fought in the Great War.'

'I did so myself. Come, come, there has to be something else. He's not one of those conscientious objectors, is he?'

'Prime Minister, I think you know Hamish was disqualified for having helped a destitute young girl out of a very bad situation. That girl lived and has gone her way, while he . . .'

'Became a country doctor in Northern Ireland and doctor to the Nazis at Tralane. My dear, please do not think ill of me. We can use him in North Africa. War provides the forgiveness time alone can never allow.'

Again he would give her a moment. Tribunals were seldom what they should be. Reaching for his glass, he found it empty. 'My dear young woman, the Nazis grind virtually the whole of Europe beneath their jackboots. Day by day men and women are being tortured and shot for having defied them. Are you aware in the slightest of what those brave souls must face?'

She wished he'd not accuse her of anything more but knew he was in a very difficult position, that Tralane and Inishtrahull, while the least of his problems, had become paramount. 'I think I know what they must feel, Prime Minister. Each day out there on the island and since, a good part of me has died. I'm not proud of what I've done. I'm ashamed of it.'

'But you have changed, haven't you?'

'Yes, I've changed and I know this.'

Churchill drew on the cigar. She was uncommonly fetching, still unassuming and not revealing any of that tough inner spirit and instinctive will and talent that had allowed her to survive and to singlehandedly accomplish so much. Indeed, though he had little use for them, she reminded him of a schoolteacher—no, a secretary. Yes, that was better. Had she the gift of languages, he wondered, a knack for learning them? She'd had a bit of college *Deutsch*. Could she take it up again in addition to polishing the French?

He thought so, he thought her a treasure but had she already been through too much? Only time would tell. 'Will you agree to go into Occupied France for me?'

The cigar was poised, the question had been given quietly. Occupied France . . .

'As an agent of the Special Operations Executive, Mrs. Fraser. Sworn to secrecy as of this moment for such "agents" do not exist beyond the minds of but a chosen few.'

Her heart still ached from Inishtrahull; she still had nightmares . . .

'We will train you, Mrs. Fraser. We will give you every benefit of our diverse knowledge.'

When she looked away from him, he realized that every last particle of her ordeal had suddenly returned. Instinctively she knew exactly what she would have to face in France, a most opportune and healthy sign.

'I . . . I'd like to talk to Hamish. The two of us . . . we've been apart, Prime Minister. I need to be with him; he . . . he needs to be with me.'

'And the rope?' he asked, despising himself for the reminder.

'Yes, I'll go to France for you but first I want a fortnight with my husband.'

'A show of anger is always refreshing, Mrs. Fraser. Don't

get yourself pregnant. See that he volunteers for service in North Africa. Everything will be taken care of. Let us get on with this war. Let us crush the Nazis so that they may never again rise up.'

The house in all its Georgian eminence lay in the gathering dusk. Seen from the top of Caitlyn Murphy's Hill, it drew the night exuding warmth and refuge.

Mary couldn't believe that she was actually seeing it again. Mrs. Haney would be in her kitchen. Bridget and William were back but the clock, the watch could never be rewound, and she knew this.

Hamish slid an arm about her waist. 'The IRA would never let us stay here in peace, lass. *Och*, we both know it and so will Ria.'

Yet they'd have a few days to themselves. 'Darling, couldn't we keep it? Couldn't you persuade Mrs. Haney to look after it for us? Then maybe when this war is over . . .'

'Is it that you've come to love the house so much you would dare to come back?'

'You know I have. These people need you, Hamish, and we both need them.'

Mary felt his hand come to rest on the back of her neck, felt him caressing her. Things had been good for them in bed, far more than she'd ever thought possible.

'There is just a slender hope,' he said. 'Let me speak to Ria about it.'

They took their time. The scent of wet hay and peat was in the air, of turf smoke too, and the distant sounds of cowbells and lolling sheep. 'I love you, Hamish. I want so much for us to have a life together and to have children of our own.'

The simple things that could never be. Mary knew this. They had four days and that was all. Getting permission to return to Ireland to settle the house had been nigh on impossible until the prime minister had intervened.

'You've friends in high places,' he said, a reminder.

'Not friends, just people who want to help because . . .'

'*Och*, I know you can't tell me where you'll be going, but I will wait and keep the house for you.'

He could be so archaic when he wanted, would see her tears and shed his own. 'This war is going to take years, Hamish, but I've this feeling inside me that in the end things will turn out for the best.'

Had it been but the kindest of lies? 'They're going to send you into France, and I know this, know exactly what you'll have to face and do. Mr. Churchill had no business . . .'

She touched his lips to silence him, said 'Hush, my darling, I will come back, you'll see, and so will you.'

Together they walked to the car and Hamish drove down the hill to the house, they sitting here for a moment more in the gathering darkness.

He'd a fistful of one- and five-pound notes, the counterfeiting so good it would have been extremely difficult to tell the difference if one didn't know that the banks had all been alerted.

'Ria will take these to someone who will see that they get into the right hands. Men died for these, Mary, but maybe if others know that the Nazis are swindlers, they'll want to keep quiet about it and will let us come home someday.'

The light of a storm lantern lit up the car. The waiting had been too patient. 'These goings on,' clucked Ria under her breath but beamed as the doctor got out and went round to hold the door open for his wife.

'Ah and sure them blackout regulations can be set aside the moment, Doctor. 'Tis terrible glad I am t' see the two of you home and safe. Now it is, it surely is. William, be sharp with them bags. Bridget . . . Bridget, girl, didn't I tell you to curtsey?'

There'd be no dust. No thoughts of anyone bothering them.

Mary found herself hugging the woman. It was as if she *had* come home, as if she would never have to leave.

EBOOKS BY J. ROBERT JANES

FROM MYSTERIOUSPRESS.COM
AND OPEN ROAD MEDIA

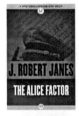  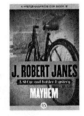 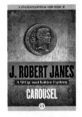 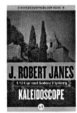

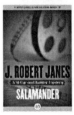 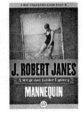 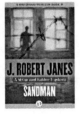 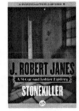 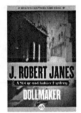

Available wherever ebooks are sold

MYSTERIOUSPRESS.COM

Otto Penzler, owner of the Mysterious Bookshop in Manhattan, founded the Mysterious Press in 1975. Penzler quickly became known for his outstanding selection of mystery, crime, and suspense books, both from his imprint and in his store. The imprint was devoted to printing the best books in these genres, using fine paper and top dust-jacket artists, as well as offering many limited, signed editions.

Now the Mysterious Press has gone digital, publishing ebooks through **MysteriousPress.com**.

MysteriousPress.com offers readers essential noir and suspense fiction, hard-boiled crime novels, and the latest thrillers from both debut authors and mystery masters. Discover classics and new voices, all from one legendary source.

FIND OUT MORE AT
WWW.MYSTERIOUSPRESS.COM

FOLLOW US:
@emysteries and Facebook.com/MysteriousPressCom

MysteriousPress.com is one of a select group of publishing partners of Open Road Integrated Media, Inc.

THE MYSTERIOUS BOOKSHOP, founded in 1979, is located in Manhattan's Tribeca neighborhood. It is the oldest and largest mystery-specialty bookstore in America.

The shop stocks the finest selection of new mystery hardcovers, paperbacks, and periodicals. It also features a superb collection of signed modern first editions, rare and collectable works, and Sherlock Holmes titles. The bookshop issues a free monthly newsletter highlighting its book clubs, new releases, events, and recently acquired books.

58 Warren Street
info@mysteriousbookshop.com
(212) 587-1011
Monday through Saturday
11:00 a.m. to 7:00 p.m.

FIND OUT MORE AT:

www.mysteriousbookshop.com

FOLLOW US:

@TheMysterious and Facebook.com/MysteriousBookshop

Open Road Integrated Media is a digital publisher and multimedia content company. Open Road creates connections between authors and their audiences by marketing its ebooks through a new proprietary online platform, which uses premium video content and social media.

Videos, Archival Documents, and New Releases

Sign up for the Open Road Media newsletter and get news delivered straight to your inbox.

Sign up now at
www.openroadmedia.com/newsletters

CPSIA information can be obtained at www.ICGtesting.com
Printed in the USA
BVOW03s0705180814

362840BV00002B/8/P